TOTAL

ANGST

by
D.C. White

ISBN: 978-0-9837355-2-6

Other books by D.C. White

The Angst Series

Capitol Angst
Angst to the Nth
Total Angst

DEDICATION

This book is dedicated to all the people of the world that don't take things at face value and have the ability to see every tree regardless of how dense the forest may be.

For all our fans who read the words, loved them, and couldn't wait for the next book. Well, here's the final installment of the Angst trilogy. I know it's hard to let go of characters, after all, they're like part of the family we've been through so much together.

Acknowledgements

We have so many people to be grateful to for all their help, time, patience and reading ability. To our beta readers without whom this series of books would never have been possible.

Thanks to my sister Terrie and friend Jon for being willing to read in the beginning words that were good but needed so very much work. You're awesome. Thanks to Debbie Wormald, Cindy Prib, Don Prib, Bettie Dye, Marlene White and Cheryl Haak for believing in us. That's probably one of the harder things done for us, but you stuck with us from the first book to the third. Thanks for your kind words and positive feedback and thanks for the constant pressure to finish the series. It certainly would have never been completed without your help! We look forward to a future of more books and hope we'll find you all ready and waiting.

We love you friends!
Cheral and Dennis
D.C. White

Table of Contents

Chapter One

Chapter Two

Chapter Three

Chapter Four

Chapter Five

Chapter Six

Chapter Seven

Chapter Eight

Chapter Nine

Chapter Ten

Chapter Eleven

Chapter Twelve

Chapter Thirteen

Chapter Fourteen

Chapter Fifteen

Chapter Sixteen

Chapter Seventeen

Chapter Eighteen

Chapter Nineteen

Chapter Twenty

Chapter Twenty-One

Chapter Twenty-Two

Chapter Twenty-Three

Chapter Twenty-Four

Chapter Twenty-Five

Chapter Twenty-Six

Chapter Twenty-Seven

Chapter Twenty-Eight

Chapter Twenty-Nine

Chapter Thirty

Chapter Thirty-One

Chapter Thirty-Two

Chapter Thirty-three

Chapter Thirty-Four

Chapter Thirty-Five

Chapter One

"NO!" Jane screams as she watches in disbelief the loss of signal on the television they were using to see her parents, held hostage in "W H E R E are they?" she yells at Quinton. "We have to find them," she cries in a panic. "I can't lose them now, not when I just found out they're still alive."

"Relax Jane, we'll find them. At least now we know that they're still alive. You were right, you would know if they were gone. You're connected to them. They're fine, I'm sure. Do you feel anything, a loss or a feeling that things are changed?"

"No, I feel the same. They're alive. I can feel it," she says more calmly. "Thanks Quinton. I needed the grounding. They're alive. I would know if there was something different."

"Let's see if there was an earthquake in the country. At least that's what it looked like. If there was then we can narrow down the area that they were located in, and start our search there."

"Awesome, thanks for thinking it through for me. We'll find them once we know the approximate location. Get me Teriq on the phone. I'll inform him of all that's happened and he can dispatch some troops to find them, before that underground group takes the hostage thing to another level. They need to get moving now, before they can gain much ground. If they get out of there before we find them, it could take months to get their location. I don't want to wait months. I want to see them now."

* * *

"Kat, where are you" Snake yells in between coughs, the heat and dust a killer; making it impossible to see more than a foot in front of himself, not to mention breathe. "Kat, WHERE are you?" he yells as he starts moving in the approximate direction that she was in last.

"Lieutenant, where are you," he hears, but no sound from Kat.

"Here, I'm here," he yells.

"Thank God, Lieutenant," Mongoose says through his coughs. "What the hell happened?" he asks loudly.

"I'm not sure," Jacob says. "I can't find Kat, have you seen her?" he asks brusquely.

"No Sir, the last I saw her, she was with the hostages, and that part of the tent is collapsed. We need to start digging to get those people out of there."

"Round up as many people as you can, we need to get everyone out before they suffocate," Jacob orders as he rushes over to the collapsed area of the tent, grabbing and throwing everything out of the way.

"Come on Kat, where are you," he mumbles, breathing shallowly until the air clears to minimize the coughing. Ah, a hand, a limp hand. After tugging a little harder to uncover the rest of the body, he discovers Jane's mother. Feeling quickly and finding a pulse in her throat, he yells for help, hands her over and continues on with the search. Where the hell is Kat, he wonders worriedly. Hold on, something soft. It's softer than the wood and debris, maybe a person he thinks. After quickly moving things off . . . Kat! "Be okay; please be okay," he mumbles as he pulls her free of her entombment in the rubble. After cleaning her eyes and mouth, he feels for a pulse, praying that she's alive. Ha, there it is a faint pulse, strong enough that she's alive, but injured, and definitely unconscious. "I've got her" he yells to Mongoose as he lifts her into his arms to carry her outside where he can see slightly better and breathe real air a little easier.

"I've got Jane's dad," Mongoose says as he reaches Jacob. "He looks a little worse for wear, but I'm sure he'll be fine," Mongoose says to Jacobs questioning look.

"Any idea where Rand is," Jacob asks as he tries to wake Kat up.

"Last I saw anyone was right after this happened, then everyone took off running, trying to grab anyone they could reach, and get them out of danger."

"See if you can find Rand, I'll stay with these three while you hunt him down. Tell him we need all the first aid supplies available. I have no idea what's wrong with any one of these people. It could be anything from a concussion to broken necks, backs, pretty much broken anything after what just happened."

"Yes Sir, I'll head out. It won't take me long."

"Thanks."

"Come on Kat, wake up now," Jacob says quietly over and over, Kat's still not responding.

"Sir" Rand says as he drops to his knees next to Kat.

"She hasn't moved since I brought her out here from the tent. She's breathing, but very faintly."

"Her pupils are equal and reactive" Rand murmurs as he starts checking her over head to toe. "Looks like she was knocked unconscious, she could have a concussion. What was on top of her?" he asks Jacob.

"Most of the tent, a couple of poles, nothing that should have damaged her too bad, at least it didn't look that way," Jacob says, thinking about how he found her. "She was pretty buried though."

"My opinion, she has a concussion and with the lack of oxygen, she's still out cold. I'm sure she'll come out of it soon. I'm not seeing anything like broken legs, arms, that kind of stuff. I'll get some water to use to clean her face with, see if that brings her out of it."

"Kat, wake up now," Jacob says after washing her face off, the dust was thick and heavy, but her skin can breathe now.

"Huh" a small gasp is heard before a bigger one, air being gasped in. "What happened?" she groans when she's able to breathe without all the coughing.

"There was another eruption," Jacob tells her, his heart slowing down after she finally takes a deeper breath. "We took a big hit here in the front

4

line but so far haven't lost anyone, that I know of. That makes us pretty lucky," he says quietly to Kat after he pulls her into his arms, unable to bear the thought of losing her. *So close, so many times*, he thinks.

"Kat, can you tell me if anything hurts?" Rand asks while Jacob holds her.

"My head hurts, and my back a little, but not terrible," she says groggily. "What happened to me?" she asks in confusion.

"The tent collapsed on you. By the looks of it, you tried to protect Jane's dad by pushing him forward. He must have tripped; I found laying on top of him, with the tent and a couple of poles laying on you. We pulled you out and then we pulled him out. We found Jane's mom first and got her outside, they're both just now regaining consciousness. Looks like we all got pretty lucky," Jacob adds on a sigh of relief.

"Ask me how lucky I feel later, right now, not so much" Kat says on a groan.

"I know, but at least you're still alive. I had my doubts about that when I first found you. Even though you were breathing, it was so faint I wasn't sure if you'd make it," Jacob says, the pain in his voice showing his fear clearly.

"I'm okay, Snake, I promise," Kat insists quietly, understanding the fear he must have experienced. "I'll be fine in just a couple of minutes," she murmurs as Snakes face gets closer, a reassuring kiss imminent. As firm lips touch her soft ones, she groans into his mouth, opening for tongues to touch, deepening the kiss, stroke by stroke, kissing like lovers finally meeting.

"You have to stop doing this Kat. I can't take much more of these close calls. Do you have any idea how many times you've come close to dying on me?" Snake says in frustration and with residual fear.

"I don't do these things on purpose Snake. I wouldn't, you know that. I would never do anything to worry or hurt you."

"I know," he says on a groan, kissing her lips lightly over and over, reassuring himself she's fine. Slowly raising himself up, he runs his fingers through her hair, and over her face before letting her go, helping her to sit up slowly while watching for any look of pain on her face.

"See, I told you, I'm fine!" she says with a quick grin after she manages to sit up.

"So I see," Snake agrees with a smile.

"Well, I guess we need to get to work. We can't expect Jane to not come looking for us, since we showed her parents to her on TV. What happened, anyway? Was it an earthquake?"

"Nope, it was an eruption from Yellowstone. Not a huge one, but this one was larger than the last. We're all going to have to start moving, since we have no idea if it's going to erupt again, and if it does, will it be the big one? We're way to close for a big one, this small one almost did us in. Any larger and that could be it for all of us! Mongoose, gather everyone together for a quick meeting. We need to get moving," Jacob orders him.

"I'll get them but where do you want me to send them? All the tents are on the ground, there are no buildings in this area, so where do you want to meet?"

"Let's meet near the truck. At least that's still standing!"

"You got it Lieutenant."

"Eli, glad to see you're okay. Mallory, no injuries, that's a relief," Jacob says as everyone starts to gather for the meeting.

"Yeah, it was close, but I'm quick. I almost got laid out by a tent pole, but dodged it, just!" Mallory admits with a grin.

"Wow, everyone sure looks a little dusty" Kat teases.

"That's the pot calling the kettle black, don't you think?" Eli says teasingly.

"Yeah, I know, but at least my face is pretty clean, if only I had a mirror," Kats adds laughing. "Let's take a seat, we need to make some decisions now about which way we want to go" Jacob says.

"I've been thinking about that," Eli says "and I think that the largest group should head south to Texas. The underground is dwindling, and there's no point in Jane getting her hands on the few of us that are left."

"Okay," Jacob says, "But why. What's your thought process?"

"Well, if the large group takes off south, and Jane hears about a large number of people, heading south towards Texas, I think she'll head after us. She won't realize that her parents aren't with us. She really can't do anything to us, since we haven't done anything and it would put her in a very bad light. That's not something she needs right now, when she's trying to go worldwide with her chips. The last thing she needs is any negativity."

"Good thought," Jacob says. "If you head south, then Kat, me, Rand and Jane's parents head a different direction, we might be able to get past her troops without them being any wiser. We're going to need some new transportation, anyway. You guys take the trucks and such, just leave us the pick-up. I think maybe we'll head to Sturgis, meet up with my biker friends. I'll make some calls. Maybe we can get a big biker group together. She'll never think to look in that direction. Then we can start heading east, through South Dakota, Minnesota, Wisconsin and then into Chicago. Then further east into New York and then south to D.C. It'll be a nice break and we can get some of my friends involved, too. It's only August, so the weather should hold, and bikes will give us more freedom than say a big truck. It'll allow us to scatter, if we need to."

Chapter Two

"Really Teriq, you've got nothing?" Jane asks quietly. "No sign, no hint of where they could possibly be? You've looked everywhere out there?" Jane asks, desperation starting to set in.

"Of course I've looked everywhere. All that we've found is some material that looks to be shirts, pants, that kind of stuff. They were burnt up pretty good, but that doesn't mean they were your parents. It could have been anything or anyone's, but I doubt they were your parents."

"Why Teriq, why wouldn't they be my parents?"

"They look like some farmer's clothes. Old beat up blue jeans, and tee shirts. They all seem a little too big for either of your parents. Not that I expect they were dressed in good clothes. After all, they've been with the underground for who knows how long. They could look like anything at the moment."

"True," Jane says, thinking. "Teriq, you know it's been over two weeks since you left here, and you're just now getting to the eruption area? I doubt you'll find anyone at the speed that you're searching," she says sarcastically.

"Jane, I told you what took so long. This area has been devastated. There's no way to move fast with what we've had to go through. Plus, I told you we had to bury a lot of people. Mostly from the heat of the eruption, but some of it was air quality. All they had to breath was ash air and you know how toxic that is, right?"

"So let me clarify this. You hold no hope that you'll find my parents. Do you think they're dead? Because I KNOW they're ALIVE! You have to find them. I'm serious about this Teriq. You DO NOT come back here without my parents. Do you UNDERSTAND?" Jane screams at him.

"Yeah Jane, I got it. Calm down. We'll find your parents, I promise. It's just taking longer because of the condition this area's in. It's freakin hot and dry. There's very little water to be found, at least where we are right now. I'm sure we'll find some if we head further south. That's our plan for now. South for water and to interview anyone we can and see if we can find someone that's seen that group. It's really too big to hide easily. There has to be someone that's seen them, and I swear I will find someone to tell me which way they went."

"Fine, then keep in touch with me, and keep me updated," Jane demands before hanging up.

"Honestly Quinton, you'd think he'd be better with all the experience he has, not to mention the title he now carries. It feels like I have to do everything myself." Jane adds in disgust. "I really can't see a good reason why this is taking him so long. The longer he takes the more danger my parents are in. Especially when that group finds out that I'm not changing anything. I'm just going about the same things in a different way. This country will never know what hit it, and the people, they're starting to love me, which I knew would happen. All I'm waiting for now, are my parents. After all they've been through, it's only right that they walk near me when I take over world power. We only have a few months before the big meeting in Brussels. And just a few weeks until the summit, where the rest of the world will receive the chips, making the United States the richest and most powerful country in the world. Like it's been meant to be, they just needed the right leader," she adds with a smile.

"You're amazing, Jane. I've worked for years and have never seen anyone with your capabilities. You make a perfect President. And you're right. The people are starting to come around. You haven't been in office that long, but you've already changed the course of the United States drastically and in a way that will never be forgotten. You're making history Jane, how's that feel?" Quinton asks with a grin.

"It feels awesome! I've dreamed this dream since I was three. My parents told me that someday I would become President of the United States, and once that was accomplished, I would become Dictator of the World. Everything is finally falling into place. Today I work on the few countries that are trying to hold out on me. They won't, and I will succeed because I will allow no one to escape. Every country, every person on this planet will bow down to me. This world will become known as one nation under Jane.

Now, I must speak with the countries that

have called to offer help. I will accept some and other's I will not. No one wants to become like China, forgotten by the world, destroyed. They are being used as the perfect example of what not to do. The world has been sitting back and watching, and I've shown them what happens to those who do not follow me, who mock and refuse to bend. They become broken."

* * *

"Hey, Eli, be careful out there. You'll find some unrest, but doubtful it will be as bad as it was. From everything that we've been hearing, the country's starting to accept Jane and the changes. After all the natural disasters that everyone's been facing, people are getting tired. They've gone into the survival mode. Like I've said before, Americans have short term memory problems. It has become a 'me' world. If it doesn't affect me, then it's okay. That's the way Jane's going to succeed, by waiting until everyone accepts. Evil becomes the accepted, and then it becomes not evil, but what everyone knows. What everyone is used to," Jacob says tiredly, rubbing his hands over his face, wishing for somewhere to relax, if only for a moment. "I promise that we will never stop working to change what has become. We can't let her continue on the way that she's going. We do know that her goal is world domination, and no one in the world will survive that. SO we will continue on with the goal of stopping Jane, at any cost."

"Don't worry Jacob there are some of us that will rally behind you, as soon as you give the word. Not everyone will follow Jane. Our group will be constantly talking to others, just to find out and to remind everyone why we must stop her. The cause is just, and trust me, there are a lot more like us out there, we just have to keep reminding them of the why. Where are you and your group heading?" Eli asks quietly.

"We're going to head for Sturgis. I've called a few of my buddies and they're working on getting nondescript bikes. They want to join us for a cross country ride. I figure it's easier to hide out in that kind of a group, than try to make it across the country by dodging shadows. Jane's parents will travel with us. There's still time to use their position against Jane and trust me, I plan on it. It won't be a fast ride, but fast enough. The goal is to stop her from leaving for the summit. I'm going to try to keep all the problems on this stratosphere. I figure it'll be easier for all of us to work from D.C. then to try to follow her across the world. It'll probably take us a week to get to D.C. from here, which leaves us a little over a week before she leaves. That's leaves plenty of time to throw a wrench in the works," Jacob says grinning.

"As soon as we get to Austin, I'll call and give you our new contact information. I don't want to lose out on the updates," Eli adds.

"Jacob, can I talk to you privately, for just a minute?" Mallory asks quietly.

"Sure Mal, let's take a walk," Jacob offers, concern in his eyes.

"What's up Mal?"

"I was wondering. Is there any way that Mongoose can go with you and Rand with us?"

"Why would you ask....never mind, I think I

know, you and Rand, huh?"

"Yeah, we hooked up a while back and believe the relationship is good, getting better. I think he would prefer to stay with me, but doesn't want to cause any problems. So what do you think? Can he switch out positions? I know this is asking a lot, but I think I'm really falling for him and believe it's mutual."

"Let me talk to Mongoose and get his opinion. He may want to go with Eli and that group."

"Okay, thanks Jacob, I appreciate it" Mallory says quietly, hugging Jacob, tears in her eyes.

* * *

"How much longer, Snake?" Kat asks around a huge yawn.

"Not till tomorrow Kat. I think everyone's pretty much done in. The past few days have been tough, between putting out fires and then the eruption, I think we could all use an early night. I know I could," he says tiredly.

"What do you say Mongoose? Ready to find some rooms for the night, get an early start in the morning?"

"Sounds good to me Lieutenant, I'm a little tired myself," he admits.

"If I remember correctly, there's an old hotel just down the road, near the Wyoming border. That'll give us maybe three hours in the morning before reaching Sturgis. We should all get there close to the same time. Another twenty minutes or so and we should see that hotel. I hope they still have food today. I'm sure everyone's a little hungry."

"Yeah, I could eat," Mongoose says as Kat says

the same thing and they both start laughing.

"Wow, you guys sure do think alike," Snake says laughing.

"I think I'd like a nice juicy steak. I haven't had one of those in so long that I don't think I can even remember how it tastes. That's just pitiful, a man shouldn't ever lose the memory of how a steak tastes!" Mongoose says with a chuckle.

"Amen to that brother. I need one of those too. It's been at least a year since I've had one, which is way too long" Snake adds thoughtfully.

"Is that all guys think about, food?" Kat asks quietly.

"No, but its right up there near the top on the '10 most important things in life' list."

"What else is on that list," she asks curiously.

"Kat, you don't know about the list," Snake says with a quick teasing look at Mongoose.

"Actually, I've never heard of the list," she says in confusion.

"Well, let me tell you what's on it," he says. "Ready?"

"Yep"

"All right, number Ten; a comfortable bed to sleep in, number Nine; a comfortable chair to sit in, number Eight; a big screen TV to watch football on, number Seven; lots of pizza to go with the football, number Six; plenty of cold beer to go with the pizza, number Five; a mid afternoon nap, number Four; a good hunting rifle, number Three; more beer, number Two; a fast motorcycle, and number One, "drum roll please. . . the most important thing on the list is a willing woman to have hot sex with. You get everything on that list and a man's a happy guy." Snake says laughing, a wide grin on his face.

"Were you teasing me Snake?" Kat asks in suspicion.

"Hell no, I wasn't teasing you! The list is real, it's just sometimes the items change places, but I've never seen number One change," he adds with a leer towards Kat whose face has turned a few shades of red.

"There's that hotel. Looks like its still open, must mean they have some rooms available. You stay here," Snake says as he parks the truck. "I'll head in and see if they have what we need. Mongoose, you're on the first babysitting shift, I'll take over in about six hours."

"No problem, Lieutenant, just point me in the direction of the food."

"Soon Mongoose, very soon."

"Okay, we're all set," Snake says when he jumps back into the truck. "I've got two rooms, one for me and Kat and the other for Jane's parents and you. They're at opposite ends from each other, so I took them. We'll grab dinner and then hit the sack. It's gonna be a busier day tomorrow than today, believe it or not. Hold on and I'll drive you down, then I'll park in the middle so no one knows where we are."

* * *

"Wow, I'm stuffed," Kat says as she drags herself into the hotel room. "I ate way too much, a lot more than I'm used to," she adds as she sits on the edge of the bed and then lays back and groans.

"Comfy" Snake asks as he watches her from

the door.

"Oh yeah, very" she mumbles, closing her eyes for just a second.

"Kat, wake up, it's just a dream, shh, there's nothing here I promise, shh," Snake says to a whimpering Kat.

"What?" Kat asks loudly as she wakes with a jolt.

"You were having a bad dream, that's all," Snake says quietly as he holds her and runs his hand up and down her arm, shoulder and back in a comforting way. 'Everything's fine' he murmurs.

"What time is it?" she asks on a yawn.

"It's close to one in the morning."

"What, it can't be, I just laid down here for a second," she adds shocked.

"Yeah, you fell instantly asleep," he teases with a grin. "You must have been exhausted."

"I was pretty tired, but I didn't think I was that tired," she confesses.

"Remember what happened yesterday?" he asks gruffly.

"Wait, the eruption, right?"

"Yeah, the one that knocked you out for a good ten minutes, a long ten minutes."

"Oh yeah, I remember the eruption, but forgot that I got hit in the head and knocked out. That must have been why I was so tired. Guess that makes sense now that I think of it."

"Yep, it makes a lot of sense. You're also not known for taking care of yourself, so it's no wonder that you forgot that you were knocked out."

"Aw Snake, that's not fair. I take care of myself, most of the time."

"No way Kitten, no you don't. You're the last person you think of, always."

"Yeah, you're right this one time," she admits.

"Right, one time," he says on a snort.

"Well, okay, maybe you're right more often," she says, taking a deep breath.

"I know I'm right," he says leaning in closer, breathing in her scent. "Kat," he murmurs.

"Snake," she breathes back as his lips touch hers gently, his hand moving slowly upward, gently oh so gently, until at last he holds her breast in his hand. On a gasp she starts to tighten in fear and he knows, showing her by kissing her more deeply, tongues touching, searching until she relaxes again, that he will never hurt her.

"Kat," he whispers as his lips move across her cheek, to her ear and down her neck, small soft kisses, small nibbles, no pain. She moves her neck further so that he can reach easier, every point that his mouth wants to reach. Gently moving his hand under her shirt, he holds her breast through her bra, but it's not enough, not until he slides his hand inside where the heavy warmth beckons. The nipple puckers for his touch. As he slowly plays with and holds that little pebble, his head moving down her neck to her chest, soft sighs are all that's heard in the room. There are just the two lovers, discovering each other, in no hurry.

"Kat," she hears as a question of yes or no, all that's needed.

"Snake, I love you," he hears and with a groan he eases his mouth back up to hers and into a deeper kiss, one that will take them both on the journey of each other. With tongues sparing, and little nips happening on both sides, excitement gains ground.

"Ohhh, Snake," she whispers as she feels him remove her shirt and bra, his head moving down to nestle between her breasts, licks and kisses covering her chest and one breast and then the other while his hands play, hold them and squeeze them together.

"I've wanted this forever, Kitten," Snake murmurs as he takes them to another level. As he slowly lowers her zipper and tugs gently on her pants, she starts breathing quickly, excited in spite of the fear she keeps pushing back. When he tosses her panties to the chair, she's open for full viewing and he's never seen anything more beautiful. With gentle hands he pets and smoothes the softest skin he's ever felt. Gently pulling her legs apart, he touches her softly, gently rubbing her clit, and catching her groan with a kiss.

She'd wanted this, no needed this forever. As his kisses deepen to raw sexual power she loses herself, her body tight with pure sexual need. There's no time to think, only demand, her body so close to orgasm that she can't breathe. One small touch could send her over and yet he slows and backs off as she groans and complains.

"Shh Kitten, shh," he says as he slowly moves his body down, kissing her puckered nipples, spending time on each one even as she demands more. With a final pull on a nipple, he licks, then moves lower, his goal obvious. Touching her with a finger, he slowly moves it over her clit and through the curls that are hiding his destination. After parting her for better viewing, he groans just as he prepares to taste that which is beckoning.

With a slow move he kisses her before drinking of the nectar that has been calling. Kat yell's softly, her heartbeat accelerating until all thought's left and only feeling remains, but oh what feeling. With him thrusting in and out with his tongue, rubbing her clit harder and harder, Kat reaches the point of no return. Her muscles become rigid and so tight she almost reaches climax, then she screams as she falls off the edge with his next move, her body shaking, lights flashing behind closed lids.

He begins the journey up slowly, kissing, nipping, and licking every inch of skin he can reach until he reaches her mouth, and kisses her deeply, tongues thrusting like a dual, she giving as good as she gets. She moves her hands to his big hard chest, playing with his nipples, making him groan into her mouth, slowly moving her hands down to touch him, so hard yet like velvet, building her excitement to breaking point. Then he nudges her legs wider giving him easy access and gently positions himself to enter, murmuring "Kat, wrap your legs around my waist." After she moves her legs to get a good grip, he starts slowly entering, waiting for the fear, the panic, but only hears her groan with pleasure, the tightening of her muscles proof that she's ready.

"Harder Snake," she whispers before claiming his lips for a deep kiss, "I need you, I need this," she murmurs.

He buries himself to the hilt, and then his thrusts become harder, faster, deeper until neither can breathe, all thoughts are gone, only feeling, exquisite feeling is all that's left. Then the moment occurs when their hearts beat as one, their bodies connect on the most fundamental level and they reach explosive climax together.

Snake moves gently off of her, afraid of hurting her he pulls her up onto his chest. They both fall quickly into a deep, soft sleep, content as never before.

Chapter Three

"We're almost there, just another couple of minutes. This area looks the same, there's not much difference considering I haven't been here in, oh, five years now," Snake says. "We'll probably find them waiting for us at the Hard Rock. It's where we used to meet up, back in the day. Yep, there they are," Snake says when he sees a couple of hundred bikes parked out front of the Hard Rock. "Mongoose, remember to call me Snake, it's what they know me as. I never told them my real name, or what I did. As far as they're all concerned, I'm a buddy with a bike and own a bike shop in Texas. That's my undercover story and I stuck with it tight. I couldn't afford for anyone to find out about the real me."

"You got it, Snake," Mongoose agrees with a grin.

"Kat, you stick close to me. This is a tough group. When they see that we're together, they won't try anything, but until then, you're open for too many things, trust me. They're actually a good group, they just don't look it."

"Snake, man, how's it going," a biker with big burly muscles and tattoo's of skulls on his head and arms yells out from the balcony of the second floor of the Hard Rock when Snake cuts the engine of his truck. "What the hell are you driving, man?"

"By bike broke down and I didn't have time to replace it, that's why I called you, you bastard," Snake yells back with a big grin.

As Kat exits the truck, she hears whistles coming from everywhere. Snake pulls her into his side establishing their relationship. Groans can be heard coming from the second floor, after his biker friends realize that she's taken, by one of the meanest of their friends.

"Let's go up, I could use a beer and I want to introduce you to my friends," Snake says to Kat and Mongoose. "The guy I just yelled at goes by the name Killer. He's the interim leader of this unruly group. Mongoose, you need to get Jane's parents and bring them up, too. Warn them though, to keep their mouths shut. If these guys find out who they are, I'm sure they'd sooner kill them then waste time and money to let them ride with us. I'll need to talk to the leaders of the group, and explain to them who they are and their importance. But first, I need to remind them of who I am, and take my leadership place back. All right, let's do this, follow my lead. Talking is best done only after you've been around them awhile. Until then, keep your mouths shut and your eyes open."

"Snake, I thought you were dead man," Killer says after the guy slap on the back and the light punching session. "Where you been, you just dropped off the face of the earth a couple of years ago and no one ever saw you again. We asked after you, everywhere we stopped, but nothing."

"I settled back in Texas, worked on bikes for awhile, visited D.C. a few times, and finally got back together with my family back east. This is the first time I've had to get back here, and I called as soon as I knew I was gonna be in the neighborhood!" he says with a laugh. "It's good to know you missed me," he adds with a wicked look in his eye and a sarcastic smile aimed at his friend Killer. With his black hair tied back in a pony and his biker clothes on, he looks like the leader of the worst of the worst, and is received back into his group as if he'd never left.

"Hey man, it's good to see you," Killer says loud enough to get the agreement from everyone else at the Hard Rock bar.

"Oh yeah," Snake asks, placing Kat in a chair at a table and moving on his friend. "So, it sure didn't take you long to take my place, now did it, Killer?"

"It's not like it seems," Killer says quietly. Then louder "Hey man, you left us, not the other way around. Someone had to take control. The top of the food chain, that's what I am. Of course I'm in charge."

"Really," Snake says, advancing closer, preparing for battle. "Who voted you in?" Snake asks. "Were you voted in?" he asks even softer.

"Tell him guys that you wanted me to lead, remember, after he dropped out of sight you said you wanted me to lead?" The demand is met by silence. There's not a person there that wants to be on the receiving end of Snakes bad mood. Besides, they like Snake. He was a good leader, fair. Now Killer, he's not a good leader, really a chicken shit is what he is. There's just been no-one that cared

24

enough to take over his leadership. They all pretty much do what they want to, most days, anyway.

"Fine," Snake says to the silence. "It looks like they don't want you as leader. What do you think I should do about this?" Snake asks quietly.

"I don't think you should do anything, except maybe have a beer," Killer says with a slight grin.

"Yeah, that sounds like a good plan. I been on the road for days, it seems. Thanks, Killer, for taking the lead while I've been tied up. I appreciate it!"

"No problem Snake. It's good to have you back, right where you belong," Killer says after a handshake and a punch on the shoulder.

"Snake, were you messing with him," Kat whispers when he comes over to where she's sitting.

"Was it that obvious?" he asks.

"To me it was, but the rest, I'm not sure. You'd have to ask them," she adds with a wicked grin.

"Not right now," he says with a wink.

"Wow, I'm exhausted," Kat says after a couple of beers and one mean bar burger.

"Me too," Snake agrees escorting her down the stairs to the truck. "It's time to hit the hotel area. I need a good night's sleep. We leave at first light. It's all set up. Our bikes are here so you'll be riding with me. Mongoose will take Jane's Mom and Killer's gonna let her Dad ride with him. I only provided specific info to Killer. The less everyone knows the better. I'm pretty tired tonight since I didn't sleep much last night, something kept scratching at me, wouldn't leave me alone!"

"What," Kat says on an indrawn breath! "Shh

25

Snake, someone might hear you" she says face flushing in embarrassment.

"Aw, don't be like that Kitten, I'm just teasing and no one heard you except me," he says quietly. "Besides, we didn't do anything wrong. As a matter of fact, we did everything right" he adds with a devilish grin, blue eyes innocent.

"Snaaake, please," she says plaintively. "Stop saying that, stop."

"If I stop, can we go back to the hotel room and do that again?" he asks teasingly yet seriously. "Kitten, you listening?" he asks when there's no sound from Kat.

'Yeah, I was just remembering last night," she admits with a wicked looked out of those oh so green eyes.

"Kitten, you better not look at me like that. If you don't stop, I won't be responsible for what everyone else around here hears or sees. That'll all be on you!"

"I believe it was all ON me anyway, last night," she says running for the truck, a laugh following her.

"Fine, that's the way you want to play, let's go," he adds with a smile as he pushes her further into the truck and jumps in to head out, revs the engine and tares out of the parking lot.

"Ummmm, Snake."

"Yeah, what is it?"

"Aren't you forgetting something?" she asks innocently.

"Now what," he growls.

"Mongoose."

"Shit, why didn't you remind me before this?"

he says as he turns the truck around to head back to the bar.

"I just figured you wouldn't leave until they got in the truck."

"You made sure my mind was occupied on something totally different," he adds with a smirk.

"You started it," she says indignantly.

"Ahh, but you certainly finished it, didn't you," he replies.

"Hey Mongoose" Snake yells out the window after pulling up to the bar. "What the hell is taking you so long?"

"We came out here once, but you were already headed that way," Mongoose says as he points to the end of the road. "What's the hurry man? Couldn't wait for us to get in? Is there a fire or something?

"Yeah, or something!" Snake agrees with devilment and a sideways glance at Kat.

***

"I think that's everyone, let's head out," Snake yells, the bike noise deafening. Taking the lead he waves to Killer who pulls out after Mongoose. *With over a hundred bikes all moving in the same direction, there's no fear of being stopped by anyone, including Jane's special-ops group. These bikers are way too intimidating. Thankfully, they'll all split off before Chicago. The logistics of this many bikes hitting restaurants all at the same time is not doable. Not to mention hotel rooms for this many. Besides, once we get to Chicago, the city will help to hide us and the rest can start back home"* Snake thinks as he rehashes the plans he made, in his head.

"I think we'll stop now," Snake informs Kat after pulling into a small, out of the way hotel about fifteen minutes from Chicago, and shutting down his bike.

"Thank God," Kat says, struggling to stand after having been on the bike for close to fifteen hours. "I thought bike riding would be fun, you know, kinda like Easy Rider or something like that," she adds disgusted. "If this is what it feels like, I don't get what the big deal is. Actually, my hips hurt so bad, I'm not sure I'll be able to get back on that bike tomorrow!"

"Sorry Kitten. Its rough riding that long if you're not used to it. I'm even a little sore, but I'll be fine by tomorrow."

"Really Snake," Kat says on a groan, "tomorrow?"

"If you're still as bad in the morning, maybe we can hang for a couple of days, instead of getting right back in the saddle tomorrow."

"Thanks I totally appreciate that," Kat says with a tired sigh, her whole body sagging.

"No problem, Kitten. Here, grab my arm I'll help you to the room."

"Ahh," Kat groans as she lies on the bed. "This room's not a very nice one, but the bed, awesome," she says to Snake, who's just standing there and watching her, a small grin playing over his lips.

"The room doesn't have to be five star, we're just staying a couple of days, not buying it or anything. Besides, it's off the beaten path, which makes it harder for anyone to find us."

"That's perfect. We don't have to worry about anyone knocking on our door then."

***

A loud pounding on the door in the middle of the night jerks Snake and Kat awake. After grabbing their guns, they check through the peep hole to see who's making the racket and when they find Mongoose, they jerk the door open.

"What the hell is so important that it couldn't wait until morning," Snake yells at Mongoose.

"Sorry, I'm really sorry Sir, but we have a problem."

"What is it," Snake asks as he puts his gun down, seeing no threat.

"Jane's parents, they're gone."

"Gone where?" Snake demands.

"I'm not sure, Sir. I left for two minutes to get some ice and when I got back, they were gone. The ice machine's not more than thirty feet from the door to the room, my back was turned less than twenty seconds and yet when I got back, they were gone. I didn't see or hear anything. It's like they disappeared in a puff of smoke."

"Well shit, Mongoose. We have to find them. Chicago's not the nicest city in the world, especially some of the outlying municipalities, like Joliette. Nice small town with a shitload of gang-bangers. The last thing we need is for them to be grabbed. Lord knows what they'll do with them. Head out, we'll start the search. We need them back before anything happens. Meet back here in a few hours, hopefully with them back in our hands. Mongoose, you go with Killer, and Kat and I will head out to search, too."

"Yes Sir. I'm really sorry, Snake."

"Yeah man, I know. Don't worry about it, we'll find them."

"Let's take the smaller areas and look at every place," Snake says to Kat as they start up the bike. "Better plan for a long day, this area's pretty densely populated. Keep your eye on any area that a group of kids hang together. They could try to get lost in the groups. If they blend, we'll have a real hard time finding them."

"I'm heading east on Jefferson, then we'll start a grid search. Go north and south off Jefferson onto Scott Street, then if we keep heading east, we'll cover the majority of Joliette. We should cross Mongoose since he'll probably do the grid thing too!"

"Shit, we just spent six hours looking for those two and nothing. Where the hell could they have got to? This place isn't that big. Something tells me that someone's got them. My question is who took them, and where the hell did they put them?" Snake bitches at Kat.

"I know really, they couldn't have gotten that far. We took off after them no more than a half hour after they took off. Obviously they know how to hide. If you think about it, they've been hiding most of their lives here in the states. I guess you could call it 'hiding in plain sight,' she says in disgust. "Oh well, so much for a good night's sleep."

"Let's get a little rest, and then we'll head out again, see if something turns up. Maybe by that time, Mongoose will be back with some good news."

"We can hope."

* * *

"Nothing, Sir, I'm sorry. I've looked everywhere I could think, and found nothing. I even stopped a few gang members and they said they saw no one with their descriptions. They could have been lying, no they probably were lying," Mongoose informs them upon his return to the hotel.

"Get some rest, Mongoose, and we'll head back out in a few hours. We'll probably have more luck after dark, since the one's that may help them would be the gangs that hang out around here after dark. No point in wasting our time with daylight hours," Snake says. "Kat, turn on the local news, and let's see if there's anything going on that's important, that we may need to know."

***

"This just in, this is Breaking News," the anchor reports. "President Jane Martin has received a hostage demand today an anonymous informant from the White House has informed us. A gang cell from Chicago has contacted her saying that they have her parents and they want ten million dollars for their release. We have no idea how they got to Chicago, especially since for the past six months or more they have been presumed dead. It must have been a relief for the President to at least know that they're alive and well. She hasn't released anything about this yet, so we're unsure what she plans on doing about this situation. Stay tuned for more information as we receive it."

***

"Damn it," Snake growls. "I had a bad feeling earlier when there was no sign of them that someone had them. Now the President knows where they are."

"No, she only knows that they're in Chicago, she doesn't know where yet. We spent hours earlier looking for them, so even if she sends her special ops, that doesn't mean that she'll find them that fast. We still have time, if we start now, right? I mean, even her special ops were probably looking for them near the eruption site, so they're not that close."

"True Kitten, but that means they're out this way already, so they don't have the long distance from D.C. to here to go. It does mean that they could get here faster than we thought. It also means that we'll have to ramp up our movements, try to find them, get them back and head out before her special ops unit gets here. No more nap's," Snake says disappointed.

"True Snake, sorry I didn't think of that," Kat says quietly, her time with Snake coming to an end. Who knows when they'll have any time again, if ever.

"Okay, we need a plan," he says to Mongoose, Kat and Killer.

"Killer, you can take off. We're done for now, but stay reachable. Things are going to start revving up real soon and we may need the whole gang as back-up."

"No problem Snake. You sure take on some big

jobs, my man."

"Yeah, so I've been told," Snake admits with a tired grin.

"All right then, I'm off. The fewer bikes together, the less chance those special ops people you been talking about will have to find you. You may be able to get the parents back if you act like your part of their gang."

"Those are the lines I'm thinking on," Snake admits.

Chapter Four

"Jane, Charles Rosenthal called a little while ago. You might be interested in what he has to say," Quinton says after reaching Jane on the phone.

"Who is Charles Rosenthal and is it about my parents," Jane asks, pacing her office, phone in hand.

"No," Quinton admits in frustration.

"Then I probably don't care what he has to say."

"Listen Jane, not everything's about your parents, no offense. However, you need to work on not just waiting for information about them but about what's happening right now. This is your chance to shine in spite of all the pressure you're under regarding your parents. Charles Rosenthal is an astronomer, and a close advisor to your predecessor. According to what he told me, he has some information that could possibly affect the whole earth."

"Oh, what's that? Are we going to be destroyed by an asteroid?" Jane asks sarcastically.

"Not quite, but I really think you should talk to

him."

"Fine Quinton, I'll talk to him, but in person, not on the phone. I make better decisions when in person. I have an opening tomorrow morning at eight thirty. Have him here at that time and I'll give him a half hour."

"Thanks Jane, I appreciate it. You won't be sorry," Quinton says in relief.

* * *

"I need to make a couple of calls Kat," Snake says while looking for his phone and the numbers he carries in his wallet. "I'm going to see if I can find Chico. He's a friend and the leader of that other special-ops unit in Iran a few months ago. We've worked together on and off for years. I have his back and he usually has mine. I'm sure he'll be happy to help. I have an idea about that gang. Chico's of Puerto Rican descent, and should blend in with the gang that took Jane's parents. If I can get him here within the next day or so, he can infiltrate that gang, grab her parents and take off for D.C. We'll gain a lot more information from Jane herself, when he delivers her parents to her. She should be grateful enough to keep him around, even if it's only for the protection of her parents. She's not going to want to take any chances with them once she has them back."

"That would be awesome Snake. A way to hear what's going on before the media gets the information. It might just allow us to keep up. Not that we were doing that bad, but hey, anything helps," she says before flopping on the bed with a groan. "I'm so tired," she complains to Snake, who doesn't hear her, he's listening to the phone connecting.

"Hey man," Snake says in relief. "I wasn't sure if this was the right number or not. I know we usually change numbers every month or so, but with everything that's been going on, the eruptions, Jane's special ops unit that we've had to dodge, the explosions; I've been a little busy."

"No doubt, Lieutenant, I planned on changing numbers but wanted to talk to you first. I can't cover your ass if I can't reach you some way. You've definitely been on the move, that's for sure." Chico says seriously. "Is everything all right?"

"It will be, if I can get your help with something I'm planning on this end," Snake says quietly.

"Whatever you need, Lieutenant," Chico assures him.

"Great. Any way you can get to Chicago, in the next few hours?" Snake asks.

"I can. I'll arrange for a Blackhawk. I have a friend that has one available, and doesn't mind flying at night, undercover. Just give me a few hours and I'll be knocking on your door. Anything else I need to know right now? Otherwise, don't say anything till we meet in person. I don't trust this phone anymore. I've had the number so long; it's probably not secure."

"My thoughts too, appreciate it. I'll see you soon. Call me when you get close to the destination."

"Yes Sir out."

"He'll be here in a couple of hours," Snake says to Kat before looking to see what's she's doing so quietly. Never mind, he thinks when he sees her sound asleep on the bed. A couple of hours sound great, he decides as he lies down next to her and closes his eyes. Chico will call when he lands, he reassures himself before falling asleep.

Kat wakes with a groan and an arm flying out to hit that stupid noise. I must have set the alarm she thinks before hitting something hard, warm and solid. With a gasp she springs into a sitting position, finding herself on the bed next to Snake who's searching for the phone that's making the racket.

"Snake, you scared me to death," Kat says hoarsely as Snake holds his hand up for quiet.

"He's here," he says to Kat after hanging up the phone. "Sorry Kitten, I didn't mean to scare you," Snake says quietly.

"That's okay. I'm sorry I fell asleep. I didn't mean to. I just laid down for a second, then hear what I thought was my alarm. I didn't mean to hit you," she says with a blush moving over her face.

"No harm no foul," Snake admits with a grin. "I fell asleep too. When I saw you, it looked like a real good idea so I did the same thing, and feel much better for it. Anyway, that was Chico. He'll be here within the next twenty minutes or so. They're looking for a place to land. Once they find that, he'll be getting some transportation, and then he'll be here. I told him a car would probably be the best bet. He just needs to have room for three, Jane's parents and himself, something that will get him to D.C. easily. Finally, our plans seem to be back on track. Once he leaves for D.C., then we can take off too, just on a different route."

"What a relief," Kat says. "We're running out

of time, Snake. The Summit's on the horizon and we're no closer to D.C. than we were a few days ago. We need to get closer to the president so that we can throw a wrench in the works. I'm going to make it my life's work to make her life miserable, in the nicest possible way," she adds with a grin.

"It'll be fun, watching her frustration level rise. I'm looking forward to all the mean spirited little things we have planned that will make her crazy!"

"Where are we going to live when we get back to D.C?" Kat asks.

"I think we should consider my parents house. There's no one there, it's got everything we need and we can hide the fact that anyone is staying there pretty easily. Mom installed blackout curtains in every room, just in case anyone needed to hide out, anyone being me of course. That was before they knew I was in the service. They just thought that I was a bad kid, always in trouble. Mom and I talked a lot when we were underground. I'm glad I had the opportunity to get to know them both before they died," Snake says with a soft smile, eyes glistening.

"I know your parents loved you and were very proud of you Snake," Kat says, tears leaving trails down her cheeks. "She told me how proud of you she was. She planned on telling you herself, but never got the chance. Things were crazy that last week that we were underground."

"Don't cry Kitten," Snake says as he pulls her close, comfort in bodies touching. "We did get some time, more than we had when I was young. I have no regrets. They saw who I really was, and I had time to tell them why. I'm glad. I'm glad I got to get to know my brothers and sister again, too."

* * *

"He's here Kat."

"Chico, come in man," Snake says after opening the door. "This is Kat. Kat, this is Chico."

"Miss," Chico says politely.

"It's nice to meet you," Kat says with a grin. "Sorry for the crappy job, though."

"No problem. Besides, the jobs not crappy, it needs to be done, we need to try to put a stop to what Jane's doing. I've heard things that should never have been thought or done. She's broken just about every law we live by in the United States."

"Yes she has, and with no conscience whatsoever," Kat says in agreement.

"How was the trip," Snake asks during the pause.

"Quiet. I had the pilot hold until I talked to you. I didn't have the criteria and wasn't sure if you needed him for anything else.

"Thanks, but I think from here on out, we'll be traveling the motor route. There's less chance of being seen that way. I thought we'd all blend easier by bike and by car or truck than by Blackhawk.

"You got that right Lieutenant."

"All right, let's head out for some food. We can talk there." Snake adds as he throws his coat on. "I'll let Mongoose know and he can meet us outside. We'll ride together, start making some plans."

"Sounds good to me," Chico says. "It's been a while since my last meal. You have to eat when you get the chance. The next time may be a day or two."

"The last few weeks has been a hit or miss. I need fuel to keep going, too!" Snake laughs as he heads out the door.

* * *

"Thanks Snake, I feel much better now," Kat says around a yawn.

"Looks like you still need some sleep. Sorry Kitten, but I doubt that's going to happen till much later tonight. We have to get Chico infiltrated into that gang and remove Jane's parents before those idiots get out of control."

"I know, Snake, I'll be fine."

* * *

"So Chico, take the spare bike that Mongoose is using. He can have it back later, but for now, you need the ability to either join the gang or find out where they're holding her parents and grab them. I'll get transportation lined up for the three of you. I'm hoping we can accomplish this today. The longer we delay, the more things that stupid gang can have in place. I still can't believe that her parents managed to escape us only to be found by a gang in Joliette. Let me know when you get them and I'll get your transportation close so you can just load them up and head out. We'll take care of all the logistics for you. New phones are the first line of business. I'll make sure your new one is in the transportation. Keep the old for now so we can connect until after you get her parents. Once you arrive in D.C., you're to contact Jane. Do not take them straight to her. Tease her with them for a few days. We need some big promises from her before she can see them. I'd actually like to use them for as long as possible before giving them up."

"I like that plan too, Lieutenant." Chico says.

"Kat, Mongoose and I will be close behind you the whole way. That way if something does happen, we can get there fast. You need to head towards Cleveland; I think route 90's the way to go. It's an interstate, so of course there's construction on it, there always is. The worst area you'll go through is just west of Chicago. That place is always backed up. Once you're through there, it's a clean shot. We'll plan on stopping somewhere in Cleveland, eat, and rest. Next we'll head to D.C. via West Virginia. It's early enough in the year that the weather should hold, notwithstanding the freak weather events that happen. Especially this year it seems. If all goes well, we'll be in D.C. within the next day, day and a half. We'll handle things as they happen. All right, you've got your orders, let's move."

"Shit," Snake yells when gunfire erupts on a side street off of North Chicago. "Hold on" he yells at Kat as he guns his bike, bringing him closer to the excitement. "Kat, get your weapon ready, Chico may need backup."

"I'm ready," she yells as they round the corner off of North Chicago onto East Van Buren, Chico taking heavy gunfire as he tries to move in closer to the auditorium authority. "Looks like we found their hideout," he says to Kat as he moves closer to the building. "Pretend like your shooting at Chico; let's let them think that we're after him."

"Looks like someone's talking to him, leading him somewhere," Kat says after they make a pass by, pretending to shoot at him, but missing with every bullet.

"Now we wait," Snake says as they pull off Van Buren on to East Jefferson.

"How much longer, Snake?" Kat asks after a long day leads to an even longer evening.

"It shouldn't be much longer, Kitten. He's been in there for quite awhile. I can't see this gang just hiding out for all this time. They have to be getting antsy. Plus, the longer they go waiting for Jane, the more chance she has of finding their hidey hole. You and I both know that's what she's doing right now. Her special-ops group is probably trying to get the exact location as we speak. We can't allow them to access the area, so I'll page Chico and tell him to get a move on ASAP. Wait, we have movement, there, see the alley? That looks like...yes it is, they're heading for the truck we parked in that lower level lot. Looks like it's time to head out. Let's go."

"Chico, its Jacob, there's no way we're going to be able to make it to Cleveland tonight. It's about seven hours away and it's too close to midnight now, so let's go for about two hours and then we'll look for somewhere to lay up for the rest of the night. We can't afford to make any mistakes this time around."

"Copy Lieutenant. We'll go until about two a.m. then stop."

* * *

"Mr. Rosenthal, thank you for coming this morning. I'm sorry that I wasn't able to talk with you last night, but I have so many things going on right now that started to culminate yesterday late. This morning is the first that I've been free."

"No, I want to thank you President Martin for agreeing to see me so quickly. I know what a busy person you are and I appreciate any time that you can give me."

"Please, have a seat," Jane says graciously.

"Thank you. Now, about what I saw in the sky in the past month. We've been tracking an asteroid for years and what we're seeing now is cause for alarm."

"If you've been watching this for years but now it's a cause for alarm, it must be something big," Jane says inquiringly.

"Oh, it is President Martin. It is."

"Can you tell me why, Mr. Rosenthal?"

"Yes, President Martin. The trajectory for the asteroid has changed dramatically in the past month. We have no idea why this has occurred. It hasn't hit anything that would have caused such a drastic change, so it really is indescribable. If what we have seen and projected comes to pass, we're looking at a month maybe more, before this hits the earth. If that happens, the destruction will be astronomical. Depending on where the asteroid hits, the population affected, we're looking at the possible end of the world. The power generated by the explosion would be one hundred times that of a nuclear bomb detonating, with as much if not more destruction."

"Wow, Mr. Rosenthal. How sure are you that

this asteroid will hit the earth? Is there any way that you could be wrong? This is some extreme news, Sir."

"I'm sorry to have to be the one to tell you this. Of course there's always a possibility that I could be wrong, but I don't believe I am. However, with the way that the asteroids course has changed in the past month, it could make more changes. We'll be monitoring it every minute and calculating the impact path every hour. If it does change trajectory, I promise you, you'll be the first to know. As to which part of the earth it will hit, that's unclear at this moment."

"Well, Mr. Rosenthal. You've definitely given me much to think about. Please keep me informed of any and all information regarding this," Jane says rising, exhibiting the end of the meeting.

"Thank you President Martin. I appreciate the time that you've given me. I promise to stay in touch and keep you apprised of any changes."

"Well, Quinton that was different. What do you think of his news?" Jane asks after Rosenthal leaves the office.

"I don't know, that's a lot of information."

"I agree with you there," Jane says as she pours herself and him a glass of whiskey. "I think I could use a drink and I'm sure you can too," she says as she hands him his.

"I'm not sure what to think. How do you prepare for something of this magnitude? There's no way we can change the trajectory of something like that, but we'll lose everything that we are if it does hit the earth. I'm just. . . I don't know what to say. Hell, I don't even know what to think," he admits sheepishly.

"Yeah, that's pretty much how I feel. I'm kind of dumbfounded." Jane admits. "I don't think I've ever been left speechless before," she admits with a smirk. "It's a different feeling, for sure. One I'm not sure I like. Oh well, with that thought in mind, I'll think on it, in the mean time I have other things that require my immediate attention. Like my parents, what's the word on finding them? Have you heard from Teriq? He has to have something by now, for crying out loud. We will not be giving in to that bunch of gang bangers. I will get my parents out and they will not get any money. A bunch of idiots, just a bunch of stupid little kids messing with the President of the United States."

"I spoke with him earlier and he's still searching for them. He's outside of Chicago, but as of when I talked to him, there's been no sign of them. He's trying to locate that gang. He did say something about no way in hell was that gang going to pull anything."

* * *

"Morning kitten," Snake says when he notices her eyes on him across the room.

"Hi," she says, blinking sleep out of her eyes. "What time is it?" she asks as she slowly gets up, yawning and stretching.

"It's early it's only about five thirty, go back to sleep for awhile. You have time."

"Naw, I'm up now. I want a shower, I need a shower" she adds with a laugh.

"Yes you do," he replies teasingly.

"Hey now" she says as she heads for the shower. After brushing her teeth and then turning on the shower, she strips to hop in. Hot water, "ahhh, that's good" she says quietly when the water's rushing over her, waking her up.

"Yeah, that's good," she hears as Snake appears on the other side of the shower curtain, more than a shower on his mind. "Need some help?" he asks as he steps in to the water spray, grabs the bar of soap out of her hands, and starts lathering her up.

"That's wonderful," she moans as she feels his hands massage her fatigue away like magic. After he lays the soap down, she grabs it to start the pleasure on him. Massage for massage she thinks with a grin and a need that continues to grow with the touching. After a thorough hair shampoo, she moves closer to him.

"Snake, I love you," she murmurs as she leans forward for a kiss.

"I love you too, Kitten," he says with a kiss, tongues lingering, stroking. As she wraps her arms around his neck, he picks her up and touches her back, her legs, up her back again until the need has grown so powerful that she can't breathe.

"I need you Snake, I need you now," she says with some urgency.

He turns her towards the wall, promising many things with a long deep kiss and a little nudging on his part until she's wrapped around him, taking him as deep as she can.

"More," she groans, until he's buried to the hilt, the pressure an all consuming wave of ecstasy, no longer able to think clearly, only the building of the pressure all than can be felt. "Faster" she groans into his mouth as he takes them higher, harder until with a gasp and slight scream that he catches in his mouth, they both go over the top, breathing suspended until thought can get back.

"You okay Kitten?" Snake asks hurriedly. "I'm sorry," he says when he hears her breathe again.

"What," she says drugged by the climax, vision still not a hundred percent. "Why are you sorry?" she asks when she can focus, the shower off and a towel being used to dry her off. "I'm not sorry," she says happily.

"I was afraid I'd hurt you. You've been through a lot lately, you know?"

"Naw, I'm fine. You could never hurt me Snake, at least not on purpose. Besides, I'm not done with you yet," she says with a look through her lashes at him and a come-hither finger crook.

"You've got me," he admits in a deep voice as he picks her up and carries her to the bed. "Now let's try this again, only this time, I'm going to savor," he says on a promise as he lays her down gently and devours her nakedness with a look so hot it can burn. Hands following eyes, he begins the- oh- so slow journey from her lips, to her neck and down over her collar bones to her heavy breasts, breast too big for such a small woman, but so perfect, so right. No spot on her body left untouched, unexplored. "You are so perfect," he whispers as he licks her nipples then suckles at her catch of breath, hands moving lower smoothing her hips, her long soft legs.

"Snake," Kat moans as he teases her most sensitive spot with his fingers, dipping and playing, smoothing and stroking until she can't lay still, the need is so great she's on fire. "Please," she begs with a whimper "I need more, I need, I . . . Please Snake" she begs on a groan as his fingers move deeper and faster, a lover with no bounds. Moving his body down, in no hurry, he slowly presses heated kisses over her stomach to her belly button, lavishing that small thing with so much attention that she feels her heartbeat increase yet again. Moving further down, he drapes her legs over his shoulders having her exactly where he wants her, open to his viewing and touch. Licking and touching, smoothing and spreading, her agitation increasing the closer she gets to climax, and with one light nip on her clit she blows wide open, a climax so big that it tries to take her under, and he licks and sucks, moaning along with her, the taste of her so sexy that he's close to losing it himself, but he won't let that happen. Slowly he moves his fingers up to her breasts again, before settling over her.

"Wrap your legs around me," he says softly, "I'll help you fly," he promises.

"Snake," Kat screams as he enters her hard and deeper than ever, so deep there's nothing left but her, him, it.

"Kat, you're so tight, so hot and wet, you're perfect," he says as he starts moving, both moving towards each other in that ancient dance of love, both reaching for fulfillment. As the movement becomes faster, faster and harder with a heart that wants out to fly, Kat gasps his name as the lights start to flash behind her eyelids and unable to think she gasps in a huge lungful of air and explodes.

"Shhh, it's okay, shhh," she hears after what seems like seconds, but is probably longer since she's comfortably covered and snuggled.

"Snake, that was wow," she says softly. "I've never experienced anything like that, wow" she says again as she smoothes her hands over his hard sweat covered chest.

"I'm glad you approved," he says with an arrogantly knowing smile.

Male arrogance such a part of him she thinks with a soft look, "I love you so much Snake. Why did it take me so long to see it?" she asks wonderingly.

"I kept you guessing, so that you wouldn't see it. I was afraid I wouldn't be able to be with you. But, I've decided that I've given my whole life to work and now, it's our time, time long past due."

"I'm glad Snake, because what I feel for you, I've never felt for anyone before. Thank you, thank you for loving me."

"Don't thank me Kat, I thank you. I've wanted you forever and I'm so grateful I have you now. Let's see if we can get a little more sleep before the day get's going. It's going to be a long one I have a feeling."

"Okay, but stay; don't leave me please," she says as she drifts off.

"Only death will separate us Kat," he promises her sleeping form before getting up quietly to head back to the shower.

"Time to get up, sleepy head," Snake says after a gentle smoothing of her hair. "We're going to need to get going again soon," he warns her, giving her a minute or two to wake up.

"Okay," she says quietly before trying to snuggle down in again.

"Kat, you need to wake up now. Chico's going to be pounding on the door any minute. It's close to seven a.m. already and we have a ways to go today. Times running out, unfortunately," he says regretfully.

"Aww, I don't want this to ever end," she says as she slowly sits up.

"This will never end, I promise," Snake says fervently.

"Good, because now that I've got you, I'm keeping you," she admits firmly.

"Good," he says in agreement, love in his eyes.

"Shit," she says as she jumps out of bed at the loud knock and runs for the bathroom. "I'll be out in five minutes, just five minutes," she promises as she slams the door.

* * *

"Hey man, come in," Snake says to Mongoose when he opens the door. "How'd the night go, you guys get any sleep?" he asks.

"Yeah, Chico and I took turns, even though they don't know I'm around or even know Chico. We're good," Mongoose says. "Chico's going to stay with them while we make plans."

"Great. Kat's in the shower, but she promised she'd be out soon. I think we need to find some food, and then hit the road. We have a lot to get done today."

Chapter Five

"Look Teriq, I'm done listening to your excuses. You promised me you'd find my parents weeks ago and I'm still waiting. You have until tomorrow to get some information on them, where they are and who's holding them. Torture those gang bangers, I don't care what you do, I want to know now," Jane yells through the cell she's on.

"Jane, please, listen," Teriq cries in frustration.

"I have listened. I'm done listening. You've had nothing to report for too long now. I'm done waiting. Tomorrow, Teriq, no later," she finishes and cuts the call.

"Jane, really, you need to calm down a little. You're doing yourself and no one else any good when you lose control like you just did" Quinton says quietly. "I'm sure he's doing everything possible to find them. Remember what it's like out that way? They've had a couple of small eruptions in Yellowstone, there's volcanic ash everywhere, it's hard to breathe and see and now they're searching Chicago. What do you want him to do? You've only sent the minimum special-ops with him. He's pretty much working under extreme conditions with less than an adequate work force.

Cut him a break, for crying out loud!" Quinton says in disgust.

"Quinton, I know exactly what's going on out there and still, there is NO excuse in the length of time this is taking. That rebel group, I'm sure, are causing some of the problem. But the blame I'm placing belongs to Teriq. He's not working as quickly as he should be and I'm done talking to him about it. This discussion is closed. Now, we need to talk with the rest of the countries that have not decided on the Summit. We have only a few short weeks left and this Summit will make the world shake in fear and excitement when everything that we planned comes to fruition. I want every country on board with this. I will be disclosing a great amount and the world will finally see who I am," Jane says arrogantly.

"Yes, Jane, they will see who you are," Quinton says and after the suspicious look she sends him he adds "and that's something to be proud of."

"You are so right," she says sarcastically while thinking *your time is running out, Quinton. I really don't need you by my side for this. As a matter of fact,* she thinks, *you won't be by my side for this. This is mine, all mine!*

"Turn the news on Quinton. I just saw a breaking news flash," Jane says as she heads for the TV area.

"This is Jim Cochran of WELT News Channel 3, Washington D.C. We have some breaking news. There's been a substantial earthquake in the St. Louis area. We don't have the measurement as of yet, but are expecting to receive it momentarily from the USGS. It sounds like it has taken place along the New Madrid fault line which extends from around the St. Louis area then further north and east into Lake Erie area, near Cleveland, Ohio. There have been reports of damage, to what extent, we do not know yet but I'm sure that information will be coming shortly. This is Breaking News. I'm Jim Cochran of WELT News Channel 3, Washington D.C. Please stay tuned for further information."

"Cleveland, damn it," Jane yells. "What the hell is going on in this world? It's been one thing after another for the past year. When is this going to calm down so that I can do my job" she demands angrily.

"Wow," Quinton says, face getting pale. "This can't be a coincidence," Quinton says accusingly to Jane. "What's been unleashed in this world, Jane?" he asks, feeling sicker by the minute.

"Excuse me," she demands. "What exactly are you accusing me of," she asks softly as she moves to stand directly in front of him.

"Nothing, nothing, I'm not accusing you of anything. I'm just finding it all a little hard to take in. Yellowstone's erupted twice in the past month, now this earthquake, not far from the eruption. It just seems a little much. That's all. I can't seem to take it all in."

"Yes, it has been quite a month," Jane says agreeably.

"This is Jim Cochran of WELT News Channel 3, Washington D.C. with more information about the recent earthquake. The quake has been measured at an approximate 7.4 magnitude on the Richter scale. That's a substantial size for an earthquake in that area of the country, especially since that fault line hasn't had a major quake in over a hundred years. We are waiting now for Mr. Jason Argonne, USGS Department Head. He'll be able to answer any questions that we may have about this earthquake. We'll be right back with Mr. Jason Argonne after this quick message."

"Thank you for agreeing to answer some questions, Mr. Argonne," Jim Cochran says, after the forty-five second commercial ends.

"No problem, Jim, and please call me Jason," Jason Argonne says quietly, seriously.

"What can you tell us, Jason, about the earthquake that occurred less than an hour ago in St. Louis?"

"We have, according to the seismograph, experienced an earthquake measuring approximately 7.4 on the Richter scale. That's a substantial earthquake for this part of the country. As you know, the more earthquake prone areas of the U.S. are out west, in the San Andreas Fault area along the California border. However, there have been large quakes in this area of the United States. Around the early nineteen hundreds there was a reported quake that measured more than 8.0 on the Richter scale. This most recent quake, a 7.4 is close to the last large quake. The difference is the type of quakes. Out west, you have the plate shift, while here in the Midwest we have the plate grind. With the shift, your quakes are large but with the grind they affect a much larger area. They can be felt nearly twice as far as the shift, causing a much wider area of damage and destruction. The areas hit were heavily occupied. There are a lot of buildings and people that occupy this area and with that size population, bigger damage and more deaths occur. We've had reports as far away as Canada with no damage, to the greater Cleveland area with more reported damage. Of course, it's early so the reported damage estimates are just starting to come in."

"Hold on just for a moment Jason. There's some breaking news coming in right now," Jim says as he listens to what's being reported through his ear piece. "Sorry about that, Mr. Argonne, Jason, but we've just had a damage report come in from the greater Cleveland area. There's been a collapse in a salt mine located just east of Cleveland, with an unknown number of miners trapped. The lake has broken through an area of the salt mine, after the ceiling collapsed, contaminating the fresh water with thousands of tons of salt. This may be a disaster of massive proportions," Jim Cochran says excitedly "we're going live to Cleveland so that we can hear what's happening and get any new information coming out of that salt mine."

"Hi Jim, this is Cali Nowacki of WEMZ News Channel 2, Cleveland."

"Cali, what can you tell us about the salt mine collapse? How many miners are trapped down there and what kind of damage has been reported?"

"Jim, the last report was about fifteen minutes ago. The CEO of Prism Salt reported that there are twenty seven people trapped about two thousand feet below the surface. He also stated that they have emergency procedures in effect and they have a positive feeling about retrieving all twenty seven trapped miners. He also reported that a part of the mine that was collapsed has been flooded with lake water and that they are trying to stop more contamination into the lake by the salt. The eco-system is of the utmost importance, he's quoted as saying and they'll be taking every measure to ensure that there will be no more contamination of salt into the fresh water lake. This is indeed a very serious problem and they are not taking it lightly."

"Wow," Jim says to Cali. "This has been a time of disasters it seems with one after another in the past year. It's as if the world's gone crazy!"

"I have to agree with you Jim. We've had our share of emergencies this past year. Let's hope that this will be the last in a long line of problems that the country's experienced in the past twelve months."

* * *

"Oh my God, what's going on," Kat exclaims loudly after listening to the news while stopped at a restaurant for lunch on their way east.

"Wow," Snake says quietly, absorbing the information that just came through the television.

"How many more disasters is the United States going to experience this year," Kat exclaims. "There aren't many more that we haven't experienced. There've been explosions, earthquakes, eruptions, crazy storms. We've had just about any and all types of disasters in one year. It's almost as if the earth is complaining or punishing. Although I know mentally that's not possible. But if you think about it..." she trails off after seeing the look on Snakes face. "What Snake, what do you think?"

"I think that there are more powers to be than the earth, don't you think?" he says.

"What do you mean? Oh, I think I get it," Kat says slowly. "Yeah, crap, that's. . . "

"I know," Snake says when Kat stops talking, shock on her face.

"You really think that this is Revelations coming true? We've had quite a few disasters. We have such devastating corruption hitting not only this country but the world in general. I guess if you think about it, it could be the end times. I'm not ready for the end of the world. I'm not that old, and I haven't done a lot of things that I want to do before I die," she says, tears gathering, slowly rolling down her cheeks.

"Don't worry Kitten," Snake says as he holds her close. "We have time; we're going to be able to do a lot of things yet. It's not the end of the world, it can't be. That's all just speculation, theory, guess work. I'm sure we won't see that happen, at least not in our lifetime. All right, enough dark talk, I'm going to contact Chico. It's time he takes Jane's parents into D.C. We have enough to do ourselves, so he can take over from here. He should be able to infiltrate Jane's group, get some news to us when possible so that we can start moving. We have to stop her from getting to the Summit Conference. She's got enough power as it is, she gets much more and she'll have too much power over the whole world. Those damn chips she's pushing will control everyone in the world nicely. The other country heads aren't going to like the consequences, if she has her way. I just can't believe how ignorant the Presidents and leaders of the world really are. She sucked them in nicely, including all those country's that couldn't get along in the Middle East."

Chapter Six

"Eli, how's it going? Is everything all right?" Snake asks after Eli answers the call.

"Yeah, we're all good here. We just arrived in Dallas, and are looking for a place to settle in, for now."

"Excellent!" Jacob says with a grin. "We're on our way towards D.C., by way of Cleveland. Kat and I both want to check out the damage caused by the earthquake. From what we hear, salt is contaminating Lake Erie, which is one of the fresh water sources in the world. Hopefully they'll be able to contain the problem; otherwise, the country's in big trouble. Destroying that water supply affects not only fresh drinking water but a rather large food source. Something we can't even come close to considering gone. Food prices will sky rocket. It's just a bad thing all around."

"That earthquake was a rather large one for that part of the country. Mal and I were talking about it and just wondered how much Yellowstone had to do with that quake. After all, Yellowstone is a super volcano, and it had a couple of mini eruptions just a few days before the quake. It all just seems so coincidental, that's all," Eli says thoughtfully.

"They have to be connected. I really don't believe in coincidences, and that one was a big one."

"Yeah, that's what we thought. Anyway, you guys be careful out there. If Jane has any inkling that you're alive and headed in her direction, she'll take you all out. You're too much of a threat to her future plans."

"I know, that's definitely a fact," Snake admits with a chuckle.

"Everything here is good for now, how about there?" Eli asks.

"Not bad. We're down to me and Kat now. I sent Chico off with Jane's parents earlier today. We had to set up a little skirmish so that Jane's parents would think that Chico saved them from us. Of course Kat and I wore disguises. We wouldn't want to be identified, at least not yet. I'd like to keep surprise on our side. But he needed that to be able to get a little closer to Jane. He is now officially on his way to D.C., but isn't planning on meeting up with her right away. He's going to find a place to hide out before he contacts her for an exchange, for safety on his part. As far as her parents are concerned, he was part of the gang banger group that grabbed them in Chicago. He looks and plays the part really well. He'll do what he needs to, to infiltrate the White House. I'm not really concerned. He's got the capability of contacting me with his plans, and any questions he has. We have a couple of days to get her parents to her and get him into the White House. If all goes right, everything should fall into place."

"Looks like it won't be long before the big fight begins. I guess we should probably take these couple of days and get things ready here. We can be in D.C. fast if needed. I've got that black hawk and the pilot staged close by in case of an emergency. I wasn't sure if we'd be needed in D.C. so I kept them close. Do you know how hard it is to hide a helicopter? The logistics are killer!" Eli adds on a groan. "But hey, we did it, at least from what I've seen and heard we did it. Hopefully there won't be any surprises!"

"I'm sure it's fine. She's not looking in that direction, she's more focused on her parents and Chicago. That gives us a little room to breathe."

"Right," Eli agrees with a nod.

"All right Eli, we're going to start moving now, so I'll let you go. Call if there's a need, otherwise I'll contact you once we get to D.C. and move in to Mom and Dad's house."

"Wait, what?" Eli asks. "You're moving in to Mom and Dad's place?"

"Yeah, it's empty, off the main drag and in an area that's been chip implanted. Everything we're looking for!" Snake adds. "Do you have a problem with it?"

"No, it was just a shock hearing that, I guess. But you're right. That is a perfect place to lie up. Keep in touch Jacob. Neither Mal nor I want to lose anyone else, so take care man!"

"You got it. Talk to you both soon. All right Kitten, let's head out." Snake says.

"Yeah, we better start moving or we won't get very far today. I'm interested in seeing what's going on up at Lake Erie. My parents and I visited that area frequently when I was young. Some of mom's family originated from there and we'd go up for reunions every few years."

"It's supposedly a pretty nice area, but with all the problems they're having with the lake, it doesn't bode well for the future of the area."

"What kind of problems? Like I said, we were there pretty frequently and I don't remember hearing about any lake problems."

"The lake seems to have broken through one of the roofs of a salt mine, just east of Cleveland. It's contaminating the fresh water lake with salt. That's changing the whole ecosystem, killing off a lot of the fresh fish supply. As you know, all the great lakes are connected, so they're scrambling to stop the salt from leaking out to protect not only Lake Erie but the other four lakes as well. It's a pretty big deal, actually."

"Wow, it sure sounds like it. Was this leak going on before the newest earthquake?"

"Yeah, but the media wasn't informed, so they really haven't been talking about the prior problems. They're now focused on the newest issues, this new earthquake. Unfortunately, with the existing problems and the size of the earthquake yesterday, I'm sure their problems just got worse."

"Wow, that's quite an issue. How in the world would you stop salt from getting into the water? It probably doesn't take much salt to destroy water. At least, when you cook, it doesn't take much salt to ruin a whole pot of water. A little goes a long ways!"

"That's why I thought we'd stop. Not only is this serious, but it would help to have friends in this area of the country. The chips are getting close to them, but we should miss them by a week or so. I'm sure there are quite a few people in that area who are followers of the old underground. We just need to find out who and get them involved with the new underground. Jane's getting close to her objectives, and we're going to need all the help we can get, if we plan on stopping her from getting to the summit. Unfortunately, that's only days away now. Time keeps on ticking."

"Check out all the damage," Snake yells to Kat as they move into the earthquake damage area.

"Wow, I wouldn't have guessed," Kat yells after scanning the area. Buildings toppled in spots, fires consuming the rest. "It's as if someone took a crane with a ball attached and sporadically hit and skipped some buildings. It's a weird concept. Why do you think only some of the buildings were affected and the rest weren't?"

"It probably had to do with age and what the buildings were made out of. Brick and block are less forgiving than wood. They don't move at all, where wood has more of a movement capability. I'm just theorizing. I don't really have the answer to that, but it sounded good, didn't it," he asks with a wink and a grin having stopped and dismounted from the bike at the first signs of earthquake damage.

"I was impressed with your knowledge," Kat teases with a toss of hair, hands on her hips "but now, not so much."

"Hey, just because I'm unfamiliar with

earthquake damage doesn't make me unimpressive. I'd love to show you what I am good at! Then you can tell me how impressed you really are" he says quietly and intensely, a look in those electric blue eyes that speaks directly to her heart and groin.

"Snaaaaake, please," she says quietly, blushing while glancing quickly around, reassuring herself that no-one overheard his comment.

"Kat, even if someone did hear what I said, it's only you that changed its context," he teases, watching as she turns a deeper shade of red.

"Stop," she says, disgusted with her fair skin and obvious emotional ups and downs. "I know my face is an open book when it comes to my thoughts. If you'd stop making sexy innuendos, I wouldn't have this problem all the time."

"Aww, I'm sorry Kitten," he says with a low chuckle as he grabs her for a hug.

"Snake, you're not making things easier," she mumbles against his chest, falsely protesting while enjoying the word play and affection. "If you'd let me go, I might be able to breathe," she mumbles.

"Fine, if you insist," he says, tugging her chest slightly tighter against his before he slowly releases her, touching as much of her as possible before she gets too far away, never tiring of finally being able to touch her whenever he wants.

After a quick look around, she steps closer to him, tugs his head down and whispers a promise in his ear that has his face turning slightly redder than normal and causes his eyes to glaze. "Later," she whispers and moves away, a spring in her step and a wicked grin on her face. "I win," she says loud enough for him and only him to hear.

Chapter Seven

"Eli, look to your six. There's someone or something moving out there," Mallory says having caught a glimpse of something in the wooded area just outside of camp.

"I think I see it. Find Rand and see if he can find out what it is. I've got a meeting scheduled in five minutes with another group of patriots. Our groups keep getting bigger and bigger. If only Jane could see all the people that really hate her, she wouldn't be so comfortable in the White House. Soon, we'll be able to take our country back. It's going to be an awesome surprise for her and her insurrectionists. I'm starting to get excited by this whole thing. Plus, if we keep growing at the rate we have been, we'll definitely have to branch out even more. It's almost to the point where the command just isn't big enough," he admits tiredly, rubbing his hands over his face, whiskers rasping, trying to rub the fatigue off.

"Yeah, I've noticed. I'm sure there are more leaders out there; you just need to pick them. It'll take some of the load off of you. Maybe you should consider that now, Eli. You're starting to look a little tired."

"Hey now, that's the pot calling the kettle," he adds with a grin, noticing her worn clothes, broken fingernails, lack of makeup. An overall appearance of worn out with fatigue creating wrinkles near her eyes and mouth. "Looks like we could all use a vacation," he says seriously.

"I know I could, but there's no time for that now. We have to be as ready as possible for when Jacob calls us in. I'll go find Rand and we can go check out who ever that is in the woods."

"Thanks Mal, I really do appreciate all that you do," Eli adds, grabbing her by the shoulders for a quick hug from brother to sister. "I never want you to think I don't care about you," he says, letting her go slowly.

"I know, Eli. I love you too."

* * *

"Eli, this is Mike. He's got a story to tell you. One that I think you'll be really interested in," Mal says after Rand and her help a middle aged man, extremely thin and weak, sit down near the door of the building they use as an office. After a quick glance around, as if seeing their office building for the first time, she notices how run down and ramshackle everything is. *At least we have food and water*, she thinks. *This poor guy looks like he hasn't eaten in months*. "Let me get him something to drink and eat before you start talking."

"Sure Mal, take your time. I could use a sit down too," Eli says comfortably, reassuring him that he means no harm, just wants a friendly talk.

"I can talk," Mike offers quietly, exhaustion in every line of his being. With sunburned skin dried so deeply that he looks like leather, and very little spark left in his pale gray eyes, he still sits up taller on his chair when he says "you need to know this right from the start. I'll never go back there. They'll have to kill me first."

"Who's they and where is there," Eli asks quietly.

"The compound, the one that I finally escaped from," Mike says in confusion. "You know, that place they call the courtesy camp!"

"Sorry, I've never heard of the courtesy camp," Eli says then "I'm Eli, by the way. We're a bunch of citizens that go by the name patriots, ones that have taken a stance on this country and how it's being run. We don't like the President and what's she's been doing to our country. There's not a person here that has that chip and not one here that would accept it either."

"If you didn't accept the chip, then how come you're not in the courtesy camp, like all the others? That's why they put us in there. They said that the courtesy camp was there for those who hadn't made the decision to take the chip. They told us it was like being on vacation and that for six months we could stay there until we decided about the chip. That was just a bunch of bull. I'll tell you, it's in no way like a vacation for anyone that goes there. More like an old concentration camp from Hitler's time. They treat you like prisoners, don't give you much food, just some watery gruel and dirty water to drink and make you work all day long out in the hot sun. Plus, they have guards surrounding you constantly, and they don't even speak English. I'm not sure what language they speak, but it's not one I've ever heard before," Mike says, voice almost to a whisper now, no energy left.

"Here Mike, drink this," Mallory says when she gets back and see's he's on the verge of collapse. "I told you to wait to question him till I got him something to eat and drink," she says in exasperation, slightly annoyed.

"I didn't question him Mal, he just started talking. I didn't ask him one question," Eli denies.

"Fine, but you'll have to wait, since he's almost too exhausted to breathe now," she says, annoyed.

"I'm fine, Miss, really," Mike says quietly, having sipped his drink.

"No you're not, but you will be in a few days," she says firmly, nudging his drink towards his mouth again.

"Thanks for being so nice," Mike says, tears slowly moving over his cheeks, sinking into the furrows before finally making it to his chin. "No one's been nice for a long time now," he admits.

"How long were you in this 'courtesy' camp?" Eli asks intensely.

"I'm not sure exactly how long, probably four or five months now."

"Hmm, this has been going on a while then," Eli mumbles, wondering how this could be the first time they've heard of this place.

"Yeah, it's been a long time. There were people there before I got there, some looking just as bad as me. My guess is this place has been there as long as they've been trying to make everyone take those chips. That would be nearly a year ago."

"How many people, would you say are in there," Eli asks quietly, while Mal, Rand and a couple more of the group all lean forward to hear the answer.

"Gosh, there's thousands, thousands. The scary part is I'm housed with only men. I know there are women and children there too, but I've never see them. Sometimes you can hear some screaming, but usually it's just the men talking or making noise. I had my wife and two kids with me, Bobby and Mary, but once they checked us in, they took my wife and kids to a different camp and put me in with the men," he says scared. "I've been quietly asking around but no one seems to know anything. Either that or they're afraid to talk about it, ask the wrong person. We already get beat when we don't move fast enough or for just standing in line for food. No one wants to make life any harder for the women and children, if they're even alive at this point."

"Crap," Eli says as he slumps back against the chair, a dumbfounded look on his once handsome face. A face now permanently lined with worry. "I can't believe this is the first that we've heard of this. How the hell can this happen," he asks outraged, voice gaining in loudness and intensity. "Where are all those people that we brought here? Why hasn't anyone said anything about this? This is an atrocity, a total freakin atrocity!"

"I'm sorry," Mike says as he cringes away from Eli, waiting for the blow.

"No man, hey, I'm sorry. I'm not yelling at you, I'm just frustrated with all this, you know. It's not you," Eli says reassuringly, not meaning to scare him. "You NEVER have to fear anyone hitting you again, at least not when you're with us. Now, I think you should rest, before we start asking questions. There's a whole lot we're going to have to know, and since you're the one that's had this experience, you'll have to tell us everything. Mal, take him to a room so he can get some rest. Make sure he's got plenty of food and clean water to drink, and see if you can round up something for him to wear. I'm going to call Snake. I'll bet he's never heard of this place either. I can't believe we haven't heard of it before now. How could this have been kept quiet for so long?"

"Come on Mike," Mal says quietly, gently pulling on his hand to help him stand. "Just a couple of minutes and you can take a nap," she promises, worry etched all over her face.

"I want to help. I don't have time to take a nap," he insists, face gray.

"We won't do anything without you, I promise. We do have to make some calls and gather some people together though, so it's going to be at least a couple of hours. You may as well rest now, you probably won't get any more for awhile. You need your strength if you're going to be able to help and not hinder us, right," she reminds him gently. "Others are depending on you to be strong and you're tired right now. But after a little nap, you'll be fine. Besides it's getting late in the day, and we won't be able to do much after dark, at least until we see what we're up against."

"Oh, right," he mumbles and follows her to a building across the way, one used as sleeping quarters.

"Here you go," she says after entering the building, turning down a long hallway and entering a door midway down. "This one's empty, the bed's made up with sheets, a blanket and a small pillow.

It's the best we can do right now," she adds by way of explanation. "There's a bathroom farther down the hall, last door on the left."

"This is perfect," he murmurs as he slowly heads for the bed, exhaustion pulling him towards the floor if he doesn't lie down soon.

"I'll come and get you before we make any moves," she promises and quietly closes the door, a little snick confirming the door latches.

***

"I can't believe this," Eli's saying as Mallory enters the room they use as an office. "How in the hell did this get by us? How could we have been traveling for nearly a year throughout the states and never heard of this place before? No one's ever said anything about such a place existing. This is unbelievable, totally unbelievable! Have any of you ever even heard a whisper about this?"

"No way! There's no way! We never would have left something like this go on if we'd have known. My god all those people being treated like they're in a concentration camp. It sounds like its right out of the Hitler nightmare," Mongoose snarls in disgust. "It's pretty damn sad when there're things like this taking place in the states, in this day and age. Unbelievable!"

"Have you gotten a hold of Jacob yet," Mallory asks quietly.

"No, I haven't had a chance. I called all the group leaders together. I was curious if anyone else had heard of this before. I filled them in on what Mike told us and you walked in right after I asked that question, so you heard what I just heard."

"Yeah, it doesn't sound like any of us have heard of this before. I suggest we talk to Jacob. I'm sure he hasn't heard of these places either or he would have said something before now. I'm kinda curious, though, to hear what his reactions going to be," she adds with a straight face and a wicked look in her blue eyes.

"I'm gonna call right now. No sense in waiting. With this going on, speed is of the utmost importance. We need to get some surveillance going, find out what's going on in there and figure out a way to rescue those poor people. But first we need to find out exactly where this place is. That was something I didn't ask Mike. He looked so bad, I was afraid he was just going to die sitting there. How can anyone do that to someone? It makes me furious," Eli snaps before dialing Jacobs's number.

"Hey bro, how's the weather," he asks as soon as Jacob answers.

"Not too bad, partly sunny, pretty warm, but not too hot right now," Jacob answers slowly. "Eli, what's the matter? You never call to ask me how the weather is" Jacob says in an abrupt tone. "What's wrong?"

"Well, nothing with me or Mallory. Everyone here is doing great, but, we met a guy today that Mal and Rand found wandering around in the woods just south of here. He claims he escaped from a place called the 'courtesy camp'. Have you ever heard of the 'courtesy camp'?

"Not that I can remember, no. Where is the place and what is it?" Jacob says.

"It sounds like a throwback to the Hitler concentration camps from way back, but it resides right here, somewhere in Texas. No one here has ever heard of this place and yet this guy, he looks like he came from a concentration camp. He can't weigh more than a hundred and twenty pounds. He looks skeletal. He's exhausted, been abused and treated like a criminal, all because he and his family refused the chip. He also claims that his wife and two children were placed in there too. He hasn't seen or heard from them since they were put there. He said the women and children are put somewhere else, where the men aren't. It's pretty bad Jacob. I can't figure out how this has been going on for close to a year and we've never heard of it. Not one person here has knowledge of this place existing. Anyway, I wanted to let you know what's happening. The next thing we're going to do here is find out exactly where this place is. Then we're going to do a little investigating and see exactly what we're up against. We would have gotten more information from Mike, but he was on the verge of collapse, so Mal gave him some food and water and put him to bed for a little while. Jacob, are you there?"

"What, yeah, I'm here. It's a little bit much to absorb. Give me a minute here."

"Sure. I totally understand. You should have been here when we first heard about this. I'm still steamed. I can't believe that Jane's soldiers are able to keep this under wraps."

"Wait, what? What about Jane's soldiers?"

"Oh, that's right, I didn't tell you. Mike said that the guards don't speak English. He actually said he didn't know what they spoke; he's never heard that language before."

"Did Mal speak to him; try to get him to pick which language it was?"

"No, he was looking so bad that we made him eat, drink and lie down before we lost him," Eli says quietly.

"It sure sounds like the army she brought in from Iran. Damn it, this shouldn't be happening. It's one thing after another," Jacob yells in frustration.

"I know. Trust me, we all know" Eli says in anger. "My job keeps getting bigger all the time. I'm going to have to make more team leaders and branch out again. I can't keep up out here."

"I hear you. There're only so many of us to go around. Now with this, it's going to be a much bigger problem for you. I wish I were close enough to help you out, but with me being half way across the states, well, that's impossible," Jacob mutters.

"Don't worry about it Jacob. We'll take care of it on our end. Somehow, we'll manage," Eli promises.

"Let me talk to Chico. Maybe he can get me some more information on this. He has friends out there too," Jacob says.

"Call me when you find out anything. In the mean time we have a shitload of work to do here, so I'll contact you when we learn more."

Chapter Eight

"Snake, what's the matter," Kat asks after he hangs up and just stands there, staring at the wall, the plain wall.

"What?" he says quietly, still staring?

"The call, what happened? You were talking to Eli, right," Kat asks worriedly?

"Yeah, sorry Kitten. My minds just trying to absorb what Eli just told me. I'm, I don't know, shocked I guess. I should have had some info on this, I mean, it makes perfect sense, but why didn't I think to look for this? This is my life, my work, I should have thought. . . "

"What Snake, what?" Kat cries in frustration. "I don't know what you're talking about. What should you have known?"

"Sorry Kitten. I forgot you weren't on the phone, you didn't hear. All right, let me try to explain. Jane had a type of concentration/prisoner camp set up in Texas that Eli just found out about. Evidently this has been set up from the beginning, for those people that chose not to accept the chip implant. They're sending them to that camp for six months and if they accept the chip, they get it and are allowed to leave. If they don't accept it, I'm not sure what happens to them, but I have a real bad feeling they don't get to leave alive. It's Jane's way of making sure that everyone conforms to her leadership."

"You're kidding right. She's killing people that don't get the chip?" Kat asks in a whisper, appalled by the thought of what's happening in the states now, the evil that's been unleashed.

"Yeah, sorry Kitten, I know it's terrible, but really, if you think about it, it's what she'd do. It's the type of leader she is. Look at all the people that died quickly, all those that could have caused her and her position a problem. She wiped them all out. We should have known that she'd be ready for those that refuse the chip. After what we learned about the chips capabilities, of course everyone would have to accept it in order for her to have total control. What I can't believe is I didn't think to look for this, for anything that would point me in that direction. That's just ignorance on my part, for crying out loud. I've worked in the services all of my adult life, special-ops no less, and I let this get by me!"

"Snake, you're not responsible for the whole world and taking care of or even knowing what's going on everywhere. You're just one man, she's not and she brought her own army over here, remember? Look at everything that you've made yourself responsible for. You can't do everything, not everything. This is a big world and it gets bigger by the day. What can you do Snake, you can't be everywhere at any one time. I think you've done an amazing service to this country, and saved an untold number of people from certain death. Now where are you headed and to stop what? Can't you think about you once in a while?"

"No Kitten, I don't have that luxury. No one does right now. Things are coming to a head real soon, that's why we're headed to D.C., to see if we can get a jump on Jane before she gets to the summit and beyond. She's still going strong in the direction she planned and I'm not even sure anymore that anyone can stop what she plans."

"Snake, stop, don't give up, you've never been one to give up, and now is not the time to start."

"I know Kitten. I'm not giving up, I'm just tired. I'm tired of the pressure, tired of the never ending work, tired of the ungrateful, just tired. Give me a couple of minutes to wallow, then I'll be back to normal. In the mean time, we're going to have to head out; we have to get to Prism salt mine sometime today."

Chapter Nine

"Uncle, its Jane, I think it's time to finish the scheduling of the peace conference. I wanted to ask your opinion on something also."

"Jane of course, please ask anything you wish."

"Thank you Uncle. I have an idea. I need the Israelis' to join in the peace conference. In order for world domination to occur, everyone must be willing to meet with me. With the Middle East the way they have been for millennia, there will be no way to obtain world peace. What do you suggest? How can we make this happen, in a short amount of time? So far, there are only six countries that have refused to meet at the summit. I can handle all but two of them those, of course, being the Israelis and Palestinians, only the two most stubborn personalities known to man."

"Ah," Jane hears then a loud laugh and a few chuckles. "Jane, I'm sorry, it's just the way you said those things. I had to laugh. You're absolutely correct they are the most stubborn people in the world, me of course, being one of them."

"I meant no offense, Uncle," she says with a sigh. "It's pretty frustrating for me, since I can't even get them to call me back, you excluded of course. So I guess what I'm really talking about are the Israelis, the more stubborn of the two at this time."

"What have you tried? Have you spoken to the President of Israel? He's not known for his friendliness, no matter who you are. But the United States and Israel have long been supporters of each other. I believe if you contact him personally, you could probably talk him in to meeting with you. You may need to meet with him first, in private, just to assuage his pride. At that time you will undoubtedly be able to talk him into pretty much anything."

"Do you think it will be so easy, Uncle?"

"I do think so Jane. You are, after all, a force to be reckoned with, are you not?"

"I am Uncle, thank you. Sometimes I forget. You must remember, after spending so much time with the infidels, I tend to forget who I am."

"You must never forget, Jane. You are, after all, the only hope that this world has. Power must be obtained in order for all your dreams to come true. You hold a world full of hope in your hands, one world, one religion, on ruler. You must succeed."

"Yes Uncle, I will succeed. I just needed the support and the reminder. I will contact President Baladan. Hopefully he'll talk with me now. I've called multiple times in the past few days and have not gotten through to him yet!"

"Keep calling Jane. Sooner or later he'll talk. Persistence seems to be the key here!"

"I promise, Uncle."

* * *

"President Baladan, thank you for consenting to speak with me," Jane says softly and respectfully. "I've been planning this discussion for ages. Now I find that I'm unsure how to start the conversation," she admits sounding uncertain.

"Please, President Martin, feel free to speak your mind. I apologize for taking so long in getting back to you, but there has been much disruption going on in my country and I needed to get things under control before I felt free to speak with you. I believe I have succeeded, so now I have more time available. What can I do for you President Martin?"

"Please call me Jane first, and that may make me feel more comfortable."

"Of course, Jane it is. Please call me Eliam."

"Thank you Eliam. What I'm calling for is the summit that's coming up at the end of next week. I did not receive your reservation and was wondering why you couldn't attend?"

"Like I said, Jane, my country has been in an upheaval, with all the strange and confusing things that have been happening worldwide. It had nothing to do with the summit. It was the opportunity and timing that was causing me a problem. I was unsure until now, whether or not I would be able to attend. Now those things seem to be quieter and more under control, I see no reason why I will not be able to attend as long as nothing major happens at that time."

"That's wonderful, Eliam. I want us to be friends. Israel has been on the United States side for eons. I will not do anything to change that relationship, I promise you," Jane vows intensely.

"Thank you Jane. That causes me considerable

relief. With the world and everything changing so rapidly, I was concerned that the United States would become enemies of this country. You are a power to be watched and reckoned with. I really did not want more trouble, but of course, would have proceeded in the right direction, had there been any. Israel is not a force to be tossed aside. We have much more strength than we allow the world to see," he warns quietly but firmly and with dignity.

"I'm very aware how strong you are, President Baladan. We will never underestimate you and your country, I promise you. I look forward to seeing you at the summit next week, President Baladan."

Chapter Ten

"We'll be reaching Fairport Harbor in about ten minutes," Snake says as they pass through Cleveland. "That's the town that the salt mine is located in, that has the leak. That's not the only thing that town has. It's not widely known, but it's also home to the only neutrino detector the United States has. It's quite a big deal actually, especially to the astrophysicists of the world."

"What's a neutrino detector?"

"A neutrino detector observes sub-atomic particles that came from a star twenty times bigger than our sun, and went supernova millions of years ago. They're studying the sub-atomic particles that came from it to learn more about the universe and what and how it's made up. This thing is so intricate that it's located about two thousand feet below the surface of Lake Erie. It's actually pretty cool, if you read about it. Unfortunately, they don't give tours."

"Bummer, I'd like to see it, and learn a little bit more about it."

"Yeah, me too, but no can do. I just hope that it wasn't damaged by this latest earthquake. I'll make a few calls and see if I can find out any more information."

"Here we are. Let's head into the office and see if we can get in touch with the supervisor of the site. We really didn't need to stop here, but after all the riding, we needed a break and what better place than here, to get more information. Besides, didn't you say that this is the area you visited when you were a kid?"

"Yeah, it's close. Actually it's more east of here. A place called Geneva. Geneva on the Lake is where we always met our family. They had a pretty neat carnival type place. We used to ride go-carts and play games, kinda like a fair, only always there," Kat says dreamily, with a smile. "It makes me remember Mom and Dad. I don't do that enough. They were the best parents ever. I was totally lost when they died; it was so hard losing them both at the same time."

"I'm sure you were kitten. It's tough losing your parents. I can't imagine losing mine at sixteen. It was hard enough losing them now, but I had years of working and not being able to even see them. I guess I wish I could have spent more time with them, before they went, but life kept getting in the way," Snake says in a gruff voice.

"They knew you loved them Snake. They understood too, I'm sure of it. They loved being part of your life, being in the underground. They loved all the people they talked with, cooked for. Those are times they really lived, and enjoyed living. You gave them purpose, Snake. They were grateful for the time they did get. This world's gone nuts. I'm sure they're happy now and out of all the bull!"

"That's true," he says clearing his voice. "Let's

head in and see what's going on."

"Can I help you?" a middle aged woman greets them as they walk in.

"Yes, we're looking for the supervisor of the site. Is he available anywhere, Nancy?" Snake asks having glanced at her name plate on the desk, while scanning the area. A few chairs, light walls, bright lights and a view of Lake Erie from a window located behind the desk.

"That would be Steve Orris. He's out in the salt mine but I'm expecting him back within a few minutes. He's got a conference call at two o'clock. That's only a few minutes from now. If you'd like to have a seat, I'm sure once he's back he'll be happy to talk with you. It's been crazy here lately. You're not from the media are you? Steve doesn't like talking to the media."

"No, we're not media, but I totally understand why he doesn't like the media," Snake reassures with a grin.

"Thanks, he won't turn into his alter personality because of the media. You'll at least get to meet him in normal mode!" she adds chuckling, a smile turning the once angry looking woman into a much prettier one.

"Tell me," Snake says "have the chips arrived here yet" he asks quietly, feeling the temperature in the room drop by a few degrees.

"No Sir, they have not," she says soberly and crisply.

"We haven't received ours yet, either," Snake says, judging feelings and attitude. "We've been traveling for days now. Just came from the outskirts of Yellowstone. We actually got into some of the ash that was expelled with the latest eruption."

"Then you haven't heard about the most recent eruption?"

"I'm not sure, when was it," Snake asks just as an older gentleman, tall, thin with black hair and silver glasses, enters the office.

"Can I help you?" he asks when he see's Snake and Kat standing near the receptionist's desk.

"I'm Lt. Jacob Callander and this is Kathleen Thomas. We're headed to D.C. and in the area so thought we'd stop in to check the status of the leak in the roof of the mine. Since our commanding officer is from this general area, he's going to want that information when we get back to Washington."

"Oh, sure, come on in to my office and we can sit and talk."

"Thanks, and thanks Nancy, for the information."

"Have a seat," Steve says after ushering them through a door into a room that looks like the last time it was decorated was turn of the century. Dark and closed in, smaller than to be expected for a supervisor of a plant large enough to supply thousands upon thousands of pounds of salt to the states and house a secret facility that few know exist.

"Thanks," Snake says quietly after sitting in one of the two chairs sitting in front of a desk that is totally covered in papers.

"Sorry about the mess," Steve says as he walks around to the other side of the desk to take his seat. "I'm not normally this messy, but then again, we don't normally have earthquakes that affect us the way this one did. Seems we've had one problem after another for the past month. I'm hoping these issues resolve sometime soon. I'm afraid with all the hours I've had to work, that my wife won't recognize me when I finally do get some home time," he adds with a grin, fatigue evident in his face, a slight bruised look under is eyes.

"We won't keep you long. I was told you have a two o'clock conference call and I certainly don't want to get in the way of that," Snake reassures him.

"It's fine, what can I do for you?"

"We wanted to check on the state of the roof collapse, and how serious it really is."

"It's pretty serious. The worst part is the trapped miners. However, it looks like we're getting close to the level that they're at and hope to have them all out by this evening. If you were the media, I wouldn't be talking to you at all, but since you're government, I thought you should know the seriousness of the problem and the close resolution."

"Thank you, I really appreciate this and so will my General, when I get back to D.C.," Snake says. "Just a couple more questions. Were you able to contain the salt release into the lake? And is the neutron detector in any trouble because of the quake?"

"As to containing the salt, we've had emergency measures in place for this exact problem, so we were able to contain the contamination. The lake water will soon be back to pre-earthquake, maybe another couple of weeks.

The miners should all be reached in a matter of hours now, and how did you find out about the neutron detector?"

"I knew about it from years ago. It was in something I read in an old magazine, written back in the eighties. I'm a diver and it was an article I read in a diving magazine."

"Oh, geez, that was from a long time ago. You have an excellent memory if I must say so."

"Yeah, it drives people nuts, usually," Snake admits with a sheepish grin, a wink and a head tilt toward Kat.

"You're telling me," Kat says on a groan. "He never forgets anything. It makes me feel stupid. I've got a good memory, but it's nothing compared to his," she admits.

"Seldom do I entertain in this office regarding the neutron detector. Really, no one knows about it, nor has it surfaced in the past few weeks, since the earthquake emergencies. I'm grateful for that, actually. I'd rather the media stays focused on the mine and miners. The less I talk about the neutron detectors, the safer they are. That's a big program that I'd hate to see ruined by the knowledge being brought forth from the archives. The scientists work much better when the media stays out of their way."

"I totally understand, Steve. I won't be saying anything about that to anyone, I can guarantee that," Snake says, voice low in a confidential manner.

"Thank you Lt. Callander, I appreciate your cooperation."

"Is the neutron detector still up and running,"

Kat asks curiously.

"Yes it is. Every month or so, some specially trained divers come out from the Proton Decay Group and inspect every photo multiplier tube and every connection maintaining its operation. As far as I know, they've never had a problem with it."

"That's awesome and damn cool!" Kat says. "Have you actually seen it?"

"I saw it shortly after it was up and running. Of course, I couldn't actually go where the detectors are, since you have to dive to get there and I'm no diver. But the room it's off of is totally cool. Very interesting, if I must say," Steve admits a smile lighting up his face. "All right, I'm going to have to . . A loud explosion covers anything else that Steve was about to say while dust fills the air and Kat lands on the floor, tossed out of the chair she'd been sitting in.

"What the hell just happened," Kat yells as she scrambles to get up.

"I'm not sure," Steve yells as he runs for the door.

"I think it was another earthquake," Snake says as they run for the door after Steve.

"If that was an earthquake, it was freakin huge," Kat says breathlessly. "It threw me to the floor, Snake. That had to be at least an 8.0 if not bigger."

"Yeah, whatever it was, it was powerful. I hope it wasn't anything to do with the trapped miners. Didn't he say they would have gotten out in the next couple of hours? God I hope it wasn't the mine collapsing on top of the miners and the rescue crew."

"Me too," Kat says as they catch up to Steve. His face drains of all color, as he listens to someone on the phone.

"She called already. Yeah, as soon as possible, I promise," Steve says wearily. "That was not good news," he says to Snake and Kat who were hovering for any information. "The mine collapsed just as they were finishing the rescue. They got all but four miners out and then the collapse. They're not sure what caused it, but it's much worse this time. The only difference is there are only four miners in there now. They said by the looks of things, there isn't as good a chance of surviving this time."

"Shit," Kat cries softly and turns to bury her face in Snakes chest.

"Shhh," Snake says, dumbfounded by what just happened, as he starts rubbing her back in comfort. "They were so close," he murmurs.

"Yeah, another ten minutes and everyone would have been out of there safely," Steve agrees, discouraged.

"Is there anything we can do? We're both trained in rescue, so if you show us where the area is, we might be able to do something to help before the fire department gets here."

"The fire department just pulled in, over near the gate. I doubt there's much anyone can do right now. But, let's head over and see if we can help anyway. I can't just stand around and do nothing."

"Is there anything that I can do?" Kat asks a crowd gathering near the mine entrance.

"No, you need to stay back so no one else gets hurt," a young guy says, barely recognizable white powder covering him from head to toe.

"I have some rescue training," Kat offers encouragingly.

"I doubt even the best trained rescuer's going to be able to help here," another dust covered guy offers quietly.

"You know those miners that didn't make it out, don't you?" Kat asks understanding dawning.

"Yeah, we know them. We've worked together most of our lives. This is bad, real bad. There was hope, before that stupid part of the mine collapsed, but now it's doubtful."

"I'm so sorry," Kat offers. "Are you sure we can't do anything?"

"Yeah, you can take the world backwards a year. That would make a huge difference. If everything would have stayed the same in this country, we wouldn't have been working so many hours just to hide from the new government and that stupid chip," the young guy says sarcastically, while others standing near shush him desperately. "What, I'm not saying anything that hasn't been said before," he complains.

"It's okay; I certainly won't be taking this information with me anywhere. I feel the same way actually, and so does my friend, here he comes now," Kat says reassuringly after a quick glance to see where Snake got to.

"Snake, these guys are friends of the still trapped miners," Kat offers by way of raised eyebrows from Snake.

"It's good to meet you," he says after glancing at the two closest.

"You too, Sir," the young guy says quietly.

"We're among friends here Snake," Kat offers quickly a slight shake of her head indicating a talk is needed.

"I want to talk to you again," Kat says to the young miner as she grabs hold of Snakes arm to tug him aside for a quick whispered conversation, weariness in her eyes, a slight film of white dust covering everything including her eyelashes.

"I know we have the information they need," she says after explaining everything that went on once she introduced herself to them. "I'll give them the information if you want to go and call Eli. His groups about to get a lot bigger, I think," Kat says as she turns back to the miners.

"This can't go anywhere but to those you absolutely trust. If this information gets into the wrong hands, a whole lot of people will be hurt, murdered or imprisoned."

"I understand."

"Perfect," Kat says and after explaining to him about the undergrounds located all over the country she finishes with "now, I need a name and a contact number so that I can let the others know about you and where you're from."

***

"Our groups keep multiplying, it's a good thing we don't have to handle this, it has gotten out of control."

"Yeah, but Eli can handle it. Plus he's got lots of people willing to help, we're going to need them real soon, Kat, real soon," Snake murmurs, thinking of the problems still facing them when they get to D.C.

"Snake, are we being followed? It seems everywhere we go, disaster follows. We went way west and they had an unheard of earthquake. We move further inland and Yellowstone erupts, a couple of times. Now we're here in the great lakes region and the mine collapses again. I'm getting freaked out about this stuff. It's as if we're bringing bad things with us," Kat says, a quiver in her voice.

"Listen Kat, we talked about this a few days ago, remember. We have not caused any of this, but, watch the times, right? We're living in really uncertain times. I'm not saying that it's a coincidence or anything like that, but where are we headed? Who wants to stop us? I'm just saying."

"Isn't there anything that we can do to stop this? Can't we save anyone, before disaster strikes?" Kat asks, tears running down her face.

"I'm sorry kitten, but we have no control over any of this. The only thing that we can do is continue on with our plans and hope no one else gets hurt in the process. We have to stop her, Kat. If not, the whole world will suffer, just as small parts are suffering now. No, the world will never be as it was, but it can be helped. We can make a difference. We just have to keep our minds focused with what really is most important. We have to get to D.C. If we linger, then whatever it is may catch up to us. I'd rather it catch up at the Whitehouse than anywhere else, where anymore innocents are, at least."

"Right, let's make our goodbyes to Steve and head out. We've got quite a few hours yet before we hit Washington. I'd kind of like to make it to your parent's house to sleep tonight. It may feel a little bit safer to me. Right now, I'll take anything," Kat says, anger and determination a glint in her eyes.

"Steve, we're getting ready to head out. There's nothing that we can do here to help, and our presence could even hinder your work, so we're out of here."

"Hold on a sec," Steve says when he see's John run out of a building, scan the area looking for something, hold up a hand with the wait signal and beeline straight for him.

"What's wrong, John?" Steve asks when John gets close enough to hear him.

"I heard there was some kind of government hot shot here and I have a theory that might be of interest."

"Oh, you're talking about the Lieutenant here?" Steve asks in confusion.

"Yeah, I am. Are you Lt. Jacob Callander?"

"Yeah, that's me, why?" Jacob asks suspiciously.

"Look, I've tried to get this news to Washington, and they won't listen. They think I'm a crackpot. I know you have contacts in Washington that may be interested in this information."

"And who are you and how do you know my name," Jacob asks as he casually moves into his fighting stance.

"Anyone that keeps up with what's going on in Washington knows your name, Lt. Jacob Callander. You're not the most popular man in the country. Besides, I heard you were dead."

"To many I am, and I'll ask one more time. Who are you?"

"My name is Dr. Jonathan Smith in charge of the Proton Decay Group."

"John Smith, really?" Kat says in disbelief.

"Yeah, sorry, it's John Smith, I know, so individual," he adds self deprecatingly. "I know all about you and your problems with the president and that's really the least of my concerns. I'm more worried about the survival of mankind and the earth and what's happening than I am about the political atmosphere in this country."

"Yeah, the earth seems to have a bad case of indigestion what with all the earthquakes, tsunamis, volcanic eruptions and extreme weather patterns." Kat adds in agreement.

"Exactly! Have you guys heard of Charles Rosenthal?" Steve asks quietly.

"Yeah, I've heard of him. Isn't he the one running around predicting that the earth's going to be struck by a meteor?" Snake asks.

"Yeah, now there's a crackpot!" Kat says sarcastically, snorting a laugh out.

"Yeah, that's the guy, however if you put that crackpots information with this crackpots calculations, then maybe we aren't the crackpots after all. When I first heard about Rosenthal's prediction I flashed back to 1990 and a large influx of neutrons detected by the neutrino detectors. Now if those neutrons came from a super nova at that time, then it's very possible that debris from that super nova could be approaching our galaxy about now. If it is debris from a super nova, then the density and gravitational pull of that meteor could be enough to have major effects on earth's magnetic fields. That could actually pull the earth out of the orbit of the sun. You do remember the extremely large earthquake that occurred a few years ago and actually knocked the earth three degree's off its axis?"

"I remember that," Jacob admits thoughtfully.

"It could make volcanoes and earthquake faults more active, and create the atmosphere for more severe weather," John says.

"You give me all the information you want them to have and I'll get it to the right person or persons. But, I'm in no position to blatantly call these people. However, I'll make sure the ones you want to have this, get it."

Chapter Eleven

"President Martin, you have a call," Karen says when Jane finally picks up.

"Who is it?"

"I'm sorry but the caller refused to give me that information. Since you're waiting for information about your parents, I assumed you'd want to take it anyway."

"Put it through please."

"President Martin?"

"Yes, what can I do for you Mr.?"

"Rodregez, Chico Rodregez."

"Mr. Rodregez, what can I do for you," Jane asks in frustration.

"It's not what you can do for me, but what I can do for you," Chico says

"All right then, what is it You can do for Me?" Jane asks, anger simmering just below the surface.

"Well President Martin, I thought you'd be happy to hear this news. I have your parents!' Chico says enthusiastically, a smile heard in his tone.

"WHAT!" Jane yells stopping and standing still, shocked by what she just heard. "You have my parents? Where, when?"

"I have them with me. They're both fine, and are ready to come home."

"Where are you, exactly, Mr. Rodregez?"

"I'm in D.C. Just got here earlier today and thought I'd give you a call and let you know about your parents."

"When can you bring them to me, Mr. Rodregez?"

"Well, that's the problem. I can't just give them to you. I rescued them from a young gang banger group in Chicago and took real good care of them while bringing them here, to D.C. I think I deserve something for that. It wasn't always easy, you know. I actually got into a shoot out with the gang, just to free them. Then there were some soldiers that tried to infiltrate that gang and were stopped. After that there was an earthquake and damage along the way. It wasn't easy getting here at all. Surely my time's worth something. Besides, I did a good deed, right? You owe me now, right?" he demands into the silence.

"What is it you want, Mr. Rodregez? Money, power, what?"

"Well, since you put it so nicely, a little money would be good, but the big thing that I want is kept in charge of your parent's safety, a place on your staff. I'll do a good job taking care of them, I promise, President Martin."

"Mr. Rodregez, you have to be kidding, right. You have my parents and now you have demands to be met before you'll release them? I call that hostage negotiations, and that makes you no better than that gang that had them in Chicago, nor the traitors that held them out west."

"What? I'm much better than all those who had them to begin with. I contacted you as soon as I arrived in D.C. and told you I had them. I went to a lot of trouble, but I'm NOT holding them hostage. This is what I call payback for doing a good deed. If I never asked for anything, I couldn't live. It takes money and a job to stay alive in this world. I'm only asking for what's right. I'll tell you what, I'll contact you in a few days and you can let me know your decision then. Until then, have a nice day."

"Wait . Damn it, he hung up," Jane screams and throws the phone across the room to bounce against the wall before hitting the floor. *I need to talk with Teriq. He'll know what to do. Damn it, I can't believe they're so close and I still haven't seen them.* "Karen, get me Teriq on the line. Now!"

"Yes President Martin, right away."

"Here he is," Karen says after Jane answers the phone.

"Teriq, where are you," Jane demands as soon as the line clicks over.

"I'm just outside of Chicago, Jane. Still in search of your parents, but I think we're a little closer now than we were yesterday. At least the kids we're questioning are slightly more knowledgeable, have at least heard their names, so yeah, we're closer. What can I do for you?"

"My parents are in D.C. I just received a call from a Chico Rodregez who claims to have them and is demanding money and a job for bringing them to me."

"Jane, are you sure he has them? Because I'm pretty sure they're still in Chicago. I can't see them being in D.C. already."

"Look Teriq, all I know is that he called, said he had my parents and wants both money and a job to watch them for me. He didn't sound like he was lying."

"Didn't you ask for any proof? Talk to them on the phone, anything that verifies their location?"

"No, I didn't. I didn't think of it at the time and now he won't be calling back for a couple of days. What the hell should I do, wait for him to call back? I'm pretty sick of all the waiting and worrying. Isn't there anything that can be done right now?"

"It doesn't sound like it. It sounds like you dropped the ball before you had all the information," Teriq replies, smirking, trying hard not to show any emotion through the phone line.

"I dropped the ball?" Jane repeats anger beneath the surface.

"Yep, sorry Jane, but it is what it is."

"I want you back here today Teriq, understand?" Jane says calmly, death in her eyes.

"I'll leave right away. Unfortunately, I'm not that close so it'll be at least eight, maybe more hours before I can be there. I guess him not calling for a couple of days is a good thing. I'll definitely be back by then."

"Fine," Jane says calmly and meticulously hangs up the phone, eyes blank, not moving just staring into space, expressionless when a soft knock sounds on the closed door of the hidden office.

"What," Jane says as she answers the door, knowing it had to be Quinton that knocked. No one else is allowed in the room without a call first.

"Everything all right Jane," he asks as he walks in slowly, noticing things on the floor that should be on the wall. "Something happen?"

"Yes, something happened," she snaps. "I'm

not in the habit of throwing things on the floor, or knocking them off the walls unless there's a problem, a rather big problem!"

"What is it," Quinton questions as he heads to the bar to poor them both a drink.

"My parents," she says softly, "it's my parents."

"What about them," he asks when she just stands and stares, no words coming out of her mouth.

"They're in D.C.," she says.

"What! How, when, how did you find them?"

"A guy called about a half hour ago and informed me that he has my parents and they're in D.C. Then he hangs up after he says he'll call back in a couple of days. A COUPLE OF DAYS! He thinks I'll wait a couple of days to talk to and see my parents! He's freakin nuts."

"That's awesome news Jane! Awesome. They're alive and close. Closer than they've been since you became President. That's wonderful," Quinton exclaims. "Here, a drink to good news for a change."

"Thanks Quinton, but it's only news. I want my parents now!" Jane demands.

"But I thought they were with some guy and he was going to call you back. . . "

"Yes, they are," she interrupts. "I have NO way to reach him, he didn't leave a number and they couldn't trace the call, so now I'm at his mercy and he knows it. He wants both money and a job for bringing my parents to me," she grinds out, anger in every movement as she starts pacing the floor of the small room. Suddenly the phone rings again,

"What," Jane demands, totally irritated now.

"President Martin, there's a commotion at the front gate. Your presence is requested by the secret service."

"Why, what's going on?"

"I'm unaware exactly what it is, just that the Secret Service want you to go to the front gate as soon as possible."

"Fine," she says irritated. "I'm needed at the front gate by the secret service, come with me Quinton and let's see just what the hell is going on now."

"What is it," she demands when she reaches the front entrance where it looks like a couple dozen people are milling around.

"President Martin," her chief of the secret service addresses her in relief.

"What's so important that you had to call me up here?"

"There's a gentleman at the front gate insisting that he has something of yours and wants to see you personally to give it to you. We checked and he's weaponless and there a two people with him. I think you'll want to see this first hand."

"Fine," she says, resigned.

"Mom? Dad? Is that you?" she screams when she catches a glimpse of the two people huddled together near a dark skinned, tall man. With the scream, they look up quickly, gasp in unison and start off at a run to meet Jane midway.

"Oh my God, it is you," she exclaims when she grabs hold of both parents, touching them for the first time in months. "You're okay, you're both okay" she says, tears in her eyes, happiness glowing on her face. "How, who, where did you come from, how did you get here," she starts rattling off questions rapid fire.

"President Martin?" Chico says in between all the talk that's going on.

"Yes," Jane answers, begrudgingly looking away from her parents, making eye contact with Chico before her gaze is drawn back to the only two people in the world that she's loved all her life.

"I brought you your parents," Chico says into the silence. "Could we talk somewhere soon" he asks hesitantly.

"Oh, absolutely we're going to talk. I thought you wanted money for them, but we'll talk about that too. Henry, take Mr. Rodregez inside to the oval office, and stay with him. I'll be there in just a few minutes, after I settle my parents in to their wing. Follow me Mom, Dad. I'm so happy you're finally here," Jane says as she leads them into the South Wing of the White House.

"Mom, Dad, I'm going to take care of this guy, Mr. Rodregez, he'll never hurt or cause harm to anyone again," Jane promises.

"Jane, he never harmed us, he was the only one that treated us good since we were taken. All we know is we were locked in a dirty run down hotel room. We heard loud arguing outside and someone said, look, children belong with their parents and I'm going to make sure they get back to where they belong. Then there were gunshots and the door flew open and Mr. Rodregez came into the room and took us with him. He took us to the outskirts of Chicago to a real nice house, a beautiful home, although I don't think it was his because he broke into the back door to get in. Once we were inside, he let us shower and clean up. He took clean clothes out of the closet for each of us then fed us and I think he stole a car, because he put us in a real nice car and we left for here."

"Sounds like Mr. Rodregez' is quite the enterprising young man!"

Chapter Twelve

"How much farther," Kat yells at Snake after riding for hours. After no answer she hits him on the back of the head to get his attention.

"What?" Snake yells.

"How much farther," Kat yells back.

"Couple of hours yet," Snake says, "but we're gonna have to get gas, next gas station."

Two exits later and a gas stations advertised, so they get off. After pulling up to something looking like an old general store from the fifties with the gas pumps out front he's surprised to see a sign on the pump that say's "Just scan your chip to start the pump."

"Shit, forgot about this. Well, let's see if they still take cash," he tells Kat after they both get off the bike, relieved to stand straight for a few minutes.

"Welcome to the town of Blue Creek," an old, skinny; long gray haired ex-hippie says when they get to the register.

"Thanks, but where's the town?" Snake asks with a grin.

"You're in it," old hippie man exclaims, laughing toothless.

"Do you still take cash for stuff," Snake asks with a smile.

"Nah, ain't no use fer cash around here no

more, don't you have the witches' magic chip yet," he asks.

"Haven't needed it up till now," Snake admits.

"Huh," old hippie man grunts. "Well now, you ain't gonna be able to do much of anything in Virginia without that chip."

"Is there any way I can get gas without the chip," Snake asks slowly.

"Depends, who are ya," old hippie man asks quietly.

"I go by Snake."

"You kinda look familiar like, maybe I seen ya here before?"

"Nope, never been here," Snake says.

"Wait a minute. I seen ya before, on TV, with your lady friend there, too," old hippie man says determinedly. "It was a while back, but I'm sure it was you."

Snake starts to reach for his gun when "Now hold on there mister," old hippie man says nervously "I recognize who you are now and I ain't got much use for that witch in Washington, neither!"

"Really," Snake says suspiciously.

"I promise, it ain't like that. She's ruining this here country with all this bull and these damn chip things. So I'll tell you what I'm gonna do. If this is gonna help you stay under her skin, then take it," old hippie man says as he pulls an envelope out from under the counter and hands it to Snake

"What's this," Snake asks as he opens the envelope and finds a chip.

"That's your ticket across Virginia. You just glue it on your arm and nobody will be any the wiser."

"Where'd you get this?" Snake asks.

"There was a government man that came wandering around this field surveying my crops that came to an untimely demise. I figured he wouldn't be needin it anymore and I thought maybe I could use it for somethin sometime."

"So you dug it out of his arm?" Kat asks.

"Yep, it was easier than skinnin a hog," the old hippie man admits with a grin.

"You killed a man for walking through your corn field?" Kat asks appalled.

"I never said it was corn!" he answered winking at Snake.

"Ohhh," Kat says biting back a smile.

"If there's ever anything that I can help you with, here's a way to reach me," Snake says as he hands the old hippie man a small piece of paper with a phone number on it.

"Thank ya and would you like a small sample of my harvest to take with ya for the road? I had a bumper crop this year," the old hippie man says as he holds a small clear bag out for inspection.

"I wish," Snake says "but I have to keep a clear head. I'll tell you what, when all this calms down, I'll be back to sample that bumper crop."

***

"Let's hit the road," Snake says after filling the bike. "We gotta get to D.C. and find out how Chico's making out. It's going to be dark soon. We should just make it to Mom and Dad's in time to be able to see what we're doing," Snake yells after exiting the highway.

"Yeah," Kat says, envisioning comfort and food in the near future when something hits the bikes left rearview mirror and blows it off. The bike starts wobbling before Snake gets firm control again and Kat stares at what used to be the mirror, but is now small pieces of metal and plastic. Once they pull over and stop the bike she gasps "what the hell just happened? Something must have hit us, there wasn't any traffic going by when that explosion occurred. What the hell?" she says as she gets off the bike shakily and pushes her hair back, and notices blood on the fingers of her left hand. "What?" she says, confused.

"Hold on Kat, let me see what you have there," Snake says as he notices smeared blood on Kat's face. "Looks like you got hit with something," he says grimly as he reaches out and tears off a piece of shirt tail to use to clean it up. "Hand me that water bottle," he says as he wipes at the blood that's seeping down her cheek. "It's not very big, but probably could use a stitch or two. Ah hell, Kitten, seems I'm always getting you hurt."

"Did you hurt me?" she asks confused.

"Not personally, but it's my bike and I was driving," he says scowling.

"What happened?" she asks "Whatever it was, it was fast. Did you see something, a bird maybe, fly into the path?"

"There was nothing, nothing but air, no dust, no birds, no other vehicles, nothing."

"Weird," she says, shaking her head. The sun's shining; birds are singing in the distance, there's no sign of anything that could have hit the bike, just nothing but a gorgeous day. "I wonder what the heck it could have been, to do that kind of damage."

"We'll probably never know. I guess we should get back on the bike and finish this trip. We've got less than an hour left and we'll be at Dad's. The sooner we can get there, the sooner I can clean that cut and fix it so it doesn't scar too bad."

"I'll be fine, I promise," she says as she climbs on.

***

"Wow, it doesn't look dusty or empty at all. Actually, it looks like someone cleaned it recently. There's no mess, I expected at least a little mess," Kat admits after roaming around the house while Snake turns the air on to freshen the unused feel. I'm gonna check the freezer and see if there's anything we can use," Kat says walking slowly out of the living room and through the dining room, remembering the last time she was there. The smiles and laughter from a close family filling her mind with happiness and sadness at the same time. Knowing that things will never be the same again, thanks to Jane and her evil plans for the future. So many things have changed" she sniffles when Snake walks up and puts his arm around her, gazing quietly out of the dining room windows.

"I know," he says quietly, remembering his family, *brothers, one now gone, the other in Texas with his sister, his parents, never to walk through these rooms again. Its hard coming back to so much change,* he thinks. "How about you look through the cabinets and freezer while I contact Eli? That'll make eating that much faster. I don't know about you, but I could use some food," Snake says as he hugs Kat. *If only you knew just how much I love you* he thinks.

"There's some homemade stew I found in the freezer. She's got it so stocked you'd think she knew this was coming. It'll be done in just a few more minutes, thanks to modern technology. I love microwaves," she admits with a grin, the smell of stew permeating the air making the house seem that much homier.

"I just got done talking to Eli. He dispatched a group of guys out to the compound that Mike (the guy they found in the woods) gave them directions to. He's expecting to hear back from them before morning to give him an idea of what they may be up against." Snake says pacing the length of the kitchen, stomach growling. "I have a feeling this is a bigger deal than any of us have thought about. I've been thinking about this and if they have one of these places, they probably have a lot more. How else would they be able to contain all the nay-sayers. I mean, if this place is full, you know they have others. It would be too blatant if they brought people in only to take lots of "stuff" out shortly afterward and no one ever saw the people leave after they went in. Yeah, the people of the U.S. may be in short memory mode but that would still be way too obvious. We never should have missed this, I still can't believe that we heard nothing about these places!" Snake growls in disgust, stomach rumbling from the smell of hot fresh stew.

"It's hard to know what's going on. We've been out of touch way too long," Kat agrees as the microwave dings and she opens the door, grabbing the stew to give it a last stir and dish it out.

"This is so good," Snake says as he shovels in the stew, mopping up the gravy with some bread that Kat found in the freezer and zapped to defrost.

"Yeah," Kat mumbles around a mouth full of stew, eyes glazed in ecstasy.

"I don't know about you but I'm so full and relaxed that I'm going to fall asleep sitting right here at the table if I don't lie down pretty fast. This has been a l o o o n n n g g g g g day," she says around a yawn.

"Yes it has. I'm going to run through the shower and see if I can find any clean clothes that may fit. The master bedrooms the last room on the left down the hall," Snake offers as he walks out.

"Wow, I'm not sure I feel comfortable sleeping in this room," Kat admits as she stares at the bed that takes up a third of the room, the curtains closed for privacy, lights on low.

"It's just a room. Mom and Dad would have loved you staying here. But if makes you really uncomfortable we can pick a spare room. It's just this bed's bigger than the others. The others are all full size, this ones the only King in the house."

"Oh, well, I don't want to sleep alone, and a king makes more sense, so if it won't bother you then I'm okay with it."

"It won't bother me," he says as he walks slowly towards her, thoughts of how she'll look laying on the bed making his breath come a little more quickly.

"Snake," Kat says softly.

"Yeah," he answers just as softly.

"Umm, I'll be right back," she says as she walks

towards the bathroom, visions of the night starting to take shape, excitement in the pit of her stomach.

* * *

"What," Kat mumbles, her hair all over her face along with a pillow. "What's that noise" she says as she slowly rolls over, bumping up against a hard male body while trying to remove all the hair from her mouth, and trapped around the bandage on her cheek.

"I'm not sure," Snake admits sleepily "I think it's, wait, is that knocking?"

"Shit," Kat says as she jumps out of bed. "Who could it be?" she asks in a panic. "No one knows we're here, who could it be?"

"I'm not sure," Snake admits as he throws some pants on and grabs his gun.

"Stay here and I'll go see what the knocking's all about."

"I'm not staying here," she says in disbelief as she grabs her clothes and starts throwing them on, trying to keep up with Snake, the gun in her left hand making it difficult to button her shirt.

Kat skids to a halt as Snake holds up a hand in the wait gesture.

"I think it's the paper boy. I didn't see any papers lying around when we got here yesterday, did you?" he asks quietly.

"No. Maybe he's trying to collect for old papers. They may have had a bill due when they left for the underground. It was pretty sudden when we all had to leave."

"True. I'll have to try to pay that without him

knowing who paid what."

"Good luck with that. You probably need the damn chip to pay," she says disparagingly.

"Good point. He may have to go without getting paid. I don't want to chance any interest being drawn here."

"No, the last thing we need is interest. It'll hamper what we need to do," she says, voice dwindling when she notices the interest that Snakes showing in her partially buttoned shirt.

"Were you ready to get up? I wasn't. How about we go back to bed? We've got plenty of time to indulge our fantasies before reality has to step in, don't you think?" he asks as he lowers his head slowly, her lips calling his.

"Haven't had enough yet?" she asks after he releases her lips from his much wanted prison.

"Never, if we live to be a hundred, I'll still not have enough, kitten. I'll always want you, like I always have."

"I don't remember you wanting me when we first met. I seem to remember you impatiently yelling at me for almost getting raped by that sleazy biker friend of yours."

"I was just yelling because I didn't want you to know how I really felt back then. I figured you'd been traumatized enough by Elroy."

"I wasn't traumatized by Elroy at all. He was nothing but a scum bag. I had it under control," she insists with pride in her abilities.

"Right," he snorts as he pulls her along, back to the bedroom they'd just exited. "Enough talk, I've got other things planned that you don't need words for," he says slowly, voice full of promise and need.

"I could get used to this," Kat says softly as he pulls off the shirt she threw on, touching her breasts with firmness and longing, making love to her with his eyes.

"Snake," she says after finding herself on the bed, her breasts being lavished with total attention, talking no longer needed. "Snake," she groans again when her hands start to smooth the soft but hard skin laying over her, a tightening in her groin causing her to gasp in excitement and need.

"Kitten," she hears after her fingers encircle that which they were searching for, that hot, velvety hard organ which is growing bigger and harder as she slides her hand up and down. "My turn," she says in a whisper and turns him on his back so she can give him the attention he needs.

After peeping at him through her lashes, she moves down taking him in her hands before bending slightly and licking his head, one hand on his shaft the other on his tight abs. With a long slow lick down the full size of him, he groans in need while she closes her eyes in ecstasy, loving him more at this moment than ever., filling her with heat and love.

"Kitten, be careful. I don't want this to end too soon," Snake says on a groan, then he lifts her off of him, lays her down and enters quickly, swallowing Kats scream with his mouth. "Okay," he asks quietly, laying still, waiting for her answer before picking up the rhythm.

"More than okay," Kat says breathily. "More," she says again "harder, faster," she groans.

That's all he needs to hear, picking up the rhythm, slamming home, the sound of their love making the only thing that can be heard. When he feels her release coming, he covers her mouth with his to absorb her scream and thrusts a couple more times before allowing himself the pleasure of release.

Chapter Thirteen

"Snake, we got here a couple of days ago. It was an easy ride since the Martins gave me no problems. They were actually pretty nice to talk with. Too bad they aren't what they seem," Chico says quietly.

"Yeah, it is too bad, but look what they've given birth to, what they've created. They can't be good but they can be good actors."

"True. Anyway, Jane called me last night. She's talking about the summit that happens in five days; at least that's what she said. She's interested in me continuing the protection of her parents here and while traveling. She wants me to head that up, with a few more chosen people to help, of course. Plus she's guaranteed me a large sum of money and free housing if I agree to her proposition."

"Excellent, it's better than we hoped for! I'm glad we made it before the summit. That's going to be our chance to get much needed information. Plan on getting some recording devices planted around her. We need to know just what she's planning on. It's definitely not all above board. Actually most of its underhanded. I just want to know what to expect. There are a few countries that haven't agreed to the chip. I think she's going to push them hard at the summit."

"I'm glad too. I'm supposed to meet with her tomorrow at zero nine hundred in the oval office with the answer. I think she'll be pleased with what I have to say. I do have a couple of questions. Do you have any background information on the Vice President, Quinton Uqbahtor? If my gut's right, which I can usually rely on, I think our Mr. Uqbahtor is a plant directly from the foreign country that she seems to favor. There's just way too many strange vibes going on. I was in the room with both of them and there are too many things left unsaid. Yes, she's the President and has all the power, but I think he's wielding a lot more power than even she's willing to acknowledge. He's just got way too much confidence in whatever he says or even suggests. I did pick up a slight amount of displeasure in a couple of the things he mentioned, but then she just backed off and left those suggestions. He wanted to talk about what's going on in the European Union in two months and she shut him down quick. I would have gotten angry myself, the way she said things to him, but he just grinned. When she saw that, she shut up real fast. In my opinion, the grin was his way of reminding her who he really is, how much power he wields and just what she can't do about it. It was pretty strange. Do you know anything about him?

"Actually, I know a little, but not as much as Mal. We had some suspicions last year, since I knew him slightly before he was given the position of Vice President. I knew he was Arab, not American Indian like he told everyone, and that he owns one of my customized bikes, but I didn't know how he could be connected. So Mal went out west last year and ended up in a restaurant allowing her to see who he pretends to be and who he hangs with. She sat just a few tables away and could hear his conversation with his cronies, in which he felt free to talk in his native tongue thinking no one else in the restaurant could understand, but Mal did. She's fluid in seven languages, one of them being Farsi. Anyway, he was talking quite a lot about Jane, her parents and the guy that shot the speaker of the house's plane out of the sky. There's definitely a connection, I just didn't realize that he held that much power. I'll have to look into that more and get back to you."

"Thanks, appreciate it, now down another path. So where is Admiral Teriq Auliya? Is he still looking around Chicago for her parents" Chico asks, a grin evident in his tone.

"I doubt that," Snake says through a snort. "I'm sure Jane's contacted him already and he's probably on his way into D.C. Never underestimate him or her. That would be your downfall."

"Don't worry about that, I know snakes when I see them, especially poisonous ones."

"That's right, that's what I want to hear," Jacob says teasingly. "Remember, don't mention me or Kat. As far as Jane's concerned, we're dead. Another thing, see what you can find out about where they're sending the citizens that refuse the chip. We've uncovered something in Texas, but after thinking about it, I doubt it's the only place. Just do your best to listen in on any discussions, especially after the General gets back. He's probably the one that set up that compound. Also, from what I heard, those Iranian forces she brought in, they're in this somehow, in charge of guarding the detainee's maybe. Eli's going to work on getting that information and get back to me sometime today, so I should know more next time we talk."

"Excellent, Sir. I've never heard of either of you, and I'll do everything I can to find out what's happening to the ones that refused the chip, too. Do you want to set up a schedule to talk on a frequent basis?"

"Yeah, how about evenings when you're off babysitting duty? Tomorrow, say at twenty two hundred hours?"

"That sounds like a good time. If I can't make it, I'll leave a message and let you know when to expect me."

"Thanks Chico, and thanks for doing everything you've done."

"My pleasure Sir, after all, this is my country too and I certainly care about what's going on in it. I'm in for the long haul."

***

"Jacob, we finally have the equipment gathered for Mal. She'll be able to get into the main programming for the chips. We can finally start making the changes to the chips so that Jane can't kill at will. It took us the longest time to actually come up with a scanner that will blast the chips information to a computer we set up with Mal. Hold on she wants to tell you herself."

"It's awesome Jacob. I can stop her. At least with those I can get scanned back to me. I know it's not everyone in the world, but when she realizes what's been done, it'll hopefully make her less sure of herself. I'm really looking forward to seeing her expression when she understands what happened," Mal says gleefully.

"Congrats Mal, this is big. I had hoped that it could be done, but when we all had to scatter and leave all your equipment behind, I wasn't sure if we'd ever get back to this position. This is really great news," he says as he grabs a hold of Kat's hand with his free one and gives it a squeeze in excitement.

"I know Jacob. I wasn't so sure either. But after a lot of scrounging and working my fingers off, I did it. This program's as good if not better than the last one I did. But you have to remember, it took me months to get where I was with the last one. I just had to remember what I did, not redo, and then figure the rest out. Anyway, it's done."

"Thanks Mal, now put Eli back on. I need to talk to him about something else. Love you Sis, bye. Eli, what have you found out about that facility with the guards?"

"I've sent a few of the guys out. Rand, Mongoose and Lucas left late last night. They contacted me earlier and said they had information and that a few others have joined them and they'll be back tonight. We're going to call a meeting as soon as they get back and see what the hell's going on with that 'courtesy camp' that she set up. This is not above board, you and I know that. I'm just not sure how bad it is nor how deeply involved it's going to be to rescue those people. We are going to rescue them, on that you can be assured," Eli promises grimly rubbing his eyes with his hands, trying to push the fatigue out of the way, hot, tired and dusty after a weeks of triple digit days.

"I know Eli. I wish I could help. I should have seen this, should have expected it..."

"Stop Jacob, you can't be everywhere and do everything. That's not realistic. Besides, we both know that it'll take an army, not just of two, but of thousands upon thousands and we still may lose the battle. But at least we're all doing what we can to make it not so easy on her. If right wins the battles then we will win. That's the best that anyone can do, you included, superhero," he adds with a smirk obvious in his voice.

"I know, I know," Jacob adds discouraged yet encouraged at the same time. *The chips can be changed, which will help protect the people, but it seems for every good thing we get done, another bad one shows up. It's almost like a chess game and she's constantly at check. Let's hope it's our turn and we can maneuver into check mate*, he thinks.

"What, sorry, my mind wandered. Could you repeat that," Jacob tells Eli after realizing he wandered from the conversation at hand.

"I said I'll call you when we start the meeting and put you on speaker so you can hear the same thing we hear at the same time. It'd be nice if we could get video conferencing going. I'll mention that to Mal and see what we need to do that. How about you, do you have what's needed for it?"

"Yeah, I think we do. We've got Mom's laptop. I'll have Kat check it out and see. If we can, then I'll have her send the information to Mal, after you give me her IP address. It's the same address that Mom was using, so she might have that already. I think Mom and Dad knew something because they stocked the freezer, the house was maintained and I checked all the utilities and they paid for two years in advance for everything. It's almost as if they had a premonition that bad things were going to happen and they might need to lay low for a while, a long while. Whatever the reason, I'm grateful. It's made my life a little easier. I don't have to think of survival but of how to change the course of what's Jane's set in motion. That's a much bigger problem than survival, but at least I have time to concentrate on just that. Now I have lots of stuff to get done here, so what time should we plan for the meeting tonight? Nine o'clock our time, yeah, that's a good time for us. That gives both of us time to get down to work. I'll talk to you tonight."

"Mal's into the chip program and ready to start changing the codes. That's good news for a lot of people, if they only knew. So now Kitten, I think we need to change appearances. You're too well known in the D.C. area and everyone thinks I'm Devon, making me too well known too. Looks like new clothes and some hair dye's in order."

"I think I'll go goth this time, with black hair, nails, clothes and a white face. That should blend right in with the others. Now, let me see," Kat says as she wanders around Snake, focused on how to change him. "I'm sorry, I just can't see you changed enough to not look like you," she says after studying him from every angle."Wait, can you walk with a limp? I think you'd make a great bum, a stringy gray wig, dirty old clothes, old army boots, yep, oh wait, that's not a disguise," she says with a giggle and quick step back, out of harm's way.

"What do you mean that's not a disguise," he asks with indignation. "You saying that I already look like that," he says with a grin back, comfortable with the teasing back and forth.

"Not me, I would never say that Snake. You're too hot to ever look old and decrepit!"

"Aww, that's nice of you Kitten," he says with a slow step forward, a gentle tug on her hand. It never pays to let the enemy know when they're trapped. Not until it's too late, like it is right now.

"Hey," she says on a gasp of surprise, held tight against that hard body that she's come to love. "I was kidding you know," she admits during her struggle to release herself, panic starting to set in. Sometimes the past does come back to haunt you.

"Shhh, it's me kitten, it's just me," he reassures her through her panicked punches, saddened by the glimpse of fear he saw.

"I know and I'm sorry. I also know that you'd never hurt me, it was an unconscious gesture. I didn't feel afraid, but my mind must have. I'm sorry Snake. I'd never hurt you or your feelings on purpose."

"It'll fade with time Kitten, I promise. Now, let's work on the disguises. I have to do some scouting and get the lay of the land. I've been out of here for so long I'll have to start fresh with my contacts. It may take a few days, days we don't really have, so let's start moving" he says briskly.

"There's a shopping center about twenty

minutes from here. It's small, so we should be able to stay under the radar for the short time it will take to get what we need. I just hope we can pay cash for what we need. I'd hate to use the chip and not be able to use it again later. That's such a waste."

"I hear you. Let's go."

Chapter Fourteen

"I told you Jane, I thought they were in Chicago. No one informed me of them leaving," Teriq says for the umpteenth time.

"Listen Teriq," Jane says face red, hair messy and her normal composure out the window. "How much longer will you have a job if you can't handle it? You certainly can't expect me to continue on with this charade. You lost my parents. In Chicago," she enunciates slowly, talking to a two year old in her mind. "Did you find them and bring them to me? N O you did not! A stranger off the streets found them, didn't like how they were being treated and brought them to me, and might I add, at great risk to himself. If he wouldn't have had someone like me to bring them to, he could have really suffered vile consequences. But since he brought them to me, he knew I wouldn't hurt him because of the huge favor he did. You, on the other hand, seem to have become unnecessary. I realize that the country is still under martial law, but it seems to be running quite nicely without you in charge. You've become nothing but a figure head. I don't need any figure heads; I have plenty of them already. Tell me, do you think you deserve to keep your job?"

"Jane, I may seem like nothing to you, but this country is pretty unstable right now. How do you think the people would handle it if you started changing things that they've finally become comfortable with? I believe you have a lot of important meetings coming up. Out of the country, might I remind you? The last thing you need right now is a civil upheaval. The people are used to me, to my orders, to the way I do things. They've become relatively happy lately. I had the opportunity to talk with quite a few on my journey back here and the atmosphere is much lighter than it was at the beginning of your regime. Since you backed off with the capital punishment on TV, people seem to be breathing easier. You can run a country without its people, but what would be the point? Are you going to leave Quinton in charge while you're gone?" he asks, a smile flitting at the corners of his mouth, his dark eyes shining with glee. *Some things are worth waiting for and this was definitely one of them, Jane at a loss for words. I'm going to pay for this, but it's well worth it. I'm a little sick of the way she's been treating me, like I'm nothing but dirt beneath her feet. She'll learn respect, very very soon! She really is naïve if she thinks she's going to be the World Dictator. How stupid,* he thinks.

"Well, where did that come from? You really believe you can get away with this attitude towards me, you, who are nothing in this whole grand scheme of things. I gave you your job, and I can take it from you. Have you no respect for the higher powers? I was groomed for this job, by someone of much greater importance than you.

Watch out Teriq, you have no power without me giving it to you."

"You're right Jane. All the power is yours. I have no power, nor do I want any power. I'm here to do your bidding, and for no other reason. When this is all said and done, I will be ready and willing to go home. I apologize for any disrespect that you heard. I'm not sure what happened to me but that is not how I feel at all. Again, I apologize, Jane," Teriq says, skin an ashen color, all glee wiped from his face, eyes. Anyone looking at him now would have never expected to hear what she heard.

"Teriq, why the sudden change," Jane asks sweetly, pocketing a small phone as she turns to look out the window.

"I'm not sure what you mean Jane," he says quietly, voice shaking slightly. "I was being totally disrespectful of you and your position and again, I apologize. That was uncalled for and not how I felt, not at all," he repeats again.

"Good, I'm glad we were able to straighten that out. You may leave now. I'll contact you when I need you, otherwise, stay out of my sight."

"Yes President Martin. Thank you," Teriq says as he salutes her then turns and heads out the door.

"Teriq, just one more thing," she says just as he grabs the door handle. "There is no where you can hide to escape me. The chip, it can't be removed. And what you just felt. That was just a small sample of my capabilities. I can cause you great pain, from anywhere in the world. I can also end your life, from anywhere in the world. You just experienced one of my new chip programs that I couldn't wait to try. Thanks for allowing me the opportunity."

***

"President Martin, you're mothers on line seven."

"Thanks Karen. I'll take it right here. Mom, what's up," Jane asks, a smile in her voice, never tired of talking to her mom.

"I was wondering if we could have lunch today, dear. Your father and I are tired of each other and would love to spend a little time with our baby girl"

"As a matter of fact, I did put you on my schedule for lunch today," Jane says as she looks out the window of the oval office, noticing for the first time today the beautiful sunshine through the tree's, dappled marks hitting the lawn, a bright cardinal sitting on a rose branch his color at odds with the soft pink petals of the roses. Looking around as if waiting on something and singing in that high pure voice of his, something sounding like pretty girl, pretty girl. "We need to talk about a few things before we leave for the summit. Only another day and we'll be leaving. Anyway, we'll talk at lunch. Give me another thirty minutes or so and I'll be available," she adds, abruptly turning from the view to concentrate on her mom, never one to gaze aimlessly.

"Thanks Jane, we'll see you soon."

"Karen, is Quinton in his office," Jane asks after calling her secretary.

"No, President Martin, he left about half an hour ago. He said he had a meeting, probably for lunch, and wouldn't be back until around three."

"Oh, all right, get me Chico Rodregez on the line then," she orders.

"Right away President Martin," she replies.

"Here he is," she says then transfers the lines after hitting the blank button on the phone.

"Mr. Rodregez, its Jane Martin."

"President Martin, what can I do for you," Chico asks after a short pause, giving him time to assimilate who just called and click the record button on his laptop.

"I need to speak with you tomorrow about the summit. We leave day after tomorrow and I want to see what you've set up for the protection of my parents, not that they'll need much once we arrive. They'll be with family, after all. Can you be here at nine am?

"Yes, that's true, and absolutely. Nine am is fine with me," he agrees quietly.

"Good, I'll see you then."

***

"Mom, Dad," Jane says as she hugs her mom while grabbing hold of her dad's hand. "This makes me so happy, you have no idea," she adds, tears in her eyes, a flush of color in her otherwise pale complexion, her hair longer and darker than normal. It's amazing what a beauty shop in the White House can do for someone with a plain appearance. "Let's sit, shall we," she commands as she leads them to the table set up by the window, a view of the shrubs surrounding the area, beautiful dark glossy green. *It's been a good year for the plants and flowers*, she thinks as she settles in to spend some long-yearned for time with her parents.

"I'm so sorry that you went through so much," she starts out. "I was so afraid after the church was bombed and there was no sign of you at home. By all appearances, you had been at the church and as far as I knew, you were gone, just like everyone else in the area. But I didn't feel it, you know, in my heart I didn't feel it. I still had the link to you. I never felt it disappear, so of course I wouldn't believe it. No matter who told me, there was no way. You were never gone as far as I was concerned" she claims fiercely. "You can't leave yet. We're not done with what was started so many years ago. This is something you need to be part of. You've been part of this whole thing from the beginning. You will see it through" she insists arrogantly, her arrogance covering the fear riding closely behind, to close for comfort.

"Shhh, my darling Jane, shhh. You can be who you are with us. We're your family, remember? It's okay to be afraid in front of us. It's okay to let us help you. We're finally here so that you can have help. We too, have yearned for this time. To be a part of the greatest thing that's ever happened to this world, to watch as you become what you were born to become. We are so proud of you and what you've accomplished, even without us," Jessica admits teary eyed.

"Thank you Mom. I've been so alone without you both," Jane says, head lowered respectfully. "From now on, you will be with me wherever I go. We're leaving the day after next for Uncles. I'm sure that he's excited to reunite with you both. You haven't seen him since you were given this job and sent here, have you," she adds, happiness and excitement building. "I can't wait to see your reactions to each other."

"No, Jane. We haven't set foot outside the United States, not since we landed in Canada and crossed the border near Minnesota. Once we arrived in Texas that was it. We established ourselves and prepared to complete our mission," Fred finishes, a proud yet insecure look in his black eyes, bottomless and still. "I do want to add that after we had you, you became more than our job, we couldn't help ourselves. We fell in love with you at first sight. We did complete our mission but I also hope you never felt that you weren't loved."

"Dad, you know I haven't! I've always felt your love. You were never anything but kind, patient and loving to me," she says misty eyed.

"And you Jane, you were the best little girl a father could want. So very smart, always happy, and truly loving. You were just the best, always!"

"Dad, thanks. That means so much to me. This has been a hard time for me. I'm surrounded by frenemies. There's not one person that I can trust, except for you and Mom. Plus I haven't had that for so long I'm not sure how to react. It's going to take me a little to get back in the right thought process, but I will. Now that we're back together, things will be so much better."

"Jane, from everything that we've seen and heard you're doing fine. You've made the right decisions and gone in the right direction with the country. The people are starting to come around, I think. You're gaining in popularity now. That's a huge deal if you think about it, especially with the rocky start that you had. But if I must say, you've accomplished so much in the short time that you've had. It's not quite a year yet, and the goal is in sight."

"Yeah, the goal, we're getting close, very close. That's another thing I wanted to talk to you about. Uncle's excited that you'll be seeing each other really soon. We leave tomorrow night for Iran. He's setting everything up, so don't be surprised if he invites old friends and has an intimate party for you. Then I'll be joining the summit in two days, where I can finally clinch the rest of the countries that have been stubbornly resisting me. This needs to be finished before the European Union's big summit at the end of next month. I want to have everything in order before I accept the seat that they've been holding for me. It's too bad they don't know that part of it yet, but they'll understand soon enough. It's getting kind of exciting yet kind of nerve racking too. Fortunately for me, I've had so many problems to deal with that I haven't had time to get really nervous," Jane admits a hint of excitement in the sparkle of her eyes, the slight flush to her otherwise pale cheeks.

Chapter Fifteen

"Wow, I'm not sure I'd recognize you anywhere," Snake says after his first glimpse of the changed Kat. "Your hair, it's so short and really black. The black makeup and lipstick, awesome, and is that a real tattoo? When did you have time for that and the piercings? The eyebrow, I wasn't expecting that. You totally look like a freak, but a good freak," he admits with a laugh.

"Excuse me, who did you say you were?" Kat asks mock seriously. "You're the one that's totally changed! The white blonde hair and mustache, and the modern black glasses that everyone seems to like nowadays, they make you look really hot! I didn't know you could grow a mustache that fast" she admits wryly. "Where'd that mole come from? That wasn't there earlier and the clothes, they all combine to make you look at least ten years younger. I'm impressed, jealous and shocked at the same time. I'm kinda anxious now to see Eli and Mallory's reactions. It ought to be interesting," she says, rubbing her hands in glee. "I love doing this kind of stuff but unfortunately it's for a bad reason, one that we have to live with. Did you set up the computer like I told you to? It's almost nine now, so they should be contacting us within minutes."

"It's all ready to go. And you have nothing to be jealous of. You look like your seventeen or eighteen, so don't complain to me. We do look like a couple though. At least we can go out and about this way and hopefully gain no new attention. It'll be nice to be able to go outside with you. Strange but nice for a change, that way I can keep an eye on you," he adds with a leer, the two of them laughing together becomes what Eli and Mallory first see when they start their camera.

"Oh, we're sorry" Mal says embarrassed, not knowing who they're seeing at first glimpse, just a couple of young people messing around with their laptop camera.

"Wait . . . " Kat says to the now empty screen. "She must have exited the program" she snorts in realization. "Our cover must be good. She had absolutely no idea before she tuned out."

"Wait, here they are again. Mal, it's us," Jacob says quickly, trying to grab her before she can click off again.

"Jacob? Is that you, it doesn't look like you at all. The voice is the only thing I recognize. WOW, you guys look amazing, and like you're having fun too," she says suspiciously, a little jealousy in the tone.

"Not really sis. We were laughing because we were envisioning your reaction and you didn't disappoint," Jacob admits with another laugh and a soft giggle from somewhere near him could be heard too.

"Hi Mal," Kat says as she steps into the camera's viewing area.

"Kat, it does sound like you. But you look nothing like yourself! You look totally modern, very goth and teenagerish! An excellent choice, but did you really get a tattoo? And the piercings are they real?"

"Naw, it's a temporary tattoo. It's supposed to last a couple of weeks, its henna, so it won't fade fast. Hopefully it'll last long enough to do the job. The piercings, unfortunately, are real. They had nothing available that looked real enough, but I figure they'll fade once this is all over and I can take the studs out. I kinda like them though. Maybe I'll keep them when we're done. Use them as a memento. We'll see . . .," Kat adds with a grin.

"Can we get down to business now," Jacob asks impatient with all the girl talk. "What did you find out about the courtesy camp? Who's responsible for it and what's going on inside?"

"We brought some of the guardsmen here that have been maintaining the security on the perimeter. Once Rand and Mongoose made contact, they were able to talk with a few of the guards and what a story. I'll let Rand tell you what they found out," Eli says as Rand steps into view.

"Hey Jacob."

"Hi Rand."

"We managed to talk with the guards that are in charge of this 'courtesy camp.' They were totally unaware of what was actually happening. Their orders were to maintain the perimeter. No one enters unless accompanied by an Iranian soldier. The guardsmen were told that this was an American facility, for citizens that were in danger. They were brought there under cover of darkness for their protection. Once inside, the soldiers took them to rooms where they could stay until the danger was past, then the soldiers returned them to their homes. They had no idea that these places were used as punishment, nor that family's were split up once they entered and the women and children were separated from their husbands and fathers. They never heard any strange things coming out of the protected area, so they haven't been concerned."

"They never heard anything? How can that be?" Jacob asks in disbelief.

"From what I can gather, from Mike the escapee, everyone is told that to make a noise is to bring punishment down on your family members, wherever they are in the facility. Since no one wanted to hurt their family, not one person ever made a sound of complaint. There was screaming occasionally from little voices, but kids scream for a lot of reasons, so it didn't concern them. There was never any prolonged screaming as is the case with pain or punishment so didn't consider anything was out of the ordinary."

"That's kind of hard to believe, but if that's what they're saying then it must be," Jacob says with a shake of his head.

"They're good guys, Snake. I've no reason to doubt them; they seem on the up and up. We brought some of them back with us, so that they could hear from Mike what's really going on in there. We're going to do this here tonight so that you can witness first hand what's happening to those people," Rand says grimly.

"Before we start with that, did they give you an idea of whose camps these are? Who started them and controls them?"

"Actually the CO has paperwork detailing

exactly what they're required to do and by whose authority. They were signed by none other than the Vice President of the United States, Quinton Uqbahtor."

"Well, the plot thickens. I can't say I'm surprised. I've been hearing some rumblings about him and his position, but we'll get into that later. Right now, let's get this class started. First, how is Mike now? Is he able to speak easier, well rested and on the road to recovery?"

"He's better than he was. At least he looks like he might live another day. He still looks like one of those people in the pictures from the Nazi concentration camps, back in the early 1900's, all skeletal, but still better than he did look. He's got more determination than most, that's for sure. He wants his family back and he wants to be the one to get them out of there. Unfortunately, I can't let him do that. It's way too dangerous," Eli says firmly. "He understands now and has promised not to get in the way of our training."

"Excellent. All right, let's start this."

"Mike, we need to ask you some questions, so if you'll have a seat over there? Jacob, I'm going to move the computer camera out more so that you can see the whole room. Let me know if you can't see."

"That's good Eli. We can see most everyone now," he says as he scans the area, seeing about eight unknowns and a few known's.

"Mike, tell us what you observed during your stay at the courtesy camp," Eli opens the discussion.

"My wife, daughter, son and I were taken to

the camp in March of this year, in the middle of the night after we had refused the chip. We felt it was against our religion, you know. We had been warned about this in the bible and didn't want to accept something that could potentially stop us from seeing our lord. They told us it was a really nice place, and we'd be there for about six weeks. At the end of that time, we'd go home. It was to stop us from talking to anyone else about not receiving the chip. I guess that at the time, we thought it was so no one would know that we said no. That way they could convince everyone to receive the chip. If those that refused were allowed to remain at home, then no one would accept the chip. It made sense to us at the time, but looking back, I can see all the stupid things that they told me and I believed. I take the blame for this and for anything bad that happened to my family because of my stupid decisions," Mike says, a tear drop rolling down his face and trembling on his chin.

"Mike, we talked about that remember?" Eli reminds him gently.

"Yeah, I know. Sorry," he says, coughs, swallows audibly then sits up straighter and begins to talk again. "Anyway, once we got there, we passed through outside guards, and were warned before we arrived to not speak or look at anyone. It was for our own safety, they said, and for the safety of all those already inside. So of course we did as we were told. None of us were expecting anything other than what we were told. We had no reason to doubt."

"What happened after you went into the building?" Eli prods gently.

"Once we were there, they told my wife that she and the kids were being taken to a pent house type suite and that I would meet them there after they introduced me to some of the other people that were staying there. They said they knew that she and the kids were tired and could use some sleep. They were right and who were we to argue. It was kind of exciting, since we're poor people and could never afford a pent house hotel suite. I guess, thinking back on it, we were pretty gullible, or ignorant, and now because of my ignorance I don't know what happened to my family. If they're even still alive," he says emotionally as Jacob notices a stir in the room, the guards standing straighter, more at an alert stance.

"What happened next, Mike," Jacob asks, pulling his attention back before he collapses inside from the guilt.

"Right," Mike says as he refocuses. "The next thing that happened that night was I was escorted to a room, given some clothes to put on, dark gray, plain clothes. They told me to change so that they could launder the stuff I had on for the next day since we weren't given time to pack much. So I went into the room, the door locked behind me and there was no knob but there was another door, so I figured that would be the one to exit from. After changing I went out the other door and a new soldier was waiting for me there. This one acted a little strange but I followed him anyway, since there was no other choice. He took me to another room, opened the door and I walked in before looking too closely. Inside were hundreds of men all dressed just like me, but really skinny and the room smelled like an outhouse. It didn't even look like a cheap hotel room, not a bed in sight. A lot of skinny smelly blankets on the floor and along the far wall lots of buckets. It was nothing more than a giant outhouse, hence the smell. I glanced around quickly, saw a few men staring at me with sadness and knew something bad had just happened. I could feel it in my bones. I spun around, looking to see if the door was still open and the guard still there, but it was closed tight and no knob again. No way to exit the room unless by a guard. I opened my mouth to yell and one of the other men shushed me, and quickly came closer to tell me why I couldn't yell. He told me in a low voice no one else in the room could hear, that if I yelled, something bad would happen to my wife or kids. Or one of their wives' or kids. You see, the only way to control everyone is if the threats are against everyone. Some people love weakly, therefore their family members would suffer, however, if what you did affected anyone of the men's family in the room, they knew that we would control ourselves. That not one man in that room would risk someone else's family, especially when that man could easily kill you if he even THOUGHT that you caused something terrible to happen to his family just because you couldn't keep your mouth shut. They knew exactly how to handle prisoners," he finishes sadly.

"Yes, I'll bet that did work well," Jacob says compassionately and thoughtfully. "You said you've been there since March? That's quite awhile ago. Have you seen or heard from your family since you've been there?"

"No and none of the other men have either."

"What can you tell . . .," Jacob starts to say before he's interrupted.

"Sir, I'd like to say a couple of things before we continue," a tall, dark haired, military strong man in his late twenties interrupts before anything else could be said.

"Your name Staff Sergeant?" Jacob asks.

"Chris, Sir, Christopher Mallone, National Guard Unit 1268 out of Toledo, Ohio.

"Thank you Staff Sgt. Mallone. Now, what is it you'd like to say?"

"This is about the guard duty that we've been doing. We were told, Sir, that the people going into the facility were not being punished, but protected. We deemed it our responsibility to follow orders to protect the citizens of the United States in any way that we could. Since this was a direct order from our leader and it was for a good cause, we fulfilled our duty. Now, after listening to this, we see that all is not as it's portrayed. Sir, I can with all honesty say, there's not one of us that would have allowed anything negative to happen to these people that we were charged with protecting. If we would have known what was going on, you can be sure that we would have stopped it. And what about the soldiers that are on the inside Sir. Why are they not protecting these people?"

"A very good question Sgt. You can be sure that I'll be finding out that answer as soon as possible. I also know that none of you would have allowed anything to happen to those that you swore to protect, therefore you are not being held responsible for things that you had no idea was happening behind closed doors. Now let's let Mike finish telling us what else he noticed happening so that we can make an informed decision. After all the facts are in, then we can decide how best to rectify these problems."

"Yes Sir, thank you Sir."

"Go ahead, Mike. If you're up to it, tell us what else you know."

"None of the men were able to find out about their wives or children, after they were separated upon arriving at the facility. The guards are there to make sure that none of us leave our room. They do come into the room many times a day, but I think it's just for their fun. They called us names; hit us with fists, sticks, anything that's close by, just because they could. If any of us asked about our family's we were told that they were doing great. That they especially like the young ones, and that they never scream long (a gasp and a sob from Mike) when they're being played with because we let them know that if they scream, we 're going to keep doing it until they stop" Mike stops talking, unable to continue because of the sobs shaking his body like a strong wind storm.

"I'm sorry Mike. We had to know, and I'm so sorry. We'll fix this, I promise you. Look around you, you're among friends now, friends that will stop this abuse and bring your family home to you," Jacob says, anger in his words, his face drained of all color.

"Eli, you'll have to handle this. I'm too far away from this to be able to take control. I have complete faith in your abilities, so will hand this off to you. I do want to be kept in the loop, though. I want to know what you else you find out and I want to know who's ultimately responsible for these terrible injustices. I'll be doing some digging at this end and see what I can find out."

"You bet Jacob. We'll talk every night at the same time and keep each other informed, if that works for you."

"It does, and thanks Eli, we're out."

"Oh my God," Kat says from the corner of the room. "What are they doing, Snake. What are they doing" she asks, tears leaving streaks down her white powdered face. "Those are just babies, just babies. They're supposed to be playing ball, playing with dolls, not being raped over and over again," she says as she rushes him, grabs him in a choke hold and hangs on for dear life.

"Shh, I know kitten. I know," he groans in anger and despair, teeth grinding as he relives the last few minutes of the interview. "Eli will handle things out there. I can't be everywhere and do everything. We have to get this country back under control and get rid of those bastards she brought in. It's our only hope. We have jobs to do that are working with the same goal in mind. You just can't see it immediately. Trust me Kitten, our work here is just as if not more important than what Eli is dealing with. He'll take care of it. Did you see the look on the faces of the guardsman? They're appalled. No way is anyone getting away with what's going on out there. There will be hell to pay and the guardsmen, they're going to collect. Now let's start taking care of problems at this end. Are you ready to head out of here and see how our disguises hold up? You probably should fix the white face thing, you have streaks now and that won't do," he says as he turns her gently towards the mirror, hoping the distraction and the orders work to take her mind off what she just heard.

"Oh, I can fix that," she says as she hurries over to the vanity, having noticed how messed up her makeup is. "Maybe you should check your shirt. It looks like most of my powder is somewhere it doesn't belong," she admits with a small grin and a roll of her eyes. "By the way, thanks Snake. I know exactly what you were trying to do, and yes it helped, so thanks. It doesn't change what I heard or envisioned, but it helps to change direction and to distract me."

"Whatever works," he answers with a shrug of his wide shoulders, made wider looking with the clothes he chose for his disguise. *One look at him and all you see is sex, plain and simple. That should take everyone's mind off of recognition. No way is anyone going to look at his face long enough to figure out they know him*, she decides with an inward smirk, her own body responding to what he's advertising. *Not that the bleach blonde white hair and bright green eyes are recognizable. He sure can disguise himself*, she realizes while wondering if he's done that to her before and gotten away with it. *Note to self: ask him about that later, much later,* she decides dreamily. "Just one quick question, where in the world are you going to hide a weapon in those clothes? It doesn't look like there's anywhere loose enough for a gun."

"Thanks for noticing," he smiles arrogantly and with a knowing flash from those sexy eyes of his. "I don't need an extra gun, I have this," he says and magically a small gun appears in his hand.

"What, where," she says in disbelief. "I was watching you and I didn't see anything. Where'd you learn magic, Snake? How'd you do that," she asks in wonder as she walks slowly forward to see how the heck he did that.

"I can't tell you that, I'd have to kill you," he says jokingly, slowly moving out of reach.

"Awww, come on. Just show me," she whines.

"Later Kitten, right now, we need to hit the road. Scope out the area and look for anyone we may know that can help us out."

"You're right, but I won't forget, you'll have to show me how you did that."

Chapter Sixteen

"What? There's one in every state? That's not possible. I know we would have heard of these places if in fact there were one in every state."

"I'm sorry, but like I said, we questioned one of the guards and he finally admitted to there being one in every state. From what he says, usually it's located as this one is, out and away from any large concentrations of people. But he was pretty insistent that there is one in every state. We can question a few more, but I doubt that he was lying. Why would he lie about that? It wouldn't benefit him at all," Jerry (a seasoned national guardsman) insists.

"Yes, I do want you to question a few more. I want the truth, not a fabrication. Now, if you don't mind, I'd like those answers by early evening. We have a daily video conference set up with Jacob in D.C. and I'd like to be able to hand this information off to him tonight. We're now in a crush for time. With the Summit tomorrow, Jane's already in Iran with her parents and preparing to gain the trust of the countries that have been hanging back from the chips. If she manages to convince those countries, she's then positioned herself to actually fit in to the dictator of the world position. That's not something we want to happen."

"I'll head back out with my troops. If we rush, we should be able to be back in time for the conference."

"Thanks, Jerry. I apologize for the abruptness, but things are starting to come to a head and we don't have time now for long 'walks on the beach,'" Eli adds with a grin.

"Right," Jerry laughs as he leaves the room.

***

We should be there in no more than a half hour Mom. I know Uncle is as excited to see you as you are to see him. It has been a very long time since you were together last," Jane says to her mom in Air Force One.

"I am nervous," Jessica says. "I'm unsure of what to expect," she adds, twisting her fingers together, her once black hair sprinkled heavily with grey, her bright sherry colored eyes dulled with age.

"He too has aged," Jane says reassuringly with a small shake of her head. "We have all aged. Especially in the past year," she murmurs looking closely at her mother and father and really seeing what the past year has done to them. New lines carved into her father's face, heavy gray in his curly black hair, his once strong body thinner than ever, his proud stance drooping with fatigue. "I'm sorry for what was done to you this past year and I promise that those whom are responsible will pay," she vows matter-of-factly.

"Jane please, it's not good to harbor anger and bitterness towards others. You must forgive them, my darling Jane. Please, let it go. It will do no good to seek revenge."

"Of course Mother, it will be as you say," Jane promises, reaching out to squeeze her mom's hand and realizing that the undercover life they've led for the past thirty plus years changed them, made them Christians. *They will pay*, she thinks, realizing for the first time to what extent her parents paid for her, to bring her into this world, and to help her reach her destiny.

"What was that," Jessica gasps as the plane shutters.

"Just a little turbulence, that's all," she reassures them as she reaches for the phone to talk with the captain.

"Jane, it was just a little air turbulence. Is everyone all right?" he asks quickly.

"Yes, we're fine, just a little nervous, that's all."

"We shall be landing within the next ten minutes or so. I've been informed that the Shah's car is waiting for you and your parents for your trip to the palace."

"Thank you Captain, I appreciate the information."

"Chico. We'll be landing in ten minutes or so. You are to stay with my parents once we leave this plane. I don't want them left unattended at all. And please stay on high alert. I will not take any chances with them ever again," she warns as the buckle sign lights up, before turning back to her mother. "Prepare for landing Mom, Dad. We'll be there very soon now," she says, the excitement in her voice making her eyes sparkle.

"That's it," Jane says as she starts unbuckling, preparing to leave the plane for the waiting limo. "Shall we," she asks her parents as they stand in preparation.

"All set," her father says quietly.

"We're just going to get in the car and begin the journey to the palace. I doubt very much if Uncle is with the car. The last time I was here, he met me at the doors to the palace."

"That's good, Jane," her mother says in trepidation, nerves showing clearly on her face.

"President Martin," the limo driver says with honor, "please, if you'll just sit here and your parents also, we will leave. We don't have a long trip the palace is only about twenty minutes from here."

"Thank you," Jane says after she ushers her parents into the car. "This is our bodyguard, Chico. He'll be riding with us."

"As you wish," the limo driver says.

"Jane, everything looks so different," Jessica murmurs to Jane, surprise evident in the wide eyed look and the awe in her voice.

"Of course it is Mother. You have been gone for well over thirty years. There must be change. It would be very unusual for it to have remained the same."

"That's true; I guess I wasn't thinking about what it would be like. I was just excited to be back again."

"The palace is just a few minutes away," Jane says as she turns to Chico. "I want you to stay in the background at the Shah's but to be present at all times with my parents. The last time I sent people here, there was a bit of confusion and one of them died. Stupid man, he thought he could cause trouble for me with Iran, but that will never happen," Jane says in warning. "There it is Mom, Dad, and there's Uncle standing on the steps outside, do you see him standing with some of his personal guards?"

"Yes," Jessica gasps in excitement and squeezes Fredericks hand with hers.

"I know darling," Frederick says to the unvoiced excitement shining out of his wife's eyes, and the tight hold she has on his hands. As they're looking at the palace looming larger the closer they get they see a small puff of dust appear on one of the body guards waiting with the Shah and then he falls to the ground.

Chico yells at the driver to "keep moving, we're under attack," causing Jessica to scream and Frederick to gasp.

"What the hell," Jane screams as they speed past the palace.

"A sniper," Chico yells back as he checks his weapon, eye's searching desperately for any movement outside of the vehicle.

"Why would they kill a body guard," Jessica asks confused.

"I'm sure it was an accident, it was this car and its occupants that they were after. Not the Shah or his body guards."

"Why didn't they wait until we exited the car? Why shoot when we could see and get away?" Jane asks in confusion.

"My guess is they were aiming for the car and misjudged, lucky for us," he answers quietly.

"Lucky for us," Jane murmurs thoughtfully. "Now what, Chico, what are your plans now" she asks.

"I think you should call the Shah and find out if they've been able to get things under control. He'll be able to tell you when it's safe to go back there. Or he may want you to go to a different entrance, one less in the public eye."

"I'll call him right away," Jane says "but why would anyone want to hurt me or my parents? I don't think it was us they were after," she adds in denial.

"President Martin, you're a target. Look at the country. You have enemies. What do enemies do, they attack. They look for a weakness. You haven't demonstrated a weakness yet, except when you first gained office. Now that you have your parents back, you have a weakness. Them."

"True, true, I guess I hadn't thought about it. It's been pretty quiet for the past couple of months. And yes, they do make me weak, but I wouldn't change that for the world. So we step up security, that's all. I'll ask Uncle and he'll provide more security for us while we're here. You can't be on duty twenty four hours a day."

"I could, but it would be pretty exhausting and I wouldn't be at my peak, so thanks for that. As it is, it will be a few days until I feel comfortable enough to leave them when they're not in their rooms, locked and secure, but we'll figure something out. Now, if you'd call please, we can't drive around forever, there's not enough gas in the limo for that."

After a few minutes of silence, Jane in control

again, dials the Shah. "Uncle, its Jane. We're fine, but one of your guards was shot, how is he? I'm so sorry Uncle. I'm sorry that my visit here has caused such a commotion and killed one of your finest body guards. I do apologize," she says formally.

"If you think so Uncle, yes, my parents are fine, unharmed thanks to the quick thinking of our own personal body guard. Thank you Uncle, we shall arrive soon, I'll let you go so that you can call your driver."

"He's calling the driver as we speak to inform him of where to drop us. I'm sure Uncle will handle everything thoroughly, he is after all, used to assassination attempts."

"Good, then we should arrive soon," Chico adds after Jane finishes talking. "No one leaves this vehicle before I do. I want to become the shield that will be needed to get you into the palace. Once inside and under the protection of the Shah, you can do as you please, but until then, we must take every precaution. I don't know who, what or where this attempt was done by but I do promise that we will find the parties involved. It looks like we're pulling up now, so please be patient. I'll get out and help each one of you into the building."

"Thank you Chico. I appreciate your diligence," Jane says thoughtfully.

The tone is quiet as Jessica, Frederick and then Jane is helped out of the vehicle and into the palace, no one comfortable with the short time exposed to a shooter.

"Uncle," Jane says happily as she sees him for the first time in months "how are you, I've thought of you a lot these past months. You're support has been so important to me, Uncle."

"Jane my dear, welcome," he says kindly with a brief pat on her shoulder, never one for hugs or touching. "I too am glad that you made this trip. I've wanted to talk with you, my dear, but prefer to talk person to person and not on a phone which can be listened in on by so many others. We have much to discuss, much that has been put to the side but can now be brought forward. I'm afraid you won't get much rest while you're here, we have so many things that need done but first, please come in, come in and I'll send for refreshments."

* * *

"Rand, I want you, Mongoose, Jerry, Lucas and a couple of the other Guardsmen to gear up and head out to the encampment. Question every guard that's on the perimeter but try to do it without letting anyone on the inside know. We need to get the word to them about what's really happening on the inside and schedule a takedown within the next twenty four hours. I'd like this done before Jane get's back into the country. I also want to know who's completely responsible for this and try to figure out a way to contact the other states for a takedown of their encampments. We can't continue to let this happen. Mal's ready with the program and thanks to you has a few scanners ready for those with the chips. We're going to cause a little chaos when she tries to use the chips for murder and mayhem" Eli says as he grins and rubs his hands together. "We're going to get our people out of that place as soon as possible and let them go home. There're enough of them that I think they'd be safest at home, surrounded by family and friends."

"I think you're right," Rand adds in agreement. "There's no way we can take on the job of keeping them here and safe. We may need to move really fast and we have more than enough people that will make fast difficult. We can't afford to take on anyone else. Besides, I'm sure they're all anxious to get home."

"No doubt, I'd be anxious too. I'd probably go somewhere far, far away and hide out until all the craziness subsides. But you're right they'll want to go home to familiar surroundings. There's comfort in familiarity. Unfortunately, if they're all in the same shape as Mike, then there's no one that will be able to leave. We're going to need some medical attention once we gain access to the camp, and all of those poor people are going to need a lot of help, including fresh water, foods and medicines. I'll make a couple of calls. I know some people with the capability of helping in that situation."

"We'll head out now and get in touch with you when things start changing," Rand yells while grabbing Mongoose by the arm, and leaving Eli to answer the now ringing phone.

"Callander," Eli says brusquely into the phone, just to stop the racket while massaging his forehead with two fingers, trying to refocus.

"Eli, everything okay?" Jacob asks when he hears the suddenness of the answer.

"What, oh, sorry Jacob, my mind was elsewhere when I answered. Rand just left to gather some of the troops and head out to

Courtesy Camp. They're going to start the questioning of the perimeter guards and decide on the best course of action to use to take out the Iranian guards on the inside."

"About that, I've been thinking. Isn't Mal capable of tweaking the chips? I think you should use those somehow to infiltrate the Iranian's that are guarding the citizens. Not to kill them or anything, but maybe wreak a little chaos inside. Knock them out or something, just a thought."

"Yeah, I've been thinking about that also. Mallory did mention that she could change the chips. We just have to be able to scan them with the scanners that Rand's taking with them, so that she can get those specific ones into the system. Somehow though, we need to gain access to them in order to scan them. I'd prefer to do it through surprise and not attack. It would save us from anyone else hearing about this before we're ready for that can of worms to be opened."

"What about some kind of drug, maybe in the food that only the guards eat?"

"Yeah, I'll contact Rand and he can find out from our guards, what the inside guards have as a specialty item. Then we can figure what kind of drug and how to employ it."

"Excellent. I'll take off now. I wanted to suggest this before they left, but looks like I missed it by minutes, so I trust you to take care of it."

"Yeah, thanks Jacob. I'll talk to you at our predetermined time tonight," Eli says while looking around at the dusty dark room he chose to use as an office. *It's no wonder I feel like a need for a shower constantly, since I probably do* he thinks watching the dust fly, in what little natural light there is. After he dials Mal on his cell, he settles in for a short talk.

"Hey Eli," Mal says when she glances at the number calling in before answering it.

"Hi, got a minute Mal?"

"Sure, what's up," she asks turning the screen off on her computer so that she can concentrate on her brother.

"I just talked with Jacob. He made a couple of suggestions regarding the Iranian soldiers and how to handle them. He also mentioned that your capabilities with the chip could really benefit us. He's not recommending that we kill them or anything, but that maybe we could knock them out for a while. I told him you probably could but that I'd talk to you first and let him know tonight when we call in. Can you knock them out?"

"Yeah, I can, but only if I have their information. That has to be done with the scanner directly with the chip, so you do have to get pretty close" she says, running her hand over her long dark hair, usually worn up, which it started out as today but that was almost a whole day ago and the rubber band was giving her a headache, so now it's down, totally uncontrollable and making her nuts.

"So if I'm hearing you right, then the chip needs to be scanned with the scanner at the site it's placed?"

"Yep, that's right. You have to get up close and personal."

"Right. Then we'll have to have Rand and Mongoose and the rest do the retrieving. It's not going to be very easy since we want to knock them out or something, certainly not kill them yet, not that they don't deserve it for the way they've been treating the people in there. I just don't want to start something that could get out to the other troops in the other states. I'd rather keep this kinda quiet until we can't keep it down anymore."

"What about feeding them something? I'm sure they don't eat the same things that the prisoners are eating. There's no way they could, they'd all go AWOL. You could always find some kind of a drug that would knock them out for long enough to scan their chips, right? You could put it in whatever it is that they don't give the prisoners. It could be juice or coffee, tea or even pop. I'm sure there's something that they all drink that's kept from the rest. Better yet, why not target the boss, the Guard that's in charge of the inside? You know there has to be one. We could make him real sick, sick enough he needs to go to a hospital and en-route, have one of our perimeter guards act as a medic in the ambulance. He could scan the guards chip, since I really only need one of the Iranian chips for processing. They're probably all programmed the same. I can do some major damage to anyone with that specific chip."

"That makes things a lot easier, yet harder. So what you're saying is with just the one chip you can control anyone that has the same programmed chip implanted? That turns this into a nationwide operation, not just the small one here in Texas. We definitely need to talk to everyone about this first, including Jacob, so let's plan on the conference tonight. I'll contact Rand in a little bit and throw him the job of finding out who's responsible for getting food supplies into the compound. There has to be a perimeter guard that's doing that, otherwise they'd never get anything since none of them leave the facility."

"That would work. Rand's going to be at the perfect place to find that out and we can get this thing on the move. In the next couple of days, we'll finally have been able to free those poor people. Like Jacob said though, they won't be in any kind of shape to even go home, judging from what Mike looked like. We'll need medics brought in and proper food and medications to help those people begin to heal. It'll take weeks before any of them will be able to go home. But at least they'll be able to go home someday."

"Yes, they'll go home, unlike the others whose luck died along with them."

"I know Mal, I know. Since this is going to be a big operation, we're going to need to give it a name to go by so that anyone working with us will know what we're talking about, but only those that know in advance. It'll make it code. You have any suggestions?"

"How about Operation Resurrection, a double edged word?"

"Double edged, how so?"

"Well, we're going to be bringing this country back from the direction that Jane's had it going."

"All right, that's one, and the other?"

"Devon, Eli. Remember our brother Devon?"

"Of course I remember Mal, how could I not," Eli asks in anger.

"Well, it just seems that everyone else has moved on and I can't seem to stop thinking about him. I miss him, Eli, I really miss him," she says sniffling, tears rolling silently down her cheeks, grateful that she's not video conferencing and the tears go unseen by others.

"Awww Mal, I know. Don't cry, please don't cry," he begs softly. "You want me to come over there?"

"No, I'm okay," she says quietly. "Anyway, Operation Resurrection, the other edge is our way of honoring Devon. He's not here anymore but he is here in our hearts. It'll just be like a pact between the three of us about never forgetting our quad."

"That's an excellent idea, Mal, excellent. I like it, and have no doubt that Jacob will feel good about the name also. You can tell him tonight when we meet up at the video conference at nine. Don't forget to be here for it. I have so much to do now that I doubt I'll see you until then. Besides, you sis, are going to need to pack up what you're using and anything you want to take with you, you're headed for D.C."

"What, wait! What are you talking about Eli? I'm headed for D.C.? When, now?" she quickly asks, confused.

"Yeah, I forgot to tell you. Jacob wants you and your computer programs in D.C. as soon as possible. I told him I'd let you know and you'd probably be leaving sometime tomorrow. Oops, sorry, I had so much going on earlier that I forgot to mention it to you. I really am sorry Mal. Don't worry though; Rand's due back later today before the video conference."

"Gee thanks Eli. How come I never seem to get

a voice in these decisions? You just arbitrarily decide who's doing what and expect everyone to fall in line at your decisions" she snaps.

"I said I'm sorry Mal" Eli growls.

"I'm sorry just doesn't cut it Eli. I'm really sick of you not even talking to me about things that affect me. You've done this before. Look, I know that things are a little difficult right now, but honestly, can't you stop and think before you make decisions regarding me? I'm not your child to be sending here and sending there. I'm also an FBI Agent, a freakin adult, have been for a long time. Just because you make these decisions doesn't mean that I'm going to do what you want. I'll think about this and get back to you" Mal says with finality, snaps the phone shut, throws it across the room and grabs her hair before screaming out loud in a fit of rage.

Chapter Seventeen

"I've talked to almost everyone on perimeter guard duty. Not one person knows anything that's going on in that building. Did you find out who's responsible for the food and the dispensing of the water?" Rand asks Mongoose and Luke when they gather at their pre-determined place and time.

"Yeah, it's Corporeal Davis. He schedules delivery time for all the food that goes through the doors. He also said that the guards have special beverages that the prisoners do not get. Hell, the prisoners barely get anything. There's some gruel that's like water, water, which is dispensed per body weight (they don't want to have waste) and that's pretty much it. The guards get full course meals of course," Luke adds in disgust. "From everything I learned today, it's like the old concentration camps the Nazi's used back during World War II. This county has really turned black on the inside. We need to stop her before she can do any further damage," he finishes.

"Good, good," Rand murmurs. "So, since the guards drink and eat separate foods, let's see if we can get some information on the guard that's in charge of the inside. Hopefully he consumes something that no one else does. That way, we can add something to his beverage that'll take him out, enough that'll make him so ill he'll need transport to a hospital. Once we separate him from the building, we can infiltrate the ambulance with our own and get a good scan of his chip. That's all Mal said she needs is one chip scanned, since they're all programmed the same."

"If we can control the guards without anyone finding out and get help for those poor people that were put in that place, all without causing a stir among the other camps, then we can move forward to the next camp. After a couple of these places, Jane's strength will diminish slightly. The awesome thing is, she won't even know. I love it!" Mongoose says quietly but determinedly. "The less power she has, the happier this whole country will be."

"What was the reaction from the perimeter guards you talked to today?" Rand asks.

"Most of the ones I talked to today didn't seem overly surprised. They, in general, admitted that they weren't comfortable with their jobs. They were suspicious about the goings on inside. They did say that they never heard any commotion coming from the inside, but did get a faint scent of something and it wasn't a pleasant one."

"Do you think they're willing to listen to us? That would mean a change of command, which could be construed as a treasonous act. They'd be going away from the order of the General of the Armies, since the country is still under Martial Law," Rand reminds them.

"Yeah, they said they were willing to leave.

None of them are very happy with the direction the country's headed in. A few of them mentioned that they didn't think this had anything to do with the President. It's only the Vice President that's ever been mentioned."

"That's interesting," Rand says thoughtfully. "Remind me to bring that up when we get back to base camp. Eli needs to hear that, and so does Jacob. Now, I need to talk to the Corporeal that's in charge of food and beverage dispensing. I'm sure we can come up with something that will knock that guard on his ass. This is going to be the most fun I've had in months," he declares, a grin on his handsome face, brown hair a little longer than customary for the military, skin darkly tanned from so much time in the unbearably hot state of Texas, uniform sweat stained, worn, and brown with dust. "Let's meet back here in an hour, so we can head out and make it back to base before the video conference tonight."

* * *

"How'd it go Snake?" Kat asks after meeting back at the restaurant that they split at.

"Good, good" he says absent mindedly.

"Snake, are you in there?" Kat asks again curiously. He's usually so alert that nothing gets by him, but at the moment, he's just standing there, staring blindly at the street. "Snake, come on Snake, you're freakin me out" she says, suddenly breathless in fear, he's acting so out of character.

"What? Oh, sorry Kat. My mind was elsewhere."

"Yeah, I know. I've been trying to get your

attention for a few minutes now. You were starting to really scare me," she admits, confused. "What were you thinking about?"

"Devon," he admits quietly.

"Oh."

"We'll talk about it later, after we get back to base," he offers. "How did it go for you today" he asks when she just stands there, perplexed.

"Good. I made a couple of contacts with my old group, the one I worked with undercover with the Homeland Security Director. I wasn't able to find Des, though. I had hoped that she was still at police headquarters but there's no sign of her. There was no mention of her name either, so she must have left shortly after we did last winter. I just hope nothing happened to her. She was too trusting, kind of naive actually, for someone in her position, and at her age."

"I'm sure she's fine. We'll probably see her while we're in town. If not, you can stop off at her apartment and see if there's any information on what happened to her or where she went."

"That's a good plan, thanks for your understanding."

"So what did you use as an excuse at police headquarters? Did you just waltz in and look around? Surely someone noticed you?"

"Oh, I went in looking for my sister. I told them she was part of the clerks, but couldn't find her, so I assumed she was in a different police department."

"They believed that?"

"Sure, why wouldn't they. I can be pretty convincing when I want to. Besides, the few that I worked directly with didn't recognize me. Not looking the way I do now," she adds with a laugh.

"I'd recognize you anywhere, Kat. If I would, then there are others that would also. You're taking too many chances. It's way too important for us to get through this part of the operations without getting caught. We have freedom of movement right now, but if we have to start hiding again, forget it. The extra time we made with the appearance change will be stripped away and we'll be moving from place to place to stay under the wire. Don't take those kinds of chances again, you hear me?" Snake demands angrily.

'I hear you Snake," she adds before angrily leaving his side.

"Kat, stop," he growls loud enough for her to hear, making her stop and slowly turn around, stubbornly refusing to move closer.

"Look, I'm sorry. It's just that there's so much at stake right now that anything happening could throw us back days, maybe even weeks. We just can't afford for that to happen."

"I know, and I'm sorry Snake. I promise that I'm not taking unreasonable chances. I would never put this whole operation in jeopardy," she says quietly.

"I know you wouldn't. The pressure's starting to take its toll, that's all. Just ignore what I said, please? We've other more important things to accomplish today. I want to get a message to Charles Rosenthal about the meteor shower that could be here at anytime. After all, my bike can attest to that, since a small one was probably what took out the driver's side mirror the other day on our way into town."

"True, I'm sure that's what it was, since we didn't see anything else around at the time. We just can't prove it, that's all," she adds agreeably, willing to move on to new areas in the discussion.

"Plus Jon Smith did say that it's probable that there are meteorites from that super nova that exploded millions of years ago that could be showing up in our atmosphere soon, possibly causing a cataclysmic affect on the world. We need to let Rosenthal know, since he's already suspicious of this anyway. It'll just confirm his discovery."

"So how are you going to contact them? I thought you had to be careful who you talked to."

"I do. I'm going to call a friend who has friends at the Smithsonian. That's where Rosenthal bases himself. Once he gets the information, I'm sure he'll contact Jane and then the media. He seemed to be the type to meet with the media frequently. Probably his line of work has thrown him into their lights many times," Snake adds with a grin. "Better him than us!"

"You can say that again," she adds laughing. "I don't do the media. Not since Sydney . . . sorry," she says wiping at the sudden tears.

"I know. She may have been media, but she'd become a friend too," Snake says gruffly. "Damn it, we've lost so many now" he adds angrily, just thinking of the many that died for a cause they didn't even know they were part of.

* * *

"I think we have the perfect thing to catch a

guard," Mongoose informs Rand when they meet-up before leaving for the base. "Corporeal Davis admitted that there is something that the guards order every week that no-one else has access to. They like something called Tiny Tubs. They're one serving size drinks that come in assorted flavors. Little plastic bottles with aluminum foil lids. He said he orders them by the pallet, usually mixed flavors. There is one flavor though that's a special request, Pina~ Colada. He did say he tried it and it wasn't too bad, but not a favorite. However, one of the guards only drinks the Pina~ Colada flavor. Anyway, he said that if we took the Pina~ Colada ones and laced them with something to make that guard sick, he knows it will work. He's did say he wasn't sure which guard drinks only that flavor, but he figured it was the boss. They're usually the only ones that get special treatment. Then he mentioned something about Visine, and how, if ingested, it makes you ill to the point of hospitalization, possibly even death. The kids smart, I'll give him that. That sounded like a winner to me, at lease, it's easy to obtain and if, like he says, the drinks have aluminum foil lids, we could inject them with the Visine. The flavor of the drink should hide any sign of the Visine. I'm not sure how long it takes to get sick from it, but waiting's not a problem."

"That does sound like a good plan, but let's take it to Eli first before we make any decisions. Maybe we can have Mal look up the severity of the poisoning from Visine and how long before the first symptoms start," Rand says, amazed at the trivial knowledge some people have.

"Awesome," Mongoose says with a grin and a small salute before leaving to find his guys and get ready to leave for base.

***

"It's time," Snake says as Kat get's ready for the nine p. m. video conference.

"They should be coming on any second," she promises after pulling up the conference address and clicking on it.

"Hi Eli, we're good here," Kat says once Eli's face comes into clear view.

"Perfect," he says at almost the same moment.

"Jacob, we have quite a bit to cover on this end tonight. So if it's all right with you, I'm going to go ahead and get started."

"Shoot," he says, quietly waiting to hear what's been going on today.

"Rand and Mongoose and the guys are back from the Courtesy camp. I'd have to say that they did real good today, but I'll let Rand tell you how that went."

"Lieutenant we have some information that I think you'll like. We managed to talk with the rest of the perimeter guards today, and we found out who's responsible for supplies being ordered and delivered to the camp. We also discovered that the perimeter guards had absolutely no idea what was actually going on in the camp. Needless to say, they all want to be a part of what our plans are. They feel pretty bad that these things have been going on right in front of their faces. Everyone of them swore to make right the wrongs that have been done to the American's inside the camp. It wasn't easy keeping them from charging right in and fixing things, but once they all understood the big plan, they backed off a little. They're good guys, Lieutenant, we're lucky to have them on our side."

"Excellent Rand, I never doubted the integrity of the guardsmen, they're soldiers and as soldiers they took an oath to serve and protect, just like the rest of us did. They can do nothing but join our group and right the wrongs. Anyway, what did you discover about the Iranian guards and how can we infiltrate them without raising an alarm?"

"We talked with the guardsmen responsible for ordering the food for the people in the camp. He's assured us that the guards do eat differently than the detainees. He orders things called Tiny Tubs, which are beverages that come in small plastic containers with sealed foil lids. He's actually the one that had the idea of poisoning them through these drinks. When asked how, he said that he'd heard either on the TV or on the internet, he wasn't sure which one, but had seen somewhere that Visine is toxic if consumed through the stomach. It has a poisoning affect but he wasn't sure if it was immediate or took more like days to accomplish, however he did hear that it can be deadly. Since Vision is an over the counter product and not something that's easily tracked, that it would be a good way to take them down."

"Hmmm," Snake says then whistles, eyes starting to sparkle. "Rand, that's great information. Good job getting these guys to open up."

"Thanks, but that's not all," Rand says, waiting for the excitement in the room to quiet down a little. "I talked with the guardsmen responsible for ordering, in detail, about what they received and his thoughts on the whole matter and he almost guaranteed that the Iranian in charge has a special order for the Tiny Tubs, since an order for a specific flavor is routine, two cases of a pina colada flavor that he says isn't very good at all. Yeah, he tried it out of curiosity. He figured that only the top dog would rate for a special order and since it's for two cases a week, he's probably the only one drinking it. So it should be easy to tamper with just those, pegging that one specific guard."

"That's good news and a pretty good idea. I'd like to meet this soldier when we have the opportunity. How soon can we put this into action?"

"I'm thinking his next orders due in two days. We should be able to obtain everything we need for this op. The Visine is found pretty much anywhere there's a pharmacy type area, and if we purchase say three or four bottles from multiple locations, that shouldn't cause any kind of suspicion for us. After all, it's hot and dry out there, so as guardsmen, we'd need something to refresh our eyes. The syringes we need are over the counter also, simple diabetic syringes, since making the smallest hole possible is the objective. That way we won't cause any obvious leaking to occur and won't draw suspicion back on us. It's a pretty simple plan, but it should work like a charm. Then once the Iranian guard falls ill, we'll be standing by ready with a rescue unit. I figure there's probably a small town nearby that's all volunteer, and they won't miss the squad unless they have a call, and then it'll be too late. We'll respond to their 911 call with a squad and a paramedic, dressed in the local uniforms. Once we get our hands on the guard we can scan his chip in the squad, what happens to him after that is up to you. Let him die or fix him, hold him hostage, whatever."

"There's no guarantee that the guard that falls ill is the leader, but it's still a good plan. I guess it doesn't matter if the guard's the leader since they all have the same chip. One chip is all it'll take," Jacob says in agreement. "Is Mal there? We can ask her right now if just one chip will do."

"Umm, about Mal," Eli says. "She left today for D.C. She should be in your neighborhood, oh, probably sometime in the middle of the night, knowing Mal. She won't stop till she gets there. Besides, she was a little irritated with me over this trip."

"Irritated? She didn't want to come here?" Jacob asks.

"She did, but not until she had a chance to see Rand. Unfortunately he just got back here not even an hour ago. She left here around 1300 hours, so was probably in Illinois, maybe, by the time Rand got back."

"You should have let her stay until tomorrow. It wouldn't have been a problem with us, one day won't make or break anything."

"I know, and I told her that, but she was so angry with me that she just left. Nothing I could do, Jacob."

"Gotch ya. Sometimes the best defense is ignorance. All right, we'll expect her sometime this morning. So we'll just go on from here, assuming that one chip is all she'll need. What else happened?"

"Not much more on this end. I thought that was quite a bit for a day," Eli says questioningly.

"It was, and thanks Eli. You're group did a great job. Now here, Kat and I have been busy too. I made contacts with quite a few of my co-workers today and set up a pretty large chain of command. I was also able to talk with Chico, who's in Iran as we speak. Jane and her entourage arrived at their destination early, before noon our time today. The only problem that occurred was someone shot at her car as they were close to the driveway of the Shah's palace, which made them speed away from the area until they got an all clear. I'm still looking into who the shooter was. I'll probably have the information before we talk again tomorrow night. In the mean time, Kat wandered into her old precinct today looking for Des, her previous partner at D.C Metro One. She wasn't able to locate her on the job, so she stopped by her house later this afternoon. It doesn't look like anyone's been there in a very long time. With the dust, the unused air, your normal neglect when you're not around, it all pointed to her not having been there for a long time. She also scoped out the precinct while wandering and it looks like they're back to full force. Everything seemed to be running smoothly just slightly quieter than normal is all," Jacob finishes with a nod from Kat.

"Tomorrow we'll gain a little more ground and set into place transportation to the G Force Summit, planned in Belgium at the seat of the European Union at the end of November. That leaves us a few months to pull a lot of things together. Looks like from here on out, we'll be working our asses off trying to get everything done that needs to be done before then. We can't let her complete that Summit. Somehow we will put a stop to this, even if we all have to travel there ourselves."

"Jacob, do you realize how many we'd have to find transportation for? You're talking thousands upon thousands of just the military not to mention all the patriots that would and should be allowed to go. This thing keeps growing by huge leaps and bounds," Eli asks with a look of dismay on his face.

"I know Eli. I just don't have the answer yet on how to fix that problem. That's going to have to wait until we have exact plans. Right now, all we know is when the Summit is and how much time we have to get everything done. It's not a perfect world, and we've been fighting this process for more than a year now with very little reprieve. All I know is we're all working as hard and fast as humanly possible."

"That's true. All right, we'll keeping thinking for resolutions of those issues. But first and foremost, we have to rescue those poor people from the Courtesy Camp, before they start dying off. Starvation's a real threat for those poor people, and the children, I don't even want to think about what they're going through. We can only do so much at once," Eli growls in frustration. "I know we're facing the same problems. There's so much to do and so little time to do it in."

Chapter Eighteen

"Good morning Uncle. Today's the big day. I'm a little nervous and a little excited," Jane says as she walks into the breakfast room, a room the size of a football field with Persian rugs, art work that looks like it's from the Louvre and Crystal Chandeliers. *Just your normal everyday palace*, she thinks with a sigh. Soon this will be mine.

"Jane my dear, today you'll be able to accomplish something that no other leader in the world has been able to do. Bring peace to the Middle East. There's nothing to fear there," he says comfortingly.

"But Uncle, how am I going to accomplish that when the Israelis refuse to participate?"

"Once you've completed the demonstration of the chip at the summit, we can discuss their reception, and if they'll be willing to accept the chips allowing our plan to move forward."

"Do you really believe that it will be that easy?"

"It's already been done Jane. Have you no faith? Have I not always been good and faithful to your goals?"

"Of course Uncle, you have always been there for me, you've always supported my destiny. If it weren't for you, I would not be where I am today."

"I support Allah's plans for you, never my plans, always Allah," he says quietly in reproof.

"Yes, I'm sorry Uncle. My life has been given to me and my destiny planned since before I was born only because of Allah," Jane murmurs, head bowed in respect.

"Never forget Jane, where you come from and what you are responsible for. Now, you have only a few hours before the summit begins so let's find a place to sit so that we can discuss your presentation. We'll start with breakfast, and then we'll talk shop," says the Shah with a smile while escorting her to the table to order breakfast.

"I'm not sure that I can eat, Uncle. I'm pretty nervous."

"Nonsense Jane, you must eat, and so you will. You are the President of the United States. That's no young girl's position. You are mature and determined, so of course you will eat. You will also stand tall and strong in front of the summit this afternoon. You will not show those nerves that you keep mentioning. This is your destiny and you will move forward."

"Thank you Uncle. You're so right. I will stand tall and strong. I am the President of the United States, the first woman to ever hold this office. Those poor people never stood a chance," she admits with a laugh.

"There's the Jane I was hoping would show up this morning. The fighter, the fearless one," he says in approval.

"Yes Uncle, I'm back. I will not let anything get in the way of my destiny. Now, Lets eat, shall we? Mother, Father, come and join us," Jane says when she notices them standing in the doorway, indecision written all over their faces. "We're just getting ready to eat. This will be nice, like a family gathering," she announces as she links her arms through her parents and leads them to the table that the Shah is standing by.

"Sit Da'wah, Tariq, please be comfortable. Were your accommodations adequate?" he asks after Tariq is seated and he has taken his own seat at the head of the table.

"They were way more than adequate Dhul. Surely Allah has blessed you with much," Tariq say quietly and with reverence.

"Ah, but Allah has favored you with more than any of us, as he has entrusted you with Abrar or 'Jane' as the world knows her," he says in kindness and respect. "You two gave up everything important to follow what Allah had planned. You've done well, Da'Wah and Tariq, you've done well. What is mine is yours for surely Allah would want it that way.

"No Dhul, no, that's not so. Allah has gifted us beyond our purpose for allowing us to be a part of this great vision, his divine purpose. Success is near, peace we look forward to," Da'Wah say solemnly.

"Let's et, shall we Mother, Father, Uncle?" Jane says "I have many things that must be done before the summit this afternoon. If we don't eat soon, it will surely be lunch time before I get my nexy chance," she adds with a smile, impatience in the glint of her eyes.

"I'm sorry Jane, let's eat," Jessica says, happy to be sitting with her daughter and beloved friends.

***

"Our guests have started to arrive. There's only one hour left before the presentation. How are you holding up, Jane?"

"I'm fine Uncle. I'm ready to finish this part of the plan so that we can begin on the final leg of our journey. The exciting times are about to begin," she say on a laugh, high on the emotions of the day. "I'm glad that all who were against this have promised to be here today. It will be easy to convince them face to face that what we have here will make them greater leaders of their people. Who wouldn't want to be greater," she demands quickly, "given the opportunity? That's all that I'm offering them, the opportunity to be greater. I don't want to rule for them, at least as far as they know. I'm just helping them as I've helped my country. I have proof that people are willing to be ruled, only in certain ways. My ways are more subtle than theirs, that's' all. I just wish that James Fahr would have been able to help me today, but unfortunately he had a previous engagement. No problem, I'm quite capable of handling this. After all, he may have designed the original chips, but I have changed them so greatly that what was his is no longer. Doubt he would recognize his own chip on a computer screen. It's now all my design."

"You amaze me Jane, with your knowledge of how to do all of those modern things and still maintain your integrity for Allah. You're a gift to all of us, my dear."

"Thank you Uncle," Jane says, surprise on her face at such a compliment. "Do I look the part today Uncle?" I will not shame you or my parent's, will I," she asks, uncertainty looming, it's hard to be pretty when you've got nothing to work with. She is known as plain Jane, after all.

"Jane, you're beautiful. Your face is glowing, your clothing is becoming for one of your position."

"Thank you Uncle," she says cheeks reddened slightly from the compliment. "Have you seen my Mother and Father?"

"Not yet, but I'm sure they'll be down soon. This is a big day for them, too."

"Yes it is. They have worked their whole life for this and it is soon to come to fruition. They must be very excited!"

"As am I," he says quietly, having lived his whole life for what she is about to finish for him. *If only she knew,* he thinks.

***

"This is Gerry Partell of World Vision Now live from Iran with coverage of the President's announcement at the highly anticipated Summit. She will be questioning those countries that to date have refused the offer of the chip. We are at the palace of the Shah, in western Iran. He opened his palace for the President, since she's a close family friend. This place is definitely large enough for this meeting and probably easier to secure. I was told that prior to the President arriving at the palace yesterday, the limo that she was a passenger in was shot at. There were no injuries, thankfully, but since then they have tightened security drastically. I was actually informed when we arrive earlier today that we may not be able to broadcast live. Fortunately for us, the President heard about this and gave us the go ahead, knowing how important it is for our country to be included in everything that she does. She'll be beginning momentarily, so please stay tuned."

"This is it then, Uncle. I'm ready," Jane says after everyone is seated and quiet, waiting for her to move forward and begin.

"Yes Jane, do what they say in the movies, break a leg,"

"Thank you Uncle. I shall hope not to actually 'break a leg," she says dryly as she moves into the spot light of the room, drawing the eyes of more heads of countries than she's ever faced at one time. Seeing so many faces turned in her direction, suits from the western world along with a Galabeya (the flowing robes seen frequently in the Middle East), the crystal chandeliers sparkling like diamonds, the aroma of the finest incense burning in the background creates an almost magical moment. The *stuff of dreams*, she thinks, eyes glistening in excitement.

"I want to thank you all for attending this meeting. The first thing that I want to say is thank you Shah Manzah, for opening your home to us for these very important proceedings. I am indebted to you for your hospitality and kindness.

"I'm honored to be in such great company today. I realize I don't have the experience that you all have but I can assure you that I am not a weak leader. As president of the most technologically advanced country of the world, with one of the largest armies in the world, I want you to know as any resident that's still living in China will tell you, I am not afraid to use the weapons that I have available. That being said, this is a peace conference, and we're here to try to bring peace to the region and the technological advancements that will help your countries to not only become more efficient but will help them to thrive. I'm hoping that each and every one of you is on board with this goal, because it will help to bring the world the peace that was intended by Allah. However, one thing I did learn in the United States as I was growing up was if you're not with me than you're against me. Now, shall we get started with our conference, beginning with our common goals?

What we discuss here is of the utmost importance to our world. I hope to explain everything to you with such satisfaction that you will have no doubts what-so-ever. There seems to be some confusion regarding our chips. I can tell you in all honesty that the chips that have been supplied to not only the United States but to most of the world are working exactly as had been demonstrated and planned. We have experienced no problems and they have been received very well by the general public. I've been notified by many of these people that they love the fact that only true citizens can receive them, and that all of the health information is readily available at any hospital or doctors office that they visit. There have been a few that have gone into much further detail, mostly reiterating the fact that had it not been for the chip, the hospital they were taken to may have accidently harmed them, but didn't because of the information obtained prior to treatment from their chip," Jane says and waits quietly while the applause dwindles.

"The chips are beneficial to any who obtain them. Our chips have special programming, not only helping with the health care controversy but they also help when you're trying to get home after a long day at work but need to stop off at a grocer's for some urgent things like milk, bread, you know the necessity's that most homes find they need. They can now purchase their items with a scan of the chip, instead of needing to lug around a purse or wallet with all those plastic charge cards and the filthy paper money that no one seems to mind doing away with. They have the ability to make an automatic payment of the needed amount right then and there, one of the more popular things that they're capable of performing. The abilities of these chips are endless. New programs are being constantly written to make the link between the person and the chip even stronger. I for one do not understand the hesitation that you have exhibited towards the chip. What is it about these chips that you choose not to embrace?" she asks earnestly. "I'll let you think on that and move on to the very reasons why you should welcome the chip into your countries.

How they were created to help you run your country much more efficiently than you have ever been able to.

I wish the creator of the chip had been able to be here today for this presentation but unfortunately he had a prior engagement that he was unable to get out of. He was comfortable with me being the one to give the presentation, since I know as much about these chips, if not more, than he does.

These chips are brilliant; indeed, they have surpassed the reason for their creation. I have my own group of programmers on staff that not only maintain the chips but are constantly developing new programs to enhance the chips capabilities. I demonstrated as much to the citizens of the United States last year, with the ability to stop a robber, and that in turn helping to cut down on the police force needs. Of course, we will always have a police force in the States; they just won't need to respond to the small problems that were eating up so much of their time.

These chips can and will be programmed for you to your specifications. You alone will have control over your people, the way that I have it over mine. The actual procedure for inserting the chips is completely painless. Mine was done on national television along with Vice President Uqbahtor and our late minister Jerry Johnston, from the People's Church in Texas. If you'll remember, that church was completely destroyed last year from an unknown terrorist group. The complete House of Representatives, the Congress and every Senator of the United States was killed in one fell swoop, along with Jerry. As President, I am still searching for the truth about that matter and who was responsible. That will be dealt with after I have the complete information.

I have had my chips programmed also for tax purposes. Each citizen of the United States has their government taxes automatically taken out of their deposits allowing them the freedom of never having to file taxes again. This is not only beneficial to them but also to the government. We have their taxes instantly available to us every time they get paid. We don't have to wait for transfers from their employer's to our departments. This allows the levels of government to run much more efficiently. Each citizen also pays a charge for the use of the chip. They are not free to produce or to program, therefore it was necessary to charge a certain amount for each chip. For children, their parents pay weekly for the chips until a minor comes to the adult age which is eighteen in the United States. That too was something that we programmed the chips for. As you can see by everything that I've said so far, the benefits far out way the costs of these chips. As head's of your countries, you will also have all the capabilities that I have. What you charge for your chips and their usage will be your business. The costs for your purchase of the chips are minimal at its highest. We are not making a fortune from that which I am offering you. We will charge only what is needed for production. If you want our help with the programming, that too will be at a minimal cost. With these chips, you will have instant knowledge of how many people live in your country. What your tax base is, enabling your countries to operate much more efficiently. There are many other programs available to you should you request them. I have requested a special program enabling me, as President of the United States, to make the decisions of life and death. The chip is capable of stopping ones heart, if so desired. Of course, I will not use them in that way unless I'm left with no choice. For instance, say one of the murderers on death row in any number of our prisons escapes. It would sometimes take days, weeks or even months to find them and capture them bringing them back to the prison. That costs a lot in tax payers money since our police forces must charge for travel and overtime. This frees up those who would be responsible for capturing that escapee allowing them to do their normal job. It also cuts way down on the costs associated with that operation. Since those people were scheduled for death anyway, it just made a lot more sense to give me that responsibility. I am, after all, the President, and as such should have that responsibility.

You, as heads of your country, should also have that responsibility. These chips also help in maintaining citizenship problems. If you are not a true citizen of the United States, that being both parents were born here and are citizens, then you are not able to have the chips from my country. Those illegal's, as we call them, are sent back to their country where they obtain those chips and use their governments insurances, pay their governments taxes. In my country, that doesn't mean that you cannot become a citizen, it just means that you must go through the correct government agency to do so. We are no longer footing the bill for anyone that doesn't pay taxes. They no longer get all the free perks of the United States for doing nothing. We take care of our own, and allow people to become citizens as long as they become one completely, through the right channels and abide by our laws.

At this point I would like to ask the media to leave do to the sensitive nature of the next stage of the negotiations. Any media coverage may compromise the security of any nations in attendance today. As soon as the negotiations are complete we will hold a press conference and answer any questions you may have. Please escort the media out of the room. Thank you.

"Wait, we weren't told that we wouldn't be able to stay for the whole meeting" Gerry Partell of World Vision Now complains loudly while the armed guards for the Shah intercepts him and escorts him from the room along with all five camera men.

"Now gentlemen, let's have an open honest discussion about your concerns regarding the chips. I know that you have some unvoiced and I'm interested in hearing just what they are. Who among would like to begin this conversation?"

"I would like to" President Murabbi Abdul-Majeed of Iran says after standing in his black silk suit, crisp white silk shirt and blazing red tie, a middle aged gentleman, power demonstrated in his elegance and quietness. "All these things that you speak of are all good things; however, you have demonstrated to the world that you don't hesitate to use your powers against other countries. How do we know that you're not going to use this technology against us?" he asks in a deep, well modulated voice, no microphone needed.

"I can see where that would be a very real concern to all of you. However, Mr. Fahr, of Fahrquest Industries has agreed to meet with each one of you on an individual basis and design the chip to your own specifications and your specifications only. You will be the only ones with the key to your chips. If you understand anything about computer technology you understand that it's is totally possible to block anyone else from getting to your chip programs. Mr. Fahr has guaranteed to me that these chips are able to be completely protected."

"Jane, could you give us a few minutes in private" Shah Manzah requests after listening to the exchange between her and President Abdul-Majeed.

"Of course" Jane says quietly, turning and leaving the room through the door nearest her.

Shah Manzah turns after watching Jane exit the room, a nod from the guard on the door acknowledging that her departure was complete "Gentleman, if that is your only concern, let me assure you that Jane Martin has no secret or personal agenda. Let us not forget what even the name of the chip means, the FIQH. This isn't a time to worry about our own interests; this is a time to begin spreading the word of Allah and Islam, to all corners of the earth.

"We meant no disrespect, but you can see where our concerns lie. If you can guarantee that you can keep President Martin under control, than I believe that I can speak for everyone in saying that we will gladly join in this endeavor, and we will except her offer of the chip in our countries" President Abdul-Majeed says.

After looking at each face and receiving their nod of approval, Shah Manzah says "you have my word. I have great influence with President Martin. Now, I have one more important piece of business that must be discussed. Having had an Arab-Israeli conflict for thousands of years, Israel has not yet accepted the chip and before you react to what I'm about to suggest, keep in mind that this is a very temporary condition that you'll have to live with, so here's what we propose" and after dropping that bombshell there's yelling and arguing in the room that needs to be brought under control before any more discussions can be had. "If I could get your attention please" he says again after a few previous try's to gain control of the room, once the room has quieted sufficiently he begins "as you know Israel and the United States have been close allies for years, therefore they trust them. Under the right circumstances they'd be willing to take the chip from the United States and trust them to develop it for them. This chip will have capabilities that none of yours will have. It could actually wipe out the Israeli nation with one push of a button. But in order to have them agree to this, we have to give them something that they've been wanting for years. We must appear to give them back all of the lands that they claim are theirs. But as I've said, this will be a very temporary inconvenience for us" barely hearing himself speak over the eruption in the room with that announcement.

"Even if we would agree to this, this would be a huge undertaking and probably with a lot of bloodshed in getting our people moved out of the area" one of the presidents from a smaller country says loudly.

"It's not like we have to have a mass exodus out of the area, just giving our word to the President of the United States and Prime Minister Baladan would be enough to get them to accept the chip. Remember, a signature on a peace treaty is only as good as the paper it's written on. Now gentlemen, I will leave the room and let you discuss this amongst yourselves. I'll be awaiting your answer by the end of the day" and Shah Manzah turns with authority and dignity, slowly exiting the room through the same door that Jane went through.

"They're convening right now; we can expect their answer by the end of the day" the Shah informs Jane when he joins her for tea.

After a lengthy wait, nerves taut with anxiety President Majeed enters the room that Jane and the Shah have been visiting in to inform them "we have decided to accept your offer and conditions, however Shah Manzah, if this does not work out the way you suggest that it will, it will be much worse for you and your family than you could imagine."

"I can assure you this will work out in Allah's favor," Shah Manzah replies.

"It will all fall into place President Majeed. Thank you for the decision, I'm sure you held a lot of sway power over the other countries present."

"You're welcome President Martin. I look forward to all that is about to transpire" he assures her with a slight bow of the head, an honor to a President and a woman, he then excuses himself and leaves.

"Well Uncle" Jane says after President Majeed leaves the room. "It will be as you predicted. Thank you for backing me in this and for your hospitality, it's been greatly appreciated. Shall we prepare to face the media? I know they're waiting impatiently and now with the departures of the countries, they'll be really getting impatient. I don't want them reporting anything that shouldn't be reported."

"Yes Jane, we had better get out there and face the music, as they say," he adds with a small smile. "I do like some of your, what do you call them, slang words?"

"Yes, they are slang. I much prefer our way of speaking, but I also must live in my country so have learned some of the more common ways of speaking."

"You do so brilliantly, my dear. You're a natural" he adds with a grin.

"Thanks, Uncle" she says, cheeks turning rosy from the compliment.

Chapter Nineteen

"Well" Snake says slowly after having watched the conference from the living room of his parents' house with Mal and Kat, and all the talk has quieted, and the media has left the hall following Jane's abrupt dismissal.

"I think she's going to pull this off, don't you?" Kat asks looking at Snake after seeing his expression while Mal just stands there staring at the TV.

"Damn it, that's it" Mal says slowly as she finally understands what's been bothering her.

"What Mal?" Snake demands "What's it?"

"The name of the chip, the FIQH chip, there's a meaning behind that word. It doesn't stand for Fahrquest Industries Quality Healthcare like we've been told. Yes it does, it's their initials. I mean there's a much deeper meaning behind those letters, that word, it's got two meanings, a hidden one. I should have caught this sooner, damn it, I know this stuff. Why didn't I pick up on this a year ago when she introduced it?"

"What's the meaning Mal, enlighten us."

"FIQH means understanding, comprehension, knowledge and jurisprudence in Islam. A jurist is called a Faqih, an expert in Islamic legal matters, passing verdicts within the rules of Islamic Law namely Shariah. The name of this chip covers everything Muslim, a religion that is very narrow and not the teachings of the Christian religion. You know that the Christian religion isn't tolerated well by the Muslims and the Islamic Shariah law is even more opposed to Christianity. That's were a lot of world fighting has occurred, this religion has created thousands of martyrs."

"I know, I was thrown into the center of that whole problem when I served in special-ops. They don't find anything wrong in sending out their children as suicide bombers. Some have twisted their religion to the point where they believe it honors them to be used in these ways. It ensures their place in heaven" Snake says quietly, sadly. "I watched this happen too many times to count and was helpless in stopping those poor children from blowing themselves up. We can't let that start happening here in the United States. They'll try to overtake our country using their religion, using our own constitution against us, which I might add" he says angrily "they've been doing for quite a few years now. There are too many ignorant bleeding-hearts in this country to allow us to stop this problem before it gets any bigger. You wouldn't believe the red tape involved in just protecting our land and our freedom of religion. They've been taking that whole freedom of religion thing way out of context, not the real reason it was written. They founded this country on the freedom to worship

God. Yes, Christianity, not Islam, not Buddha, not atheism, Christianity. I have a quote memorized because it had such impact on our founding fathers. John Adams said 'the general principles on which the fathers achieved independence were the general principles of Christianity' and actually the first amendment was not to keep religion out of government, it was to keep government from establishing a "National Denomination," and even when Jefferson wrote to the Baptists he made it clear that the wall of separation was to insure that Government would never interfere with religious activities because religious freedom came from God, not Government, not Allah, not Buddha, that one of the first high courts of this country back in 1799 declared 'by our form of government, the Christian religion is the established religion' . . . Sorry, I jumped on my soap box, anyway, you already know that, but this, this is going to be hard if not impossible to stop, but it MUST be stopped."

"Wow Snake, I never realized how religious you are. I'm glad, and Mom and Dad would be so proud of you for knowing all those things, for being able to quote those people!" Mal says in awe. "I agree we have to do something before this country is completely destroyed. But what can we do. We're so few compared to all those that have just followed Jane like she's the second coming. It's not looking good, and this is happening really fast, what can we do? Even as we stand here, she's setting the whole freakin world up for dictatorship, her being the dictator!"

"I know," he says a groan, rubbing his hands rubbing his face, tired beyond belief, the thought of fixing this problem overwhelming.

"Wait, we can't fix this problem, just the few of us, but we can cause her problems which will have an effect on the outcome," Kat say quietly. "You have to keep this in perspective. As just a few compared to the country, no, the world, we can't stop anything from happening, but we can make a difference. I'm sure if we find the right key, we can throw everything we have at her, causing a slight stumble. Maybe that's all it'll take."

"Kat's right," Mal says thoughtfully. "We have enough people on our side that we can do something to cause problems. Sometimes problems can stop things, kinda like a train derailment. For example, if even one car derails, then the whole track's screwed up and no other train can go through there. If we can cause a problem like that, it can stop, well maybe not stop, but it can change the outcome."

"Yeah it can" Snake says "and that's actually what I've been trying to do. I've been thinking about this non-stop for months now somehow knowing the direction this has been headed in. We have to find that one small thing that can change the direction that she's set in motion. After all, it's only been a little over a year since this really started for us, but I have a feeling it started a lot longer ago than a year for her. It's only been the last year that it's come to the front for viewing, I think this has been going on for years, maybe even decades."

"I wonder what time the rest of the news briefing will be. How long do you think before she goes back on the air to let everyone know?" Kat asks.

"Who knows? It could be today or even tomorrow before we hear what the outcome is. I can't see every one of those countries following her without problems. If they do then it'll show us how big her backing really is."

"What time is it? Don't we have a video conference scheduled with Eli at nine o'clock?" Mal reminds them.

"Yep, we do and it's," Snake says as he glances at his watch "almost nine. We better get that computer set up. I don't want to miss this. We should have some information about that 'Courtesy Camp' and what they've got intel wise."

"Yeah, we need to get those people out of there as soon as possible. I don't dare think what's going on there behind closed doors, it would bring me to my knees in anguish," Kat says, voice getting quieter and quieter.

"I know," Snake says compassion heavy in his tone. "Don't think about it Kat. You don't need to go there ever again. Keep focused on what we're doing and thinking about how to change the outcome of what Jane's put into motion."

"There, it's on and ready. I don't see Eli yet, but he's got a couple of minutes, so we wait," Mal says, taking a seat on a chair not far from the camera or the computer screen, excited about seeing Rand for a few minutes while talking with Eli and the rest of the group out west.

"Hey" Mal says when Eli's face pops up on the screen in a blink. "You almost scared me," she says teasingly as Snake and Kat walk over to take a seat next to her.

"Sorry Mal, wouldn't want to do that," he says with a grin, teasing her back "except with a snake, oops, sorry Jacob, not you, I mean, sorry Snake, not you, oh hell, who are you today?" Eli asks tongue in cheek.

"Stop it Eli," Jacob says, face a serious mask hiding the humor in his dancing eyes.

"Sir yes Sir," Eli says with a formal salute.

"Nicely done, Eli, now, let's get down to business, we've got a lot to cover tonight," Jacob says authoritatively.

"Eli, you start since we're all waiting here to find out how the courtesy camp issue went today."

"Sure. We were able to lace two whole cases of those drinks that the guards like, Tiny Tubs, with enough Visine to make a horse sick. Whether he survives that, we have no clue, but we do know that it will make him really sick. Sick enough that I have no doubt we'll get called for an ambulance. We left ten soldiers there for when that occurs. They'll be picking him up in a local fire departments ambulance, wearing paramedic clothes, the whole nine yards. No way would anyone know that they weren't the real deal. Anyway, once we have him in the ambulance, we can scan his chip and send that off to you Mal. Then you can work your magic. That should enable us, hopefully anyway, to take over the camp completely. We're thinking of switching positions between the guards and the prisoners, but doubt there would be enough room. We have no idea how bad the prisoners are and don't want to take any chances harming anyone of them. So, the next thought is, just kill them all. It kinda goes against our consciences' but we'll do what we need to," Eli says with determination, the goal in sight.

"No, don't kill them all. How about if I contact some of my military buddies at the nearest base? Maybe we can work out a deal. We'll let them handle that problem, and just deliver them up with bows in their hair," he offers as he grins with anticipation.

"I like it," Eli says, "but I want to be there too and so do all of these guys," he adds with a wave of one hand towards the room in general.

"Don't worry Eli. You and your guys will have lot's more action coming your way. Missing this one small thing won't be a big deal."

"Not true Jacob. These guys were duped into believing that they were protecting those people when they were protecting a building only. Those poor people have been . . ."

"Stop Eli, I haven't forgotten what's been going on. Just because I'm not there with you doesn't mean that I don't know what's happening out west. Of course they can be involved. Make them the guards for transport to the base after I get the clearance. Not everyone is aware yet of what's been going on. I have to be very careful when contacting the base to only talk to the ones I know are following us. They may not even want them at the base, but somewhere else. I'll find out and get back to you. You can work out the details at your end. Just don't kill them all. It's not who we are, remember?"

"Yeah, yeah, I got it," Eli admits tiredly. "I wasn't thinking of the big picture, just of immediate gratification. Sorry Jacob."

"No problem, I totally understand. Now, anything else we need to know about at this end?"

"Let's see. I see Mal made it there safe and sound, no problems sis?"

"Nope, I made it. It was a long, boring drive but no problems on the way. I'm sorry too, Eli, for being such a bitch before I left," she says flushing slightly.

"It's all right, really, Mal. I didn't give you any heads up on this, really because I didn't know until right before I told you. I didn't have any time to break it to you, anyway, it worked out, you're there where you were needed and as soon as we get the scan, you'll have it, promise," he says relief in his tone.

"Thanks Eli. I don't want there to be a rift between us, not now, not after everything, not with what's happening in the world . . ."

"I know me either. Thanks Mal."

"How's everything going in D.C Jacob? Have you had any problems?"

"Actually we're moving along at a good speed. I still have a few people that I haven't been able to reach, but hope to within the next few days. Jane's going to be back in the states soon and I want to have everything in place by that time. The earthquakes have quieted, so let's hope mother nature starts behaving. There's only been a few small meteorites hit the earth in the past week or so, so we've gotten lucky there, although from what my source tells me, the worst is yet to come.

Pay attention to the news when you can. Also, did you by chance see the news conference from Iran today?"

"I only caught the tail end. What's going on out there? Now what's she planning on doing. No matter how powerful she believes she is, I can't see her creating peace in the Middle East. No one's been able to do that, ever!"

"I know, but trust me, she's got something up her sleeve, something that will put her in the position that she's been aiming for, a position that the world will definitely regret. Can you imagine what would happen if she became dictator of the world? These are scary times were living in. I don't believe anything will ever be as it was. The world we knew two years ago is gone and won't be back. All we can do is crimp her style. I'll do that gladly, just to make her life miserable. It's the least I can do!" Jacob says determinedly.

"I hear you Bro. I want in on that and I know a few hundred more that feel the same way. Now if there's nothing more, I'm going to head out. I want to find out if there's been any illness reported at the courtesy camp. I'd like to get this ball rolling. The sooner we can get to those people, the better."

"Sounds good" Jacob says, "talk to you tomorrow night unless something happens then I'll call or you can call me if you have news."

"Will do, Jacob. Out."

"Snake, check out the TV. There's a breaking news alert coming on," Kat says after glancing at the television.

"This is Gerry Partell of world Vision Now reporting live from Iran, on the Summit that was held today between the Middle Eastern leaders and the President. We were in the conference room with them but were escorted out by the Shah's guards when the President announced that privacy was needed. We are now awaiting her arrival to inform the United States what occurred, what decision was made today. I've just been told that she's ready let's hear what she has to say;

"Thank you for your patience. I am pleased to announce that after seeing the great success that the chip has had in the United States and the rest of the world, the Arab nations have all agreed to accepting the chip. This is a major step towards the world peace that we've all hoped for. Not only have they agreed to the chip, but we also had a discussion of how to bring Israel the only remaining country without the chip, a way to offer Israel the opportunity to also take advantage of all the chip has to offer. We have scheduled a meeting with the Prime minister of Israel for tomorrow to discuss the possibility of bringing peace to Israel for the first time in history. I cannot go into any particulars at this time due to the sensitive nature of these talks, but I will be glad to answer any questions that you have now and will definitely report to you tomorrow night on the outcome of our meeting with the Prime Minister."

"How did you convince all these countries that were so adamantly against the chip to finely accept it?" asks a reporter from Iran.

"I explained in detail the FIQH chips, how they're made and programmed. It was a matter of miscommunication that delayed their acceptance. Now that they're aware of all of the benefits the chip offers, they are very ready and willing to move forward as we have."

"How do you think that you're going to get Israel to accept this?"

"I believe that once the Prime Minister is informed of the benefits and how they can advance his needs within the country that he will undoubtedly accept them as has the rest of the world. The chips can only help him to maintain his government and his people in the manner that he would want. He's a reasonable man, I'm sure that he just doesn't have the information he needs to make this magnitude of a decision. I have no doubt that he will be in favor of the chip once he understands its capabilities."

"No offense President Martin, but you're an American and you don't know him as we know him. We've been dealing with him for years and he's anything but a reasonable man," says the Iranian reporter, while small laughs can be heard throughout the crowd.

"I actually know him better than anyone here believes obviously, and as the President of the United States, our relationship has always been honest. We've been allies for generations and expect that to continue on. The chip will help him move towards the peace that's been just out of reach. If that's all, I want to thank you all for your time and I am looking forward to seeing you again tomorrow evening after my meeting with the

Prime Minister, hopefully with some very good news," Jane says, turns slowly and leaves the podium.

"Well that was interesting," Gerry Partell says as the camera's turn back to him having watched the President until she was out of sight. "You just heard President Martin announce the success of the chip summit with the Arab Nations. All but Israel is on board, and the goal is to have Israel accept the chip by tomorrow. If she can pull this off, it will be the greatest accomplishment by any world leader in the history of this planet. This is Gerry Partell in Iran going back to the studios of World Vision Now, back to you Christine."

"Thank you Gerry. Do you have any idea what she said after you were evicted from the meeting, to convince them to accept the chip?" Christine asks Gerry while he's still on air.

"Actually, no, but I can say this. We have got an amazing President."

"What the hell just happened here?" Kat asks dumbfounded as she looks at Snake and then at Mal, mirroring their expressions.

"Amazing, AMAZING, I'll tell you what's amazing. It's amazing that anyone would buy this shit, that's what's amazing," Snake yells at the TV, scrubbing his hands over his face, beard rasping so loud it could be heard outside.

"What just happened? Did they really agree to the chip? How can that be, why are we the only ones who can see through her façade, can see the real person behind this," Mal asks in disbelief.

"Probably because we've been following this story right from the start, and we know things that the public has no idea of. Maybe we should let them know?" Kat says.

"There are a couple reasons that we shouldn't let them know. One, is no one knows we even exist. Remember I'm dead. Two, is right now the average citizen of the United States is so caught up in what they're getting free that they would never believe anything negative about our darling Jane. So anyone that would speak against her would be conceived as an enemy. We watched the televised capital punishments when she first took office. Everyone remembers those occasions and no one wants to be brought into the light for fear of the same things happening to them. It's neighbor against neighbor."

"Who could be calling at this hour," Kat says after hearing a cell phone go off. "Snake, what is it?" she asks after noticing him take his phone out of his pocket.

"Hold on Eli, let me put you on speaker, all right, go ahead," Snake says after moving the phone so they can all hear and turning up the volume.

"It seems that the Visine works faster than any of us could have imagined. But don't worry, we were ready for it. We got the call and our men picked up the Captain of the Guards ten minutes ago. It doesn't look like he's even going to make it through the night. This Visine is bad ass shit. We had one little glitch in our plan. It seems that the Captains aid insisted on riding along in the ambulance. But I'm thinking this might work to our advantage. We now have a live guard in custody. And once Mallory activates the chips, we'll be able to tell up close and personal if her new program works. Mallory, we scanned the chip and are sending you the information as we speak. You should receive it right about now."

"Excellent news, good job guys, I knew I could rely on you. Mal will get right on this. We'll let you know when we're ready on our end, but it shouldn't be long," Jacob promises.

"Thanks Jacob, we'll be ready and waiting, I only hope that I can control these soldiers, they're all pretty angry about what's been going on under their noses," Eli says before hanging up.

"Oh god Jacob, what if it doesn't work. I don't want to be responsible for anything that may jeopardize the safety of not only the captives but also our troops." Mal admits nervously.

"That's nonsense Mallory. There's no one else that could pull this off. You're the only one on earth that can be trusted with this responsibility," Kat says. "When I was working as a detective I worked with a lot of high tech computer geeks and none of them had your talent! Now let's do this together."

"You'll do fine Mal, I know you will. You're not going to be hurting our people; they need your help to get them out of that damn camp to safety. How they're living right now is not living at all. You're doing them a service, Mal. You're helping them to live again," Jacob says.

'Thanks Jacob, thanks Kat. All right, let's do this," Mal says as she moves into position at her computer. "I set up a field around the towers that supply the signals to the camp. No one outside of that camp should be affected. I didn't want all the soldiers in all the camps to collapse at the same time, since the other states aren't ready for this. Eli said they'd pass this info to those other camps after we took care of this one. That way the guardsman can be prepared to take care of the prisoners and the guards when I knock them out. I don't want to kill them all. I figure we can take care of that problem when the time comes."

"Excellent Mal! Let me know when it's done so I can get the ground troops moving in."

"Five minutes Jacob; it will all be done in five minutes. You can call Eli and tell him to have the troops move into position. The guards should be out for about thirty minute's total, so they'll need to move fast. Tell them it's done, they can move now," Mal says after some frantic typing on her computer.

"Eli, move your men into position, this will all go down in just a couple of minutes."

Chapter Twenty

"Alpha team, are you in place?" Eli asks into the radio.

"Alpha team in place on north side of main entrance, Mike is with me to guide us through the area," Mongoose replies.

"Bravo team, ready?" Eli asks.

"Bravo team on the east side of the building, east entrance, ready." Replies Rand.

"Charlie team ready?" Eli asks.

"Charlie team ready," Jerry replies.

"Delta team ready?" Eli asks.

"Delta team ready," Luke replies speaking quietly to Staff Sergeant Mallone.

"Delta team is the chopper in place and ready if needed?" Eli asks quickly.

"That's affirmative Sir, and ready to fly," Luke responds.

"Eli, it's a go, send them in now. Leave the radio connection open for monitoring," Jacob orders.

"This is operation resurrection, it's a go, Go . . . GO," Eli yells into his radio.

"Let's go guys, operation resurrection, go, Go, GO . . ." Mongoose repeats dumping water on the lithium rope wrapped around the locks on the door causing the locks to blow off. "Man that stuff works awesome. Whoever came up with it was brilliant," Mongoose says as he grabs Mike to keep him near unsure what's on the other side of the door. Kicking the door open, Mongoose looks around quickly seeing nothing. No movement, no bodies, nothing, no people, just a long tunnel leading into the inner portions of the building. "Mike, this is where we need your memory. Which way do we go?" Mongoose asks as he turns and see's Mike running down the tunnel. "We're going to have to hurry to keep up with that guy," Mongoose says to the rest of his guys, "it looks like he's on his own mission," as he catches up with Mike, he's entering a door on the left of the tunnel. After walking through the door they get their first view of the power of the chip. There are five, no six guards lying on the floor, unconscious. Immediately two of Mongoose's men split off and begin using zip ties to immobilize the guards before they regain consciousness, while two more begin to secure the guards weapons. Looking straight ahead, he sees another door with a padlock on it and Mike tugging desperately on the door. He pulls Mike back and strikes the lock with the butt of his gun busting it open, allowing access into the room. As he enters the room, he sees a sight that's he's only seen in history books, pictures from the death camps of World War II, yet it's not the vision that affects him, but the smell emanating from the room and the shadows lining the walls, some sitting, helplessness a heavy pall over everything, skeletons with dead eyes staring back at him as he glances around the room. Mike runs to one of the men, falls to his knees and begins hugging him.

"Jim, I told you I'd get us out of here," Mike says.

"Get pictures of all of this, we need proof to take to the other camps. We can't let this go without recording everything," Mongoose orders his Lieutenant.

"Come on Mike, we have other places to go. Don't worry, we're aren't leaving until this is taken care of, but I have other men I need to check on and you need to guide us," Mongoose says grabbing Mike by the arm and turning him away from his friend, who looks like he's about to collapse.

"Delta team, north perimeter secured, send in medics," Mongoose orders. "This is Alpha team to Bravo team, Charlie team, have you secured your area? Bravo team, come on, . . Charlie team . . ?"

"This is Charlie team, east quadrant secured, we have found the kids, the guards are subdued, weapons secured, but we've got a bunch of kids here that need some help."

"Copy Charlie team this is Alpha. Delta team we need medics east quadrant, this is Alpha team," Mongoose orders.

"Bravo team, this is Alpha team; Rand, what the hell is going on?" Mongoose snaps into his radio.

"This is Bravo team, west side is secure but we have some problems down here. One of our men is injured and all the guards are dead. It seems we have a sniper in the room somewhere. We have been unable to locate the exact position."

"Ten four, understand, continue to search out sniper in west quadrant. Alpha team and Charley team will move to the south quadrant to secure."

"Ten four Alpha, Bravo out."

"Charlie team, begin moving to the south quadrant. We'll meet you there." As they move back into the tunnel, they begin heading up a ramp to the south end of the building. Just as they reach the top of the ramp, they hear a gunshot coming from behind the doorway on the left. Mongoose slowly and quietly opens the door and sees an average size brunette with a gun almost as big as her, shooting through a small hole in the wall. Moving quietly and methodically, he grabs her from behind knocking the gun from her hand, and pulling her away from the opening. "It's okay, we're here to help you, this nightmare's over," he tries to reassure the kicking, yelling wildcat that he's trying to subdue, the language coming out of her mouth convinces him it's not a woman after all but a trucker in disguise. "Stop, stop, will you just stop," he yells, trying to gain her attention. After calming down slightly he's able to finally push her a little distance away from him and get a good look. It is a she, not a he and she looks like she's been through hell.

"As far as I'm concerned, it's not over until every one of those bastards is dead. They've got to pay for what they did to us."

"Oh, they'll pay, but I think there's been enough killing for today. Now, maybe you can help us get the rest of the captives to a safer place?" Mongoose suggests to her.

"Take her back to where we found the kids, maybe she can help calm them down," Mongoose orders a guardsman as he hands her off.

"Bravo team, sniper is secured, this is Alpha, over."

"Rand to Mongoose, did you kill the bastard that tried to kill me?"

"No, I left that for you," Mongoose admits wickedly. "Rand, take bravo team and split up, transfer all the guards into the north quadrant before they wake up. Bravo and Charlie team are going to continue to secure the south quadrant. We'll meet you there after we secure the rest of the building."

"Copy Alpha, out."

"Let's move out, we need to finish securing this area. I'm heading up," Mongoose says to the rest of his team as he continues up the ramp. A pair or heavy steel doors stop his progress, multiple security cameras are aimed at the entryway. "Take'em out," he orders the team members closest to him. "On my six" he says as he moves to grab the handles, pulling the doors towards him. He waves his team off to the right as he heads to the left once they're through the doors. Bright light is spilling through a large bank of windows, flat screen TV's line one wall, a overly large sectional in jewel tones takes up the other two walls, with end tables in a highly polished wood, looks like teak, placed throughout. Everything is spotlessly clean except for the guards that are lying around unconscious, having succumbed to the chip program that Mal had instituted. "We need to hurry and get these guys contained before they wake up. Check all those doors lining the hall back there behind the living quarters. We don't have much time left. It's been over twenty minutes since the initial entrance. That leaves us less than ten minutes before these guys come out of their temporary coma. Use the zip ties and let's get ready for transport," he orders as he proceeds to restrain those lying nearest him. "Anyone else in the back" he asks as his team members start coming back into the area that he's working in.

"Just a couple, they were still out so we restrained them. We'll start transport when you're ready."

"Excellent. What's back there?"

"You wouldn't believe it. All bedrooms and bathrooms, most of the bedrooms with two full size beds in them, all used but meticulously clean. If I didn't know where we were right now, I'd think we were at a five star hotel; everything's very high quality and barely used. They must have had house keeping up here, there's no way these guys kept this place this clean!"

"Yeah, I'll bet they had housekeeping," Mongoose agrees sarcastically. "Housekeepers by way of the female prisoners, and I'll bet that's not all they had them up here for, either," he adds angrily. "Let's get these bastards down into the prisoner's room. I'll bet they're gonna be excited when they wake up there. Start moving them now."

"Yes sir."

"I'm headed to that small southeastern area where the kids are. You can get me on the radio if you need me otherwise make sure all the guards are in the northern room that the captive men were held in. After all, they should get the same experience that they gave to the guys!"

"Copy Alpha. We'll meet up with you there when we're through here."

Two minutes later, Mongoose reaches the section of the building that housed the kids. *At least the smells not as bad in this area as where the men were being held,* he thinks. Opening one of the doors to see if it's empty he notices plain walls, sleeping bags scattered over the floor with small blankets tossed helter-skelter. *This must have been the sleeping room*, he thinks, about to close the door when he glimpses a very small head peak around the door of the closet. Slowly so as not to scare the little thing he wanders closer to the door, making no fast movements, being as friendly looking as possible while in his fatigues.

"Hey, it's all right" he says quietly. "I'm here to help you, not hurt you. Want to go and find your mommy?" he asks cautiously. Big eyes just keep looking at him, a tiny body curled up as close to the corner of the closet as possible. *She really blends in*, he thinks. *I would have never seen her had she not peaked around the door. It's probably what protected her from the soldiers, or maybe they had an ounce of feeling keeping them from hurting her,* he thinks. *Nah, she was good at hiding that's all. Those bastards have no feelings. They'd have killed her had they known about her.* "I promise to take you to your mommy, honey. I won't touch you, you can walk there all by yourself if you want to" he says coaxingly seeing a slight reaction to his words in eyes that grew a little larger with the news. "Come on, follow me. She might have some food for you, if you're hungry," he adds trying to find the trigger that'll cause her to move on her own. And on that note, she moves very slowly so he turns away from her showing her he meant what he said. With slow movements he moves towards the door hoping she'll follow when she senses no lies. After a couple of minutes he finds the room, a huge dorm type room, where the rest of the kids are and a lot of women, the noise so low it's hard to believe all these people are in this room together. *Guess they've learned to stay as quiet as possible to avoid any undue attention from the guards. What a sad way to live*, he's thinking to himself when his little captive finally see's her mom and runs full force to her, a greeting involving silent tears from mother and daughter and from anyone that witnessed it, the quietness of it all a very uncomfortable and sad experience. After a quick glance he finds the hellcat that held them at bay with the gun and moves towards her in a nonthreatening way, her watching him like a hawk.

"I need you to come with me," he tells her quietly watching for any reaction. After a small nod of agreement, he turns expecting her to follow. "We need to talk," he says quietly "but I don't want it to be in front of anyone. I have some questions and you're gonna give me the answers to them," he states firmly.

"I'm not telling you anything," she mutters quietly in defiance.

"Here, we'll go in here," he says as they pass a room down the hall. After entering and checking to make sure they're alone, he turns to face her, seeing the gaunt face, unkempt appearance, and noticing for the first time the real color of her hair. *A dirty blonde, not the brown I thought at first. I bet she's pretty when she's got more meat on her bones, but right now she's almost skeletal* he thinks all while waiting for her to look at him. "What's your name?"

"Desdemona," is all she offers.

"That's it, just Desdemona?" he asks dryly.

"Actually my name is Desdemona but I'm known as Des," she says feeling compelled into adding in defense of her name.

"Where are you from?"

"Washington."

"The state of Washington, you're pretty far from home? How'd you get all the way to Texas and into the courtesy camp?"

"Not the state, D.C., I'm from the D.C. area."

"That's still pretty far from home. So how'd you get into Texas's courtesy camp?" he asks again, with a little less patience.

"I volunteered, how do you think I got here?" she says anger starting to churn.

"What!"

"I volunteered, that's how I got in here. If you believe that then you're stupider than I thought," she says sarcastically. "Look, let's not even pretend we're friends here. We're not! So why would I tell you anything? Because you think I owe you for rescuing us from those bastards? That's a load of crap. Your men made sure we stayed inside these walls. You people are no rescuers, more like prison guards. Close your ears to any big problems going on in here, that's all you did. While those poor kids were being abused, the women were being made to prostitute themselves to earn extras for their kids and even some of the children being molested and raped. You make me sick," she yells, face red, blood pressure surely rising.

"Hold on a second. My men didn't do any of those things." Mongoose says in defense of all she said.

"Bull, that's bull. If they didn't do any of those things, then why were we being held prisoner in here? I've been here almost six months and was sure that I would be one of the next ones to 'disappear' with no one being the wiser. That's what happens to them, you know. If they continue to refuse the chip, they leave this place and are never heard from again. My guess, they kill them. If you'll look around the area, I'm sure you'll find a mass grave somewhere, where all the people that have disappeared from here are buried."

"What are you talking about?" Mongoose asks quietly face a whiter shade of pale. "How do you know that the people disappear? Maybe they just get released and go home from here."

"No way, there's not a person in here that would leave of their own accord without their family. People barely survive this place. The food is extremely minimal to the point of starvation. The guards are vicious with their beatings over nothing or their rape when the urge is there. No way would anyone leave this place leaving behind their loved ones," she finishes adamantly a slight sway to her body.

"Here, sit down there," Mongoose says as he pushes a chair towards her "before you pass out. When was the last time you had any food?"

"I don't know, it doesn't matter, does it. Just let me go. I just want to go home."

"Sorry, no can do. We're sending medics in here to take care of all the prisoners, get them back on their feet. Then we'll make sure they all get home. In the mean time, these places exist in every state and we have to do something about them soon. Before any of the other ones get word on what went down here. You're coming with us to base. You tried to kill a soldier and you need to answer for that."

"Yeah, whatever." she says tiredly. "He's not the only one I tried to kill," she admits.

"I figured after I saw all the dead guards and assumed you were the one responsible. I don't care about them, but I do care about my guys," Mongoose says.

"Right," she says wishing he's just stop talking already, too tired to even care what happens next as she slowly slides like a boneless mass to the floor, darkness and peace enveloping her.

"Shit," Mongoose grumbles as he tries unsuccessfully to grab her before she hits the floor.

"This is Alpha. I need a medic in the room next to the kid's room, south area of building."

"Copy Alpha, on our way. Out."

"What's the problem" Rand asks as he walks through the now open door noticing a woman lying on the floor near Mongoose.

"She passed out while we were talking. It's probably nothing more than too much excitement in a short amount of time, and not enough food for a long time."

"Yeah, she looks pretty bad. It doesn't look like she eaten in weeks. Poor thing," Rand adds as he drops to his knees to check for a pulse. "Who is she," he asks curiously as he starts checking her for any major injuries.

"She said her name is Desdemona, but she goes by Des, she's from the D.C. area and that's as far as we got before she just slithered onto the floor in a dead faint," Mongoose says watching Rand check her over.

"Her blood sugar probably crashed from all the excitement she felt. No food and too much excitement do it every time. She's looks bad, really bad, worse than the guys I just spent the last few minutes checking out. I'd hate to hear what was done to her to make her look this bad. There's some bruising, some old and some new, some old and new scars from injuries. It's impossible to tell what caused the faint, since she can't weigh more than eighty pounds or so, she's not much bigger than some of the kids I glimpsed. She's in bad shape."

"She had enough energy to tell me off in so many words," Mongoose says dryly.

"That was probably the last of her energy store. What are you planning on doing with her?"

"She goes with us when we leave. I'm taking her to base," Mongoose says matter-of-factly.

"What, why? She's not up to traveling, not right now. She may be in a few weeks if she gets past today, but no way can she make the trip in the next day or so, sorry Mongoose."

"Oh, she's going if I have to carry her the whole way."

"You just may have to, why are you so insistent? What is she to you?"

"Well, she's from D.C. she's feisty, swears like a trucker and has real good aim with weapons. That all leads me to believe there's more to her than she wants anyone to know."

"What do you mean she's good with weapons? How do you know that?" Rand asks in confusion.

"Well, you know the sniper that was trying to take you out?"

"Yeah, what about . . . Wait, you saying she's the sniper that was trying to kill me?"

"Yep, one and the same."

"She doesn't look strong enough to pick up a weapon let alone have enough energy to use one. You said feisty? No way did she act feisty. She couldn't even stand let alone do everything that you're claiming she did!"

"Trust me Rand, she's the sniper. Good skills too. There's definitely more to her than meets the eye. It should be interesting to find out more about her," he says thoughtfully, concern in his eyes at the stillness of the small woman lying on the floor.

"What are you gonna do," he asks Rand when he sees him rifling through his medic bag.

"She needs some IV fluids or she'll never come out of this. Her electrolytes are off, I'm sure, which is what's keeping her from regaining consciousness. I'm hoping once her body starts to receive those electrolytes she'll wake up."

"So you're still going to help her, even though she tried to kill you," Mongoose asks quietly.

"What, of course I'm going to help her. Look at her. She wasn't trying to kill me in particular I'm sure. It was probably anyone that she felt threatened by."

"You're right. She's the one that killed the guards we found lying dead up here. Unfortunately, she didn't get them all, but they'll suffer for what they did, trust me," Mongoose admits, anger in his glance at Rand.

"All right, I'm going to go and see if I can find somewhere to put her that's more comfortable than the floor, I'll be right back," Mongoose says as he leaves while receiving radio contact from one of the teams.

"Come on Miss, wake up now," Rand says quietly when he notices her breathing change, wakefulness near.

"What," she gasps when she wakes, confused about where she is and who he is.

"You're all right," he says reassuringly, holding her arm down so she doesn't try to get up. "You passed out sitting in the chair and ended up on the floor. Just give yourself a couple of minutes, you'll be fine. I'm giving you IV fluids to help you out a little. You're severely malnourished and very dehydrated so I'm sure with a little fluids you'll start feeling better soon."

"Who are you?" she asks in a whisper.

"My name's Rand, I'm here with the National guardsmen that were guarding this facility. Poor guys, they had no idea what was going on behind closed doors, but I'll bet those damn Iranian guards are really regretting their duties right about now," he says in satisfaction.

"What do you mean they're regretting their duties?" she repeats slowly.

"Oh, we gave their futures over to the National guardsmen for punishment. We thought it would be the right thing to do since after all, the guardsmen were really upset when they found out what was happening to the people they thought they were protecting."

"Huh, I don't understand," she says.

"Our guardsmen were placed on the perimeter for protection of the citizens that were brought here. They were told that because they refused the chip, they were in danger from the other American's that chose the chips and chose to follow the President, so they were brought here for their own safety. They just found out the reality of what was happening here after one of the men escaped and found his way to our compound. Now that everyone knows what was really happening, they're taking it pretty hard."

"So they should. They didn't know what they were doing to us? Couldn't they hear any screams, anything?"

"No and before you judge them guilty, let me tell you the strange quietness that we found after we stormed the place. There wasn't one captive that spoke above a whisper. Even the children were quiet, wouldn't speak and cried silent tears. It was a terrible experience for all of us. We've never experience a phenomenon such as that silence."

"It was so the guards wouldn't hurt anyone. We weren't allowed to make noise. Terrible things happened to anyone that made any, or it would happen to their children or vice versa, so to protect their loved ones from further harm, we all stayed quiet, no matter what. But that wasn't in the beginning, but after we learned the hard way what happened to the ones that made noise. They should have heard something then."

"They did, but they also said it didn't sound any different than when kids fight. No prolonged agony screams, or anything like that."

"Yeah, that was a while ago. No one made any noise recently; it was too painful knowing what was happening to those who did."

"That's what I told them, I figured it had to be something like that. To endure in that manner everything that's happened here is totally amazing," he adds in awe and with respect.

"You do what you have to do to protect the little ones, it's all done out of love. The innocents of this world, they did nothing to deserve any of this and yet they were caught right in the middle."

"Don't worry, justice will be done. There's no way that one of the guards placed inside these facilities will escape their punishment. There's also no one that will want to help them."

"That's so good," she murmurs, tired beyond belief.

"Go ahead and close your eyes, you're safe now. You can rest and we'll watch over you. There's no one here now that wants to hurt you," Rand says as she closes her eyes slowly and looses consciousness again.

"Is she still out?" Mongoose asks when he walks back into the room, having found a private room for her to be taken to.

"She was here a minute ago but must have exhausted herself, then fell back under. More rest and she'll do. Did you find a place for her to rest in?"

"Yeah, all the way at the end of the hall is a bedroom perfectly made up. It's all set for her. It's far enough away to give her privacy and quiet. Things are going to get a little noisier as soon as everyone realizes and believes that it's okay to make noise. No one's going to hurt them for it anymore, those bastards. I can't even think about what was being done and how they kept everyone under control," Mongoose says, face red, anger barely under control.

"I know, it's shocking how low humans can go, to do what they want in any perverted manner they want."

"Want to help me move her? I'll carry her she doesn't weigh much of anything. My backpack weighs more than she does. It's going to take a long time for her to regain her normal strength. I'm looking for a large car for transport, so that she can sleep during the trip to base. But that won't be for a couple of days, so she'll have a little time to rest before then."

"She may come back quickly with the fluids and some nourishment. A couple of days will help. It's going to take a long time for her to get back to normal though, but with care she'll get there."

"Good. I'll grab her, you grab the attachments and we'll get her to her room. I'm going to want a guard on her door, just to keep everybody away and give her time to rest. She's got me interested. After seeing the way she handled the gun and took me on even in her weakened state, I'm curious as to who she really is. I'm thinking there's more to her than anyone here knows. It'll be interesting to find out," Mongoose says thoughtfully.

"Follow me," Mongoose says after he picks her up, waits for Rand to grab the IV bag and begins the short walk to the end of the hall.

"Here you go," he says gently to the sleeping Des, pity stirring him at her pale look and weightlessness.

"All right, I'm going to call Eli and let him know what happened today. We'll probably head back to base within the next seventy-two hours or so. That should give all of us time to accomplish a lot. We need to question all our guardsmen and let them decide who'll take on the next stage of the trip. We need to disperse them to the bordering states so that those compounds are notified and they can schedule their takeovers. Hopefully we'll keep this going quickly and quietly, before anyone in D.C. gets wind of it. We're on the right track now, so let's not do anything to slow it down."

"Yeah, hopefully no-one got word about it but there's always something that you can't plan for. You never know, maybe a radio connection was missed within the guard group when they were unconscious. Even though we think we have everything covered, there's always the unknown!" Rand adds.

"Yeah, let's hope not," Mongoose mutters, brain frantically searching for anything that may have been left out.

"How're the prisoners holding up? Anybody come out of the shock Mal caused through their chip?" Mongoose asks Lucas when he gets to the northern area of the compound, having searched the rest of the southern portion and finding nothing unusual. *It was definitely a lot nicer than where they were holding the men captive*, he thinks.

"Yeah, they're coming to," Lucas says with a smirk. "I don't think they like their new quarters, judging by all the screaming coming out of there. They sure are a lot nosier than they let their prisoners be. Bunch of pansy-asses if you ask me," he adds with a laugh.

"Awww, they don't like our hospitality? I'm crushed," Mongoose adds dryly but with deep satisfaction.

"Let's gather a well armed group so we can go inside and get some answers," Mongoose orders Rand and Lucas.

"You got it," Rand says as they both head out to find who's available.

Chapter Twenty-One

"Prime Minister Baladan, thank you so much for agreeing to speak with me," Jane says entering a room at the palace that she'd never seen before. After a quick glance around noticing a lot of white with gilded mirrors, and a beautiful dark gleaming table, set with the finest gold in-laid ivory china that money can buy, she stops at the table as he rises to help her with her chair registering amazing floral pieces scattered throughout, leaving a faint hint of rose wafting in the air of the room. I *feel pretty plain* Jane thinks just before continuing "Thank you," she says after he finishes helping her. "It is an honor to me that you have agreed to this meeting" she continues once he is seated. "I'm hoping that I can dispel any rumors that you have heard regarding the chip."

"I look forward to hearing what you have to say, President Martin," he replies formally, a dignified handsome man with a regal bearing, dressed in a westernized suit in light charcoal, a black tie with gold embellishments, showcasing his smooth golden skin, black hair with distinguished gray sprinkled throughout the temple area.

"Please, can I get you anything before we begin?"Jane asks looking to the guard that's standing at attention at the door she just closed.

"No thank you, I'm fine," he replies, black eyes gleaming with gold flashes, gesturing at the water and coffee on the table before him along with a small plate of cookies.

"Good, then we can talk right away," she says happily, courtesy's taken care of. "The people of my country have taken on the chip with enthusiasm. They're happy with all that the chip is capable of doing. They now receive rapid health care, no matter where they are. They can even be outside of the country, and as long as they have the chip, they can be treated as who they are. With all of the information available, they are treated faster and better. They can also use their chips for everyday needs, since they no longer need to carry the filthy paper money that they used to. I'm sure that alone will cut down on disease that's transferred from person to person in the normal course of a day. Those are just a few of the things that the chips are capable of, and what they are aware of. Of course, as President, I have many more responsibilities. The chip allows me to protect my people from dangerous things. They don't have to worry about being robbed. For one, there's nothing to take. They no longer carry money, which is what they were usually robbed for. The chip is not compatible for anyone beside's the one it was programmed for, so there is no gain for anyone to take the chips. The chips are capable of having special programs run them, of course of your choosing," she adds, "but no one need know except you. You will be the only one capable of having anything added to the programs, if that was a concern," she says finishing her spiel.

"It all sounds very good, President Martin, and yes that has been a concern of mine. However, I find it difficult to believe that no one else will have the same capabilities that I have. What about the ones that actually do the programming. Don't they have those capabilities?"

"Of course they do. I myself can't program the chips. I'm not that computer literate. But we have safety layers in place so that I must be contacted and use a special code along with a specific programmer before any special program can be run. I had to be able to make someone responsible for the chip maintenance besides myself. I'm too busy to be constantly interrupted for minor things. However, the big things must go through me. You can set up the programmers, decide who will be responsible and all the rule or laws, if you will, of your chips. No one but you will know what safety measures you have put in place."

"That's all good news, but our country has experienced something that they call 'hackers.' Those that have that capability don't seem to have limits to what they do or what they're capable of doing. These things concern me. I don't want to bring something new into the country that 'hackers' may be able to get into, change and do all kinds of damage to, not only the chips programming but to the people wearing the chips. You do not seem to have a guarantee that these things won't happen."

"We too have people capable of breaking into all manner of things, but I can promise you that under penalty of death in the United States, we have much fewer hacker problems than anyone in the world. I do admit that I control the country and its people with an iron fist. They can be pulled in front of the people on a whim and judged. The verdict, of course, is always the one that I want, but the people need not know this. You, too, can promise the same outcome and will find that you will have much more control over your country, as I do," Jane says arrogantly and knowingly.

"So you do guarantee, then, that I will not have problems with the chip?" Prime Minister Baladan reiterates.

"If you would like to call it a 'guarantee' then you may. I call it control; the people in my country call it peace. They are comfortable with my ability to protect them, knowing that I do things only in the best interest of them," she adds softly with compassion, transparent compassion seen only by the very few she allows through her many layers of falsehood.

"I see" Prime Minister Baladan murmurs, black eyes blank, face expressionless.

"Do you?" Jane asks kindly.

"Yes, President Martin, I do," Prime Minister Baladan says.

"Good, then I can expect a show of solidarity from you and your country? I can't stress the importance of all that's transpiring. I will make a promise to you now, Sir that these things will come to pass. The chips will allow you freedoms that you have never before experienced. They will grant you peace in your country, peace that has been illusive since time beginning. I bring to the Middle East, peace. Yours is the last country left holding out against the chips. All others have already agreed to these things, seeing the great benefits they are gaining. You too, will become rich beyond measure and your country will stop the fighting that has been going on. President Majeed has guaranteed that there will be no more firing on the Israelis, that from the moment you accept the chip, he will order his country, his people to stand down, even at the Gaza strip. I am scheduled for a press conference immediately following our meeting to notify the world of your decision. At the time your decision is announced, peace will begin everywhere in the world. It will be an amazing experience the moment that it happens. The world will finally be united."

"What makes you believe that you, a new leader, and a woman no less, can be the one that will finally bring peace to the Middle East? We have been in turmoil for millennia and yet you, who have no experience, can finally be the one to succeed? I don't believe that this is possible. I have been ruler of this country for more than twenty years and have been unsuccessful; and you who have led not more than a year will finally succeed. Forgive me for sounding incredulous, but it is how I feel. I have ruled strongly and would not be fulfilling my duties to my country, to my people, if I jumped, as you say, into the fire with the rest."

"I'm really sorry, Prime Minister Baladan that you feel that way. Is there nothing that I can do or say that will convince you that this is the right thing to do, the right way to go?" she asks very still, anger simmering below the surface.

"At this time, I do not feel that there is anything that can be said. You have been convincing, your argument has been tempting, very tempting and yet, something keeps telling me that this is not going to work to our benefit. That there are things involved here that are unknown. I cannot in good conscience allow something to occur that would harm either my people or my country. God has brought us this far and he guides me in all things. In this matter, I'm afraid I will have to pass until possibly at a future date when all things come to light and this is proven to be beneficial. Our countries have been supporters of each other for many years and I hope that that will continue into the future regardless of my decision here today."

"Prime Minister Baladan, you speak of support for each other, and yes, I agree that we have been supportive of each other. But you must remember, this is the new regime, not the old. The old has come and gone. What you talk to now is a Woman in charge of the largest power in the world. I believe when all, yes all of the other countries complied with my request, that they were aware of the power I do yield. Out of respect for my leadership capabilities and also to better control their countries and people, they have jumped at this opportunity, knowing that it will be offered once only. How is it they say it? If you are with me, you're with me, and if you're not, then you're not. You will not have another opportunity Sir. I cannot and will not guarantee you my support if you will not step forward in front of the world and show your support."

"That almost sounds like a threat, Jane," he says warningly.

"It's President Martin not Jane to you Sir. Does it, Prime Minister Baladan? I'm sure you're mistaken. Countries follow me of their own volition, not out of fear. I do need to remind you though, all the countries of the world, except for you and yours have come on board with the chip. That would make me uncomfortable, to be the only country that has refused. It's almost as if it's a slight towards me and my people. That would make me uncomfortable, as it should you. Now, I will give you an hour to sit here and make your decision. After that I will be holding that press conference to inform the world of your decision. I'll leave you to your time now. I'm a busy person and have much to do today besides this," Jane says, then turns and walks with dignity to the door, the silence in the room deafening.

* * *

"Uncle, I don't know what to do next. Why is he not jumping at this offer? We have never done anything to cause his distrust. What will I tell the media, and the other countries when I have the conference in an hour. What if other countries back out because he refuses to accept this gift that he is being offered. What if he makes others feel the same way that he does?"

"Jane, calm, please calm yourself. I think at the end of the hour you will be surprised. There's no way that he will not join. He just needed to show you his control and power, something that he will never give up easily. I believe that's the point that he's making and I assure you, he will decide in your favor soon."

"How can you know that, Uncle? Has he said something to you about this?"

"My dear, of course he has not talked with me about this, but I've known him for many years. I know how he thinks and how very protective he is of not only his position but of his country."

"Okay Uncle, I believe you," Jane says, really smiling for the first time all day.

"I need to speak to you before we leave, tomorrow. I would have liked to have stayed a week or so, but things are starting to pick up at home and I need to be there. We still search for those that have caused trouble for me at home. I believe we are getting closer all the time. I'm anxious to be home to finish that problem. I do need you to do me a favor though, if you would."

"Of course Jane, anything, you know that I would do anything for you."

"There's a person I need you to contact. They have something that I will need for the New World Summit in Brussels in a few weeks. I promised my country a surprise and I want to make sure that all is in place for that moment. A moment that will never be forgotten, that will affect the whole world. What better place to announce it, show it, than at the New World Summit. Everyone in the world will be watching what's happening on that day."

"What is it Jane. What have you found?" the Shah asks, confused.

"I want it to be a surprise Uncle, and if I tell you, you won't be surprised. Can you please just contact this person for me? I promise, you'll love the surprise, but I won't tell you until I tell the world."

"Who is this person and where can I find him?"

"It's a her not a him, and she resides in Ethiopia, on a small island in the Blue Nile called Kidane Melesse. She answers to Kayin and doesn't speak English very well, but she gets by. She's waiting for this notification; she's been waiting for a long time. Please, don't ask anything more, let me surprise you. I promise it will be a very pleasant surprise, for you and everyone in the world."

"As you say Jane, I will send a couple of people to find her and bring her back for the New World Summit. That is where you want her to meet you, yes?"

"Yes, yes, thank you Uncle, thank you, I promise you won't regret this!" Jane says, excitement underlying her words, gleaming out of her eyes, visions dancing through her head, her day fast approaching when the world will know her for who she is, an abrupt knock on the door interrupting her dreams. "Come in" she says, the hall guard entering and informing her that Prime Minister Baladan wishes to speak with her. "Thank you, tell him I'll be right there," and with a short bow, he turns and leaves to do her bidding. "This is it Uncle. The final decision must have been made. We'll see what choice he has decided on. I hope for his sake it's the right one, oh and I have something you need to take to Kayin, otherwise she will listen but then without this item, she'll disappear. You need it in order for her to come along with you," she says quietly before leaving the room. As she walks down the hall, the excitement building in her because her day is finally drawing closer, all that she and her parents have worked their whole lives for soon to come to fruition, she automatically stands taller and enters the room in a much more regal manner, complete confidence in herself returning tenfold.

"President Martin," Prime Minister Baladan says quietly when she comes to a stop in front of him, arrogance staring back at him, a woman of true power facing him.

"Prime Minister Baladan," she says quietly yet with confidence.

"I have made my decision," he offers.

"I await your answer," she returns,

"I've decided to accept your offer, President Martin. What you have offered seems to be in good faith. I want the world to get along and if this is the means then so be it," he says graciously.

"Thank you, Sir. You will not regret your decision, I promise you," she offers with confidence. "Your chips have already been started, and can be delivered within the next few weeks. By the time of the New World Summit, your people will have had their chips started. I can't promise you that everyone will have theirs by then, but a good start will have been made."

"Thank you, President Martin, I appreciated you confidence in yourself to sell these chips to me," he adds dryly.

"I had confidence in your decision making process sir, not in your actual decision. I knew that if you had time to think about what all this could do for you, then the outcome would be the right one. And so it is, Sir," she says, a smile on her face, a glitter to her eyes.

"Yes, that's right. These will help me to rule my country. Why I had doubts, well, you would understand. It's a huge responsibility to take care of a country, to only want to do what will help the people and not harm them. There was much I needed to think over. I appreciate the time you allowed me, and your graciousness. I will not forget these things, President Martin."

"You're more than welcome, Sir. Now, the media's waiting. I promised them an interview after the decision was made. Would you like to attend this with me Sir?" she asks invitingly.

"I believe I'll let you do the honors, President Martin. I've been gone too long from my country and need to return as soon as possible. I'll leave you to give the announcement, and will be speaking with you soon?"

"Yes Sir. I'll contact you after I speak with Mr. Fahr about your chips, and if I have anything to add that I haven't thought of yet. I too am returning home tomorrow, I've been gone too long, also. It's hard to find someone to leave in control when you're not available and I feel more comfortable handling the reins to the country myself."

"I agree. I'll leave you now to your media briefing," he says black eyes glittering with gold sparks, before tipping his head in respect and leaving the room quietly, proudly.

After a quick glance around making sure she's alone she throws out her arms as far as they can go to her sides, palms up and with her head tipped back, a smile of pure joy on her face, she spins around the room, a quiet giggle all that's heard in a room of shiny glass, mirrors and white on white, the scent of flowers swirling through her head, a happiness flowing out of her that she's never felt before. When she stops spinning, she turns and see's both her parents standing near the door, happiness shinning on their faces, glowing from their eyes, her mother's face wet with tears.

"Ab'rar, you have succeeded! All our years of sacrifice and you've done it. It's coming together," she cries softly, turning to her husband her face glowing in happiness.

Chapter Twenty-Two

"Okay, we're back at camp now, let's see what we can get set up. We need to let Eli know everything that happened. This is definitely bigger than expected!" Mongoose says, truck squealing to a stop at base.

"He's probably in the office," Rand says loudly as he jumps out of the truck, Mongoose helping a tired Des out of the rear driver's side.

"What, did you say something?" Mongoose asks as he slams the truck door.

"I said," Rand starts to say before seeing the look on Mongoose's face. "Jerk," he adds with a grin, when they meet up in front of the office.

"Yeah, yeah, I know," Mongoose chuckles "get's him every time," he murmurs to Des in a calming voice while she's trying not to cower from the tone of Rand's voice. "Hey now, you don't need to be afraid, remember, I promised you, you never need to be afraid again," he reminds her.

"I know," she says quietly, teeth gritted, fear trying to push forward.

"It'll take time, but you'll get it, I promise."

"Yes I will," she says, standing slightly taller.

'Hey, you guys coming?" Rand asks loudly the door almost shut behind him. "I thought you left," he complains to Mongoose "when you didn't follow me in.

"No, we were just talking," Mongoose admits with a sheepish look, walking through the door with Des.

"Eli's in back, I already checked."

"Hey Eli," Mongoose says as he enters the last room at the back of the building, the makeshift office.

"Mongoose, Rand, it's good to see you both back in one piece," he admits as he slaps each one on the back. "Hello, Miss, welcome," he says to Des, who looks like a holocaust survivor, afraid to even meet his eyes. He glances at Mongoose, eyebrows raised in question, and see's the quick head shake and the word later mouthed.

"Eli, can we get together in about an hour?" Mongoose asks quickly before anyone has the chance to say anything. "Oh, sorry, this is Des. She's was at the camp. I'll tell you all about it after I get her settled. She's a little tired today, but a nap should help. I'll introduce her later to everyone, promise," he says after receiving an affirmative head shake from Eli. "Thanks man, appreciate it," he murmurs to Eli as he's leaving the room.

"So Rand, who was that and what was that all about?" Eli asks as he stares after Mongoose.

"That's a woman named Des. She held off our team by opening fire. We actually had a hard time stopping her she's a hell of a sniper. I think she gained Mongoose's respect and then maybe his pity when he finally got a good look at her. She's only about 5'5 or so, but doesn't even weigh a hundred pounds. She also carries around with her a haunted look, but she bends, she hasn't broken yet, so she has spine. I think maybe he's interested in her because of her steel spine. You gotta respect that!"

"True, true, so fill me in, will ya? How did it really go? What did you see? Was it as bad as we expected?"

"Oh hell Eli, it was worse, worse than anything we could have imagined. The smells, the looks of the poor people that were trapped in that building, how the guards abused and used them, it was bad, really, really bad! I'm not sure how they all survived, or why they even wanted to," Rand says, mixed expressions of disgust and pity crossing his face. "We made sure the medics arrived before we left. They're in good hands now, but God knows how long it'll take before they can leave. They haven't had food more than once a week for a long time, and at that it was the most minimal. It'll be a while before anyone of them are healthy enough to leave. But let me tell you, what Mal did, that worked like a charm. I sure am glad she's on our side," he adds with a smile, eyes sparkling just thinking of her now in D.C. but still managing to help out.

"Me too, who would have thought she'd be so smart. I mean, that stuff needs to be done it's really important stuff, but only someone like Mal would be able to figure it out. She constantly surprises me too," he admits with a shrug while walking towards the front door with Rand. "Anyway we're scheduled for a nine o'clock tonight with Jacob and Kat, so if you want to take off and get a little rest or something to eat, go ahead. I've got a few things to finish now that you guys are back, so let me get those things done so I'm ready for the next stage. We'll talk all about that later, before the video conference. Stop and let Mongoose know about the conference. He may be able to fit in a little rest too, before it begins again," he adds quickly when he see's Rand open his mouth with questions.

"You got it boss. I'll be back later. Sleep sounds pretty good right now. At this rate, I would only hinder the next stage, not help it and with everything that's going on now, we can't afford for anyone to slow us down. We're in for the fight of our lives," he mutters as he leaves the room, the sunlight causing him to squint, but in appreciation when he thinks of how those people were held, glad for his freedom.

***

"Hey everyone, let's quiet it down a little. Jacob should be showing up at any, wait, he's there, quiet," Eli yells when he gets no cooperation. In the sudden silence of the room he finally hears Jacob yelling his name over the connection, a look of frustration crossing his features when he finally says "Eli, it's about time you got control on your end, although I must say the conversations were pretty interesting," Jacob adds dryly.

'Sorry Jacob. Mongoose and Rand just got back today and this is the first that we've all gotten together. There's a lot of emotion happening and voices tend to get a little excited sounding when they've heard what we've heard. Anyway, we're here now so I'm going to give Mongoose and Rand the floor so they can get everyone caught up on what happened at the camp."

"Hey Jacob, glad to see you," Mongoose says as he moves closer to the computer screen so they can see him too.

"Mongoose, it's good to talk to you. I'm really glad you made it back. So, can you tell us what happened?"

"Sure, but I want to have Rand add his observations and experience too," Mongoose says waving for Rand to move closer to the camera too.

"Excellent, hey Rand, we're glad to see you made it out too," he says glancing at Mal and her full eyes as she stares at Rand through the monitor.

"Hey Mal," he says quietly with a wink as he sees her looking at him.

"Hi" she says softly as she moves a little further away so that the room on the other end of the video can't see her as clearly.

"Now, what we found when we got there, it's going to be hard to explain. Shocking, really shocking," Mongoose says as he begins the tale of how they took over the camp.

"The guards were all out when we got there; it couldn't have been too long after Mal initiated the chips. It was really weird and very cool," he adds with a grin towards Mal. "I don't know and really don't want to know how you did it Mal, but it worked like a charm. The only one's affected were the inside guards, like you said. I've also talked with a few of the perimeter guards who moved on to the next camp. None of those guards were affected either, so however you blocked them from knowing worked like a charm. Unfortunately, I'm not sure if they were all affected at the same time and we did find a very advanced radio system hidden off of the guard's dorm rooms. We checked inside, the guard in there was out but we're unable to determine if he had the time to get a message out to a different camp or even to the bosses in D.C. only time will tell," he adds seriously.

"The only shots fired were by one of the hostages. She's quite a sniper, maybe even good enough to give you some competition, Kat," he says teasingly.

"A hostage, you were fired on by a hostage?" she asks in disbelief, anger coming to the surface.

"You bet, Kat. She wasn't going to be taken again by anyone and after all she's endured, I totally understand her reasoning. She's here tonight, and I'll introduce you two in a few minutes. I want to finish this part of the report before we head in that direction."

"Fine," she snaps out, face cold, anger simmering, waiting for release.

"When we arrived at the camp, the perimeter guards were waiting for us. They had been gathering information for a few days and everything was ready. They were all pretty angry over the way they'd been duped. I think they all wanted justice. When we entered, we found an empty hallway, with doors that lead off of it, so we chose the first door on the right, just to start our sweep and we hit pay dirt. Inside that room was the room with all the men. The smells about knocked us to our knees. It was more like we'd entered a huge outhouse. I mean, it was dark in there, with a little light from the windows that were boarded up coming through. All the guys in there were either huddled together or on their own and sitting against the wall. It was eerily quiet, no one talked, no one even made a sound. Of course there were no guards in there either, but they probably never went in there. If they did they either used respirators or held their breath. We didn't get much of a reaction with the guys. I think they were expecting the worst and when they didn't get it then they started moving a little bit. They never said anything about themselves, but were genuinely concerned for their families. That was pretty much the only thing they asked about. We promised them we'd find them and come back, not one of them was in any condition to move through the camp in search of their families.

After that, we started a thorough search of the premise. Every guard was lying where he had been standing, so whatever you did to their chips, it took them out fast. It looked like they didn't have much time, they probably just passed out."

"Yeah, that's what the program was meant to do. I'm glad it worked like that. It gives you guys more time to rescue and them no time to prepare," Mal says relief in her voice.

"Yeah Mal, it worked exactly like that, so good job," Mongoose says sincerely, bringing a pleased blush to Mallory's face.

"It took us a few minutes to take care of a sniper, but once that was handled, we found the kids, and then the women, at least all the ones that were alive. From what we were told, the guards took the ones that had been there the longest, said they were taking them home, and would come back without them. No one ever asked the guards about that, I think they were afraid to know the truth, but did find out that whether it was man, woman or child, six months was the longest anyone had been there.

"Shit man, that's not good news, not good at all. Any idea what happened to them?"

"Yeah, we did a little investigating. It looks like they were all taken about fifty miles away, to a desolate area, a lot of acres with not a sign of anything. They probably have a mass grave there and just keep liming it when they bring more victims," Mongoose says, a loud gasp heard close by causing him to jerk his face in that direction, a look of pity seen crossing his features quickly before he recovers. "Rand, take over for a couple of minutes, thanks."

"Jacob, it was a war move that was done. I've heard of this before, during a war, but this is U.S. property and we are not at war at the moment. I think there's a bigger meaning behind this, but don't have any answers yet," Rand acknowledges, a low sound of weeping can be heard now in the room.

"Who is that," Jacob asks quietly.

"It's one of the women that were being held at the camp. She's actually the one that held us at bay for a few minutes, the sniper."

"Why is she in that room with you during this discussion? She needs to be removed, right now," Jacob orders.

"Wait sir, wait. I want to introduce you to Desdemona. She only shot at us to protect the children from us. It was totally understandable after everything she saw and heard," Mongoose says as he pulls Des closer so that the camera can see her face. Another loud gasp can be heard when Kat see's the woman's face for the first time.

"Des, is that really you?" Kat screams.

"Kat" Des questions once her eyes clear up and she can see who's talking to her.

"Oh my god, what happened to you?" Kat asks her face covered in shock, barely recognizing the woman who was her partner for years at D.C. Metro One, now a mere shadow of her former self, literally and figuratively.

"I was put in the camp when I told them I wanted my chip removed. I'd changed my mind," she admits slowly before slumping sideways in a faint.

"Whoa," Rand says as he tries to grab her before she hits the floor. "Help me take her to her room," Rand says.

"I'm sorry Jacob, I'll be right back," Mongoose says as he lifts Des, whose dead weight's not even enough to slump his back. He moves her with care, like a fragile piece of glass that could be shattered at any time.

"Eli, what's going on there? Why was she in the room during this meeting? She, of all people, should not have been present. We don't know what her allegiance is. She says she changed her mind, but did she really? From what I remember, she was pretty excited to get the chip, loved the President and all she promised and was firmly entrenched in the police in D.C. even after everything started changing for the worse. That doesn't sound terribly trustworthy to me." Jacob says.

"I agree, but if you'd seen her and Mongoose protecting her, I'd have to say things changed. Mongoose would never fall for that if it weren't true."

'I'd like to believe that, but with everything that Jane's pulled recently, we can't trust anyone. You'll have to guard her 24/7 from now on. She knows too much and could really hurt our work. We're running out of time, and can't afford for any of that to happen now! Jane's on her way back as we speak, and should be landing within the hour. Things are going to become even more heated now. We have to move faster if we're going to save anymore citizens and none of us can afford to have any new problems introduced into the mix. We're not even sure right at the moment how far Jane is involved in this. Chico should have some answers, which I'll have once he's back in town. She's coming home to get ready for the New World Summit which happens in less than two months. Not a lot of time with so many things to accomplish. We're all going to have to step up our game. It's a matter of life and death, the world as we know it."

"Wait now Snake, I know her. Sure she was seemingly entrenched in the ways of the president and fell for the whole 'this will only help you' propaganda that was going on last year, but she may have seen the truth. It's sounds as if she changed her opinions of the chip and wanted to rid herself of it. If she were working undercover for the President or anyone else for that matter, she certainly wouldn't look as if she'd been a prison detainee. That was too much even for her, trust me, I was her partner for years before this happened, no way could she starve herself like that, not for any job," Kat says, tears in her eyes.

"You're probably right, but I'm gonna need more proof before I can commit to that. I'm too cynical and Jane is way too ambitious, not to mention evil as far as I'm concerned."

"I agree, but I have no doubt that she'll prove to you that she is as she says."

"Fine, but for now we need to move the meeting on. What else have you got Eli? We'll come back to the camp info when Mongoose returns."

"I have men ready for the word for the rest of the camps. I wasn't sure how Mal wanted to work that. There's no way to accomplish this all in a day, but I am hoping for maybe a week, two tops?"

"I should be able to handle two weeks Eli. I've got the hardest part done, I just have to block the outgoing signals from each state and the towers they bounce off of before we can move on. I can do that probably seven to eight camps at a time. I'll figure that out tonight and let you know for tomorrow's meeting. Once that's figured out, it'll go fast, really fast, so you have to be completely sure before we begin. We can't change our minds once this is started."

"That's excellent Mal, I knew you could do it. Your computer skills are totally amazing," he adds with a grin.

"Thanks," she murmurs with a blush after seeing the grin on Rand's face and the promise in his eyes.

"What about you Jacob. How's transportation

246

going for the Summit?" Eli asks curiously.

"It's lining up. I've actually got transportation lined up for you guys a couple of weeks before the Summit, if you want to join us in D.C., prepare a little more and do some spying. There's something going on that she's excited about, I've heard chatter. It should be easy to find out what once she gets back here in the states. Chico may already know, I'm not sure, but I expect to talk with him before tomorrow night's video conference. Hang on, there's breaking news coming in right now."

"This is Jim Cochran of WELT News Channel 3, Washington D.C. This is breaking news from earlier today. We have also collected opinions from U.S. citizens on how they feel about this announcement. The meeting in Iran was completed and the President is making the announcement to our media counterparts, here she is now,"

"Thank you everyone," Jane says as she arrives at the podium elegant in a long sleek black gown, hair swept up and off her face, "for waiting such a long time for this announcement. The meetings are finally finished and I wanted to be the first to announce that every country in the entire world has agreed on the chips and the invaluable help they are going to give to each and every country. I can honestly say that this is the first time in history that there is PEACE IN THE MIDDLE EAST and in the whole world. At no time in history has this occurred. These are indeed exciting times," she finishes with a laugh of excitement, almost pretty with her face flushed and glowing in pleasure, applause growing louder and louder becoming uncontrollable and making any further comments impossible.

"Kat, tape that please, I'm interested in hearing the comments from the citizens, but I don't want to waste our time on that now," Jacob orders while turning back to Eli at the camp in Texas, a look of unbelief on his brothers face.

"That's the first that you heard that message, Eli?"

"Yeah, I believe it's the first for any of us," he says, shaking his head. "I'm finding these things harder and harder to take in Jacob. What has happened to the people in this country? They're just going along with everything that she says. Have they all lost their minds?" he asks disgust and fear evident in his voice.

"Unfortunately, yes, they've lost their minds and live in constant fear. You know this has been 'a me' world for so long that no one thinks of the long term. They concentrate totally on the now, how they're affected and what good it can do for them, to hell with anyone or anything else," Jacob reminds him curtly.

"I know, but I had hoped that common sense would prevail and things would get a little easier on the home front, especially in protecting our people against them."

"Right . . "

"Mongoose, glad you made it back," Jacob says when he sees him enter the room again.

"Now, I can honestly say that you're wrong about Des. She's straight. I trust her, especially after everything that she's been through. I know that I haven't known her long, what can I say? I may not have known her as long as Kat has but I've certainly known her as well if not better. I met her at her lowest point in life, just before death, I'm sure. We've spent a lot of time talking, about before, what happened and regrets."

"Whoa, Mongoose. No need to get defensive. I trust you and your opinions completely. If I didn't you wouldn't be a part of this," Jacob reminds him.

"Yes sir, thanks sir. I appreciate it. We have worked together a long time."

"Damn right we have, now report soldier."

"Yes sir! We arrived at the camp early seven days ago. We entered minutes after Mal gave the all clear signal. Upon entry, we were directed by Dave, the escaped hostage into the men's area. The room was dark and like walking into an open outhouse, which I believe it was nothing more than that. The living arrangements were deplorable sir. Anyone left in there longer than the six months would certainly have died an early death from disease. I'm hoping that those that were close to the six months that they were usually left inside don't have disease already. Once we got inside, all the guards were unconscious. The program worked like a charm Mal. You did awesome!"

"Thanks Mongoose, appreciate it."

"After inspecting the ground floor and retrieving any guards (we then stashed them where the male prisoners were kept, we all thought it would be a just reward) we started clearing out the whole compound. The women didn't have it much better, they were closer to the guard rooms, but I believe that was only for the guard's convenience. The children were kept close to their quarters too, but I can't talk about why yet. It makes my blood boil. After getting half way to the upstairs, we came under attack from an (unknown at that time) sniper. After finally being able to get close enough, I was able to disarm her, she was definitely in a weakened state, but totally determined that no one was going to touch a child, not with her around! Once all signs of threat were taken care of, we contacted the guardsmen and they sent in medics. Everyone there needed medical help, some worse than others. We helped clean up the areas where the prisoners are at this time recovering, before being allowed to leave for home. During that time, I spent a lot of time talking with any prisoner that was up to conversation and willing to talk. Some of the stories are very disturbing, sir."

"I'm sure they are. We can discuss them at another time unless they pertain to what we're in the middle of doing?"

"Another time, sir, is fine."

"Good, then continue."

"I have spent the past few days retrieving any information that Des had, even the smallest of things. Like I said, she wasn't involved. She stated that she took the chip in good faith. She was positive that it was a good thing that was being done and would help every citizen in the states, just like Jane promised. But then she noticed strange things happening, in places that should have been safe. She said she watched someone in a grocery store steal something, just something small, that they probably would have been hand slapped for by the law, scream, and drop whatever it was they had stolen and fall to the ground. Just a minute or two later a soldier showed up to take them to jail. She said it was by no means a coincidence. Someone had to have used the chip for other than what Jane promised. After that, she paid closer attention to things. She said it was as if someone was watching everything everyone did and then they sent some kind of a command to the chips, since this only happened to those with the chips. Depending on the command, something would happen to them. Whether they screamed, were shocked or even knocked unconscious, something always happened. That's when she decided to get rid of hers. She didn't want some stranger capable of making her do things to have that right. She went to the people who placed the chips and was told they could not be removed. Once you had the chip, it was there. Well, after talking to her, I know her enough by now that there's no way she would have stood for that answer, and she didn't. She went home and removed the chip herself. I'm sure it wasn't pleasant but it wasn't as bad as what they could have done to her."

"Wow, they actually told her they couldn't remove it?" Kat asks appalled.

"Yep, they did. But they also told her it couldn't be removed. That they put a special chemical on it and if you tried to remove it, they would know and hurt her before she had the time to get it out. She of course didn't believe everything she heard, but she said she'd have removed it anyway, that she'd rather die before allowing them to do that to her. They pretty much take all your freedoms away."

"Wow," Jacob murmurs, dismayed at the

potential.

"But she removed it, and didn't die, so they must have lied about that too!"

"No sir, she removed it in such a way as to keep the removing hidden from them. She removed it so fast that they couldn't have had the time to do something to her. She did place it somewhere where they'll never figure out, at least until it's too late," he says with a smirk.

"Where, where'd she put it?" Kat asks.

"She said you'd know Kat. She mentioned it a long time ago during one of your investigations, something about a cemetery for pets?"

"Yeah, I remember," Kat says before losing it and collapsing in laughter. "It's the pet cemetery, the one in PA. The one we investigated for the murder that started this whole process. I remember she was pretty impressed with it, said it was probably more expensive than a lot of people cemetery's."

"That's what she said too," Mongoose adds thoughtfully. "Anyway, after she removed it a mark showed up, similar to a tattoo in a green color and it's still there, non-faded. It informs them that she had a chip placed and either tried or successfully removed it. Either way, if they find you with that mark, they send you to the camps. The people believe the camps are just that, a place to go and think about getting the chip. Not somewhere that you're punished for not taking the chip or for removing it."

"Thank you Jane Martin for making the United States a dictatorial state, instead of the free choice that so many generations fought for and have grown used to," Jacob says angrily.

"If only the people would have paid attention, this could have been stopped," Eli says quietly. "Unfortunately, it's too late now. It's gone way too far for an easy fix."

"But something has to be done," Des says as she comes through the door that she'd been standing outside of, listening in on the conversation. "You can't let this continue on. People are dying," she says, tears streaming down her cheeks.

"I thought I told you to stay put," Mongoose says when he reaches her side.

"I couldn't, I'm part of this. I have to do something I can't just stand back and watch the innocents end up where I was. Suffer even greater torture than I did."

"How did they catch you Des?" Kat asks during a lull in the conversation.

"I went out to Texas's The Peoples Church, I was hoping for sanctuary and some answers to questions that have popped into my mind, with everything that's been going on. Between the strange weather, the volcanos, and the President, I was starting to get a little uncomfortable. I went to a Methodist church when I was growing up, and I don't remember a lot of the things I learned, but there was some talk back then about Revelations and the terrible things that would happen during the end times. For some reason, I connected what's happening now with what could happen. If you take out of Revelations the fanciful things and interconnect them to things from now, you'll see a definite similarity. Two thousand years ago, they didn't know what airplanes were, nor cars, or even the internet, but our modern society is connected to all of those things in Revelations, we just call them different names. If you think about it, plagues don't have to be "old time plagues," but could be our time plagues, like biological weapons or nuclear weapons! We've had tons of earthquakes, volcanic eruptions in places that we haven't had in hundreds of thousands of years, tsunamis that have destroyed whole countries, and now we have the chip. I also think I heard about meteor's (wouldn't that be comparable to fire from the sky, like the bible proclaims) on target to hit the earth? Or maybe even multiple meteors? There are places right now on this earth where people are dying from lack of water, lack of food. It's all there it's just how you look at it. If you take it literally, then you'll believe that maybe someday this will happen, but can't imagine it because things are so different now compared to two thousand years ago. But if you look around and exchange old words with new, then I think it'll scare you. I know it does me."

"F*$#k, she's right," Kat yells into the quiet after Des' impassioned speech. "She's right, why, why didn't I think in that direction? I knew there was something that was there, something big, but I never considered this. Tell me Des did you hear the news release a couple of minutes ago?"

"No I didn't, why?" Des asks hesitantly, tiredly.

"Well, President Martin came over the satellite from Iran earlier today and told the world that every country in the world has finally accepted the chip. She was really excited about it, and then she proceeded to notify the world that there is now officially PEACE IN THE MIDDLE EAST" Kat exclaims and watches helplessly as Des gasps and collapses to the floor in a dead faint.

"Nice catch Mongoose," Jacob says dryly as Mongoose sits on the floor with Des a dead weight in his lap, having caught her milliseconds before she hit.

"Thanks," he says surprised, not expecting to really catch her, but trying anyways. "Rand, a little help here," he orders before noticing he's on his way.

"Look Eli, let's meet back here tomorrow night, same time. Just make sure Des is available, I know Kat's gonna want to talk to her."

"Sounds good, Jacob, we'll see you tomorrow night."

Chapter Twenty-Three

"It's good to be home," Jane says with a deep sigh, tired beyond her years. "I think I'll head into my rooms and try to get some sleep. I won't be able to function like this for long, and I have a feeling I'm going to need all my faculties about me after my media announcement earlier today. I'm doubtful that the whole country took that news good, the majority probably did, but not everyone," she finishes with a small smile.

"Yes, darling, you need to rest. You have important duties to work on. Your father and I will retire to our rooms also. I believe we could use some rest too."

"Good idea Mom. Chico, take the rest of the day off. We're home, safe and sound. My parents won't leave the building without you, so you're no longer needed today."

"Thank you President Martin. I could use some rest, too. It's been a busy week."

"Yes it has. Good night then Chico," Jane says dismissively. "Night Mom, Dad," she says kissing their cheeks before leaving the room.

"Lt. Callander, its Chico. We just arrived, no more than thirty minutes ago. I think we should meet up somewhere safe. I have a lot to fill you in on."

"I agree Chico. Glad you made it back in one piece. Let me think," Jacob says after acknowledging him. "There's an old coffee shop about ten minutes from where you are now. It was called Mike's Coffee House. I believe it's abandoned now so we should be able to meet there without problems. How about half an hour? It takes me that long to get there from where we are."

"Sounds good, I'll meet you there at about twenty-two thirty, Sir."

"Chico, you here," Jacob asks after he and Kat arrive at Mike's, doors all closed, no sign of anyone, darkness covering the building inside and out.

"It looks so deserted, ramshackle almost," Kat murmurs as they walk around the building to the back. "This place used to be so busy, bright and full of life," she says sadly. "So much happened here, it's where we met the first time," she adds.

"I know kitten, I remember. Mike's gone, Devon's gone, so many things have changed."

"yeah, so many things . . ." she agrees almost silently.

"Wait, did you see that? I slight shift in shadows, shh, you stay with me, cover my back," Snake says as they approach an area near the back door.

"Chico," Snake says almost silently. "Sir," he hears as he gets closer to the shadow. "Chico, glad you could make it," Snake says as he re-holsters his weapon, relieved that no one else is lurking in the area. "Let's go in where we can talk. Not many people venture out at this time anymore or in this area. It's become pretty desolate."

"Yes Sir," he hears, "Ms."

"Come on Kat, " Snake says as he enters the back room, moving around the dark interior pulling all the shades, keeping the dark inside and out before lighting a small bulb near the corner of the room. "Chico, it's good to see you again. It's been awhile," Snake says as he makes contact with Chico and reaches out a hand to shake.

"It has been, Sir," Chico says shaking the hand of his superior officer.

"Let's sit," Kat says as she gathers some chairs near the light, far enough away from any window or door to feel comfortable that even if someone were trying to hear what's being said, they'd be unable to.

"So, how was Iran," Snake asks after everyone's seated.

"The palace was amazing, Sir. The shah, very polite and his money just ooze's from him, but he seemed friendly enough. There's definitely a familial connection between the Shah, Jane and her parents. It's not a close relation, maybe a cousin four or five times removed. But they are blood. Someone was definitely after either Jane or her parents. We had a small problem when we first arrived, during the trip between airport and palace. We were actually caught unaware when a sniper started shooting at us and we had to take some special precautions. The guard standing with the Shah was injured, but overall, we made it safely. I think Jane's parents about had a heart attack during the skirmish, and even though they come from that type of background, they've been out of that area since Jane was borne. Once we were in the palace, my duties were more restricted. Jane didn't feel her parents needed me much while inside since the palace is extremely well guarded. That just gave me the time I needed to explore. I heard a few things on my jaunt through the palace, though. Found a few hiding places so I could pick up some information. Sir, Jane really believes she's the one running everything, but she's been kept in the dark. I overheard the Shah talking to someone on the phone, someone from here in the states. Best guess, by what was said, is the Vice President. It sounds like there's a whole lot between those two and that Jane is just a figurehead. The Shah did say that the world was ready for a woman, but that the real power lay beneath her, not in her hands. Then he laughed at something the other one said and he said 'not to worry Quinton, it will all be exactly as you've prepared for. She'll never see it coming, and in the end, you'll be the rightful ruler of the world."

"What!" Kat gasps as Snake just looks at Chico, his mind reeling, thoughts flying.

"Yeah, Jane's not the leader of this; she's just a puppet a very dangerous puppet but a puppet nonetheless.

"Wow," Snake murmurs shaking his head.

"Sir, the things she has planned have been fed to her, encouraged by Quinton. He's planted ideas and helped to shape what's happening then stood in the back ground and watched all hell break lose. He even made her believe that she's the one responsible, the next ruler of the world. Quinton's the real leader and his second, none other than the General of the Armies. The United States is screwed, but then they positioned themselves in such a way as to guarantee our total collapse and their total control.

"Holy shit, this wasn't expected. I never saw that coming, Jane's worked in such a way that she's made sure to claim and have all the power. The people have followed her, they've turned a blind eye to the bad things that she's done and focused on what she's done to help them. As expected, the country's fallen right into what they had planned. Now, with the chips and all the foreign soldiers in the states, not to mention the politicians mostly gone, all but a few of her close friends, we really have no head to the country except her. Is Quinton going to lead through her, do you think, or is he going to get rid of her and take over her position?"

"I'm not sure what the final plans are, Sir, I can only guess. I know she's like a kid in a candy shop. She's got something planned, and truthfully, I don't think even Quinton knows about it. She set it in motion while in Iran, sent some of the Shah's men out to retrieve something, a gift for the people, she calls it. She says it's a huge surprise, and the Shah just smiles like a doting uncle would."

"Hmm, I'll have to look further into that. Thanks for all the info. We've got quite a bit too. You can catch up on all of that if you want to join us tomorrow night for our nightly video-conference. We check in with Eli and that group nightly, and have been pretty busy there with the Courtesy Camp take down and the schedule of further camp takeovers."

"The courtesy camp, Sir, I'm not sure I'm familiar with that," Chico says in confusion, fatigue starting to cloud his thinking.

"Come to the meeting tomorrow night, twenty-one hundred. I'll give you the address; just make sure you're not tailed. You'll hear all about the camps and what we found."

"Glad to Sir!"

"Good, now go home, get some sleep. You look like you're starting to fade."

"I am Sir; it's been a long day."

"It looks like we'll need to step up our preparations. We're going to need more transportation for Brussels. I'll call Stan again, and see what he recommends. You contact Professor Rosenthal and get an update on the meteor. It has to be getting really close by now. It's been about a month since his talk with Jane," Snake says to Kat as they leave the coffee shop.

"I'll get on the Professor thing. It feels like there are a lot of things starting to wind up. We're getting close to something; I'm just not sure what. My whole body feels like it's hyped."

"Yeah, I can feel it too. Maybe we should use up some of this excess energy," he says with a grin, thoughts of what they can do to fix the problem giving him that intense look of want, eyes narrowed in memory, concentration and promise causing Kat to flush with memory, her groin clenching in need.

"Stop Snake, don't look at me that way," she says breathlessly.

"No problem kitten, I can wait, a few minutes at least," he promises. "We'll be home in just a few more minutes," me murmurs seductively, heat in every tone, every movement.

"God Snake, you better speed this car up, I can't wait much longer," she gasps.

"I'm already going ninety Kitten, and we can't afford to be stopped by the cops, for more than one reason," he adds teasingly.

"Ohhh, stop Snake, please," she groans, discomfort enclosing her temporarily.

"Shh, it's okay," he says as he grabs her hand to steady her.

"Here we" he says as he feels her hand pulled from his and hears her door slam shut, and finds her waiting at the door for him, clothes half off already.

"In a hurry Kitten?" he asks innocently.

"Shut up and go in Snake, now or I won't be responsible for my actions. I know it's dark out, but for all those neighbors that can see in the dark, they're going to get an eyeful in about two seconds if you don't get in and shut up," she says breathlessly as she jumps him, wrapping her legs around him as soon as she shuts the door behind them.

"Now this is what I was thinking," she groans into his mouth, lips attached firmly to his, hands working frantically to touch him wherever possible, removing clothes as she goes.

"Yeah, me too," he whispers back, hands just as busy but faster, much faster than hers she realizes when she feels the room air touching bare skin everywhere as he walks her down the hall, attached to his waist with her strong thighs. With a slight movement, he slowly lowers her to the bed, filling her to the max firmly, the whole process causing her to groan with excitement and need.

"Ahhh, yes, that's it Snake, that's it," she says breathlessly as he covers her with his body, hands cupping her buttocks, keeping her firmly positioned, raising her to take even more of him.

"I love you Kitten," Snake murmurs before kissing her mouth, her cheeks, her neck and then her breasts, breasts that harden him even more with excitement. "You're so tight, so hot Kat, I can't wait any longer, hold on, ahhh, yeah, that's it," he says as he starts slamming home, over and over until both are gasping for air, the edge coming closer, closer until with a gasp out of both mouths, a tightening and a hardening causing an explosion of mass proportion, lights flashing behind closed lids they slowly loosen their hold on each other, keeping the other close, not willing to lose the feeling they just experienced.

"Wow," he whispers in awe, his breathing labored yet slowing, awareness coming back. "Are you okay?" he asks worriedly.

"Yeah, I'm fine, I'm more than fine," she answers breathlessly. "Wow, Snake, that was . . ." she finishes, unable to put into words what just happened.

"Yeah, it was . . ." he agrees but "I'm not done yet, I just got started," he adds as his body slows to normal and he tightens his hold on her again.

"Whoa Snake, give me a couple of minutes. I'm tired," she says, eyes closed, body almost sleeping.

"Sure sweetheart, just a couple of minutes," he says hearing a slight snore come from her lips, and with a soft smile he tucks her next to him tightly, lays his head near her breast and finds comfort in sleep.

Chapter Twenty-Four

"Quinton, it's good to be back," Jane says upon entering the oval office.

"Welcome Jane. I hope everything went well with you during your visit," he says as he stands to meet her, having waited for the past hour for her to show up.

"It was awesome, Quinton. Everyone is finally on board. I had doubts, I must say about Israel, but they finally came around."

"So I heard," he says quietly.

"Now, we need to move on with our plans. The New World Summit is coming up, and I have prepared the way. The next step, of course, will be to formally accept their offer," she says, voice brusque, all business.

"Their offer being the final available seat at the table?" he says acknowledging his knowledge of her plans.

"That's right, the seat that's been waiting for me," she informs him arrogantly.

"When will you be notifying them of your decision?" he asks carefully.

"Not right away, it's always good to keep something back. Anyway, I prefer to wait till the last moment before letting that information out. Anything happen here while I was gone?" she asks curiously.

"A few small things, some that shouldn't bother you, but there are a few things you need to know," he says.

"Oh, what things?" she asks busy sorting through her mail, listening with one ear.

"It seems that the courtesy camps have been infiltrated," he says, waiting for her reaction.

"What's a courtesy camp," she asks attention split while reading a letter addressed to her from her friend the professor.

"A courtesy camp is something that I created for the Americans that have refused to take your chip. They think it's a vacation area where they can go for a few weeks to think about the chips and what the future holds for them when they accept them or what happens to them if they don't. A place where they can gain information from both sides while being pampered in a luxurious manner," he adds contemptuously.

"It isn't a place like that, I take it from the tone of your voice. Also, who gave you the right to 'create' something like this for MY people," she asks sharply.

"I don't need your permission, Jane. Remember?" he snaps sarcastically.

"Oh contraire' Quinton, you need my permission for everything. This is my country, remember? I will not tolerate you overstepping your boundaries. You are nothing, I'm the President, remember?"

"Jane, I am the Vice President, am I not," he

reminds her.

"Yes, of course you are, but only because the people expected me to appoint one. I thought you understood that your position is nothing, just a figure head, nothing more," she snaps.

"I did not, nor will I act as just a 'figure head'. I will stand beside you Jane, for now, but in future, I may do more," he warns her.

"No way, Quinton, you will never be more. I warn you now, I have many friends, friends that helped me, guided me and created who I am to do what I am doing. Nothing you say or do will alter the course that I am embarked on. This is what I was born to do and I will succeed! Now tell me about these camps that you created, what exactly happened. I have a feeling they can be detrimental to what I have accomplished thus far."

"Jane," he says around a laugh "they have worked for the past year, a year may I remind you, that you had no idea they existed. There may be many more things that are happening in this country that you are totally unaware of. How does that make you feel, President Martin," he sneers dragging out her name in a derogatory manner, anger smoldering beneath his words.

"That's enough Quinton. Leave me now. I'll gain the information from other sources. I suggest you make yourself scarce, you're about to cross a very dangerous line," she says coldly, anger snapping her spine straight, eyes icy cold.

"I'll leave you now, Jane. But be warned, we're not through here. This is not over," he snaps as he slams the door closed after him.

"Good morning to me," she says huffily. *What*

the hell's been going on around here? Why did that just happen, she wonders as she walks to the window looking out on a sunny cloudless day, pondering. "Get me the General," she snaps into the phone before tossing it back on the desk.

"Teriq?" she says when she picks up the ringing phone.

"President Martin, you wanted to talk with me?" he asks politely.

"Yes, where are you right now?" she demands.

"I'm at the Pentagon, what can I do for you?" he asks.

"I need you at the White House. There have been some things that have happened while I was gone that I need to discuss with you."

"I can be there in about an hour, if that would be okay. I just need to finish a couple of things then I'm all yours, Jane."

"Excellent Teriq, I'll order lunch. We can eat and talk."

"Come in Teriq," Jane says when she spy's him standing in the door. "Have a seat, lunch is ready," she finishes once he walks towards her.

"Hi Jane, I hope everything went well in Iran, and you had a good visit," he says quietly as he gets to the table.

"It was great, really great. It's always nice to visit family and the small summit that I had went extremely well. In case you hadn't heard, every country is now on board for the chips. This will make my goals that much easier," she adds, smiling.

"It will indeed. It's good to know that those

leaders understand the true need for the chips and how beneficial they'll be for them."

"Well, it did take a little longer to convince Israel, but they finally committed, so it was worth the extra time. I can honestly say now things will be as they should have been for a long, long time."

"Excellent, Jane, that's wonderful."

"Yes it is, and now, I have a few questions for you. I spoke with Quinton this morning and he informed me of something that happened in the states that I was not aware of. Maybe you can shed some light on this subject. What is it that you can tell me about the 'courtesy camps?' I was not aware that there was such a thing, so anything you can tell me would be appreciated."

"The 'Courtesy Camps," Jane, "you were the one that gave the orders to set these places up, were you not, President Martin?"

"No, I didn't give any such orders. However, a man in your position should have looked for orders from me regarding these places, shouldn't you have? I mean, you work for me, don't you Teriq?"

"Of course I do, President Martin. You made me your General of the Armies, after General Bossley was killed. It's an honor to be in this position for you," he murmurs, slightly nervous now.

"That's right Teriq; it is an honor for you to have been chosen by me for this position. When you were placed into that position, I remember telling you that you take your orders from me, and only me. I gave you the position and can take it away at will, but you still have not answered my question completely, Teriq. What can you tell me about these places?"

"Umm, well, there's one located in each of the fifty contiguous United States along with one in Puerto Rico and in Alaska. We didn't put one in Hawaii, we just fly them to California, to that camp, since the logistics for Hawaii were too difficult to maintain. The citizens go to the camp, usually voluntarily, if they reject the chips. They're told the camps are like a vacation, giving them more info about the chips to help them make their decisions. The program has worked very well, I must say Jane."

"Good, good," she murmurs. "What happens to them if they still choose not to take the chips?"

"Well, if after six months, they still choose not to take the chips, they're escorted from the camp and killed. We've made sure that their bodies will never be found."

"Who escorts them, who are actually in control of these camps?"

"Quinton told me you wanted the Iranian guards in charge of the camps, and since it frees up our own soldiers, I thought it made sense knowing that the United States military would hardly want involved in this whole process. They guard the perimeter of the camps, and the Iranian guards are on the inside with the prisoners."

"I see," she says thoughtfully, eyes downcast, fire roaring through them. "Well Teriq, it looks as if you made a very big mistake. Instead of taking orders only from me, you've been doing Quinton's bidding. You should have checked with me first, before you started this. I understand it was a while ago, but now, now we pay for your foolishness," her voice gaining in loudness as she pushes away from the table, the food all but forgotten. "I can't condone what you've done. You, you who were put into one of the highest positions in this country, you've betrayed me. You've acted on orders that should never have been given. I can't turn my back for a second and you help to create this, damn it," she yells finally, throwing her napkin down and then her water glass across the room, a tinkling sound all that's left from the crash of glass and mirror.

"President Martin, wait, I was under the impression that you knew all about these camps. That Quinton was doing what you had requested of him. Besides, I was told that Quinton would be taking charge, would become the new Pres i d e n t . . ." he says, voice dwindling after he realizes what he just said, recognizing sudden awareness light up her eyes, feeling the danger emanating from her now still figure.

"Well, well," she says softly, watching him thoughtfully as she walks towards her desk, disappointment teaming with anger just below the surface, expressionless as she stops by her desk. "Teriq," she says as she reaches for her phone, "remember what I demonstrated for you a few months ago? My capabilities and how they felt for you that day?"

"Yes President Martin, I remember perfectly," resignation in his voice, knowledge of his own death moments away.

"Then you should have been more careful in your choices. Quinton will never be President; Quinton will never have that power."

"I beg to differ with you President Martin. Since I'm to die shortly anyway, I will say what needs to be said. You are President only by Quinton's grace and by the Shah's as well. You know as well as anyone that we will not answer to a woman. Your place was never to be true President; you've only ever been just a figure head. The power that you had was just for looks. The true power comes from Quinton. He answers to no one, not even the Shah . . ." he gasps out as she pushes the button, his life drains from his body and he slumps to the floor.

"Sorry to cut you short Teriq, but you are wrong. I am the power, the one born to do this job, the one and only," she finishes, a smile in her voice and a fierce look of pride and ownership on her face. "Dana, please send for the medics," she says to her receptionist. "I think the General just had a heart attack. He's not breathing, please hurry," she orders, fake concern in her voice.

Chapter Twenty-Five

"Morning Kitten, how did you sleep," Snake asks pouring her a cup of coffee as she wanders towards him, combing her fingers through her hair to get it to lay down, *a waste of time since it looks like she slept standing on her head*, he thinks with a grin.

"Morning Snake," she murmurs pink cheeked "what are you grinning about?"

"How beautiful you are in the mornings," he lies smoothly, eyes sparkling with devilment.

"Yeah, right," she snorts back at him as she grabs her cup, not one to turn down coffee. "So what's on target for today?"

"Let's turn on the TV and see if there are any new developments out there. Then we can talk about priorities."

"I'll get the TV, you got the coffee."

"Great, I'll meet you in the living room. You want some breakfast?" he yells as she leaves the room.

"Not right now, I'm not awake enough yet, but thanks," Kat yells back while grabbing the remote and hitting the local stations.

"Hi, I'm Jim Cochran of WELT News Channel 3, Washington D.C. with breaking news," Snake hears as he walks into the living room. "Good timing," he adds as he settles next to Kat on the couch.

"General Teriq Auliya has been pronounced dead today shortly after arriving at the White House for brunch with the President. President Martin herself requested that 911 be called after claiming that the General seemed to have had a heart attack. The Coroner will make that call but agrees that it does indeed look like a heart attack. He'll have the results after he performs the autopsy, later today. President Marten admits to being "slightly shook up since she and the General were alone when he collapsed. She stated that she's saddened by his loss, and that she depended on his help in keeping the country running smoothly what with all the new things that have been instituted. She did say that 'he will be hard to replace.' This is the second General that has died in the past year, since President Martin became president, the first one found murdered. She'll need to appoint a new General as soon as possible since the country is still under martial law and the General is the one in charge of that. Let's hope the third appointee will be the charm. I'm sure there'll be more information forth coming. You can be assured that as soon as that information is available, you'll have it."

"And now, more breaking news, a larger eruption has occurred at Yellowstone, the phones have been ringing off the hook at the United States Geological Survey with reports of multiple small eruptions being reported in all corners of the world. The cause of all of these eruptions has yet to be determined. There are reports of deaths that have occurred, especially in the high population areas. Yellowstone is a very low population area while in other parts of the world the people are definitely being affected. Due to the toxic air that occurs because of the eruptions, people are being asked to please stay indoors as much as possible. If you do need to go outside for anything, please cover your nose and mouth. Hospitals are being inundated by the injured and won't be able to maintain a high level of care if everyone in the areas affected show up. So please, if you're not seriously injured, please stay home, inside, close all your windows and doors, and also any air conditioners or furnaces that use outside air. By turning those things off you'll be able to keep your inside air cleaner longer. Thankfully, that's all the immediate breaking news for now. We'll be back with any new information regarding both the General and the eruptions that are occurring right now. This is Jim Cochran of WELT News Channel 3, Washington D.C."

"Wow," Kat says shocked. "I'm to the point that I don't want to watch the news anymore. Every time we turn it on, something bad has happened. What'll be next, do you think?" she asks Snake who's sitting as if he's made out of stone. "Snake," she says as she jabs him with her elbow. A grunt is all she hears for a couple of seconds before he finally focus's.

"Wow," he says, parroting her before he realizes what he just said. "This is big, kitten, really big. It's as if the worlds gone crazy. I don't believe that the General died from a heart attack either. Shit, things are starting to go crazy. We talked about this but I guess I never really thought it would happen. What's our next move, what do we need to do next?" he murmurs, eyes still slightly glazed with all the information, a cell phone ringing in the back ground.

"I'll get it," Kat says as she jumps up, eyes scanning the room for the ringing noise. "Ha," she breathes "there you are," grabbing the phone on the dining room table. "This is Kat," she answers, then becomes silent as she listens to the speaker on the other end, eyes getting larger as she hears what's being said. "You're sure, absolutely positive?" she asks, voice louder than she realizes. "I'm not sure what we can do, but I'll talk with Jacob and we'll get back to you. Thank you, thank you very much for letting me know this, I really appreciate it," she says breathlessly before hanging up, spinning around and with half a step finding herself chest to face again with Snake, and with a sense of déjà vu, she shakes her head quickly as he reaches out to steady her while telling him who just called, "that was Rosenthal, and he said it would be within the next seventy-two hours. Seventy-two hours, that's all the notice we get," she cries loudly and in disbelief. "Why didn't he call us sooner," she asks knowing he doesn't have the answer, yet hoping that he can do something.

"You're sure that was Rosenthal, you didn't get him mixed up with someone else," he asks, mind spinning with all the ramifications of what the hell just happened in the world.

"Of course I'm sure," she snaps disbelief on her face that he even asked that stupid question. "What do you take me for, and imbecile? Of course

I know who I talked to," she finishes in disgust. "That doesn't answer the question of what we're going to do, Snake, What are we going to do," she screams as he pulls her forward and tucks her under his chin, finding comfort in her touch, grounding him during all the craziness surrounding them right now.

"I was just stalling, that's all. I know you know who you were talking to, I just needed a minute to gather my thoughts. I wasn't expecting anything like this, well, maybe I was, but not everything happening at once. I don't know what to do next. Let me think for a few minutes. Let's watch the TV and see if there are any more updates," he says calmly as he walks her back to the couch. "I think one of the first things we need to do is call Eli. We're going to need them here, sooner than we thought. That's the first order of business. Then maybe talk to Chico. He can help with info from inside the White House. There will probably be a news briefing soon from Jane since she never misses an opportunity to talk to the press and now she's got lots to talk about," he finishes matter-of-factly, feeling her muscles unclench finally.

"This is Jim Cochran of WELT News Channel 3, Washington D.C. with some updates on the volcanic eruptions that have occurred worldwide today. The death count has risen sharply since our last news briefing due to an eruption at the Karanetang (Api Siau) volcano in Indonesia. The volcano is the most active one in that country, and it actually contains five summit craters. Unfortunately, the location of this huge volcano affected a huge population. The heat, the ash and the lava flow have created an unequivocal disaster. That country has never seen an eruption this large, and it's still erupting. They have contacted the President for help, stating that more than half of the population that lived at the base of the volcano is gone, some buried, some suffocated from the ash while the majority got caught up in the lava zones and perished trying to escape. As of this moment, there have been eleven reported eruptions from eleven different volcanoes out of eleven different countries. Let's hope that's the total and there are no unreported incidents. The United States has suffered a large eruption in the heart of the West. This eruption affects the United States as none other in our more than two-hundred years. We have reports from as far out as western Wyoming to as near as Kentucky and places surrounding Yellowstone, reports of deaths, ash burials, lava fires and yet through all of this we can't compare to what Indonesia is experiencing, the world's gone crazy. We've sent our best reporters out to get video, so they'll have pictures and interviews as soon as they're able. Tune back in later today for those updates. We have also been in contact with some experts at the USGS and will have a Mr. Jeff MacCormick, a volcanologist with the USGS, Washington D.C. branch. He's agreed to an interview this afternoon, as soon as he's available. This is Jim Cochran of WELT News Channel 3, Washington D.C."

"Well, I wonder what time that'll be on. It's not as if we can just sit here and wait for him to become available," Kat says disappointed.

"Actually, what else can we do? There's chaos anywhere that there was an eruption. I'm sure some of the General's troops have taken over until the next appointment. Jane needs to be careful though; there are a lot of Iranian troops on this soil, a takeover try would not be good right now. Even though the American troops could handle them, it's just the rallying of our guys. There's a little bit of discontent among our troops, not that I can blame them. But it is what it is. This is the United States of America, they signed on to protect and honor and so they will. Sometimes they just need a small reminder. Anyway, there's nothing we can do outside of here that we can't do here for now. We'll make all our calls, connections and get things moving. You contact Charles and I'll get on the phone with Eli. That way we can monitor the news briefs. Jane should be doing a brief pretty soon. She never lets that go too long, I guess it comes from her background in journalism who knows."

* * *

"Charles, it's Kat again. You caught me off guard a few minutes ago. Now that my brain seems to be functioning again" she says derogatorily about herself "could you please tell me again about the meteorites and when you've estimated them to appear, and maybe strike the earth?"

"Sure Kat. I knew you were shocked. I guess I'm so used to the science behind everything that I forget that talking to people is different. So, I'm sorry about the abrupt news bulletin. Yes, I've done all the research that can possibly be done and I wish the information were different, but I can't change what's really happening. I've projected the meteorites; the angle of trajectory, speed of travel and best case scenario. The larger of the meteorites may just miss the earth, but in no way will all of them. They're clustered, at least as far as space is concerned, which is miles apart, so if the largest is just missing, then some of the smaller ones that are clustered nearby will most definitely hit," he says grimly.

"How big are the ones that will hit? What are we talking, small explosions, big explosions, super large? Can you be more specific?"

"I can only say that the projections that I've made using every scrap of data that I could get my hands on say that we may be in the projection line of some meteorites that can cause nuclear like damage since they're traveling at high rates of speed. Their velocity is large enough to impact the earth creating a shockwave that would be similar to a nuclear bomb being unleashed, depending on where they hit. This is not an exact science, you know, only projections or best guess estimates, but one of these hitting a populated area could kill millions. It's actually possible that they've started hitting the earth already, causing the large amounts of earthquakes that we've experienced lately. They do hit with such a huge force that it's not uncommon for them to create an earthquake. If they do hit as projected, and we've been having so many volcanic eruptions, our air will be even more problematic. This projection on top of current events could very well cause the next ice age, or the total opposite. The heat buildup from the volcanoes and the nuclear affect of the meteorites may create a greenhouse affect causing temperatures to increase exponentially. Either way, the future of the earth doesn't look very promising."

"That's not very good news, Charles. Is there anything at all that can be done to help our world? Are there any preparations that can be made to save lives?"

"I'm sorry Kat. There's absolutely nothing that can be done, to either protect or prepare."

"Do you think then, that with the no hope theory, that the people of the world should be informed? What good will it do to tell people that this is going to happen, and then tell them there's nothing they can do. There'll be mass hysteria, mass panic. I'm afraid of what will happen to the people if they have no hope. The world will become a war world, even if it's just for a short time. People may decide to do anything they want without worrying about the repercussions, since they won't be around to face any, the earth will no longer be."

"I understand your concern. It's an understandable dilemma, but as a scientist my job has been to study, understand, project and inform. I can see the possibilities of all you've said, they're good points, but now that you know the projections, don't you think that every human being also has that right? That it's our job to inform them and they're choice how to live out their last days on earth? Yes, I'm a scientist, but I'm also human and a Christian. I would want to know so that I can spend my last moments alive with my loved ones. Not going about my normal life, to work or wherever and not knowing it's my last chance, last chance to see them, talk to them, and hold them."

"Wow," she says quietly, heart pounding in her chest, fear and despair dragging her down. "I understand Charles. What are your plans, if you don't mind me asking?"

"Absolutely! I've contacted President Martin, and left a message for her. I haven't heard back from her yet so I'm hoping that will happen this morning, but I do understand her time demands right now with everything that's been going on. However, the longer I wait to announce this, the shorter the time span will be before the first major meteor strike occurs."

"Thank you Charles. If you wouldn't mind, could you give me a heads up on when you'll be making the announcement? I'd appreciate it. We're going to continue to do what we believe is necessary to maintain the peace in the United States. Help with all the damage and injured from the last couple of days and all the volcanoes that have erupted. People are hurt and need as much help as they can get. That's what we've been doing now for months. If you say there's no hope, I believe you. But I can't just sit by enjoying my loved ones when I know there are people out there that need me. I may not be able to give them long term hope, but for today I can help them. That will have to be enough. We'll never give up, not when we can do some good. On the off chance that things don't go the way you've projected, we need to be able to live. In doing that, there are urgent things that need to be handled for the world to continue on in a steady and peaceful way."

"You're a good person Kat and your group, they're good people. What this world needed was more like you. I promise to let you know prior to the announcement being made. Good luck Kat," he finishes before quietly hanging up saddened that he only now, at the end, met these true Americans."

"All right Eli. We'll talk again tonight at the same time as usual. Make sure Des is there, Kat wants to talk with her. I'm gonna go now, it looks like Kat's done on the phone and you've got a lot to get done before tonight, as do I," Snake says, hanging up with one hand and grabbing Kat with the other to pull her close noticing the despondency in her walk, the fear in her eyes.

"What's up Kitten? Why the long face," he asks as he holds her close, worry a deep ache in his chest.

"Snake, Charles doesn't think the earth has a future. He says that we're going to get hit with a meteor that could end the world, at least as we've known it," she says, tired of all the drama lately, subconsciously giving up.

"Kat, you know those scientist types. They've predicted this before and nothing ever came of it. It's become such a common occurrence that very few people actually listen to them anymore. You can't believe everything you hear, you know that. You have too much common sense to fall for these every time."

"I know that sometimes they don't actually happen, but they could, right? Besides, he's an expert, why would he make things up?"

"I didn't say he made it up, I said they aren't always right. Besides, even if he is right, we're here now and right now there are things we have to do. If he's wrong and we haven't done everything in our power to stop what Jane has planned, then we'll have to live in the world she's creating and I for one can't stand that thought! We have to live now, not in whatever future Rosenthal has predicted. I'm a realist and Jane's definitely up to something, something that means real bad things for the world. Since we haven't seen anyone else trying to stop her, then we move forward with our plans. You can tell everyone tonight what was said and get the consensus on how they feel, but honestly, I think you'll find that most of them believe the same way that I do. We're here now, people are hurt, and earthquakes are happening, God knows why, but they are. We have to help and we have to continue on with preparations for Brussels, unless we can finish our problem with Jane before then, but I doubt it. The New World Summit is only two weeks away now. It's going to take every bit of that time to prepare for whatever surprise she has up her sleeve. I, for one, know it's not a pleasant surprise, hers never are."

"How can you just ignore what Charles said and go on as if nothing is different?" she asks, confused and scared.

"It's how I'm made. I've never been one to borrow trouble. I'm more of the prepared type. I like to be ready when the shit hits the fan, and the shits going to hit the fan with Jane as president. She's already created massive trouble and is planning more, from everything that I've heard. I'd really like to know what the huge surprise is that she's got planned. It's giving me an uncomfortable feeling in the pit of my stomach. It's also telling me to prepare for a shock. Who knows, it could be everything that's going on, but I think its more lack of preparation on my end. Besides, it doesn't do me any good to worry about something that I can do nothing about. So instead of worrying, I'll prepare as much as possible for something that Jane is planning. That's hard enough when I'm not sure what and how to plan."

"Okay, I guess I understand. It doesn't do any good to worry, and it takes a lot of energy to continue to worry so I guess you're right. I'll start thinking only about what's really happening and how I can help, where I'm really needed," she says, reluctant but determined to do something for the cause.

"Good to hear that," he says with relief, glad at least for the temporary reprieve from her fears. "We've got a video conference tonight, just a few hours from now and I've got a few more things to do, but first I think we need to eat, since breakfast was non-existent and we're going to need the energy."

Chapter Twenty-Six

"Dana, thank you for taking over these duties, my last receptionist decided to move out west for some reason and with everything that's happened out there lately, I'm sure she's regretting that decision now," Jane says with a knowing smile.

"I love working for you President Martin. I think you're the best President that this country has ever had," Dana says happily, sitting straighter with pride finding it nice to be recognized, especially by someone as important as the President.

"I'm waiting for the media; they're due at the front gates soon. Let me know when they arrive, please, I have a news briefing scheduled and like to be prompt."

"Absolutely President Martin, I will definitely call you the moment they arrive."

***

"Good evening, I'm Jim Cochran of WELT News Channel 3, Washington D.C. live here at the White House where President Jane Martin is prepared to issue a news briefing regarding all that has occurred in the past few days. It's certainly been a trying time for President Martin, but she seems to be in control, here she is now:

"Good evening people of the United States. We have had many unfortunate things happen in the past twenty four hours, but I want to reassure you that I am in control. As you're aware, my General, General Teriq Auliya has died, here in the White House. The coroner has pronounced him as having a massive heart attack. I've contacted his family with this sad news. All I can say is I'm glad I was there to offer what little comfort I was able in his time of need. Our medical examiner, Dr. Steven Zorgath, did state that there was nothing anyone could have done to save him, for which I'm grateful because I felt really terrible when my CPR was unsuccessful. At least I tried and I did notify his loved ones myself," she finishes wiping the small tear from her eye in her show of compassion.

"Now onto other occurrences," she says as she straightens her spine in arrogance. "With the death of my General of the Armies, I found myself in the position of who to choose to fill that spot. This is the one position that can't be left open or unattended. Therefore, my choice for this position is Mr. Nicholas Rantrall, the current Director of Homeland Security. He's more than capable of handling all the duties that this position requires. He has loyalty and experience in the matters that are at hand, making him the obvious choice. That being said, he will take over this position right away and will also maintain the position of Director of

Homeland Security until a choice for that position has been made. I have no doubt that he will handle both jobs with due diligence. He's also assuming all the jobs that General Auliya was handling, without interruption. If there are problems or questions, please don't hesitate to contact him, he reports directly to me," she finishes before standing straighter and clapping her hands together, the feeling of excitement caught by the media, a stir seen moving throughout the reporter's.

"And now, something so exciting I can't wait to tell you. The date for the New World Summit is only two weeks away. I've received a special invitation for this summit, and I believe the reason will greatly benefit the country so of course I have accepted. It's what the United States has been working so hard for, for so long. At that time, I will be unveiling a huge surprise, a surprise of such magnitude that everyone in the world will finally understand and every citizen of these great United States will gaze upon with joy. I won't say anymore, I want it to be the best surprise you've ever had," she adds, voice sounding higher in her excitement. "Let me calm myself please, as you can tell, I'm a little excited by this surprise, unfortunately, I've saved the worst information for last.

Now, there have been eleven volcanic eruptions occurring nearly consecutively, within minutes of each other actually, all over the world. In the United States, Yellowstone has erupted again, only much larger this time than the last. There have been reports of injuries and even deaths caused by this tragedy. We have been fortunate however, not losing nearly the count that

Indonesia has had. They've lost millions. Their volcano had the largest eruption and with it located in such a highly populated area it was impossible for the majority of their citizens to evacuate. There have been other eruptions, like I said previously, but without the catastrophic damage that occurred in Indonesia. I'm sure as the day progresses we'll learn more about the severity of this disaster. I've had calls from most of the countries affected and through it all Indonesia is by far the worst hit. As soon as I know more about the damages and future issues, I will hold another briefing. For now, praying for those affected would not be out of bounds. If we can help with the recoveries, we will gladly do that. Until that time, I have no further information about the volcanoes. However, I have heard from a friend, a Mr. Charles Rosenthal, out of the D.C. branch of the USGS. He called a little while ago to give me a heads up. It looks like all his studying has paid off. He informed me that within the next week or so, there will likely be a meteor shower that may or may not hit the earth. We've had these warning before and nothing has ever happened from them, but I'm not taking that chance. I promised you that you have the right to know if something is going to affect you, and this really could affect you should it be accurate. He tells me that they're closer to the earth than ever before and if their trajectory stays the way it is, then we most assuredly will be hit. There's no way of telling by what size meteor, or even what kind of damage could occur. I do take this seriously and indeed will be in contact with him frequently in the next few days, but truthfully,

I will not panic from this kind of news. Like I said, we've had these warnings before with nothing happening. I believe we'll see the same thing this time around. I've done my duty to you by informing you of his warning. What you want to do with that warning is now up to you. I think that pretty much covers everything that I wanted to inform you of. You'll be hearing from me again in the next day or so, with updates or new information," she says with finality before once more glancing around and seeing the shock on the faces of the media, and with a small smile she turns and leaves.

"I'm Jim Cochran of WELT News Channel 3, Washington D.C. here on the White House lawn. President Martin has just finished her news briefing regarding General Auliya's early demise, poor man, to have died so young of something that could have been prevented. With the volcanic eruptions that have affected the world and the information about Indonesia and the devastation that's happened from that. It's a terrible thing that we all seem to be going through. Indeed this has been a most disturbing briefing. And now some information that we had not heard before, Professor Charles Rosenthal, of the USGS will be contacted for an interview as soon as possible regarding the possible meteorite shower that appears to be imminent. It looks to be a dangerous situation that the world seems to be finding itself in. I would almost say, if I didn't know better, that these are the end of the world scenarios," he admits, confusion and concern lighting his face, the cameras panning behind him following the

President as she makes her way back inside the White House, her side noticeably empty, the side that the Vice President usually occupies, nervousness in the shaking of the papers he's playing with. "I'm sure that we'll be hearing those words more and more frequently in the future. After all, there has to be some explanation for everything that's happening. I'm Jim Cochran of WELT News Channel 3, Washington D.C.

"Well," Snake says after a commercial comes on the television.

"That was, I don't know, what I expected I guess but the way she comes across, it always puts my teeth on edge," Kat says, anger in her movements as she gets up to pace the confines of the living room, reviewing everything Jane said and what she didn't say.

"I know what you mean. She always seems to be gloating, as if she has this huge agenda and it's exactly the way she ordered it."

"She probably does," Kat says dryly, disliking Jane to the point of hate.

"I know, you're right, I just wish things were different, but hell, they're not. We only have an hour or so before our video conference and I'm a little hungry so let's hit the freezer and see what's available. You know, I'm almost glad mom and dad aren't alive to witness what's happening in this world. They'd be so upset with all the evil and corruption that's around, not to mention the natural or unnatural disasters that are overtaking the world. These are definitely crazy times, Kitten, crazy times," he says as he grabs her hand and walks side by side with her to the kitchen.

"Let's see," she says as she pulls open the door to the stuffed freezer, looking for something that will fill them up not only with food but with good memories. Something to help them escape, if only for a couple of minutes, the chaos that's surrounding them. "Look, let's have this," she says as she pulls a container of stuffed cabbage off of a shelf.

"What is it?" he asks curiously.

"It says stuffed cabbage on the container, and it's only from about nine months ago, so it's still good,"

"Oh yeah, it's good. I haven't had those in years. Mom used to make them in the winter time," he adds, nostalgia softening his face. "They were one of my favorites. I hadn't been around for a long time and that's about how long it's been since I've tasted those. They sound really good, let's stick'em in the microwave," he suggests with the first real smile in an hour or more, showing her more than he knows. Showing her how very much he misses his parents, and his brother, and normalcy, making her eyes shimmer with unshed tears.

"You got it, Snake. They'll be ready in about ten minutes. Since we have that long, let's see if there are any homemade rolls to go with them. Those would be the perfect final touch to a perfect meal," she adds happily, seeing what she was looking for. "Got some, *thank you Sandra*," she murmurs under her breath *"for being so efficient and organized*. Turn on the oven; we're going to eat like royalty!"

Chapter Twenty-Seven

"Eli, how are you?" Jacob asks when he see's Eli come on the video screen.

"We're doing okay, busy, super busy but good, how about you two?"

"The same, busy. Just finished some of Mom's famous cabbage rolls and some fresh baked rolls she had in the freezer too. They were excellent!" Jacob says, gloating.

"I'll bet they were," Eli growls good naturedly.

"So, did you by chance watch the Presidents televised news briefing? What did you think about what she had to say?"

"I think it's a load of crap, but that's just me," he says.

"And me," Kat agrees as she walks into the viewing area.

"Hi Kat, it's good to see you," Eli says "it sounds like you agree with Jacob on the President's opinions," he adds with a small smile.

"I do, and you probably do too," she adds

teasingly.

"Yeah, that's pretty much the consensus around here."

"Hey Mal, it's good to see you," Eli adds when he notices Mallory walk into the viewing area.

"Hi, I just got done checking the computer. I wanted to make sure it finished what it was set up to do. All complete. Here's the report I printed off. It will tell you the name and address of all fifty facilities that we put a stop to," she boasts.

"That's awesome work Mal," he says when a loud pounding sounds on the door and Mongoose can be seen running out of the room. "What the Hel . . . ," Eli exclaims when he too jumps to his feet, turning for the door when Lucas charges into the room, out of breath. "What, what is it?" Eli asks quickly, glancing around for the unseen threat.

"It blew up, it's gone," Lucas yells in unbelief. "I was talking to one of our guards stationed at the courtesy camp and all I heard was a really loud explosion, and then nothing. I tried to contact him, but there's no answer. I don't know what the hell happened, but no-one's answering any radios. It sounded like something blew up. It was really loud, really loud!"

"What blew up," Eli yells, trying to get everyone's attention.

"I don't know!" Lucas yells back, flustered.

"Quiet down everyone!" Eli yells into the commotion. "Now, tell me exactly what you heard," he says to Lucas after the room's quiet enough to talk in.

"I was talking to one of our guards, Chris, I check in everyday to make sure they don't need anything. Today seemed no different than any other day; we talked about the camp, then about normal everyday things, like the weather, the news, that kind of stuff. We were right in the middle of talking about the newest Presidential briefing when I heard a loud explosion of some sort and then just static. He didn't answer when I yelled for him, so I clicked off the radio and tried again. There's nothing now. No static, nothing. I've tried to reach someone else, anyone, but I've gotten no answer. No sounds at all, from anyone." Lucas finishes then scrubs his hands over his face, whiskers rasping, hair in disarray from running his hands through it, dread clouding his eyes.

"All right, we need to get out there and see what the hell just happened. Sorry Jacob, we'll have to pick up here when we get back. It takes over an hour just to get there and then by the time we figure out what's happening and get back here, forget tonight. I'll call you from the camp, and we can decide what the next step is. We probably won't be able to do this conference until tomorrow, at the earliest, but at least we'll have the answers to what happened by then."

"Good, get moving, just let me know when you can," Jacob orders, frustration on his too handsome face causing his electric blue eyes to glow, creating a formidable picture.

"What was that about," Kat asks seriously. "The compound blew up? What could have caused that?"

"I'm not sure. It could have been any number of things. The thing is, I don't believe in coincidences. Sure, shit happens," he adds while pacing the living room, rubbing his hands over his face as he thinks. Not realizing that it's the exact same move his brother just demonstrated during the video conference "but this is not a coincidence. Mark my words Jane's involved in this somewhere. I'm sure she's in it. I have a gut feeling that this was not accidental."

"You're probably right," she adds quietly, not wishing to wake the sleeping dragon, but enthralled none the less by his pacing, while watching him think. *That man really touches me, somewhere deep*, she thinks, thoughts turning dangerously wanton.

"All right, there's nothing we can do from here to help them, but I can try and find out as much as possible before Eli get's in touch. You contact your CI's and I'll see if I can reach Chico. He might know something about this."

"Will do Snake, thanks," she replies with a sigh of relief and a wicked small grin.

"For what," he mumbles absently, not paying close enough attention to her to pick up on the innuendo.

"What," she says into the silence, knowing what he's asking but unwilling to reciprocate. "I'm gonna go and see who I can find and if anyone knows anything. I'll be back later."

"Take care out there Kitten," he replies absently, moving to make his calls.

"Chico, we need to talk, call me and we'll set up a time, ASAP," Jacob says quietly into the phone, unsuccessful in contacting Chico. "Stan, its Jacob, I need to get together with you, meet me at the park same place as usual," he orders after a short silence listening to the phone while walking out the front door.

"Jacob, what's up?" a sandy haired man approximately thirty five years old, six foot, average build wearing khaki tan pants and a black t-shirt asks after walking over to the bench that he's been sitting at, reading his phone apps, just like the other fifty or so people wandering around.

"Hey Stan, it's good to see you," Jacob acknowledges surprise in his tone and body language for the speediness of his arrival "what have you been up to?"

"The usual," Stan says as he takes a seat next to Jacob, casually looking around, longer at the women then the men, a look of appreciation and curiosity on his handsome face.

"We're starting the roundup," Jacob says casually to Stan, he too glancing around especially at the women, noticing everything, alert mode in high gear.

"When?" Stan asks casually.

"A week from today, since things are getting way to dangerous now, we're going to need to start our transports to Brussels. She's headed there in two weeks and I want everything to be in place before she gets to the meeting. We're only going to get one chance to stop this, and it's better to happen off our soil. What size should I expect?"

"Well," Stan drawls out, pulling on his lower lip as he thinks. "I'm pretty sure you can guestimate, but I'll say at least ten thousand. The numbers are growing substantially and don't include everyone, of course. All civilians have been turned down, but the trained military that have crossed over, at least ten thousand. I know we can't bring everyone, so any more will be left here to guard these shores. I hate taking chances with our people, wouldn't want to leave them here to take care of themselves."

"Good thinking. Glad you crossed over and joined the team," Jacob says earnestly.

"It was the only thing to do. I'm just glad there was someplace to join. I hated thinking I was the only one, so thank you Sir!"

"I've got a videoconference later today. Something's happened at the Texas compound. Eli was headed out that way to figure out what happened and fix it if possible. I won't know more unless he calls or for sure later today. I can get back with you after that. In the mean time, I've got a few more people to contact, so I'm gonna head out. I'll call you sometime later tonight or early tomorrow. Depends on what time we get everything worked out. I think logistics is going to be a killer for this, but we'll do it. We don't have a choice. I'll talk to you later," Jacob murmurs as he wanders away, still looking at his phone apps, while scanning the area for suspicious looking individuals.

"Greg, hey, you look great," Kat says breathlessly, the Goth wardrobe a little stifling in the heat of the day. *I sure am tired of black*, she thinks, surreptitiously wiping her brow of sweat without damaging her makeup.

"You're beautiful as usual," he says, admiration in him for the strong young woman standing in front of him acting like a teen.

"Yeah, right," she replies, a small smile on the otherwise straight face, eyes glowing greener than usual because of the black hair.

"Let's walk," he offers. "We might just find a breeze that will help you out a little more than just standing here. Besides, it makes us easy targets. I'm definitely more comfortable moving than just standing, waiting to be seen."

"I know how you feel I am a sniper after all. I see opportunities everywhere," she adds with a laugh. "So what have you got? Anything new?" she asks casually while walking, the public seeing two young adults dressed similarly, tattoos frequently seen on both.

"It sounds like there are thousands of people that aren't happy with the President, but are afraid of coming forward. There's news of people disappearing because of their negative opinions and they don't want to end up gone, too."

"Have your people been spreading any news to them, help them out a little bit," she asks seriously, sadness in her heart for her people, the citizens that fear life in the United States more than anything else.

"We've been starting that. I couldn't help it. It really bothers me to have taken an oath to protect these people and I've had to stand by and watch the corruption take over, the power shifting where it never should have gone. Unfortunately, I don't want to create a problem before the real help can begin. I wouldn't want any hint of what's about to take place to get into the wrong hands."

"You got that right. We've only got the one chance and we have to make good on it. So how much transportation are you going to need?"

"I've got probably close to ten thousand on

standby, awaiting transport. "

"Wow, so many," she gasps, worry in her while wondering where in the hell she's supposed to get transportation for that many, yet knowing that it's going to take that many plus a lot more to complete what they have planned in Brussels.

"That's not all of them. I told a lot that not everyone could go, that we need people here to protect this land. There was quite a bit of grumbling, but after they heard me explain how important the protection here is, they begrudgingly agreed," he finishes with a smile.

"That's probably good, since I know Snake's got people gathering troops and so does Eli and probably Mal too, but she's been so busy with the computer stuff that I doubt she's had time to do much else. I sure am glad we had her, she's freakin brilliant with those computers, and thanks to her we've been able to do what we have."

"I think Jane needs to beware, she's not as in control as she thinks," he says conspiratorially, a new bounce in his step. *Times getting close, maybe, just maybe the United States can get back to how it was not even two years ago. It may not have been great, but it was a whole lot better than it is now*, he thinks. "What, sorry, my mind wandered," he says guiltily after noticing Kat staring at him, confused.

"That's all right," she adds before repeating herself "how long do you need to get those people prepared to move?"

"I can get word moving today, and by the time it reaches them, maybe four days," he says questioningly.

"Good, then start the word moving. I'll schedule your transport starting a week from today. Keep your phone on and I'll let you know where and what time as soon as I have it. I need to move, I've been gone longer than I wanted and need to find out what's happening now. Things happen so quickly," she mutters as her walk turns into a brisk pace, leaving her friend behind standing staring after her.

"This is Jim Cochran of WELT News Channel 3, Washington D.C. we have breaking news. There have been reported explosions in multiple states tonight. We're waiting for confirmation from our sister stations, and as soon as we get that we can pinpoint more easily where these explosions have occurred. As you're aware, Professor Rosenthal was interviewed earlier this week because of his meteorite predictions. Could he have been right? It's possible that the reported explosions were indeed caused by meteorites, but those are not facts. That's just supposition on my part. I promise that as soon as we have word on what caused the explosions, you'll be notified. Stay tuned to News Channel 3 for further updates. I'm Jim Cochran, WELT News Channel 3 we're returning you now to your local scheduled programs."

* * *

"Kat, good you're back. They just broke in with news about explosions, and they did say multiple states, but we still have no idea what caused them. Unfortunately, they didn't have any confirmed reasons, just a guess by the newscaster. But they'll be back, as soon as they get confirmation of cause, so I guess all we can do is play the waiting game. I haven't even heard back from Eli yet, so no news from that direction," Mallory says.

"Bummer, I was hoping he at least called," Kat admits, disappointed.

"He will, Kat. Eli will call, as soon as he gets a chance and has some answers. You have to remember, he had to physically go to the site and that takes time. It's only been a couple of hours, so he may call real soon," Mal reassures her from the recliner.

"You look comfy," Kat says teasingly with a grin. "Do I need to go back out tonight," she asks turning back to find Snake wandering around the room, picking up this knick-knack and that, gently blowing the dust off before carefully putting them back in the precise spot he picked it up from.

"I don't know. I guess it depends on what we hear on the news and what Eli has to report, but I highly doubt it," he says absently still wandering and looking.

"I'll take that as a no and change, because these clothes are dragging me down. I'm getting into my sweats. I just wish I would have thought to pick up some black ones, to keep me in disguise," she adds wistfully.

"Sure, why don't you," he says quietly, not really paying attention.

"What's up with you Jacob?" Mal asks after Kat leaves the room, a confused look on her face.

"What, sorry, I was thinking about something else," he admits.

"You, you're acting strange. Distant, moody,

quiet, you're not acting like yourself."

"Sorry Mal. I've had a lot to think about, and I'm still not sure what to do, so give me a break!" he adds angrily, his wandering brought to an abrupt halt as he turns to face his twin sister.

"Jacob, please, I'm not picking on you. I just wanted to make sure you were all right."

"I'm fine Mal. There's so much going on right now, that my minds boggled with everything that needs done before the Summit, and what may happen because of it. It's a lot to think about, and a lot to plan for. Some dread goes along with it, of course. This is unheard of territory that we're crossing into."

"I know," she agrees quietly, fear filling her. "We've all been thinking the same thoughts, we're all a little scared but we're together so what happens, happens to all of us at once. We can get through it regardless of what happens. We'll meet this together," she promises as she stands to hug her brother, comforting herself and him.

"Hi, I'm Jim Cochran of WELT News Channel 3, Washington D.C. with more breaking news. Sources have indicated that there have been explosions, multiple explosions in different areas. They've been happening in small resort type areas housing thousands of people on mini vacations. Why these specific places have blown we have no idea. It's believed that the facilities were full to capacity and with some of the video that we've obtained, there can't be any survivors. The damage looks too extensive; we'll be running that video shortly so please bear with us."

'We should be hearing something pretty soon," Jacob says just as his cell rings. "Jacob," he answers on the third ring "yeah, I hear you. You're sure Eli? Where else, yeah, we're ready, I've talked with Cantrell, he's ready. It's a go then. Start moving your people. Right, I'll let them know. Thanks and Eli, be careful out there," he says then clicks his phone off as Mal and Kat move closer, anxious to hear what just went on. "That was Eli,' he says unnecessarily.

"We heard," Mal says impatiently "what did he say, Jacob" Mal demands, her stomach fluttering with anxiety.

"The compound is totally destroyed. There were no survivors on the inside. There were, however, guards on the outside that managed to escape with their lives. Some injuries, but overall, the numbers are good there. Not for the poor bastards that were on the inside, guarding the Iranians. None of them made it. The explosion looks like it was caused by a deeply buried explosive device. Something we never would have found. The crater it left was worse than the ones by the Capitol buildings that were destroyed. Eli believes that our President's hands were involved in this. There are just too many similarities," he finishes, hands scrubbing his eyes, his face, rasping his whiskers. "Damn it, I should have had them check deeper," he yells in frustration. "This is war," he declares "now we start moving our people out. I've been in touch with Cantrell. He's got around thirty five or so pilots on standby with cargo planes. All we have to do is notify our people on this end and they'll be transported out. He's got them staged in large private airports across the country with special orders waiting. They won't have any problem getting our troops into Brussels. They'll start moving them on Cantrell's orders. Thank God he's part of this, that a lot of our military are part of this. Jane's never going to believe the extent of hatred that she's created in this country. Ladies, it now begins in earnest. Kat, make the call; we need to get our people moving sooner than we thought. Start sending them out. Mal, I'll get you the list of the airports, what they need to do and how soon they need to be there. My guess is now. I realize that it'll take a little while, but that's all right. I don't want to draw any undue attention on anyone headed out. The less Jane knows, especially now, the better. I'm going to try and reach Chico again, hopefully he's available now. We're going to need your computer skills again Mal. Once we can get the planes in the air, you'll need to block them from visibility. It'll be a little dangerous, but the pilots we're using have battle experience and are used to flying under the wire. Cantrell has set up receiving airports, non-military, so we should be okay. They're used to illegal shipments coming in, so their planes seldom fly into areas where they're seen. We've infiltrated those sites with our own people and have things ready for them so they can disappear."

"Hi, I'm Jim Cochran of WELT News Channel 3, Washington D.C with information regarding the explosions that occurred no more than an hour ago. It appears they've occurred in facilities that are maintained by our government for citizens that needed some time to decide on accepting the chips that have been offered by our President. They arrive at these hotel like facilities, are treated to a vacation lasting upwards of a month when they are then offered the chips for the last time. Most decide to accept them, those that don't are allowed to go back home but reminded that by beginning next year, they won't be able to purchase anything without them and to then receive them, they will need to pay, a substantial amount given that at this very moment they're free. Free doesn't last forever. After all, the President can't continue offering them for free on everyone else's time frame. That's just way to costly for our government to pick up the tabs. Anyway, the building in Texas that was used as the hotel area has blown up, exploded as you will. Word from the Whitehouse is the President will be holding a news briefing within the hour to notify us of exactly what happened. Please stay tuned right here to WELT News Channel 3 for breaking news."

"Of course Jane has to do things on her schedule. She's show boating because she can, damn it," Jacob grouses.

"She'll be on soon, Jacob, I'm sure," Mal offers calmly.

"Yeah, she will, it just pisses me off that she takes her own good time to let anyone know anything."

"Well, she doesn't have to let anyone know anything; she is the President after all, not the reporter she used to be."

"I know," he says, "I know."

"Make your calls then and I'll get started on my computer programming. How big an explosion, again," Mal asks.

"Ten times the Capitol buildings. This place is a lot bigger than that was and newly built, so it has a stronger foundation."

"Wow," Mal whispers as Kat whistles at the size, dread in the pit of her stomach.

"How can anyone survive that?" Kat asks quietly.

"You can't that's why they're planning it that way," Jacob acknowledges, surprised they thought there was a chance of survival.

"So then, this is it," Kat yells anxiety and fear crowding her thoughts. "Why haven't you said anything until now? Were you going to bother to let anyone else know? All those troops we're sending, are they flying into their deaths? Damn it Snake, how could you not share this info with us. What the hell!"

"Kat, calm yourself, please. Would I do something like that and not say anything? You don't know me very well, do you Kitten?" he adds bitterly.

"I know you as well as anyone can," she says quietly, hurt in her eyes, her voice gaining strength. "You never talk, you keep everything to yourself and only share what you think is pertinent. I'm sure you're siblings will agree with me there. It's as if you're so much better than anyone else, never trusting anyone with anything important unless you absolutely have to! You're a fucking micromanager, that's what you are" she yells face red, body shaking as if in the midst of a wind storm.

"Kat, stop screaming at me," Jacob yells, slamming the last thing he touched back onto the shelf, breaking the fragile frame in his hands, a crack running down the length of the picture obscuring Devon's face from view, clouding his features.

"Ohhh," Kat gasps when she sees what happened, tears clouding her vision.

"I'm sorry, I'm sorry," he finishes quietly. "Screaming, yelling, none of it will do any good. Not now, not ever. We are at the point of no return, Kat. Surely you've seen it coming. Some will survive this and some won't, but tell me, what choice do we have? You want to commit yourself to the U.S. and the way it's going? You and I both know that what Jane has started must be stopped. We all agreed on this awhile back, you stood firm in your decision. What did you expect would happen? That we'd get Jane to change her mind on things, change the way she wants the states to be, the world to be? If so, you were living in a fairy tale. It's not going to happen. We only have one chance, just one. We have to stop her, Kat, before it's too late. The window of opportunity is almost upon us."

"You want me to call my people, send them to the pick-up zone and have them flown into certain death? I'm not sure I can give that order, Snake. It's a terrible thing you're making me do," she adds in anguish.

"I'm sorry Kat, if there was anything else that could be done, trust me, I would have done it. I'm sorry, but make the call. Time has run out, everything's in place and we will win this battle.

Failure is not an option. Think of all the people, all the lives that are praying for something, anything to stop this madness. They're depending on us to stop her. They all want to live. Sometimes we have to decide if the sacrifice is too great, but in this case it's not the few for the many. Believe me, this is the only hope that anyone has. She can't be allowed to destroy the world!"

Chapter Twenty-Eight

"What the hell have you done?" Jane yells at Quinton after learning what blew up and why. "You never had permission to create anything like this. How dare you," she yells, eyes flashing red with anger.

"You were busy," he says indifferently.

"I was busy?"

"Yeah, you've always had your own agenda. You never really cared what happened to these people. What's the big deal," he asks with disdain.

"You're kidding right? I've always taken care of the citizens. They are what I rule, are they not? You, on the other hand, you are who you are only because of me," she states flatly.

"I beg to differ Jane. It's the other way around there, don't you think," he murmurs advancing on her.

"Actually, no it's not. This is my country, I'm the one with the power to take care of issues, you were appointed by me, to stand by me, since our world believes it needs a man in a power position. How wrong they are, but I did that to appease them. I NEVER gave you any power without my control. Why you believe opposite is beyond me."

"It's because I've been the one to give you the power, not the other way around. You believe you were raised to be what you have become. You were not. You were raised to hold the position you are holding so that I, I, could take over. You were never meant to be Supreme Ruler of the world. That position has always been meant for me," he adds smoothly, power radiating from him. "Unfortunately, it's too early to show my hand yet, therefore I must insist that you play along. The timing's not quite right for the big reveal."

"The big reveal?" she asks quietly, "Whose big reveal," she demands, pressing a small button on the bar, summoning help.

"The New World leader, that would be me," he says as the door bangs open and six secret service agents swarm him.

"Stop, you have NO authority over me," he yells as they grab and secure him, awaiting the Presidents order.

"What do you want us to do with him, President Martin" the head security agent asks quietly of Jane after making sure the door's closed behind him, putting the soundproof room back in order.

"We need to take him into a secure facility, but it needs to be under darkness. I don't want this getting out to anyone besides the eight of us standing here at this time. Take him through the secret passageway. As far as I know, only a few know of that area. The media can't find out about this. He's become delusional, so put him somewhere that he can't be heard. Drug him if necessary. Just what I needed," she adds while rubbing her hands together, angry that she didn't notice this problem earlier. "I don't care what happens to him, wait, keep him safe. I do have something he needs to do for me," she adds.

"Yes President Martin," he says sending two agents out to scout out the halls leading towards the tunnel entrance. "We can get him in the there before the meetings let out. The media's still outside waiting for your briefing on the explosions," he reminds her kindly.

"Thanks Scott," Jane says turning away, trying to gather her thoughts for the press, grateful for blind following secret service agents.

"You won't get away with this Jane, believe me, I am the true leader and there's nothing you can do to stop me," Quentin warns angrily as he's silenced and manhandled out of the room, eyes blazing with fury.

"The big reveal, what's the big reveal," Jane murmurs to herself before picking up the phone and dialing Chico. "Where are my parents," she demands as soon as the phone is answered.

"President Martin?"

"I said, where are my parents?" she repeats firmly.

"They're in their room, have been for the past hour," Chico replies wariness in is tone.

"Keep them there I want to talk to them, I'll be there in a minute," she informs him before slamming the phone down.

I wonder what that was about he thinks as he prepares for her visit.

"You can go, they won't need you the rest of the day," he's informed as she enters their rooms.

"Yes President Martin." *Hmm, fine. That gives me time to get in touch with Jacob and see if he knows what's going on.*

***

"Lieutenant Callander, its Chico. I was just dismissed from work for the rest of the day and I was hoping we could get together. There are some strange things going on up here and I'd kinda like to compare notes, if that's all right with you,"

"Actually, that's perfect. I was just getting ready to call you. Can you meet me at thirteen eighty nine Wayside Road, a brown ranch that sits back off the road a little ways?"

"Sure, I'll be there in about half an hour or so, I just need to check out and grab my car."

"Come in Chico, come in. You made it in good time," Jacob says as he shuts the front door.

"Yes Sir, traffic was strangely light today, it cut quite a few minutes off my time," he adds with a grin.

"Let's go into the sitting room. Kat and Mal are set up in there waiting for more news. So what's going on," Jacob asks quietly as they wander farther into the house.

"I'm not sure, actually. I was hoping you might have some insight."

"I may, what happened?"

"Jane called me about half an hour ago, demanded to know where her parents were, and when I told her right there with me, she said I'll be right there and then she dismissed me when she arrived. It was really abrupt and kinda strange."

"Hmm, sounds like she might have heard the newest information coming in."

"Oh, you mean about the explosion?"

"Yeah, but if that's the case, she shouldn't have been any more upset than normal. I wonder what caused that."

"She was different, she even looked different. Her eyes, they were pissed. She never seemed to get mad at her parents, but that's almost what it looked like. None of my business, that. If she's angry with her parents, that's her business. I'd sure have liked to have been a fly on the wall in there today, though."

"Hey Chico," Kat says as he enters with Jacob. "How the heck are you," she asks as she hugs him.

"I'm good, Kat. You look good, different, but good," he adds with a grin, admiring her goth look.

"Yeah," she laughs. "I'm ready for Halloween," she admits eyes sparkling. "Just kidding, but I am ready to go back to old me. I'm getting a little tired of black."

"Anything going on, Kitten?"

"Just the constant news about the explosions," she says. "They did say Jane was going to be live soon from the Whitehouse. You know Jane and her love of the media."

"Yeah," Jacob snorts. "I think that's her coming on now," he says noticing the front of the

Whitehouse coming into view on the TV. "Let's see what she has to say, then we can update you on where we are," Jacob says to Chico as he moves closer to the TV.

"This is Jim Cochran of WELT News Channel 3, Washington D.C here live at the Whitehouse. President Jane Martin is about to hold a conference momentarily regarding the explosions that have occurred a short while ago. Our information has started streaming in. From all reports, the explosions have occurred in every state in this country. In each state was a rather large facility that housed insurgents, actually the insurgents are the people in the United States that have refused to take the chip immediately. They were taken to these villages, vacation or not, we are unsure of the exact nature of these facilities, but needless to say, they were taken there until they agreed to accept the chip. Here she comes now. Let's see what she has to say about these places and these explosions. I'm Jim Cochran of WELT News Channel 3, Washington, here's President Martin now," he finishes, voice growing quieter and quieter.

"...as I was saying," Jane continues, "these facilities were to help the people to make the decision to accept the chip. People were taken to these vacation camps to give them the opportunity to have a small vacation, enjoy their families away from the stress of home and work, and give us the opportunity to show them and explain to them the exact nature of the chip. Everyone that went to these all expense paid camps, agreed to accept the chips once they finally understood all the good things that they can and will do for them."

"It greatly saddens me that we have groups out there that take something innocent and helpful, destroy it and the people in it all for the name of our country? They don't care about our country, nor do they or have they ever cared about the people in this country. How could they, when they have blown up every facility that was meant to help our people not hurt them, murdering anyone inside, every man, woman and child. Yes, you can blame the followers of Jacob Callander, the same ones that have been a thorn in my side since I took office. It seems he is as dangerous dead as he was alive. Those that have gone up against your beloved President," she adds, voice gaining in strength, posture growing taller in anger and indignation. "They have destroyed any and everyone that was in those camps this morning. Mark my words, ladies and gentlemen of this country. I will not let this go. I will hunt them down and destroy them, in the same manner that they have chosen to destroy all those innocents. Their days are numbered; they need to watch their backs. From this day forward I will not rest until I have captured and destroyed them all, just like I did Mr. Callander. I cannot and will not tolerate acts of terrorism being committed in our country by home grown terrorists, which is exactly what they have done. You have my word on this!" she promises passionately before taking a deep breath, turning and leaving the podium.

"Wow that was a powerful promise that President Martin made just now. She had to stand strong at this time. She's been the best President that we've ever have and considering the way that she had to assume office, and all that she inherited prior to her gaining office, she has always put the people of this country first. Finally she's someone who cares about more than power and money. She cares about the people of this country. This is Jim Cochran of WELT News Channel 3, Washington, live here at the Whitehouse. We just witnessed a powerful declaration of war, if you will, from our President who's ready to take on the world if she must, to protect the citizens of this country. Stay tuned for more updates."

"Oh my god, Jacob, she just blamed all the explosions on us. Now what are we going to do?"

"Yeah, she did, didn't she," he says with a strange look on his face. "I guess we move our plans up a little. We need to disappear and the best way for that to happen is to move our plans up. We'll have to get out of the country earlier than we expected. But, I'm not really surprised. She had to blame someone. She can't allow anything like this to change the course she's set for herself. We've slightly less than a week before the One World Summit, leaving a little earlier isn't an issue. I'll make the call today. Chico, you need to decide what your course is. You can hitch a ride with us, or you can go back to the Whitehouse and maintain your cover, leaving with them when they go.

"I need to think about it," he admits, confused. "I'm sorry, but I guess I've been out of the loop for too long. I knew about an explosion, somewhere in Texas, but no more than one. And what does she mean that you and your 'group' are terrorists and now wanted? By the way, you look good for a corpse."

"Sorry Chico, I forgot that just because you're stationed in the Whitehouse doesn't mean that you know what's really going on. You only hear what she wants you to hear. I'll back up a little. There have been forty-seven explosions this morning, one in every continental state. They occurred in her facilities, the 'courtesy camps' that she set up to make the people take her chip, the places that you went to and disappeared from if you still refused. We've seen pictures, talked with guards and rescued prisoners after taking the first camp down. The people that went were physically abused, had no food, little water, the women and children were horribly abused before they were disposed of. They looked like old concentration camp survivors and the treatment was no better that what Hitler doled out to the Jews back during the war. It would have made you sick."

"Man, no shit. I never would have thought those things. Sure, she's not what you think, but that evil? Wow. I think I'll pay closer attention to her and less on her parents."

"My 'group' Jacob adds mockingly "are leaving within the next few days for Brussels. We've got a couple of surprises in the works for Jane's big day. You do know that she's accepting the last seat at the table? Not only does she want power, but she wants total world dominance. No way can we allow that to happen. Later today, Eli and the group should be arriving here. Then we can get everything ready and head out for our transportation, early the day after tomorrow.

There's room for you if you want to take this opportunity, but it would work better for us if you maintained your Whitehouse staff position, that way Jane's world goes on as usual. I'd kind of like her to be as surprised as possible in Brussels."

"Sure man, we can meet up when I get there."

"Absolutely, you're part of this. We wouldn't be where we are now without you. You should be with our group when everything starts. I won't say more now. I'm not putting into words what exactly is going to happen, that way there's no way she can get the information before we're ready," Jacob adds grimly, "the game, I believe, is about to end."

Chapter Twenty-Nine

"Eli, welcome home, man," Jacob says as he hugs his brother. "You don't look too bad considering the long travel time you just put in."

"Oh, that was nothing," he says, rolling his eyes, tired beyond belief.

"Right," Kat adds as she steps in to give a hug too.

"Eli," Mal squeals with excitement when she sees him through the doorway, everyone moving out of the way, afraid to be bowled over by her in all her excitement, a smile touching every face that witnessed the reunion.

"Sis," he yells as she reaches him and he grabs her around the waist to swing her around, glad to finally see his family again.

"I've got so much to tell you," she starts babbling through her tears, eyes trying hard not to scan the crowd, looking for that one face. . .

"He's right behind you," Eli whispers in her ear before releasing her slowly and with a slight touch on the shoulder turns her to face the one she's been looking for.

'Hi," she whispers as she takes the one step that will take her home.

"Hi to you," Rand says with a small smile as he finally gets to see her face for the first time in too long. "I've missed you," he murmurs as he pulls her close, tightens his hold, catcalls coming from around him, advice like "get a room" the loudest part of the good natured ribbing getting to his ears.

"Hey, let's meet in the other room, this one seems a little crowded," Jacob says with humor as he leads the rest of the group into the room being used as the situation room. "I want to hear an update, if possible, or you can take a short break first," he offers after noticing the fatigue on every ones faces. "Go, take a couple of hours. We can spare it. Once things start moving here, no one's going to get much rest. Find a place to rest and use it. There're bedrooms, the other living room, anywhere. Kat and I will see if we can do something in the line of food for you. There must be something, my Mom was pretty prepared. We'll meet in the dining room in say two hours?"

"Thanks man," Mongoose says as he starts to wander away, in search of quiet and maybe some sleep, but not without Des.

"Help yourselves," Jacob says to the stragglers wandering into the dining room. "It's a hodge-podge; there was lots of stuff, just not a lot of one thing, so it's like a buffet. After we eat, we'll meet in the situation room and talk," he promises as he grabs a dish and starts the line moving.

"Des, Des?" Kat says as she notices a small body tucked next to Mongoose. "Oh my God, Des," she cries as she grabs her and holds her. "How are you?"

"I'm better," Des admits quietly, eyes haunted by the past, pinched at the corners by fatigue, the light streaming in through the huge windows not lending a kind view to a face carved by the horror of the past year.

"Come, sit by me, we can talk," Kat says kindly. "So much has happened that I wanted to tell you, but couldn't find you. I let you down Des, I'm sorry. I should have searched for you harder," Kat admits tearfully.

"Kat, you didn't do anything wrong. You weren't responsible for me. You were never responsible for me. We were partners, co-workers, nothing more. I'm glad you went and did what you did, because we wouldn't be where we are now if you hadn't. There are many things that happened to me, all by my own decisions. Most were stupid, ignorant decisions, but I made them, therefore I have to live with them."

"We all make mistakes, Des. This country, with everything that's now happening, it's bad. But I think we're on the right track. I trust Snake, Eli, and Mal they're good people, smart people. If anyone can change the course that this world is headed in, I really believe they can. I hope they can, because if they can't, then there's nothing anyone can do. I prefer to think we can change things. Enough about that, now tell me how did you end up in that courtesy camp? Did they take you there? Were you forced?"

"No, idiot that I was, I went there to help actually. I thought I was going to help. I thought it was a "courtesy camp" someplace people could go to have a mini vacation while making the chip decision. That's what everyone believes when they go there. It's so far from the truth that I was shocked so deeply I didn't know what to do. It was horrible Kat. I had no power to stop anything, I had to watch as people were hurt, abused, murdered, starved, the children, the poor children," she says in a sob. "There are things that happened so bad that they're forever burned into my memories. I've had to learn to not think, not let myself relax, because when I do, I see everything over and over. It's like living a nightmare."

"I can't even imagine. I've seen some pretty bad stuff, but from what I've heard, it doesn't compare to what you've experienced. I'm sorry Des, so sorry," Kat adds softly, compassionately.

'Finish up ladies we're going to meet in the situation room in five minutes. Des, you need to eat, at least a little. You'll never gain strength without food," Mongoose says protectively eyes gently searching Des' face, noticing the fatigue and pain that can't be hidden from him. "You can talk more after but for now what we need to do is prepare. I have a feeling that this is going to be the most important time of our lives'."

"Welcome everyone," Jacob says as he starts the meeting. "Today we're going to start deploying. Transportation's arranged, we'll be able to fly out ten at a time. The reason I did ten is I don't want everyone on the same plane. There's too much risk of taking us all out at once. If something were to happen, which I hope it doesn't then there will be others that can continue on, and finish what we've started. It's important to not only those present, but to the United States people, the people of the world. Jane has put into play her plans of which will begin at the One World Summit next week when she officially takes the last seat at the table, the One World table. Once she's been placed there, her plans for world domination will be complete. Her chips, as you're all aware have been accepted worldwide. What the people of our country and the other countries of the world do not know is that hidden deeply in her chips is her capability to control each and every individual even to the point of death. Thankfully for us, we have someone more than capable of hacking into the chip's database, tweaking the program to our benefit without her programmers ever getting a whiff of it. We've been able to stop a few of her plans because of that. So we've had a little practice, and have set up in advance everything we're going to need to stop her and her murderous acts. Of course, there's never a guarantee, especially where Jane's concerned. She always seems to have something up her sleeve, a surprise waiting in the wings. It's almost as if she's being guided by someone, someone a hell of a lot more devious and evil than we've ever been up against."

"Oh my God," Des gasps, loud enough for most of the room to hear her.

"What's the matter," Mongoose asks quickly when she just sits there, eyes wide yet unfocused.

"It's the end," she murmurs. "It's the end" she repeats, head turning slowly to face him.

"The end of what?"

"The end, you know, the end times. It was foretold," she adds assuming everyone would understand.

"The end times of what," Jacob demands impatiently.

"The world, the prophecy, you know, in Revelations, the bible."

"You think these are the end times?" he asks in disbelief.

"Y e s," she says slowly. "It makes sense now, don't you see? Everything that's been happening, the strange weather, the volcanic eruptions, the explosions, everything! The chip, Oh My GOD! It's his, its evil, oh no, it's happening!" she sobs heartbroken. "I never believed, I never believed," she cries out. "It's too late, what are we going to do, it's too late!" she utters as she slides to the floor in a dead faint, Kat looking on in disbelief, Mongoose trying to cushion her fall.

"Snake, she's right. I never thought totally along those lines, but it all adds up. The way she got office, the chips, the evil that she brought into the country all the while manipulating the people not just of this country but of the world, making everyone else responsible for all the bad that's occurred. The strange way that everyone follows her guidance. The murders, the atrocities that have occurred, the way the world's natural weather has been disrupted. Even down to the asteroids that may hit the earth soon, the cosmos is in an uproar. A power has been unleashed and it's fighting for complete control. It all points to one thing, the apocalypse! We've been going through the tribulations and didn't even know it," Kat finishes, dismayed while the entire room disrupts in heated discussions, loud arguments, complete chaos.

"You really think that with everything that we've been through for the past year and a half that this was all pre-ordained? From Jane's taking office to all the deaths, all the eruptions, all the strange things that have happened, it's all out of the bible? I've read the bible, granted it was when I was younger, but I don't remember anything in it comparable to what we've experienced lately!" Jacob says loudly to Kat before yelling at the room to "tone it down!' "I understand that the bible was written in old world language with mostly parables, which in turn has to be put into our time, our language," he continues "but I still think you're stretching it."

"I'm not stretching it any farther than Nostradamus did, but he still didn't put things into our language either and look at how many things that he predicted came true!"

"That's beside the point. We can stand here and discuss this till we're both blue in the face, but in reality, we don't have time. Jane's about to do something that we have to stop and we're running out of time. I say first we finish what we need to do right now, then we can discuss this 'end of the world theory' more. Now," he says as he moves his attention from Kat to the room in general "if I can get everyone's attention again . . . We're running on a tight schedule. I have close to 50,000 people that need transportation to Brussels by the end of this week. We're going to need all if not more when it comes down to the war, and war is definitely what it's going to be. It'll be Americans against pretty much the rest of the world. The only thing we'll have going for us is surprise, and that's not even guaranteed. It's considerably difficult to keep these kinds of numbers, this kind of movement on the down low, but so far, so good. I spoke with Chico and there's nothing in the President's circle, no rumors, no sign of knowledge, unfortunately, Jane does have a way of appearing just when you think you're home free. Next, I would like a report on the latest from the compound. The news has covered the explosions, Jane of course has given the media their due, but I want reality, not through the grape vine news. Eli, Rand, Mongoose, stay after so you can report on everything thoroughly, I'd appreciate it. Now," he says as he faces the room "there are flights taking off frequently out of fifteen airports throughout the country. We're using the Civilian Reserve Air Fleet along with a few of our larger military planes like the C-5's, all under the radar. You'd be surprised at how many civilians don't follow the President. The logistics for this whole mission has been unbelievable but so far we've managed to do it. Every plane has been asked to land at specific bases as close as a hundred miles or so from Brussels and as inconspicuously as possible, no tail lights, no logos, actually they've been ordered to land without lights. Under normal circumstances, this is not requested, but these are not normal times. We can't surprise Jane if we let her know that we're coming. We've got all the info you'll need to get your flight out, where you're going and when you'll arrive. All I ask is that you keep this on a need to know basis, the fewer that know, the less chance of premature discovery. Just see Mallory on your way out for your assignments.

"Kat, help me get Des to her room. She's not snapping out of it very fast," Mongoose mutters worriedly. "Rand, can you give us a hand," he yells.

"Sure, here, pick her up and I'll follow you back," Kat says as Rand hurries over.

"She's not coming out of it," Mongoose warns Rand on his way out of the room.

"She'll be fine she just needed the rest more than usual. She has been through a lot in the past year."

"I know, that's why this has me a little worried," Mongoose adds with a scowl.

"She's just in a deep sleep now. Probably the best she's had in a long time. She'll be fine. Put her on the bed, I'll check her vitals then let her sleep for awhile, give her mind a chance to rest."

"I'll stay with her until she comes out of it, you two head back to the situation room. You can let me know what I miss later," Mongoose says as he settles into a chair by the bed.

"She'll be fine, and I promise to take notes if I need to and let you know what the next phase is," Rand promises as he heads out the door.

"It was unbelievable Jacob; you had to see it to believe it. I've never seen a fire so consuming. It burned hot and black. It had to have been from C4 but something else too. From all the calls I received, every state experienced the same thing. Ring any bells?"

"Oh yeah, she did the same thing to every capitol building in every state. What a bitch. She doesn't care who gets hurt or killed as long as it accomplishes her agenda. She's got no conscience; she's got a goal and nothing will stop or deter her from reaching it."

"I'll be glad when we can finish this. I'm tired of waking up every morning not knowing what to expect. We've been in a war zone for the past year and I need a vacation," Eli adds wearily, fatigue having added unkind years to his once youthful countenance.

"I hear ya brother, believe me I think we're all sick and tired of this. A few more days and it will be over, at least I hope so," Jacob adds as Kat walks back into the room.

"What do you hope so?" she asks as she leans into him, just to be closer.

"Hoping our lives change next week. We're all tired of the bull . . ."

"Do you think we're going to be able to make a difference? Are we enough to change the course of things?"

"I don't know if we're enough, what I do know is we have to go in with open minds and lots of determination. We've come this far and we can't back down now. Win or lose, we're in this till the end," he states as his cell phone comes to life. "Now what," he asks as he answers it while turning away. It's always easier to talk and concentrate when you're not looking at someone and they're not looking at you. "That's awesome; we've already started people out. You should be seeing a few here and there with a full transport arriving every four hours. Hey, I've got a lot of good people out there helping make this happen, it's not all me, trust me," he says quietly. "Yeah, I promise. I'll call you when we're getting ready to board," he adds as he turns to face his siblings. "That was Nick Rantrall, my ex-boss," Jacob offers with a small grin.

"What," Kat asks on a gasp. "How'd he get your cell number? What did he want?" she asks nervously.

"Shhh, stop Kitten, don't worry, he's on our side. We've been working together towards the same goal for a couple of months now. He just called to see if things were on schedule. Fortunately, they are. He's providing transportation near here for the people headed on the first trips out. He wanted to make sure the first load was on its way. Thankfully they are. The first trip should commence in about four hours from now, at least the one leaving from Richmond. We have fourteen other sites that will be taking off soon too. We have to be very cautious, now is the time that we could be found out. Our airspace is monitored very closely, fortunately we have Mal and we've worked hard on getting into the satellites and rerouting the system that monitors our air space. Let's hope it works. A lot of good all this planning will be if they see us, because you know they'll stop us if they can. Now, I think it's time to pack up the stuff we're going to need for the next week, including weapons and ammo. Let's get started on that, I plan on taking off tomorrow morning early. Can you be ready Eli?"

"No problem. That gives me time for a shower and some sleep. I don't need much, a sleeping bag, ammo, just the basics. I've gotten used to living on pretty much nothing," he adds with a weary smile.

"You can sleep during the flight too," Kat adds compassionately.

"That's right, I can, thanks Kat," Eli says as he turns to head to his old bedroom.

Chapter Thirty

"There's something going on, I'm just not sure what and where," Jane mutters as she paces the handmade cashmere rug of her private suite sunlight spilling in through the bank of windows as her mother and father sit quietly and watch. "Something's happened here in the states and I don't know what it is," she yells, her father jumping in his chair at the sudden loud outburst.

"Jane, what do you mean," he asks nervously.

"I can feel it father, something's going on and I'm not sure what. I need to know about everything, how can I stay prepared when something happens if I don't know in advance?"

"It's impossible to know everything before it happens, things sometimes happen."

"I know that," she yells sarcastically.

"Oh," her mother gasps at the tone of her voice towards her father.

"What mother?"

"Jane, that was disrespectful of you towards your father," she murmurs hesitantly.

"Sorry father," she snaps. "As the President, my position demands respect, however, I would never do anything to hurt you or be disrespectful towards you. Please forgive me," she requests quietly.

"Of course Jane."

"Now, have you heard anything that I should know about?"

"I've heard a few murmurs, but nothing that I would call substantial. Just through security and staff, but I thought they were just rumors. If I thought there was anything to worry about I would have mentioned them to you,"

"Father, anything that concerns me, needs to be mentioned to me. What did you hear?"

"That Quinton is power hungry. He doesn't have the personality for following, especially a female. He's too dominant a personality to follow anyone. I just thought people were blowing off steam, that there was nothing to worry about there. Usually when people talk it's to complain, probably about a perceived wrong that was done to them. Most of the time, it leads to nothing."

"Well, this time it has lead to something. He actually had a takeover planned for the summit. I can't take any chances that everything we've worked for won't come to pass because a stupid man wants to be in charge. The problem is I don't know how large his group is. I've had to put him in lock down for now until I decide how to move forward with this. Do you have any ideas?"

"I'll think on it, but you're the one that's always known how to handle problems, Jane. We just stood by to assist you when you made the decisions."

"I know, and thanks' Dad. I need you to keep your ears open now though and see if you can find out how far this problem got, how many people were involved. We leave soon for Brussels, and once I'm in the air, it'll be hard to take care of problems here. I still can't believe that this happened at all. I must have had my head in the clouds to have missed this. I just wonder what the hell the surprise was that he had planned, and did it put a stop to it by locking him up, or are there more, ready to jump in where he left off? I've worked my whole life for the final destination of Brussels and my special seat at the One World table. I've even got a huge surprise for the United States, actually the whole world that I plan on sharing with them after I take the seat officially. I won't tolerate anyone coming between me and my goal. I'm so close now," she adds excitement building just thinking about what's happening for her soon.

"We're excited too Jane. We have planned for this our whole adult lives. We will be able to watch you succeed, the way we've always dreamed."

* * *

"What are you looking at," Snake whispers into Kat's ear after finding her standing at the window quietly, watching the sun set, the sky a beautiful dark blue shot with gold.

"Nothing," she murmurs leaning back against this man that she loves, wondering what tomorrow will bring, realizing that this may well be the last peaceful moments of her life. Wishing she could have had more time, more days to spend discovering her feelings for Snake. More time to live and love.

"Things will work out," he promises quietly,

feeling her introspection, her sadness, quietness, the room as dark as her thoughts now. "There's never been a guarantee, kitten. We have each other, at least we do now. I wish we would have had more time too, but at least we've had this time. Let's not waste any of the time we have tonight. This is our time, we have until tomorrow morning. Time enough to love, do those things that turn you and me into us. I like that word," he admits as he tightens his hold on her, bends to kiss her neck, that vulnerable, sweet neck.

"I love you Snake," she whispers as she turns in his arms, stares into his eyes, eyes of such a crystal blue that you can drown in them, arms so big and strong that you can feel safe in them, a man of such strength not only physically but mentally who can and will stand between her and all her fears.

"Kitten, I love you," he says quietly as he gently guides her to the bed, the room dark, shadows covering items and hiding them from immediate view, a slight crack of light coming in from the hall before he closes the door blanketing them in the softness of dark. Two lovers finally alone, ready to consummate their love for the last night before all hell breaks loose, life getting in the way again. "Shh, no tears kitten, not tonight. Tonight we lock out the world, think only about us, our wants and needs. We don't waste our time or energy on anything else but this," he says slowly, voice raspy with want, hands touching slowly and thoroughly as he kisses her, tongues gliding against each other, lips sucking, teeth nipping, while gently lowering her onto the bed after stripping her of her clothes, then quickly divesting himself so they're finally skin against skin, hands, and lips touching everywhere.

"Snake," she moans as she finds him kissing and sucking his way down her neck, her chest, lavishing her breasts thoroughly while she smoothes, touches him everywhere, more urgently now matching fire for fire. Her body going molten with desire as his wandering mouth reaches lower, the most intimate of sharing upon her, her breath quickening, the excitement level so high feelings so intense she can't breathe in enough air. Her body tightening, no going back, no escaping until that moment when the explosion is so great she gasps, lights flashing under closed eyelids, limp with exhaustion she welcomes the feel of him kissing his way back up to her mouth, covering her body with his, winding her up to the point of no return, again.

"My turn," she whispers flipping him on his back, "tit for tat," she adds as she starts her journey in the same exact route that he took while paying particular attention to his nipples, creating hard little pebbles, thoroughly enjoying his groans knowing she's giving him the same pleasure she got, and enjoying it just as much as he did. She loves this man with all her being, gifting him with a night that he will never forget, one that will stay in his thoughts and get him through the next chapter of this life.

"Kitten," he says as he hauls her up, kissing her with abandon while trading places, spreading her thighs with his knee's and settling between, a quick move finds him sheathed tightly, a gasp caught by his mouth while continuing where he left off.

"Snake," she groans loudly as he increases his strength and speed, the rhythm as old as time and as necessary as life, sweat starting to gather on both bodies, the slipperiness adding to the excitement, the smell primal, the essence of life.

"Ahh," he groans "hold on babe," he mutters quickening his pace, her body tightening around his like a vise, unable to hold much longer when she screams his name into his mouth shattering him, a climax exploding both bodies, a new feeling for each, the melding of two souls.

"Kitten, it's time to wake up. We have to leave in an hour and I figured you'd want a shower," she hears as she opens her eyes finding the light of dawn entering the room.

"Hmmm, that was the shortest night of sleep I've ever had," she admits, studying his face in the pre-lit room, loving every sharp angle, the glittering blue of his eyes the windows to his soul.

"Sorry," he says quietly with a smile "you didn't get much sleep, but I'm not r-e-a-l-l-y sorry," he adds watching her face bloom pink from his remarks before moving out of her way so she can sit up.

"I'm not sorry either," she admits in happiness hustling out of bed and running into the shower before her body can do anything else to embarrass her.

"This is it then," she says finishing pulling her hair into a pony and out of the way, a sadness filling her heart as she looks in the mirror seeing an average sized woman with died black hair, pale skin, and shadows in her green eyes, nerves building for the day for the unknown.

"Yeah, this is it," he admits moving behind her as she stares, his size dwarfing hers, but the two creating a picture of love united as he wraps his arms around her, bends down for one more kiss. "Everything's packed and ready we just have to grab our jackets and vests. I took care of the weapons last night. We've got plenty of ammo. I think I got everything we're going to need. They're waiting for us at the airport and since it's only about a half hour from here, we've got enough time," he adds backing away while letting go, mind already occupied with his plans for the day.

* * *

"That's what we're flying in," she gasps when he comes to a stop near the ugliest plane she'd ever seen.

"You bet, why, what's wrong with it?"

"Snake, really? What's not wrong with it," she retorts, dread and suspicion warring in her head.

"It's the best transportation for our purpose. It can land with short notice, fly under the wire, it has no markings, it's a Cadillac of planes, and it's not picked up on radar."

"Well if that thing," she says pointing at a hulking carbon black monster "is what I'm getting in, I should have had a bottle of whisky before we left the house."

"Ahhh, now don't worry, it'll be fun," he grins while ushering her up the stairs and through the top of the 'plane' where the pilot sits. "Don't touch anything, see that seat right there to the left behind the pilot's seat, that's yours, and I'll sit next to you. This plane wasn't built for people, but for a single person, the pilot. It's been specially outfitted for three, for this one flight."

"What kind of plane is this, Snake?"

"We call it a Goblin. But it's actually a stealth fighter. They not used anymore, they're retired, but this is in a private airport, and not too many people know about this little treasure. It'll get us where we need to go pretty fast, and hopefully undetected. I wanted to wait as long as possible to leave so that if it does draw attention, it won't draw it to all the other transports that are going on right now. We'll be close to the last leaving and may even beat some of them getting there."

"You don't have to sound so excited to be in here," she adds, looking around at all the switches, buttons and the extremely cramped space finding no comfort in anything no familiarity, dread settling like a lead ball into her stomach.

"This is my first time," he admits with a laugh "but it's going to be awesome. Start strapping in, it'll take awhile. That's also an ejector seat for emergency purposes which I'm sure we won't need," he adds hastily when he sees her eyes narrow in suspicion.

"It better not be, I'm NOT jumping or, what you said, being freakin ejected!"

"Me either! Put on the helmet, and the face mask, it's for oxygen and it's our way to communicate."

"What!"

"It's because we're going to go so fast," he says soothingly. "You don't have to worry, you'll love it," he promises refusing to look her in the eye. "Here's our pilot now," he adds noticing Lt. Jeff Watts climbing into the cockpit.

"Good morning Sir," Jeff says as he steps into the cockpit and starts flipping switches while situating himself in his seat, an average sized twenty something with intelligent hazel eyes, brown military short hair and an aura of professionalism suited more for an older man.

"Lieutenant this is Kat Thomas, Kat, this is Lt. Jeff Watts formerly with the USAF, now with the People's Liberation Group. He'll be our pilot until we get to Beek, Netherlands where we pick up our next stage of the journey. So for the next six hours or so, we'll be sharing the cockpit."

"Snake, what's in Beek, Netherlands? I've never heard of that place before. You sure it even exists?"

"Oh yeah, it exists. As a matter of fact it's got the perfect airport for landing the Goblin, totally up to date, modern and neutral."

"Oh . . . .neutral, I get it," she mumbles.

"It's nice to meet you Kat. This flight won't last long; all the logistics' have been arranged so all we need to do now is sit back and enjoy the flight."

"We are clear to go," Jeff says as the plane starts moving forward. "Hold on, the take off's the worst part," he reassures them as they gain speed very quickly, Kat's head is thrown back against the high seat back, her body shaking as if in a palsy, unable to move her hands easily, let alone any other part of her body. *This is going to suck me right into the seat*, fear taking hold.

"Ahhh," she screams, the G force something she's never experienced before. "Snake," she cries unable to move. *I'm going to die* she decides before everything narrows to a small viewing area, just prior to lights going out completely.

"Breathe Kat, breathe!" Snake yells when he notices her stillness, "we're almost there," he adds urgently, "You're going to be okay, I promise. The force is almost over, just another few seconds."

"We are at speed, altitude still climbing," Jeff says into the microphone. "You should notice a lessening of the G force, breathing should be a little easier," he adds calmly, checking all the instrument gauges and panels.

"Snake, you could have warned me," she mutters when she's finally able to breathe and see again.

"I was afraid to warn you. I didn't want you refusing to get on the plane. Plus, there was no need to scare you in advance; you were freaked out enough during the take off."

"Yeah, can you blame me?" she asks quietly. "You know Snake, pay backs a bitch; you just wait till we get on the ground again. You had better be afraid, be very afraid."

Jeff breaks in thinking to diffuse the situation, "We'll be arriving at our destination in approximately six hours. We'll be refueling in air in multiple places, part of the logistics that was pre-scheduled. We are now at 50,000 feet and holding, unfortunately at this height you're unable to see anything below, but the sky's a beautiful blue from here, the clouds no more than big white fluffs."

"Thanks Jeff, for trying to distract me. The sky is beautiful, but I won't forget about this. Snake can tell you my memory's pretty good," she adds with a smirk, her green eyes still vivid in a face gone too pale.

"Oh, I can attest to that. She never forgets anything, spoken, read or experienced," he admits dryly.

A loud crackle, static, almost white noise starts interrupting her voice as she gets ready to reply to his last statement, cutting her off when "White horse this is zero one zero, come on," crackles through the radio, all three of them hearing the message in between the static.

"Zero one zero this is Whitehorse," Jeff replies "talk quick we've got radio interference here."

"Copy Whitehorse, we just had a few planes knocked" crackle, static * ' * ' * air force fighter jets were dispatched from an *' * ' * unknown area."

"Zero one zero, repeat, you're breaking up."

"Copy Whitehorse, we just had a few planes knocked" crackle, * ' out of the sky after air force fighter jets were *' * ' * unknown area."

"Zero one zero this is Whitehorse, which aircrafts?" Jeff replies over Kats gasp.

"Whitehorse this is zero one zero. The aircrafts * ' * ' * of Ohio, C-5's loaded to the max. Estimate is * ' * ' * ree hundred and fifty passengers, * ' * ' * vivors," the radio voice crackles and finishes.

"Zero one zero this is Whitehorse, any danger * ' * ' * 'our transport?"

"That's a negative * ' * ' * ehorse. I was able to put the word out * ' * ' * ' NOT terrorists. I didn't give the * ' * ' * ' * ' ation but informed them * ' * ' * ' friendlies, this is zero one zero * ' *ut."

"Copy * ' * ' * ne zero, Whitehorse is out."

"Breathe Kitten," Snake says after glancing

over at her, reeling from the news just heard on the radio.

Tears streaming down her checks she grabs his hand squeezing so tight that her knuckles turn white, fear radiating off her in waves.

"It wasn't Eli or Mal, Kitten, relax," he reassures her through his teeth knowing what she's thinking, fury taking over his body as he thinks about all those that were lost. "They may not have been blood relatives, but they were still part of the family, and now I'm really pissed," he states flatly, teeth grinding.

"Were there any survivors?"

"Doubtful but I couldn't make out everything they were saying, too much interference."

"Yeah, I couldn't hear everything either."

"It's possible I suppose, but not usual when planes are shot down."

"What about Mongoose, Rand, Des? They could have been on one of those flights, couldn't they?"

"They could have, but it won't do any good worrying about it from here. We'll find out soon enough when we land, for now, I'm going to rest my brain, think about non-important things for a change."

"I wish I could do that, but my brain doesn't shut down very easy. I can't help thinking about that, and them, and Jane, and what's happened till now. She's so unbelievably evil, I can't believe it."

"She won't be for much longer. I refuse to believe that we can't change this. I'm going there knowing in my heart that we will fix this. We can change what's happening. The United States, NO, the World, will never again be what it used to be, but we can stop her from destroying it completely. We can begin to rebuild. Maybe make things better than they were, who knows, but I do know that we are going to stop her, no matter the cost," Snake vows quietly with strength and determination.

"Sorry to interrupt Sir, but we're going to be refueling shortly. You've got nothing to fear, it's just a little nerve wracking for someone that's never seen it done before. I can assure you that this is not the first time I've had to do this and it won't be the last since we'll be doing this again in a couple of hours," Jeff adds seeing the fuel carrier to the right slightly above their position. "To your right, see him, that's our goal."

"Don't you think we're a little close?" Kat gasps out as they get even closer.

"It's going to look like they're sitting on us in about five seconds, but we'll never touch anything except the hose. If you feel too close, I would recommend closing your eyes. We'll be like this for a couple of minutes, we have to hook up, load up and then release and close. It's all done through switches and electronics; no one is ever in any danger."

"I can't believe how nonchalant you seem, we're going how fast and we're how far up in the sky. If we're this high and fast, and they're going the same speed, if we hit each other, there would be nothing left," she murmurs facts flying through her head.

"That's true, but we're not going to touch so there's nothing to worry about," he adds firmly, correcting the panic he hears in her voice.

"If you say something," she begins to say and screams a little when she feels something bump them.

"That's just the hose. We're getting ready to attach and load the fuel. Nothing to worry about," he adds while pushing buttons to start the process. "Just a couple of minutes and we'll be on our way again. I can speed this baby back to normal speed."

"What, normal speed? What the heck are we doing right now?"

"We had to slow down a little to fuel, but it only takes approximately three and a half minutes, total. And we are. . . there, done, now just have to release the hose, shut all the fuel equipment down, wait until the computer recognizes the fuel and adjusts the amounts and there, we're done. Wave good bye, we'll be seeing someone else in a couple of hours to do the same thing all over again."

"That's it, we're done already," Kat says, amazement in her voice.

"Yep, that's it," he agrees as he engages and they pick up speed.

"Awesome, that wasn't bad at all," she finishes with a sigh of relief.

"Good, then can I have my hand back," Snake asks in amusement.

"Oh," she says, embarrassed after realizing she had a death grip on him as he starts to rub the blood back into his hand, a smirk on that too handsome face. "Sorry," she murmurs, a smile replacing the fear of moments ago.

"No problem Kitten," he says quietly. "Glad to be able to help."

Chapter Thirty-One

"President Martin, we have some news," Nick Rantrall says quietly as he enters her office unannounced.

"What is it Nick?"

"Multiple unrecognized planes were found in our air space. We were unable to find out who they were but according to law, we had to take them out. We can't have anything in our airspace unknown, it poses too big of a threat, especially post 9/11. I wanted to personally inform you that the problem has been taken care of by our security forces. We followed standard operating procedure and dispatched fighter jets shortly after discovering them and when there was no response they were fired on. There's nothing left, unfortunately for the, but fortunately for us the planes went down mostly over water. We have the coast guard moving into the recovery areas and hopefully we'll know shortly who they were and why they were in our space."

"Excellent Nick, any guesses who they were," she asks calmly moving to the window to look out at the bright blue sky, the people walking around unaware, amazed how peaceful things look knowing that some planes were just blown out of the sky.

"Actually I don't, but things have been awfully

quiet lately, who knows, it could have been anything, anyone."

"True, but it just seems coincidental that it happens on the day I leave for the summit. I think you'll find they were up to no good, and probably headed for Brussels."

"You may think what you will, President Martin, but until we have some proof, I'm going to believe that they were plane's in distress with possible radio problems. They were just in the wrong place at the wrong time."

"No way Nick, there's too much of a coincidence in the timing. I'm sure it had to do with the summit. Fortunately for us, I've got everything totally prepared. It wouldn't have mattered had they made it, there's little to nothing that can be done now to stop the progress. In another day I will become the most powerful woman in the world as is my due, and everyone on this planet will know when that happens. I'm getting pretty excited about the surprise that I've prepared for the world. It will only reinforce my position."

"Can I ask what that surprise is President Martin?"

"Sure you can ask, but you won't get the answer from my lips. This surprise will be announced as I take my rightful seat at the One World table. Once that's accomplished, I'll present the gift. The world will see it through every television and hear it over every radio station in the world, simultaneously. I've told no-one since I didn't want it leaked anywhere, and I trust no-one, therefore you'll have to wait just like everyone else has had to! Now if we're done here, I'm going to check and make sure my parents are packed. We leave in less than twenty-four hours. My life will finally be complete. And now if you'll excuse me, I need to see me parents, make sure they're ready to get on the plane. I expect you to keep me informed on the planes that we shot down, find out who and what they were and keep me informed of anything that needs my attention."

"Absolutely President Martin, you can always depend on me."

***

"Mother, there you are," Jane says after entering the rooms provided to her parents. "Are you ready? We're leaving here in less than an hour and will be in Brussels before bedtime tonight. Tomorrow's the day, the day planned for, the day I was born for. All your hard work and sacrifice will finally pay off. Every dream that you had will finally be within reach," Jane says her voice excited, eyes sparkling, face flushed. "Oh, Chico, I didn't know you were here," she says quieter now, watching Chico's expression which doesn't change, remains bland, expressionless yet watchful. "I'm sorry. You actually slipped my mind. I was going to let you know that for the next few days, you won't be needed. There's no reason to take you to Brussels with me, my parents will be fine with me and all the security that the European Union offers freely. So please, consider this some time off, well earned if I must say. Also, I wanted to thank you for the great care that you've given to my parents for the last couple of weeks. It's made my life much easier and it's appreciated."

"It's been my pleasure, President Martin."

"Thank you. I believe you can go now, go and do something for yourself, go have fun, whatever it is that you do in your time off."

"Thank you President Martin. If you're sure that I won't be needed, then I will leave."

* * *

"Eli, its Chico. Jane just released me from my duties. This is the first opportunity that I've had to contact you all freakin day. I had ears in the oval office when the General came in to give Jane the info about the planes being shot down. Seven planes, man. Our people killed on seven different planes. Have you been able to let the Lt. know? We lost hundreds of troops today, I'm not even sure who yet. I doubt if the General knows who was on those planes. From what I was able to overhear they were in multiple places over the states at the time they were targeted. Most landed in water, but there were some that were taken out over the ground. No survivors from any of the planes that were taken out."

"Yeah, thanks Chico. I've had information filtering in all afternoon about the damage and losses. I haven't been able to reach Jacob yet; they're getting ready for landing, they turned in their cell phones before they left. They'll be picking up their new ones once they reach Brussels. Unfortunately they won't be reachable until they arrive at their destination. They may hear through their pilot about this, but it probably won't be helpful in telling them what happened. You know how air speak is. Just enough to make them think and probably worry them but there's nothing that can be done about that now."

"That's unfortunate Eli. What do you need me to do? I'm officially off duty now; Jane released me until after her return from Brussels."

"I'll have to get back to you about that, Chico. Things are crazy right now. I've had to cancel a shit load of flights. It's too dangerous for anyone to try to get there, especially after they shot so many of ours down. But I promise to get back to you within the hour and let you know our new plans."

"Thanks man, and anytime you need me, just call."

"Will do."

Chapter Thirty-Two

"We'll be landing in just a few minutes in Beek. Once there, I've got transportation lined up. We just need to unload our bags. It won't take long to reach our destination, and get everything set up. We've got a full day and a half before the big event."

"I'll be glad to be back on firm footing," Kat says quietly with a quick glance at Snake, unspoken promises in her eyes, "but where is Beek?"

"Beek is where we're landing, however technically it's not really Beek, it's Maastricht Aachen Airport, located in the town of Beek" he replies teasingly.

"Snake!"

"Sorry, I couldn't help myself. Beek is technically in The Netherlands near the border of Brussels. Transportation from there was easy to arrange. Unfortunately there are few airports that are neutral, especially for asking questions. But luckily I've got a good friend that lives near the airport and arranged for our flight in. We're cleared for landing this baby with no questions asked. He's also arranged transportation for the two of us in a non-descript black older vehicle, something that's frequently seen on the local roads. I wanted to be sure we didn't have any problems reaching our destination. Too much depends on us getting there on time."

"Can you believe it's time? That so much has passed, so many things have happened and we've reached this point in time. Life went by fast Snake, faster than I thought possible. I can't believe we've reached this point in time. That we have to do what we are about to do," her voice getting quieter, and more introspective.

"I know. It's been quite a ride, Kitten. I'm glad it was with you, these past months. I wish things were different, and they could be but we can't see the future so have no idea what's really going to happen. I suggest we just take all of this a moment at a time. That's really all we can do," he adds a quick squeeze to her hand, and intense look in his eyes.

"Look," she says breathlessly as they drop altitude and she see's land for the first time in hours.

"A couple of more minutes and we'll be back on the ground."

"Just another couple of days and the future will be witnessed by everyone in the world."

"You got that right Kitten," he says as he feels the plane slow and bank, readying for landing. "I have to say you've been an awesome pilot, Lt."

"Please, call me Jeff, Sir. We're part of the same team. If there's anything that I can do to help, please let me know. I'm here for the next 24 hours at least, unless you want me to hang in case you need a ride back?"

"I've already arranged for return transportation, but thanks. We can get together next month back in the states and talk about everything that happened, if you'd like."

"That would be awesome, Sir. I'm stationed near Arlington and am in the book, so give me a call when you're back and we'll get together."

"You got it Jeff, thanks."

"Here's our destination. I'm not sure where you're meeting your next step, but I wish both of you luck."

"Thanks Jeff," Snake says as the pilot opens the door to get out after having taxied to his parking area, this part of the airport nearly deserted.

"Thank God," Kat murmurs unhooking her safety belts, head phones and shimmying to get out of her seat. "I really like land," she admits to Snake after climbing down the ladder to get out of the cockpit.

"I figured. I kinda like it too but you have to admit that the ride wasn't that bad. Plus we made excellent time."

"Yeah, we made excellent time but remember what I said Snake, paybacks a Bitch. Now I say first stops a restaurant with a ladies room."

"There's one just a couple of minutes from here and in the right direction. I thought maybe we'd look around a little before heading to Brussels. We've got a little time and could maybe get a little sightseeing in on the way."

"Thanks Snake! I was hoping for a little down time."

"I think we deserve it. Besides, we know our plans but can't see the repercussions, so I have know idea what's going to happen. This may be our last chance to see this part of the world. I've heard the Netherlands is a beautiful country. It'd be nice if we could find a quaint little town with the old buildings, old shops. Just saying, that might be a nice way to spend some time together."

"That's so romantic Snake. I didn't realize you had that streak. But I'm glad you do," she finishes hastily at his narrow eyed glance.

"We really never had the chance to discover that part of us. We've always had too big of an agenda going and no time for the fun stuff. Since we could be done in a day and a half or so, then this may be the last opportunity to do anything like this together."

"You're so right," she agrees quietly glancing quickly away to hide the evidence of tears filling her eyes, knowledge of loss filling her soul.

"Here's our ride, hop in. I'll just throw these duffels in the back and we'll be good to go. Check the glove box and see if there are any shades in there since it looks like we're going to need them!"

"Yeah, it's a beautiful day. Blue, blue sky, puffers, and low wind, it's a perfect afternoon!"

"Once we clear this area, I'll stop at the first gas station so you can use the facilities. Then we'll head to Maastricht. It's the oldest city in the Netherlands and supposed to be truly beautiful. I guess it could be worse," he adds with a grin after getting out of the gates and onto the main road.

"I think I've heard about this area. Isn't this town also known as the 'Crown jewel of the South'?

"I don't know about that. It sounds to me like you know more about this place than I do," he adds a smirk making her want to kiss him into silence.

"Well, I guess we'll find out pretty soon. It's only a few miles from here, if I remember correctly. What I didn't remember was Beek. I should have, because it's close to here also, but technically we didn't land in Beek. We're actually near both Beek and Maastricht but because Maastricht overshadows Beek, well, the lesser known of the two, you know," she adds haughtily eyes sparkling full of mischief.

"Of course," he adds playing along. "There's a station, I'll pull in there for you."

"Thanks Snake, you're a life saver," she says checking to make sure her fanny-packs on and it's got everything she needs to freshen-up in it. "I'll be out in a few minutes."

"Take your time, we're in no hurry right now. Just starting our mini vacation, that's all."

"I'd like some food too," she admits "the flight amped me up and now I'm starving," she admits as she opens the door letting the cool air from the inside meet the warm air from the outside, the smell of clean air surrounding her, a slight hint of flowers and freshly mowed grass invigorating as she shuts the door quickly cutting off any response he was getting ready to make. She stops to enjoy the view surrounding her, a gas station and a small convenience store close but the view from beyond full of grass, a few tree's and some wild flowers growing here and there with little or no traffic at this time of the day. She finishes the walk slowly to the restroom and is pleasantly surprised that it's so nice, clean smelling, neat as a pin and well lighted. After using the facilities and washing her hands, she just stands and stares at herself in the mirror, seeing the black hair for a face too pale, a look that she's had to use for months in order to maintain her cover, but she wishes now she'd had time to go back to her natural blonde. Wondering if he sees her as she is now or as she was, and hoping it doesn't make a difference. After rinsing her face, adding a little more blush and lip gloss and brushing her hair quickly she decides that's as good as it gets, and heads back out to the car.

"You look beautiful Kitten," he murmurs and leans close to hold her gently before kissing her senseless.

"Wow," she breathes before clearing her throat, emotion riding high "I should add lip gloss more often if this is the kind of reaction it's going to get."

"It wasn't the lip gloss but the person wearing it," he contradicts and proceeds to kiss her again before she can make another comment, breathing her in like a man starving for air. "I think we better go before someone comes this way and see's something we don't want to share with anyone," he admits with a grin as he lets her go slowly, holding her steady until she regains her balance.

"Right," she says dreamily on a sigh, then louder when she realizes he's standing there staring at her dazed look with a small grin on his face. "Sorry, you see what you do to me," she adds in a husky voice, the need factor skyrocketing.

"Of course I do," he adds reaching for her and missing as she backs away too quickly taking her out of easy reach. "I plan on continuing this later, probably all night long," he promises before getting in the car and turning the air up, realizing it's much hotter out than he originally thought.

"We won't be able to take the car into the city. The roads are to narrow for vehicles. There should be parking though and walking will allow us to experience the city, not just view it from the windows."

"I like that idea. I've been sitting too long anyways. Beside, you can't see anything but the basics from the car. Maybe they've got the right idea by leaving the roads narrow and forcing people to walk, meander, and stop here and there."

"All right, here's a parking facility, let's dump the car. Make sure it's locked. I wouldn't want anyone taking our duffels. They'd be in for a slight surprise if they saw how we packed," he finishes with a chuckle.

"I wonder what the crime rate is here."

"Let's hope it's good, and when we get back to the car, it's just like we left it."

"I'm ready when you are," she says when she moves to his side of the car.

"Let's look for some dinner first. Then we can just walk around and take in the views."

"Sounds like a plan to me," she agrees eyes sparkling in excitement, something fun to do before the big event. "Look at the buildings, they're so old. You can feel the history here."

"Yeah, it looks pretty cool. The states aren't old enough to have anything like this around. But here, yeah, it goes back a ways."

"Hey, check out the walk ways. They're old rocks, stones. How cool is that. I wonder how bad this gets in the winter. I don't think I'd want to be walking everywhere with snow and cold. I'm not a cold or snow type person. I deal with it, but usually with my car heater running full. I seldom walk in the winter around home."

"You're so spoiled, Kitten."

"There's a restaurant right across the street. Want to check it out?"

"You bet, I'm hungry enough to eat a horse."

"I was hoping for more than horse. I wouldn't mind a nice thick t-bone steak, rare, with maybe a baked potato on the side."

"Yum, that sounds good to me, too."

"Let's see what they have to offer," he says as he guides her across the street and into a quaint little building with sparkling windows and a quiet air of old money. "Look's upscale," he murmurs while glancing around to see what the occupants look like and wait for the hostess to show them a seat.

"Yeah it does. Hey, did we bring money and do you think they take American money here?"

"I had some put in the car for us for when we arrived, and it's in euro, so it should be acceptable here. Let's hope so anyways. I'll ask her after we get our seats."

"Please, this way Miss, Sir" they're told after a petite brunette in a black silk dress and extremely high heels walks up to them from the back of the restaurant, a welcoming smile on her classically pretty face.

"Thank you," Kat says after arriving at a table for two set next to a window with a view of a beautiful old stone bridge that crosses a small river and was made for people to walk across, way too narrow for a vehicle.

"It's no wonder there's no vehicles allowed. Most of the roads and bridges are way too small for cars. Maybe a motorcycle would be all right, but it would ruin the whole ambience of the area. I think they've got it right here. Keep out all the modern stuff and maintain the old. It was build to last and enjoy."

"Yeah, it's really beautiful, I love it. Thanks for thinking about doing this today Snake. It means a lot and I'll cherish these memories today. I want today to last forever."

"Me too Kitten. It'd be nice if today was the first day of our lives together. But soon we'll be able to say that, there are just a couple of small things to take care of tomorrow and then we'll be done with our responsibilities.

"I don't know about that Snake. Can you picture the lack of responsibilities, for either one of us? I can't even begin to imagine what that would feel like or even mean."

"I just know that I for one would like to experience it, at least for a week or two. What could it hurt? Besides it's one of those things that I've never experienced therefore I deserve to at least try it."

"That's true. I like trying new things too, so in that we're a set. Can you read this menu? I'm not sure what language it is. I kinda wish Mal were here. She's so fluent in so many languages she'd probably know what this one is. It looks kind of like maybe Dutch or German. I didn't take either of those foreign languages, so I'm not sure."

"It's actually French," he adds with a grin.

"It's not French, idiot," she says with a snort and a laugh. "I took French and trust me, this is not French."

"Oh, well then it's probably Dutch. I'll ask when she comes back if they have anything in English and if not if she could tell us what's on the menu!"

"That works for me. My stomach doesn't care what language it is as long as the foods edible."

"Can I take your order?" a waiter asks in English with a heavy accent.

"Please. We don't speak whatever language that is on the menu, but we already know what we want. We just hope you have it."

"I'm sure we do, what would you like, and oh, the language is Dutch," she's told.

"Oh, thanks. I want a steak, rare with a baked potato loaded and a side salad with a light dressing, a roll and butter," Kat says before looking to Snake for his order.

"I'll have the same," he says coolly, waiting for any reaction from the waiter.

"Actually, we have that on the menu, so you're not ordering anything out of the ordinary. What would you like to drink?"

"I think a bottle of your house red would be perfect," Snake adds and watches the waiter leave after a quick excellent choice is commented on. "I'll be right back with your wine, one moment."

"Well that was easier than I expected," Kat murmurs in relief. "I feel better already!"

"Yeah, me too, but I'll feel a lot better once I have food in me."

"Excuse me, I'm sorry to intrude," a gentleman sitting at the table next to theirs interrupts.

"No intrusion, what can I do for you," Snake turns with a smile, finding an elderly gentleman with clear gray eyes, thin white hair, and a small white mustache in a very ruddy plump face looking at him from the next table over, waiting politely with a smile.

"I noticed your English language, and I'm assuming that you're from the states somewhere. Not southern, I'm not hearing that accent, but maybe northern?"

"Actually the D.C area, so a little southern but we don't have the southern drawl that a lot of people do from further south."

"Then let me ask, since you're from that area. What happened, why were so many planes shot down recently? Is there something going on that we need to be aware of? We're from the UK," he says gesturing to the elderly woman sitting next to him, "and we get the world news on our phones."

"What?"

"Why were so many planes shot down," he repeats confusion on his face.

"When did you hear there were planes shot down and how many," Snake repeats slightly louder.

"Earlier today, am I not right? Did the news report something that didn't happen?"

"I haven't heard the news. We only arrived about an hour ago and only stopped here for something to eat. We're on our way to Brussels."

"Oh, I'm sorry. I shouldn't have presumed that just because you're American you would know everything that went on, my apologies, Sir."

"No, no, that's all right. Can you tell me what you heard, please," he repeats.

"It was reported on the news earlier that there were seven planes that were shot down in different areas of the United States. The newscasters didn't go into a lot of details but they did say seven. One near D.C., one out west, they didn't go in to too many details, just said that they were shot down and would let everyone know when they had more details. But they were pretty sure there were no survivors. It's probably on constant coverage in the states, but only the basics are covered on world news."

"Wow," Snake murmurs expressionless, glancing at Kat to see how she's handling the news, finding her staring straight ahead, pale, eyes glazed.

"I take it from both your expressions and your questions that you hadn't heard about this. I'm sorry to be the one to break the news."

"Oh, no problem, thanks for sharing the news. No matter how we'd have heard of it, it would have been a shock."

"Here's our food," he says with relief when he notices his waiter headed in their direction.

"Good luck to you then, and it was nice speaking with you," the older gentleman says as he stands and helps his partner out of her seat and leaves.

"Snake, what," Kat says stopping when the waiter sets the food down, refills their glasses and inquires to their need for anything else.

"I don't know, Kat. We heard there was one

shot down, on the way here. Remember, it was kind of broken up but we still got the gist of what was happening. We didn't have any information then regarding who, what or where, but we'll make that our first job after we eat. We're going to need the energy so eat up. Then we can get moving and get our phones changed so that we can get the information we're missing. We'll figure it out. I refuse to think negative about our friends and family until we know more."

"You're right, but I can't help but think," she starts.

"Shh, just don't," he says briskly.

"All right, but as soon as," she starts again.

"I know, I promise," he interrupts.

"Fine," she says quietly, starting to eat.

Chapter Thirty-Three

"We've only got about an hour and a half before we hit Brussels and I've set up what we're going to need to be delivered and have waiting there. This is the end of the line, Kitten. After tomorrow, we'll know what's going to happen. Our cell phones will be waiting for us and we can contact Mal and Eli and see what the hell went down today. I'm sure everything's fine," he adds quickly when he notices her eyes tear up, her teeth gnawing on her bottom lip in worry, her face a paler shade of white considering they just had lunch.

"Everything's not fine," she says quietly. "It will never be fine again, Snake. Tomorrow the whole world will change, for better or worse, I don't know but it will change. We'll be hunted and our own government will be the hunters. We won't be able to go home, not for a long time, if ever."

"We'll make a new home, for the two of us. You're all I need now,' he promises softly. "As long as we're together, we're fine. And this is a pretty nice area of the world, but maybe something more tropical would be good. How much of a hardship would it be to live somewhere where no one knows us? Somewhere that the sun shines every day, the weathers warm and beautiful and we can sleep with each other, wake up together. Sounds like the perfect thing. Kind of like a retirement. A really early retirement, but truthfully, I'm ready for it. More than ready for it," he adds honestly.

"This is really pretty countryside, the rolling hills, the different shades of green, the blue, blue sky with an occasional bright white puffer cloud and flowers showing up in the middle of the green, a spot of color against a beautiful backdrop. But I think I'd rather be in warm weather, no chance of snow. I guess that I'm kinda sick of the cold."

"See, now you're talking," he adds grabbing her hand and kissing her knuckles softly, a promise in his eyes to her, forever. "No matter what we find out when we get to Brussels, the thing that matters to me is we're stopping Jane, and we're together. I'm focusing on those two things. I can't think about anything else until we finish the job that we started a year ago. You know how important this is. Even if what we find is worse case scenario we will still finish the job. It's what we have to do."

"I know, I just hope that it's a lot better than worse case."

"Me too, Kitten, me too!"

"What is that," she asks pointing to the road ahead and a large bird of some type that looks to be attacking something.

"I think it's a sea eagle. That's so cool," he adds as they get close enough to watch the eagle grab what looks like a snake off of the road and fly just above their wind shield as they meet at the road point, the bird massively large with a wing span of at least six feet and a long snake draping from its talons.

"That looked like a bald eagle, Snake. Not a sea eagle, but a bald eagle."

"That's what a sea eagle is. They were called sea eagles way before they were named bald eagles and become the United States national and protected bird."

"Oh, I didn't know," she admits as she cranes her neck to watch the eagle in flight. "That was beautiful, just beautiful," she adds softly, turning back in her seat to watch the road ahead. "Do you think it was a sign?"

"No, I think it was coincidence, that's all. We're not far from water, and they live near water, and will hunt many miles from home. They like snakes, I guess it gives them something different than fish all the time. It was a nice specimen and probably was a female since it was so big. I know the female eagle is substantially larger than the male. They have to be, since they need room for the eggs to form, but they're both excellent parents. They'll hunt for the young, keep them warm, take care of them, and probably push them out of the nests when it's time. That was a mature eagle though, its head was bright white, and it had all the right markings for a mature bald eagle. A pretty impressive sighting, I have to say. We were definitely in the right place at the right time for a change and it's still light enough to have seen that. Another few minutes and we'd have missed it, but then, another few minutes and they wouldn't have been hunting. A few more miles and we'll be entering Brussels. Look in the glove box, would you. There should be an address in there for our little flat along with directions on how to get in, where the key will be hidden."

"Is this what you're talking about?" she asks pulling out a small square postal card with a picture of the European Union Parliamentary building on the front, the woman on the beast metal statue in front of the building.

"Looks like it."

"It's got an address and a room number and what looks like a phone number on the back."

"Excellent, that's what we're going to need. If you look in the distance you can see a somewhat large looking town. I believe that's our destination. That should be Brussels."

"I'm getting a little nervous, Snake. Life's about to change, at least from what we're used to, I just hope what we're doing's the right thing. What if this is a big mistake? What will we do if we screw everything up?"

"Kitten, how can you even ask those questions? You've lived the last year in the front lines. Is everything we've experience, everything we've learned and all those loved ones we've lost worth so little?"

"No, of course they aren't, but Snake, we're talking WORLD now. This is a huge deal. Millions of people all over the world will be affected by what we're about to do. How can I not worry about it, about the rights and wrongs?"

"Well I guess you can not worry, but think about all that's gone on before and in your heart you'll know that this is our only choice. If we don't do something to stop Jane, she will take over the world and everyone on it and rule it as she's done in the states. As far as I'm concerned, that's definitely not living, not justly at least. That would be just surviving. She's been held slightly in check because of us, our groups and similar groups all over the states that were all but hidden for the past few months. Trust me, there's a lot more of us, worldwide, than Jane has any idea of. This is going to be a pretty big surprise for her and her followers. I'm just curious about that surprise that she's been promising for the world. I wish I could figure out just what it is. I'd rather have some idea than go into this totally blind."

"Yeah, she did promise it would be big, but just how big and in what direction. She's a scary individual. So yes, you're right. We need to stop her. I believe that what we're about to do is the right thing to do. That's all I can hope, at least," her voice dwindles on a sigh.

"We're entering the city now, let's see if we can find our flat. I'm kinda anxious to get my phone, and contact Eli. I want to know just what the hell happened in the US today, what planes were shot down. I won't be comfortable until I know exactly what happened."

"Yeah, I totally understand, I've had a bad feeling for hours now."

"No sense in worrying Kitten, until we've established what to worry about."

"That's why I didn't show you how worried I was," she says dryly. "I know what you would have said."

"I think this might be it," he says after pulling up to an older looking building on the outskirts of town, in a quiet looking kind of dilapidated area. "It's not the most expensive area," he admits with a smirk, "but it's off the beaten track and we should be able to get inside and probably come and go with no nosey neighbors."

"Yeah, as long as we can leave the car unattended," she adds quietly, a worried frown covering her face.

"Relax, we'll be fine, no problem," he reassures her as he opens his door, looking the old two story building over, a gray weathered wood with an open second story balcony, access to it from a large set of old wood steps, the same gray as the building and probably just as old. Not a speck of paint to be seen anywhere on the building. "Let's see what we've got," he murmurs as he grabs the large duffels out of the trunk while she gets the small suitcase and follows him up.

"This is it," he says stopping at room 237, the last room on the second floor, a corner room.

"Wow," she says, "it's a throw-back to the forties, or it is from the forties, same wall paper, same carpet, and even the same bedspread."

"Looks like it," he says placing his duffels on the single full size bed in the room. "Just remember, we're only sleeping here and probably for one night, tonight. After tomorrow, who knows where we'll be sleeping."

"True, but do you always have to be so practical? It's pretty frustrating, you know?"

"I know, at least I've been told by many people the same thing so it must be true. Me, I'm just stating a fact while trying to make something good out of reality."

"I appreciate it, Snake, really I do, but sometimes I just want to have a pity party for myself," she snipes, frustration clear in her voice. "Sometimes it just makes you feel better, don't you think?"

"Nope, it never makes you feel better to have a pity party. That only encourages sadness and bad moods. I prefer to look on the bright side. Now, let's see what was stocked for us. There should be cell phones, a lap top computer that's satellite capable since I doubt this place has Wi-Fi, and plenty of ammo for our weapons. Maybe some snacks and stuff, which I'd be grateful for. I really don't want to shop tonight, but we can if we need to since we do need to get out later and scope things out."

"Here's a box of stuff, in the closet."

"That should be what I'm looking for. I'll try and get a hold of Eli and see what the hell happened today. I'm never this hard to get in touch with so who knows what the news is going to be like," he murmurs as he dials. "Eli, its Jacob, we just got into Brussels and what a trip. Anyway we stopped for dinner and heard a rumor about planes being shot down over the states. What the hell's going on now? What! Who? Right, hold on," he orders as he takes a deep breath trying to refocus while Kat grabs his free hand and holds on tight knowing something bad happened just by the look of disbelief on his face. "Sorry, go on," he says concentrating on what's being said, anger, and now denial clearly written on his face. "Yeah, I'm here. Sorry. I'm just having a little bit of trouble accepting what happened. What about the plans, what can I expect? Is there anyone here that's going to be available or," he stops talking abruptly, listening closely. "All right, yeah copy that," he says, takes a deep breath and hangs up, staring at the phone before looking at Kat.

"What. . . what happened Snake?"

"You better sit down Kitten. A lot's happened while we were en-route. It's freakin unbelievable. Wow, I'm really having trouble with this," he says as he sits on the side of the bed, pulling her down with him.

"Tell me what's happened Snake. Please," she implores, tears swimming in her eyes, dread in her stomach.

"We lost a lot today, Kitten. Eli's fine and so is Mal and Rand but Mongoose, and Des, they were on one of the planes that that Bitch had shot down, them and hundreds of others when they shot down seven planes total. I can't believe they did that. No, I believe, I'm just so pissed that she shot down her own people. Her own citizens, those she swore to protect. Damn it," he growls before noticing Kat sobbing quietly after hearing her friends are gone, her old partner. *After everything that was done to Des and to make it out alive and close to starved, now dead and all for what?* "I'm sorry Kitten, I'm sorry," he says as he gathers her close, noticing how thin she's become, almost frail, in the past few months. Thinking how much trouble there's been, how unstable the United States have been, how much Hell the country and the world is going to be going through tomorrow. "Shh Kitten, calm down, you're just going to make yourself sick. I'm sorry, I know it's hard, but we have to get ready for tomorrow. I promise I'll think of something special for them all, to honor them somehow, but not until after we finish the job. Actually that may be the best way to honor them now. Stop Jane from corrupting the world. Stop Jane from ever being able to come back to the States again. Better yet, just stop Jane, period!" he finishes in a deadly voice, while rubbing her back in a comforting motion before gently pushing her upright, opening her fist to release his shirt, looking into her eyes to judge her stability.

"Yes, yes we're going to stop Jane. She needs to pay for all that's she's done to this world, those poor people, every last one of them that died on her whim. Let's help justice be served Snake. It's time to put the ball in motion," she finishes anger and determination lighting her face.

"All right, then the first line of business is to make sure our weapons are ready to go. I brought what I thought would do the job. Since you're the sniper here, you'll have the honor of stopping Jane personally. For everything that's happened to you since this started, it will be fitting. You personally will help justice to be served."

"Awesome Snake, that means a lot to me, especially after today. I will get pay back for Mongoose and Des and for the other hundreds that have died during her cause. She won't become ruler of the world, if I have to meet her face to face to end this. It ends tomorrow!"

"Good, then we have much to accomplish before tomorrow afternoon. We'll get the weapons in order, then we'll head out and scope out the best area to go to, we may have to move into position while it's still dark outside so probably sometime early morning would be best. I'll contact our source here and set up a meet for later tonight so that we can fine tune everything. I'm not going to expect any help since the troops couldn't get out of the states but I'm confident that we can do this. We really have no other choice. It's not the first time that I've had to complete a mission on my own. So what do you say Kitten? Are you ready to start the beginning of the end of Jane?"

"I'll say probably about as badly as you," she grins at him, excitement brewing.

Chapter Thirty-Four

"This is it Mother, Father. We're here, finally, and the world will be a different place when we leave here in a few days."

"Yes Jane, it will be, all our plans, our work, will meet its completion. I never thought I'd see the day, I had hoped, but never thought I'd be here for it, especially after the last few months."

"Let's get going. I'm so excited that I can't wait any longer," Jane urges, eyes sparkling with glee.

"President Martin, you have a guest waiting for you at the hotel. She's been there all day but insists she see you at your first opportunity," Darius, head of the Secret Service detail for this trip informs her quietly once she's out of the plane and headed for her transportation.

"I'll see her after I get my parents safely to the hotel. Give me about a half hour to get my thoughts in order, and then bring her to me."

"As you wish President Martin," he answers quietly slowing his walk to take up the rear of the small group in a protective manner, eyes scanning constantly for any sign of suspicion or danger.

"Wow, this is nice," Tariq murmurs after seeing the lobby of the hotel they're staying at.

"Of course it is Mother. I AM the President of the United States, the most powerful country in the world. I'm no small deal. I'm treated with respect now where ever I go, as it should be," Jane murmurs back arrogantly.

"Yes, I tend to forget Jane. I'm not used to being around you nor remembering all the time just who you really are now. Please forgive me, my daughter."

"Of course Mother, now, here are your rooms. There will be a guard standing outside your door at all times. If you need anything, just mention it to them and they will see to it that you have whatever you've requested. Unfortunately I'm going to be rather busy for awhile tonight but I promise to keep you informed of anything exciting that happens and you will be present tomorrow when I reveal my surprise for the world. Shh, soon you will know," she says quickly when she sees the question forming on her parents faces "but I will not tell you either until tomorrow when I reveal it to the world. You'll just have to wait. Now I have an appointment waiting for me, so please excuse me. Until later," she finishes with a quick touch on the shoulder of her father before turning and heading down the hall to the elevator, her rooms on an entirely different floor for security purposes.

"Darius, please escort Ms. Zeru to my rooms. I'll see her now," she says as she gets off the elevator on her floor.

"Right away President Martin," he says as he motions to the door guard to run the errand.

"Nice," she thinks after entering her rooms which take up most of the floor. Exquisitely done in creams and blues the crystal lighting sparkling in the light from the windows, a couch and loveseat waiting enticingly with a coffee service sitting on the table, steam wafting gently through its spout, along with a plate of pastries sitting nearby and some plates and napkins. "Fit for a King," she murmurs with a small smile playing over her lips. "Come in," she says as she opens the door after hearing the knock meeting Kayin Zeru for the first time face to face. A tall woman of regal bearing, a small smile and a look of inquisition on her face, nerves noticeable only in the hand grasp in front of her waist, a heavy accent to her words.

"President Martin, I am Kayin here at your insistence."

"Yes Kayin, please come in," Jane says as she moves to the side allowing her entrance. "Thank you for making the trip. Did you bring the item I requested?" Jane asks once they enter the sitting room and refreshments have been offered.

"I did bring it, although it brings me discomfort to take it from its home. It has been in that building for nearly two thousand years. It should not be here now, but on its alter where it belongs. The utmost care must be taken of it for its powers are great, it represents greatness to many. People have been searching for this item since it was placed on its alter on Kidane Melesse. My ancestors have always taken care of it, kept it hidden from everyone; it was our duty which we took on with great honor. If I may ask, why do you need it here, and how did you find it? It was with great care that its location has never been mentioned. Surely someone told you where it was?"

"Actually, no, no one that I'm aware of knows about it, nor does anyone know that I have located it and requested you, it's guardian to bring it here."

"Hmm, that is interesting."

"Where is it," Jane asks. "Have you left it alone, unguarded?"

"No, it is guarded, the guards just have no idea what it is they are guarding. I can assure you it is safe."

"I will need it tomorrow for a brief time. I am to be seated at the table of the New World Union, a seat that has been reserved for me and because of this honor, I want to present this proof to the world, that I am the chosen one for this position. I will promise you that it will come back to you for safe keeping, since you have done so well for millennium."

"You plan on showing it to the world? Does that not put it in jeopardy? Are you going to tell anyone where you found it, and who has guarded it for thousands of years?"

"I had not planned on disclosing its hiding spot, to do so would jeopardize not only it but you and your family as well. I have kept you hidden, a secret from any and all, no one knows exactly why I asked to see you, nor how I know you. You see, before becoming President of the United States, many years ago, I was a reporter, a journalist and have traveled the world thoroughly. I have informed those that needed to know who you are and why, and that I had met you during those days and we had become very friendly. I informed them that because of the greatness of this position I wanted to share it with one of my closest friends. I gave you that honor. In reality I want to surprise the world with this treasure since so many people have wondered about it since it was used. There have been questions about it, followers looking for it, people dreaming of it. Since I am the President of the United States, soon to be Ruler of the World, who better than me to show the world just who has the power? I will, however, guarantee that you will get it back approximately a half hour after I have shown it to the world, none the less for wear. There will be no damage to it, and you will be escorted to your plane, in which you will be transported in a roundabout way, back to your little island in the Blue Nile. You will be escorted right to your doorway and they will actually wait until the item is secured in its place. Is that sufficient for you Kayin?"

"Of course, President Martin, the only thing is, this treasure has never been out of my families hands, not for seconds no less a half hour. Are you sure I cannot hold it for you while you show it to the world?"

"Of course I'm sure, you will however be just outside the door, you will hand it to me, I will hand it back, so it will either be in your hands or in mine. You do trust me, do you not Kayin?"

"It is not so much that I do not trust you, but that of the honor of my family. If I did not do my duty and protect this with my life, then all the time that has been given freely to it will be for nothing. We will not be able to honestly say that this item has never left our hands, not for seconds when it is not on it's alter, where no one can get to it, no one has ever found it. But because no one has ever found it but you, you must have special powers also. So in this instance and because of what you've just explained I will do as you have asked."

"Thank you Kayin. It is with honor that I meet with you and arrange this. I know how much this is costing you. The world will be grateful but believe me, they will never find out where it is kept. I have kept that a secret. Did you not wonder why it took so long for you to get here? We flew you in many directions in order to keep your island off of the radar of all those people that think they need to know everything, especially when it's attached to me. And now if you will excuse me, I have many things to finish tonight before the big day begins for me, and believe me it will be a very big day," Jane assures her as she escorts her to the door. "Please be sure to ask your guards if there's anything that can be gotten for you. You have only to ask and it will be found."

"Thank you President Martin, your hospitality is very generous. My rooms are like living in a castle," she admits shyly as she takes her leave.

Of course they are Jane thinks while closing the door a small sneer on her normally blank face. *You live in the woods in a tiny house with rock floors. Oh well, that's done, now I need to go over my acceptance speech.*

* * *

"I think that might be the best place to stand," Snake says after searching the area, circling around and finding no obvious opening. "The place was certainly built like a fortress, down to the high narrow windows. You definitely can't see inside at all, so they must have planned for this exact scenario. I hate it when someone takes security into consideration when building something of this nature."

"So, how are we going to get the shot? When she's getting ready to go in the building?" Kat asks confusingly.

"I was thinking more of when she's leaving, when she's feeling victorious, full of herself, her newly obtained power. Besides, she's promised the world a surprise and I'm kind of curious, aren't you?"

"I guess, but I believe I'm more ready to end this thing than really care about some stupid surprise from Jane. All she brings to this world is bad, so what kind of a surprise could she possibly have?"

"That's what got me so curious and concerned," he admits, blue eyes narrowed as he thinks about all the nasty surprises Jane has pulled in the past.

"Yeah, . . .r . . . i. . .g . . . h. . . t . . . " she says slowly, her mind moving in the same direction now as his, a look of worry replacing the confusion that consumed her expression previously. "You think she's going to pull something really bad. What's going through your mind? I mean, I know she's capable, but is she gutsy enough? She's in a foreign land, among strangers, and taking part of a group. I can't believe she'd do something to offend anyone in that room with her. I mean, she doesn't really know anyone here, it's more of an honor type thing that she's accepting, at least that's what she's led the people in the States to think," she finishes worry clouding her vision now, her black hair plus blonde roots (it sucks trying to grow your hair out to natural after looking Goth for so long) in disarray from the wind not to mention the multiple times she scrubbed her hands through her hair whether in frustration or worry, both seem to have the same affect on her.

"I know, but she's mentioned this 'World Surprise' multiple times in the past month and it's always sounded sort of threatening when she says it. Not like a promise of something good, but the opposite actually. Something really bad, more like a threat, not like a happy surprise," he finishes suspicion growing by leaps and bounds the more he states his thoughts out loud.

"Okay, yeah, I see where you're coming from. I think the only reason I didn't see it was I didn't want to. She's done so much Snake, I can't take much more. It's a good thing that this ends tomorrow. What happens, happens. It will be my pleasure to end this for the world. It's not going to benefit only us, it will benefit the world. If only they knew what her plans were ahead of time. We never learn from history which is a shame. Power corrupts, and absolute power absolutely corrupts, why can't people remember these things. Look at what Hitler did, and Stalin and look at Hussein. Evil in every form, every country, sometimes you get a warning but most times not. You'd think we'd have learned, but look at us now," she finishes, tears clouding her green eyes, emotion making her look years older than reality.

"Tomorrow Kitten, it ends tomorrow. Let's finish our plans here and head back. I could use some down time and I'm sure you could too," he says tugging her close worry hazing his brain to the point of exhaustion.

"Oh yeah, and besides, if this is our last night, and it probably is, than I don't want to waste it with worries, I'd rather waste it with you," she says as she grabs him by the neck and hugs tight. "I never want to forget how we feel together," she whispers against his ear, wistful of a normal happy life, a normal happy time for just the two of them.

"I couldn't agree more," he promises as he turns them towards the car and the road back to their own little, albeit old and worn, paradise.

Chapter Thirty-Five

"I'm going to call Eli before we head out. I just want to make sure he's all right and he knows our plans for today, which he's does, but I just want to finalize things," Snake murmurs after he kisses Kat for the final time, still warm and pliant after the rather vigorous love making they just finished.

"Do you have to move so fast? Can't we just stay like this forever," she murmurs as she grabs him and holds on tight, nuzzling her face into his neck, inhaling his scent as if it's the giver of life, unwilling to move, to begin the day, the day that will change their lives hopefully for the better.

"Sorry Kitten," he grins that sexy devil may care grin, his ice blue eyes reading that face that shows every emotion, and knowing, his gut in turmoil as his mind flashes to what's in store for today.

"Fine," she says softly, sadness in her green eyed gaze, the feeling of loss heavy when he shifts his weight off of her, loneliness already replacing the feeling of peace that completed her moments ago.

"This is it," he says softly. "We have a job to finish and today's the day, but don't worry, I have plans for tonight. I thought a repeat of this morning would be a nice starter to our new life together without Jane. Just remember, the sky's the limit and after today, we're free to live our lives without all the damn aggravation that she's caused. It may not be an easy transition, but it will change. However, nothing will take you away from me. Never again will we be separate but a unit, the two of us," he promises as he stands naked and proud in front of her, her last glimpse of him through the dull dawn light creeping into the dark and dreary room is his taut butt moving with that long strong stride of his into the bathroom.

'*The man emanates sex*,' she thinks her eyes becoming blurry as she relives their lovemaking from moments ago, although it was way more than your average lovemaking with what they did together, they probably broke every law ever made. *Yeah, I'm sure we broke some laws*, she thinks as she realizes that he's back already and staring at her in puzzlement, and realizing she's still in bed she throws back the sheet that covers her, and heads for the shower, her cheeks a brilliant pink, his mouth carrying that knowing grin that he's perfected.

"Really, that sucks Eli. I'm not sure, we're six hours ahead here, it's close to eight in the morning. You should get some sleep since it's going to be another rough day. No, we've had no big problems, but the day's just starting for us. Kat just got out of the shower, sure, I'll tell her, yeah, I'll talk to you tonight," he finishes as she reaches him from the bathroom.

"You already talked to Eli? That was a fast conversation," she says quietly, studying his face trying to get a read on his mood, his feelings, anything that may give her a hint on that conversation.

"Yeah, I called him not thinking about the time differences. It's the middle of the night over there and from what he was saying, yesterday was a rough day for everyone, the whole country. We lost a lot of good people when they blew them out of the skies, not only because of that but it seems they woke the sleeping giant. A lot of the people of the states have taken up arms. They're protecting themselves from Jane's troops, having no choice since she gave more orders to them after the planes, not that I'm defending their actions because I'm not," he says angrily, frustration evident in his words.

"What are they doing, what's happening?"

"They're shooting first and asking questions later. That stupid bitch, she's caused a war and she's not even there to witness it. Thousands of innocents are going to die, all because of her selfish greed. I can't wait until she's no longer a threat to our people, to the country, no, better yet, to the freaking world. This is going to be the best thing that's ever happened to our country. I just hate it that I'm not there helping right now. It's what my service life has been for, to protect and serve, yet here I am thousands of miles from the people that need me the most."

"Snake, you can't be everywhere, do everything. You're only one person, and you have to believe that those that stayed back are working to help the people. There were a lot of them so surely they're making a difference. We just have to trust them and know that if, after this is done, they still need our help we'll head back and do what we can. I know you'll want to and I go where you go, so WE will make the trip back home. As long as we're together from now on, I'm good with that!"

"You don't understand," he says in frustration, teeth grinding with helpless rage. "Those people are my family, not just blood family but friends, co-workers, citizens of the United States. They're being slaughtered and I'm not there helping to protect them."

"You may not be there protecting them but you are protecting them. You're here and we're going to end the reason the States are in such bad shape. Once Jane's gone, things will quiet down. Eli, Mal, all the people that are there now will wrestle control away from Jane's minions and things will get back to normal. Maybe not what we've known our whole lives as normal, but it will be a better place than it has been the past year or so. You have to step back and view what's happening. How it will work out. But for right now, we need to start to prepare for our day. It's a big one and our Country is depending on us to perform this task successfully. Lives are depending on us," she finishes hugging him hard around the waist, waiting for him to gain control again, realizing that she's never seen him so uncontrollably angry before. "Let's do this," she orders as she steps back watching him become the warrior again as he takes a deep breath while straightening his shoulders, his face still familiar but with a look on it that scares even her.

"Sorry about that Kitten," he says quietly having gained control again.

"No problem. I want to be there for you no matter what. I've always been the one you've had to help and it felt kinda good to be on the other side for a change."

"Yeah, well don't get used to it," he warns softly. "I don't usually have that issue with emotions. All I can think is that you've made me weak. Whatever it is you do to me has made me softer."

"There's nothing wrong with that! Besides, you needed to be a little softer and I really like you that way," she grins, the sparkle back in her eyes, a teasing smirk on her lips.

"All right, this isn't moving in the direction that it needs to move. First things, we pack up everything, get our weapons ready, dress for the day and find some food. We're going to need the energy for everything we have to do and who knows when the next meal will be, since we've no idea what's going to happen after we take out Jane. We'll definitely be on the run and need every spare minute we can make. So, you've got your orders, hop to it," he says firmly as he turns and pats her ass quickly when she moves, a wicked smile on his face at her outrageous little scream.

"Is that everything?" she asks after her last load to the car is done.

"That's it. I checked everything and we've got it all. Now we need to find some food. At least all the work gave me an appetite. But I am hoping for some normal food. I'm just not the fish for breakfast kind of guy, so I'm hoping for a traditional breakfast, you know?"

"Yeah, I do know," she agrees as she gets in the car not bothering to buckle since they're not leaving the immediate area and the roads are all but empty right now.

"Where are all the people," she asks curiously after noticing how quiet it is in the area.

"They're probably still sleeping. In case you didn't notice, we were in a working neighborhood and by that I mean, they work all night and sleep most of the day."

"Oh, well, I hadn't thought I guess. I didn't notice anyone around last night when I arrived so just assumed they were all in bed or something."

"They may have been," he laughs wickedly "that's what I was talking about."

"Oh," she gasps realizing what he meant, and her face starts to glow with red, she's so easy to make blush.

"That was luck finding that restaurant here serving a real American breakfast. I'm so full I won't need to eat until tomorrow!" Kat says on a laugh and a groan, rubbing her belly as they exit the little hole in the wall restaurant.

"Yeah, I noticed you were pretty hungry," he adds on a laugh when she swats at him for the rude comment.

"Check out that sky Snake, I've never seen a sky so brilliant, the sun so bright and the birds, listen," she says breathlessly as she grabs his hand. "It's the most perfect day I've ever seen," she adds wonder in her voice.

"Weird huh, the day so perfect yet what's going to happen in a few short hours. Let's head over to our spot. I don't want anything getting in the way of our duty," he murmurs as he guides her to the car.

"This is it, this is the spot we scouted out, and we've got plenty of cover, a perfect view and a perfectly clear sky today. Looks like all the stars have aligned for us. I'm feeling pretty good about this right now."

"Let's unpack and head up."

"Man, we should have brought a picnic, this is perfect," Kat says wistfully.

"Check it out," Kat says as she hands the binoculars to Snake.

"Excellent," he murmurs after looking through them "they've got the big screen up. We may not need the binoculars once they're done with that screen. Man, that's top of the line. This certainly is being treated like a very big deal. That's excellent for our cause."

"There are so many satellite trucks down there it looks like a field of mushrooms. She did promise that the world would be watching this and every radio station too. These are pretty nice binoculars, I can see faces in the crowd, shit look, there's Jim Cochran of Channel 3, back home. He's really moved up hasn't he?" she adds with a laugh handing back the binoculars that she grabbed from him to see the big screen.

"Yeah, up Jane's ass, that's why he here, that's how he got the invite. I can guarantee you that every reporter down there's been screened by Jane and her group in order to get an up close spot."

"At least we're not crowed here. We've got the whole hill to ourselves. Everyone probably thinks this area's too far away. What they don't know . . ." she snorts.

"We still need to take precautions and keep our equipment covered just in case someone wanders up here. This will help some things," he says as he removes a small electronic scrambler used to scramble video feed and any digital signals. "It will help to stop those," he says as he points to the sky at three o'clock where a drone is just coming into view.

"Let me see those binoculars," Kat demands as she grabs for them.

"What for," he asks quietly.

"I think they're starting to get there. Yes," she says as she scans the area, long black limo's lining up near the entrance, people small as ants getting out of the cars amidst yells from the crowd that you can just hear all the way up here.

"Looks like this is getting started, soon, Jane, soon you'll be done," Jacob mutters, heart starting to hammer in excitement.

"Here, take the binoculars. I want to get my stuff the way I want it," Kat says quietly.

"There's Jane, I see her now," Snake says.

"So do I," Kat says and as Snake whips his head toward her to see what she means he finds her staring through the scope of her rifle. "I've got the shot, I could do it right now," she says breathlessly.

"No, let her reveal her surprise to the world before we reveal our surprise."

"It's been a long time since everyone's gotten

here, when are they going to show something," Kat demands, tired of the sitting and waiting when the screen suddenly comes on and the video showing all the chairs but one filled, before panning to the acting President of the One World Summit. Who's the acting President Snake, I can't remember?"

"I'm not sure but I think it's the leader of Spain."

"Here they go," Kat says as she hears the screen face come to life.

"Welcome world citizens. As you know we have had one seat empty and waiting for the most qualified candidate possible, and for the first time in the history of the One World Union we have had a unanimous vote on the very first ballot. We are honored and privileged to present to you the President of the United States, Jane Martin, the new occupant of our last seat that truly makes us now One World, One Union, One Body," he finishes as Jane steps into the room amidst loud applause both inside the building and outside as well.

"Thank you President Delgado, I am honored," she says after she regally steps up to the podium to assume the leadership position, her clothing a royal blue power suit, her hair styled neatly not to detract from her position, no jewelry to be seen.

"I promised the world that I would show them I had a great surprise for them all. But let me start first by telling you a story. A story of a little girl who was born with a special mission, the story of a little girl whose roots are from a country where girls are thought of as second class citizens, a place where men ruled not only the country but made all the religious laws and decisions. Fortunately there was a ruler at the time with a different view for the future, one with the ability to see and plan far ahead, to think of the world as a whole, in order to achieve his goal of world leadership.

It began with my parents who were hand chosen because they were extremely high ranked special operatives and sent to the United States, not as husband and wife, but as partners, in which they were and had been for many years. In order to achieve the farsighted goal they married to conceive me rightfully. I was born in the United States and am a legal citizen. I was raised Muslim on the inside, and Christian on the outside for safety in life and in the states. They chose the soon to be largest Christian church in the western world and became devoted parishioners, always with their goal in mind. My true name is Ab'ar Muhsin although I go by Jane Martin which is the name that you will find on my official birth certificate not that that matters at all where I am concerned. You see, there is nothing that anyone can now do about the who's and why's of me. This discussion is in reality a professional kindness for you, my people of the world. Yes, I do enjoy saying that, MY PEOPLE of the world. I have decided that it is time that you find out just who I am. I do have a special gift for the world which I will be giving to you momentarily, a gift that many people of the world have searched for, for thousands of years. A search that I found not so difficult, but if you would have had the power that I have, you also would have located it, a search that found the most valuable of items to your Christian friends and allies in the simplest of places, the least of places may I say.

Please, bring in the box," she orders arrogantly to a door guard.

"What's she getting," Kat whispers to Snake as she watches the screen intently. "What's she going to do?"

"I'm not sure but I have a bad feeling that this is going to go downhill really fast, really soon."

"There it is, it's not very big," Kat says in disappointment, a box no larger than a shoe box in Jane's hands as she turns back to the podium, an average brown type shipping box. "It looks pretty plain," she says before Jane starts speaking again.

"This small parcel holds inside of it, the hopes, the dreams, the faith of a multitude whom will learn exactly how crushing it feels to see the truth, to see what others have not seen. In this small plain box that I have located in a small Ethiopian village is your precious Holy Grail" she mocks with a smile of pure malice on her face as she slowly opens the box sitting on the podium in front of her, a box that appeared plain and dull until the first flap was slowly pulled back, a gleam beginning to emanate from the top, where the first flap had been, causing her to take a slight but noticeable step back before reaching for the other flap. "I will show you, the faithful, exactly what you have been following blindly, but which now I will bring to the light" she adds before screaming as a blinding white light strikes her where she stands causing everything in the room, in the building, in the outside, throughout the country, throughout the world to become shockingly blown to the ground as a great wave of energy, powerful enough

to deafen and blind the World occurs. In a second, a blink when realism and realms open, when few, yet some, have the opportunity to see albeit briefly people everywhere fallen where they stood, to their knees, shock and disbelief on every face and the faint coo of a lone dove all that can be heard . .
.

Isaiah   45:22-24